PRAISE F

What If

"Oftentimes you read books and love them but rarely do you read a book that touches your soul. For me, WHAT IF is one of those unique books. I not only loved this story, it left me pondering my own life and relationships with those around me."

—DesertDivasBookAddiction.wordpress.com

"Emotionally captivating. This book exceeded my expectations. Rebecca Donovan's writing is beautifully moving."

—GiveMeBooksBlog.blogspot.com

"This book was just beautiful and heartbreaking. I fell in love with Cal and needed to know everything I could about Nyelle. This is a beautiful story about second chances, and how you can make the most of them... Bravo, Ms. Donovan. Thank you for such an enchanting read." —ChicksControlledbyBooks12.blogspot.com

"In the world of fiction so vast and ever-changing, it is nice to come across a story that sucks me in because of the storyline and the characters, rather than just superficial things... I don't know what more to say about this book other than you will regret not picking it up."

—TheBookTrollop.blogspot.com

"Powerful and breathtaking." —BiblioBelles.com

"A beautifully written story of love, loss, coming of age, and learning to love again." —KylietheBookaholick.blogspot.com

"The mystery, the intrigue, and the culmination of it all propelled me to keep reading... Donovan built the bones of the story really well and the writing was good."

—ReadingBooksLikeaBoss.com

"A very touching and emotional read with just a hint of mystery... This is my first Rebecca Donovan book, but it won't be my last. I loved the characters, the writing, and the way the story unfolded."

—BadAssBookReviews.com

What If

REBECCA
DONOVAN

FOREVER

NEW YORK BOSTON

This book is a work of fiction. Names, characters, places, and incidents are the product of the author's imagination or are used fictitiously. Any resemblance to actual events, locales, or persons, living or dead, is coincidental.

Forever
Hachette Book Group
1290 Avenue of the Americas
New York, NY 10104

www.HachetteBookGroup.com

Printed in the United States of America

RRD-C

Originally published as an ebook

First trade paperback edition: January 2015
10 9 8 7 6 5 4 3 2 1

Forever is an imprint of Grand Central Publishing.
The Forever name and logo are trademarks of Hachette Book Group, Inc.

The publisher is not responsible for websites (or their content) that are not owned by the publisher.

The Hachette Speakers Bureau provides a wide range of authors for speaking events. To find out more, go to www.hachettespeakersbureau.com or call (866) 376-6591.

Library of Congress Cataloging-in-Publication Data

Donovan, Rebecca (Novelist)
What if / Rebecca Donovan. — First trade paperback edition.
pages ; cm
ISBN 978-1-4555-3311-4 (softcover) — ISBN 978-1-4789-8534-1 (audio download) — ISBN 978-1-4789-8688-1 (audio book) — ISBN 978-1-4555-3309-1 (ebook) 1. Young women—Fiction. 2. Man-woman relationships—Fiction. I. Title.
PS3604.O56736W48 2015
813'.6—dc23

2014041172

To my son, Brian. The bravest person I know.

~I wished for you.~

ACKNOWLEDGMENTS

The concept of *What If* came to me while I was listening to a song. Executing the inspiration became a complex layering of storytelling. Creating this world challenged me throughout the entire process. But after writing, rewriting and rewriting again several more times over, the result is a story that I love, about living the life you want, not the one you're given. I believe this arduous process allowed me to grow as a writer, demanding more of myself with each attempt, until every word was expressed with the passion and intensity it deserved.

I couldn't have survived the trials of rewrites without the support and encouragement of these two incredible people: My agent, Erica Silverman, was always encouraging and provided essential feedback to strengthen Cal's voice. And my partner in all things literary, Elizabeth. She is a trusted friend, and an extremely talented person. I could gush over her for an eternity. I wouldn't be half the author I have become without her.

I am very appreciative to Leah and the entire team at Grand Central Publishing for allowing me to express myself, and accepting my neurotic need for perfection. In the end, it's all about the story.

I usually have a team of readers who help shape the story as I write. After starting over for the third time, I decided not to torture them any longer and held them off from reading *What If* until the story was complete. I am grateful for each and every one of these wonderful people who voluntarily read my words, even when I was struggling to form them. They kept me going when I questioned if I should have. It's because of them that I didn't give up. There was a great story to be told, and they knew it. Their belief in me is what makes them invaluable people in my life. As friends. As readers. As spectacular humans. So, I thank you, Amy, Emily, Faith, Courtney and Carrie.

It can be intimidating to have other authors read my work. They look at it with a different perspective than other readers. They are creators themselves, so they understand the struggles, along with the rush that comes with getting it right. These authors listened to me conceptualize the plot. They advised me when I knew something was missing. I have the greatest respect and admiration for these women. Thank you for making me a better writer, Jenn. Thank you for wanting to read whatever I attempt to write, even when it's not perfect, Colleen. Thank you for making me feel, Jessica. Thank you for seeing the potential for greatness in this story, Jillian. And if it wasn't for you, Tarryn, this novel would never have been written. Thank you, my talented and exceptional friends. This story is exactly what I wanted it to be because you understood me.

What If is a story about love, loss and friendship. Above all, it's about second chances. Recognizing those moments in life when a decision can change the course of your life. Embrace those moments. Live each day knowing there is a choice to make it better. You can begin again…every day. All that is important is your happiness, and being exactly who you are supposed to be. Be happy.

What If

PROLOGUE

Why the hell are we here, Cal?" Rae asks as she hands me a beer. "I didn't like these people when we were in high school. And I still don't. Nothing's changed."

But something *has* changed.

I sit on the tailgate of my truck, taking a few gulps, and casually scan the crowd, clustered in the predictable groups they were in when we graduated last year: the athletes, the dramatics, the tokers and, of course, the elites.

They're why I'm here. Sort of.

"I'm giving this one hour, and then we're out of here," Rae declares, taking a sip of her beer. She slowly lowers her cup, staring across the field. "Holy shit. Is Heather Townsend walking over here?"

I look up just as Heather appears in front of me, twisting a strand of blond hair around her finger.

"Hi, Cal. I'm glad you showed up," she says, wearing a flirtatious smile.

"Hey," I respond. She takes a step closer, moving between my dangling legs.

"Partying in the woods is so...high school." She exhales dramatically. "I mean, you'd think we would've grown up a little since we left for college."

"Yeah, but we still have parents who won't willingly let us drink and trash their houses," I note. She laughs like I said the funniest thing she's ever heard.

Rae groans. "You've got to be kidding me."

Heather leans in so I can feel her breath on my mouth. "I think we're going to have a fun summer together."

I swallow, unable to back away any farther without lying down.

"I'm only here for the week," I tell her. Her lower lip juts out in a pout. Not attractive.

"Where are you going?" she asks, setting a hand on my knee. My entire body tenses.

"Oregon. I'm working for my uncle for the summer."

"But you just got here, like... today."

I hear Rae grumble something under her breath.

"Sorry," I say with a shrug. "So, umm. Where is everyone? I don't see Nicole with you guys."

Heather steps back with a roll of her eyes, crossing her arms. I've struck a nerve.

"I don't know. I guess she thinks she's better than us now that she's at Harvard."

I pry a little more. "Have you heard from her since graduation?" I can feel Rae staring at me.

"Not even a stupid text. I mean, we were her *best friends* for like... ever. And nothing. Bitch."

My eyes widen at her hostility.

"Heather." Vi is standing behind her with her hands on her hips. "The party's over here." She nods toward the other elites, all clustered around Kyle's BMW.

"I'll be right there," Heather responds to Vi; then she looks back to me. "Maybe we can do something before you go."

"Maybe," I reply, knowing we won't. Heather turns and walks with Vi back to where she belongs. I slide off the truck and watch them walk away, back to the crowd that never gave us a second glance before today.

I'm forcefully bumped forward by a shoulder and end up spilling beer on my pants.

"Not for you to look at," Neil Talbert threatens from behind me.

I close my eyes and take a breath to restrain myself, wanting so badly to turn around and punch him in the face. My fist clenches with just the thought of it.

"You're such a dick," Rae snaps when I finally face him.

I look past Neil—who's trying to make himself look bigger, flexing his arms at his sides—to Rae and give her a quick shake of my head.

"Still having girls fight for you," Neil scoffs. "You really haven't changed, no matter what you look like."

I don't say anything. There's no point. He's as much of an ass as he was in high school, and nothing I say will make a difference.

"Neil!" yells some guy from a distance. "Where the hell have you been? We've been waiting for the Beam for like an hour. Get over here."

The tension in my shoulders eases when he starts walking toward his brother's BMW.

"Cal, I don't know why you still let him treat you like that. Hell, you're bigger than he is now. You know you could take him," she says, still glowering over my shoulder.

"He's not worth it." I lift myself back up onto the tailgate.

"And what the hell was that about with Heather Townsend? Seriously? Sure, you grew three inches, ditched the glasses for contacts and somehow put on muscle I didn't know your scrawny body could handle, but you don't look *that* different. You're still you."

"Thanks for keeping my ego in check, Rae. I appreciate it."

She continues, ignoring me. "And Nicole Bentley? Really, Cal? I thought you gave up on her years ago."

"But don't you think it's weird she didn't come back this summer?"

Something felt off when I didn't see her walking alongside the girls earlier today. And it still does. *She's* the reason I'm here.

I look over as Ashley straddles Kyle, kissing him like she's marking her territory. Kyle was Nicole's boyfriend throughout most of high school. And Ashley, Heather and Vi were supposed to be her best friends. I was never convinced she belonged with them, even if she was at the top of their hierarchy. She always seemed uncomfortable with the attention. Or maybe I was the only one who thought that. I stopped trying to defend Nicole from her ice queen reputation a long time ago because it pisses Rae off.

"Why do you care?" Rae questions. "We haven't been friends with her since Richelle moved away in eighth grade. Nicole chose *them*, remember?" There's a bite in Rae's tone. I know it's to cover up the hurt that she still feels from losing two of our closest friends in one summer. We don't talk about it. But we never do. I've known Rae my entire life, so I *know* her, even when she doesn't say anything.

The four of us grew up together in the same small-town California neighborhood. Rae lives next door, although she's pretty much an extension of my family at this point. Nicole and Richelle were neighbors a few houses down the street. When we were kids, we were inseparable. But things changed as we got older.

Richelle moved away. We stayed in touch for a while. And then we didn't. Nicole chose popularity over our friendship soon after. Rae never got over Nicole's betrayal. And I never got over Nicole. I will never admit this to Rae, or to anyone else for that matter, but I miss them. I know I can't do anything about it now. It's been too long.

I look to Rae. "Isn't it strange that the most popular girl in school hasn't been heard from in over a year and no one seems to care?"

"Besides you?" Rae counters with a scoff. "Get over her, Cal. She became the queen elite bitch, and now Ashley has taken over her reign. They don't care about her. They never did. I don't know why you do."

"It's like she just…disappeared," I say quietly, staring unfocused at the ground.

Within the recesses of a faded memory, I can hear Nicole screaming. It was the last thing I heard before no one saw her again.

"You can't make it go away by pretending nothing happened."

ONE

You understand, right?" Carly says. "I feel really bad breaking it off at a party, but I didn't think it was fair to wait and do it later, when we're drunk." She crosses her arms over her chest, accentuating what little her genie costume is covering up.

"Yeah," I respond, with a nod—too shocked to say anything else. I eye the cowboy I'd found her talking to, standing a safe distance away with two red cups in his hands. I can only assume he's the reason she wants to talk now instead of later.

It's not like we're that serious. I mean, it's only been three weeks. Carly pulls me down by the brim of my baseball hat and kisses me on the cheek before vanishing into the artificial fog of the Halloween party. I look down at the two cups I'm carrying and shake my head. This sucks. Draining one of the beers, I make my way out of the house through the back door. There's no way I want to stick around now.

As I round the corner, I find a couple pinned up against the side of the house, reminding me of what I *won't* be doing tonight. Not what I need right now. But as I get closer, I realize they're not hooking up; they're arguing…or more like she's telling him off.

"You don't get to touch me," seethes the girl, dressed head to toe in black. I don't realize she's wearing a ninja costume at first, since she practically blends in with the shadows of the house. Then I see what looks like a blade reflecting in her hand. "This ass is not yours to touch, and if you so much as look at it, I'm going to shred your balls. Got it?"

The guy in scrubs nods; his eyes flicker between her glare and the sai held under his chin. The weapon looks legit. And she looks pissed enough to use it. I wouldn't be able to speak either if I were in his position.

I take a sip of my beer, anticipating what she'll do next. But she just walks away. I'm disappointed. I expected her to at least knee him or something.

"Fucking psycho," the surgeon spits out—but not loud enough for her to hear him. I think he prefers to protect his balls.

He elects to use the back entrance, staying clear of the ninja. Smart move. I gulp down the rest of the beer, toss the cup on the lawn, and follow after her—curious to see where she's heading. I locate her striding toward the sidewalk and continue in the same direction.

"Nyelle!" a girl yells, rushing from the front door. "Nyelle, where are you going?" Strawberry Shortcake almost runs into me, chasing after her friend. She looks up, and her eyes widen in surprise. "Oh. Hi, Cal!" She smiles, her painted cheeks blossoming.

It takes me a moment to recognize her. "Tess! How are you?"

"Um." She glances to the sidewalk where Nyelle has stopped. "I'm okay, but I think I have to go." She starts toward her friend and says as she walks, "It was great to see you. We should—"

"You two need a ride?" I ask, glancing between her and the spitfire with her hands on her hips.

"Sure."

"No!"

My eyes bounce between the two girls, not sure which answer to go with.

"Come on, Nyelle. It's cold. Let him give us a ride."

"I need to walk." Nyelle turns and continues down the sidewalk. I look at Tess, questioning. She sighs and rushes after her. I can't help it—I'm intrigued and have to follow.

"Fucking stupid boys," the ninja grumbles beneath the mask, focused on her steps.

"She's having a bad night," Tess tries to explain.

I examine the girl in black more carefully. Her face is hidden, with only a slit revealing her eyes. The black robe and pants aren't tight, but they don't hide the fact that there's a girl beneath them either. Let's just say this girl would make a trash bag sexy. Add the mystique of not knowing what she looks like, and I'm suddenly aware of the turn-on. Dumbass should have kept his hands to himself.

"How are your classes this semester? Have you decided on a major yet?" Tess asks, her attention set on me. I redirect my focus away from the fuming ninja, who continues to ramble in expletives. I'm beginning to think she might go back to the party and give the surgeon a need for an operation.

"They're okay. And no, I still have no idea what I want to be when I grow up."

Tess laughs. "I was hoping we'd have another class together. You saved me in art history last semester. I don't think I would've been able to stay awake if you hadn't made up your own commentary for the slides." Tess smiles up at me. I can see the shy flirtation glimmering in her eyes. I choose to ignore it.

"I wish you would've let him drive us," Tess complains to her friend. "It's cold." She wraps her arms around herself with a shiver.

I stop to take off the lined flannel shirt I have on over my T-shirt. "Here."

"Thanks." Tess beams, taking it and wrapping it around her shoulders.

Nyelle waits for us with her arms crossed, scanning me with judgment. I look down at my shirt, thinking maybe it's ripped or stained. I didn't really inspect it closely when I threw it on earlier.

"What?"

"Who are you supposed to be?" Nyelle asks, turning abruptly to start walking again.

"A drunk college guy."

"That's original." Her voice is heavy with sarcasm.

"What? You saw another one at the party tonight? I thought I was the only one."

Tess giggles. Nyelle scoffs.

I inspect the shiny metal tucked into her belt. The weapons *are* legit. "Do you know how to use those?"

"Do you want to find out?" she snaps.

"Nyelle!" Tess scolds. She looks to me apologetically. "Sorry. She's not usually so unfiltered...Okay, yes, she is. But I'm sorry anyway."

"You don't have to apologize for me. Especially when I'm standing right here."

"I'm not offended," I assure Tess, glancing over at Nyelle, whose eyes tighten ever so slightly. It's too dark to tell what color they are, shadowed by the mask, but they have an exotic shape to them that seem eerily familiar. "I'm not going to take you up on your offer to demonstrate your weaponry skills, though. Even if you don't know what you're doing, it would probably hurt. And pain and I don't get along."

The edges of Nyelle's eyes crease slightly, and I'm convinced I got her to smile.

We continue in our bizarre semisilence, with Tess trying to keep warm and Nyelle grumbling.

I try to get a better look at her, but she keeps her head down with her fists clenched tight. I'm thinking she may be the angriest girl I've ever met.

We finally come to a stop in front of their dorm under a bright orange light.

"Thanks for walking us back," Tess says, a little more deflated when she notices my attention focused on her friend. She removes the flannel shirt from her shoulders and hands it to me.

"Sure," I reply, smiling quickly before looking back at Nyelle. "It was nice to meet you."

"We haven't—" she begins. Her words cut short when our eyes meet. Everything fades, and I can't look away. I'm looking into the most incredible blue eyes I've ever seen. They're the kind of eyes that could keep me standing here like an idiot, staring into them all night. I know, because I've stared into them before.

"Good night," Tess says. I blink.

"Good night, Tess," I reply in a rasp. When I look back, the girl in black is already walking across the lobby.

I've never really looked at an eye for this long before. There are so many shapes and lines. The longer I look, the more colors I find. There's a shade of blue near the center that's so light, it barely looks like a color at all. Then the colors seem to get darker as they spread out, like a storm parting for a clear sky. The line around her eye is so dark, it's almost purple, like… midnight. I swear there's every shade of blue in her eyes, even specks of silver. Focusing on the different colors keeps me from blinking. I want to move closer to see them all.

"Richelle, stop that. You're going to make them blink," I suddenly hear Rae say behind me. "What? Are you jealous that he's not looking into your *eyes?"*

"Shut up, Rae!" Richelle huffs as Rae laughs.

Nicole's long, dark lashes flutter shut.

"Cal wins!" Richelle declares.

I lean back and blink a few times. My eyes are dry from keeping them open for so long.

Nicole looks to me and smiles lightly, her cheeks pink. "You win."

"There's no way it's her," I mutter. I lean against the bar, which is really a plank of wood set across two stacks of milk crates. It shifts beneath my weight, because it's not meant to hold people up.

"Dude, what are you talking about?" Eric asks from the other side. "You've been going on about eyes for the past hour. You're drunk, and you're not making any sense."

"You don't understand!" I exclaim. "She has *her* eyes."

"Okay. Whatever you say. There's no way you're driving back to our apartment. Crash here tonight. The couch is all yours."

I nod, blinking heavily. I stumble to the dark brown couch and collapse. Eric tosses me a blanket, which lands across my legs. I leave it there, not bothering to cover up. I flop my arm across my face and close my eyes.

I try to convince myself that I've imagined it. I got a glimpse of the ninja's eyes for only a few seconds. But I swear I was looking into Nicole Bentley's eyes.

I'm jolted awake when I roll over and practically fall off the couch. It takes a second for me to realize where I am. Then the memories of the previous night start floating to the surface.

Getting dumped. A ninja. Strawberry Shortcake. Nicole's eyes. Walking to Eric's fraternity. Drinking. More drinking.

I sit up slowly, letting the spinning in my head settle before reaching for my boots. I run my dry tongue along the roof of my mouth, cringing at the awful taste.

"Hey," Eric says hoarsely from the bottom bunk on the other side of the bedroom. "You have class?"

"It's Sunday," I inform him as I stuff my feet in my boots.

"That's right," he says, rolling over and covering his head with the blanket.

The clock reads after ten in the morning. I really want to go back to sleep, but I have a paper to write—and a hangover to conquer. Not necessarily in that order.

I throw on my flannel shirt and find my way out of the fraternity house. I have to walk a few blocks back to where I parked my truck for the Halloween party last night. Taking a sobering breath of the cold, crisp air, I start the truck. The freezing vinyl seeping through my jeans and the chill in the air do little to clear my head. I need coffee.

I'm in desperate need of caffeine to kick my ass as I wait in line at Bean Buzz. Especially today. I lived up to the role of "the drunk college guy" last night. I don't do it often. But it was such a messed-up night.

I thank Mel behind the register as she hands me my cup. I'm half-convinced I'm sleepwalking as I head toward the door, my eyes barely open. I focus on the light coming from the exit and concentrate on moving my body in that direction.

"Cal?"

I stretch my eyes wide and inhale deeply through my nose in an attempt to focus. Carly is standing in front of me. How did she know I'd be here? I never brought her here. I never bring any girls here. I picked the most inconvenient coffee shop off campus so I could avoid accidentally running into them.

"Carly, what are you doing here?" I ask, too surprised to be filtered.

"Uh, getting coffee," she answers, holding up the cup.

"Right," I say with a slight nod, feeling like an ass.

"Do you have a second? I was hoping we could talk."

"Uh..." I hesitate. Right now just standing is a challenge, forget about talking.

"It'll be quick. I promise."

"Okay." I reluctantly follow her to a table that opens up in front of the large picture window. I have no idea what I'm walking into. I'm assuming she wants to apologize for how she ended things last night.

"I think I made a mistake," she says as I lower myself onto the chair. "I shouldn't have broken up with you."

I definitely didn't see this coming.

My stunned silence encourages her to continue. "I guess I freaked because I'm starting to have feelings for you. But after you left the party last night, I realized how many douche-wads there are on campus. You're not like them. I screwed up, and I want to give us another chance."

Shit. I am not coherent enough for this. So I stall and take a slow sip of my coffee, looking everywhere but at the girl sitting across from me waiting for an answer. That's when I see those same damn blue eyes from last night, staring at me from the leather sofa on the far side of the café—without the mask.

"Cal?" Carly calls to me.

"No way," I murmur, transfixed.

"What?" Carly questions, a hint of panic in her voice. "No?"

"Sorry." I recover quickly, reluctantly looking away. "Um, I thought I saw... Never mind." I shake my head and try to focus. She gave me an out last night. So I'm taking it. It's not like it would've lasted much longer anyway, especially if she wanted more from me.

I take a quick breath and say, "Yeah, no. I can't get back together with you."

"Uh... what?" Carly's eyes narrow. "Why?"

"Sorry, Carly. I just can't." I stand and walk away before I can see her reaction. I really should keep walking out the door. But I don't. Instead, I cross the café to the brown leather sofa where the unmasked girl from last night is reading with her feet propped up on the coffee table.

Then I just stand there and stare at her. She doesn't notice me, and that's probably a good thing because I know I look like a creep hovering above her. I have no idea what to say because I'm standing in front of *Nicole Bentley*. But this girl looks... different. She doesn't look *exactly* like the girl who moved into my neighborhood eleven years ago. So maybe she's not her. It doesn't make sense for her to be here. Except... those are her eyes.

"Nicole?"

She doesn't look up. I'm about to call to her again when someone brushes against my arm.

"Here you go, Nyelle," Tess says, reaching over the coffee table to hand Nicole a mug. "Hot chocolate with two pumps of mocha and whipped cream. How can you drink that much sugar in the morning? It makes my stomach hurt just thinking about it." Then Tess looks up at me and smiles brightly. "Hey, Cal."

"Uh, hi," I reply, completely confused. I glance from Tess to Nicole and back again. "Um, *you're* Nyelle?" Maybe I'm still drunk.

Nicole smiles gently. "Yeah. Nyelle Preston." She reaches out her hand. "Sorry I was a bitch to you last night." She's looking right at me, waiting for me to take her hand, which is covered by a knit glove with the fingers cut off. There isn't a single hint of recognition on her face. "I was a little drunk and wasn't having the best night."

"Yeah, uh, no problem," I say slowly, reaching over and taking her thin hand in mine. "Nice to meet you." I'm convinced I'm either sleeping, drunk, or in some fucked-up episode of *The Twilight Zone*. I swear I'm staring at the face of Nicole Bentley, the girl I spent way too many hours of my life thinking about. But she's looking at me like she has no idea who I am. It's freaking me out.

"I'm sorry, but don't I know—"

"You're such a fucker! You should have told me there was someone else. I can't believe I begged you to take me back!"

I turn just as Carly thrusts her coffee cup in my direction. I bow away, but it's too late. My body clenches in pain as the hot liquid collides with my chest. Stunned, I watch Carly's blond curls bounce out the door.

Sucking in through clenched teeth, I pull the soaked T-shirt away from my skin.

"Omigod," Tess gasps. She grabs napkins from the coffee table and begins to frantically blot my shirt. "Why would she do that? Are you okay?"

Mel appears in front of me and hands me a fistful of napkins. "Do you need anything?"

"My dignity," I mutter. Nicole laughs. I'm suddenly wishing I was still passed out on Eric's couch. "I look like an idiot, don't I?"

Nicole smiles. "Well... kinda. But she looked like a psycho. So she wins."

Just shoot me already.

"Oh, Cal, I can't believe she did that. Who was she?"

"An ex," I grumble, taking the napkins from Tess. "Thanks for your help. But I'm going to go." I can feel every pair of eyes on me, including the ones that kept me from taking that exit I should've made earlier. "I'll see you later."

I dump the napkins in the trash before I walk out the door. I look over my shoulder to find the girl who looks like Nicole Bentley still watching me.

NICOLE

June—Before Fourth Grade

I watch the houses go by out the window, wondering when we're going to stop and which one will be ours. I'm nervous. I'm not going to know anyone. What if they don't like me?

I flatten the skirt of my yellow dress, trying not to think about it. Mom says that they'll like me, so I have to believe her because I really want them to. I had two friends in our old town. Our moms would visit each other, so it was easy to be friends. They liked to play with dolls and make believe like I do. They were my friends at school too.

"Well, here we are," my daddy announces, turning onto the street. I see the big moving truck in front of a sunshine-yellow house. It matches my dress, which makes me smile.

"Who's that?" my mom asks, watching a girl with brown hair run toward the car.

"She probably lives next door," my daddy says. She has on blue polka dot shorts and a white T-shirt. Her hair is in a ponytail that swings behind her head as she hurries toward us.

"She's very...*forward*, isn't she?" my mother says, opening the car door. The girl is standing by the car, breathing fast like she just ran a race. I can't take my eyes off of her. I slowly unbuckle my seat belt and open the door.

"Hi. I'm Richelle. I live next door in the blue house," she announces without the tiniest bit of fear. My mouth pops open because she may be the bravest girl I've ever seen.

"Hi, Richelle. I'm Mrs. Bentley." My mother reaches back to urge me forward. I take a slow step and grab my mom's hand, standing close beside her. "And this is my daughter, Nicole."

"Hi," Richelle says to me with a wave. Her eyes are big and brown, and she smiles like she's excited to see me. "Do you want to play?"

I look up at my mom, not sure what to do. I wasn't ready for this. I know just a few minutes ago I was scared that I wouldn't make friends. But now I'm not sure I'm ready to leave my parents.

"That's very nice of you, Richelle," my mom says, "but we have a lot of unpacking to do. Maybe tomorrow would be better. You're welcome to come by then."

Richelle switches her eyes from me to my mom. She's still waiting for me to answer, but I never say a word.

"Okay," she finally says. "Bye, Nicole. See you tomorrow!"

Just as I turn toward the house, I notice a boy and a girl across the street on the sidewalk, watching the whole thing. The boy has brown hair and is wearing black glasses. And the girl has blond hair that's in a messy braid. She narrows her eyes at me like she's trying to decide what kind of animal I am or something. I turn away quickly and walk with my mom into the house, not letting go of her hand until we're safely inside.

TWO

"Wha—tha—no…" Rae is laughing so hard she can't form a single word. I yank my shirt over my head and wait impatiently for her to calm down.

"Rae, focus," I demand, examining the red blotches on my chest.

"You really picked a good one this time," Rae says, still laughing. "God. I wish I could've seen that."

"Great," I grumble. "But that's not the point. Nicole Bentley is *here*, at Crenshaw."

"And now I think you're delusional," she says, slowly sobering from her fit of laughter. "Nicole got into *Harvard*. Unless she flunked out, which we know she'd never do, she wouldn't *choose* Crenshaw…ever. It's in the middle-of-nowhere upstate New York. There's no way she'd be there."

"Then she was separated at birth from her identical twin, because I swear to you, I saw her. Besides, do we know she's really at Harvard? No one's seen or heard from her since graduation."

"I know she got in. I saw her acceptance letter, along with everyone in the entire school. She wouldn't shut up about it." She sighs heavily. "It can't be Nicole. And I'll tell you the same thing when I come visit you next month. I think you've convinced yourself that this girl, who looks kinda like Nicole, *is* her. And it better not snow this time. I can't deal with the snow."

"Fine. You'll see when you get here." I realize there's no use in trying to convince her.

"Cal, did you even ask her if she's Nicole?" Rae asks.

"Uh...I tried," I reply slowly. "We were interrupted by the coffee, remember?"

This sets Rae off in hysterics again. I hang up on her.

I toss the phone on my bed and walk into the bathroom to dig around in the cabinet for a tube of ointment that claims to be for burns. I have no idea how old it is, since it was here before we moved in, but I'm hoping it'll help. I gently dab the clear gel on my tender skin.

Returning to my room, I sit on the edge of my bed and run my hands over my face, trying to picture the girl in the coffee shop again. There's definitely something different about her. Her face looks like Nicole's, but...not. Nicole Bentley was always flawlessly put together, like she'd just stepped out of a magazine. The girl calling herself Nyelle doesn't seem to care what she looks like, wearing her brown hair wavy, like she's just stepped out of a shower and let it do whatever it wanted—a sexy mess. Nicole is a perfectly wrapped present tied with a nice neat bow. And Nyelle is wrapping paper strewn across the floor on Christmas morning.

Maybe Nyelle isn't Nicole. I try to compare them again, putting them side by side in my head. But it's hard, because I haven't seen Nicole since graduation. I still can't remember what happened the night after we graduated. I was drunk...Okay, I was wasted. But I know I heard her screaming at her parents inside their house.

"You can't make it go away by pretending nothing happened. Because then you might as well erase me too, Daddy."

What the hell happened that night? And what would've happened if I hadn't walked away?

I don't see Nicole—or Nyelle, or whoever she is—the next day. Or the day after. But I do have a couple of close calls with Carly at Bean Buzz. As I pull up to the coffee shop on Wednesday morning, I wonder if I'm pushing my luck. She's left a couple ranting voice mails on my phone. I deleted them after listening to the first ten seconds. She's crazy. And I don't do crazy. The girls I usually date are the nice girls. The kind guys take home to meet their mothers. Except I don't stay with them long enough for it to get *that* serious.

Just as I approach the large picture window with *Bean Buzz* arched across it in large white font, I notice Carly's curly blond hair inside. I slam my back up against the building, hoping she didn't see me. I do not want to deal with an overly emotional girl this morning.

I tentatively look back up. Carly's staring out the window. I quickly press my head back against the brick. "Shit."

I remain flattened against the building, trying to decide my next move. There's always a chance she's *not* waiting for me. I glance up as she cups her hands on the glass, scouring the sidewalk. Yeah, I doubt it.

"Who are we hiding from?"

I turn with a start.

Nicole is leaning against the chipped brick, with a dark brown knit cap pulled low on her brow. Her hair is sticking out from under it, flowing over the shoulders of a thick navy-blue sweater. Her nose is red from the cold, and clouds of air pass through her lips as she grins up at me. Despite the differences, I still see Nicole looking back at me.

"Is Psycho looking for you or something?"

"Uh, it appears that way," I fumble, looking away when I feel like I've been staring at her too long. "I guess she's still pretty pissed."

She peeks up and laughs when she finds Carly posted in front of the window. "What did you do to her?"

"She broke up with me, and I wouldn't take her back."

"Are you sure you didn't run over her cat too?" Nicole snickers.

"Probably should've. I hate that cat," I mutter. She smiles bigger.

"Dammit. I'm going to be late for class." I check the time on my phone. "Forget it. I can't keep standing out here hoping she'll leave. This is stupid. I guess I'll go without."

"What?! That's just crazy talk," Nicole says. "If I tell the girl at the counter 'Cal's usual—' "

"Mel," I interrupt.

"*Mel* will know what that is, right?"

I nod.

"Okay. Wait here," she instructs. "I'll be right back."

I don't wait in that exact spot. I mean, I feel like an idiot crushed up against the building, hiding from an ex who barely comes up to my shoulders. So I pace back and forth in the alley next to the coffee shop. I keep expecting Carly to whip around the corner. I'm being paranoid. I know this. And I'm not proud.

I start thinking again about how much this girl looks like Nicole, except she acts nothing like her. Nicole never said a word to anyone outside of the elites when we were in high school. And Nyelle has no issue voicing her opinion. These girls are too different to be the same. Unless... something happened to Nicole. Maybe she was in an accident. Or hell, perhaps she really was separated at birth.

"Here you go."

I spin around quickly, startling Nic—Nyelle. Shit. Now I'm getting confused.

"Geez, Cal. Relax. I'm unarmed." Then she looks down at the cup of coffee and laughs. "Well, sorta."

"Thanks," I mumble. She's making fun of me. Great.

Nyelle smirks and hands me my cup with a napkin folded on the side. "Mel asked me to give this to you," she says, before blowing on her hot chocolate.

I unfold the napkin to read, *Dignity will not be found in the alley.*

Nyelle laughs when I crumple the napkin and glare at the brick wall in offense. Thanks, Mel.

"Did you read it?"

"Of course," she admits without hesitation. "If I'm going to be passing a note in the alley, I want to know what it says."

Her continued amusement isn't helping with the whole dignity thing.

"I'm going to be late. Thanks for getting my coffee." I start past her, then pause. "Do you need a ride anywhere?"

"Nope. I like to walk."

"We're pretty far from campus."

"I know," she replies, walking with me to my truck. As I open the door, she asks again, "Are you sure you didn't do anything to her?"

"I swear," I answer, then add after a moment of thought, "I guess I wasn't who she wanted me to be."

"Are we ever?"

Nyelle smiles weakly and continues walking down the sidewalk, taking small sips from her cup without looking back. I watch until she turns the corner, her last comment stuck in my head.

Over the past week, I've looked for Nyelle everywhere without bumping into her once. We have a pretty large campus, so it's easy enough to avoid someone. I know. I've mastered it over the past year. But if you look hard enough, you usually find the person you're searching for eventually. I've even run into Tess a couple of times, but Nyelle's never with her.

"Not hiding in alleys anymore?" I hear beside me as I'm waiting in line for my coffee. I turn my head to find the girl I've been looking for.

"Hey. Uh...yeah, I haven't seen her in a while, so I figured it was safe to come back inside." Carly left a voice message and a few drunken texts over the weekend, but she seems to have given up.

I step up in line as Nyelle waits for her order at the end of the counter.

"Good morning, Mel."

"Cal." She greets me in her monotone voice like she does every morning. She hands me my cup with my name written on it while swiping my card.

"Thanks," I say and walk away.

I'm trying to come up with any excuse to talk to Nyelle, so I say the first dumb thing that comes to mind. "Haven't seen you this past week."

"I've been...around," she answers evasively. "Hey!" She eyes the cup in my hand. "How do you have your order already?"

"I guess because I get the same thing every morning," I answer with a shrug.

Her order is called out and she takes the cup that's handed to her. I walk beside her toward the door, stealing glances at her like maybe I can figure her out if I look hard enough. Her dark brown hair is tossed on top of her head, sticking out of a messy bun. There isn't a trace of makeup on her. And she's wearing a sweater that's too large for her, hanging low over her hips and sliding off her shoulder, exposing the thick strap of a tank top. She's cut holes for her thumbs to stick through since the sleeves practically cover her fingers. Her jeans are faded and torn, and her brown boots are scuffed and broken in. Despite the lack of effort, she's still unmistakably gorgeous, like Nicole, without actually being anything like her. I don't get it.

"What?" she asks, catching me looking her over.

"You look so much like..." I stop. I can't bring myself to say it. What if she really is Nicole? Then that would mean she's lying. And why would she do that? Unless...she's got something to hide. Or she has no idea who she is.

"Who?" Nyelle asks as I hold the door open for her.

I hesitate again. If I call her out on being Nicole, there's a chance I may never see her again. And I just got her back, well...sort of.

"No one," I recover quickly as she walks past me. "Forget it."

I bump into someone as I exit. I look down to find Carly. Before I realize what's happening, a stinging slap lands across my cheek.

"Holy hell, Carly! What was that for?!"

"You *are* just like the rest of them. I can't believe I was so stupid."

I've had enough. She's been making my life miserable for the past week, and this time, I know I didn't deserve it.

So as she's about to turn away, I raise my voice. "You ended things, Carly. *You* did, so you could hook up with another guy. So just...leave me alone!"

Carly's eyes grow wide with shock, and her face flushes. She opens her mouth, but nothing comes out. Finally, she says, "Don't worry. I will." Before storming off, she adds, "But I'm keeping the *Cal* sweatshirt."

I shake my head in amused disbelief. I think she got the point.

"Well, that was entertaining." Nyelle laughs. She begins to walk away.

Unsure of when I'll see her again, I quickly call after her, "Need a ride?"

Nyelle hesitates, and just when I think she's about to accept, she shakes her head. "No thanks. I'll walk. But maybe I'll see you tomorrow." She smiles and starts down the sidewalk.

"She *slapped* you?" Rae laughs. "Seriously?"

"Rae," I say sternly into the phone, quieting her. "You're not listening. I think—I'm almost positive—this girl is Nicole."

"What is with you lately?" Rae asks. "You've been weird about Nicole for a while now. You need to stop obsessing. I'm starting to become embarrassed for you."

"I'm not obsessing. And this has nothing to do with her ditching us in eighth grade, Rae. There's something really messed up going on. And I don't know what it is. This girl looks so much like Nicole Bentley, it's crazy. But she acts *nothing* like her. She doesn't even talk like her. I'm really starting to think she was in an accident or something. Head trauma can cause amnesia and alter your personality."

"You've watched way too much *House*," Rae accuses. "We live in a small town. Don't you think someone would've said something? You know the vipers would've been all over any rumors about Nicole."

Rae's right. And after watching them carry on like she never existed this past summer, I know they have no idea Nicole's here, or how much she's changed. They would've said something.

"Check her Facebook status. See when she posted last," I say.

"I'm not friends with her, remember? On Facebook or anywhere else."

"Right." I'm not either.

While we're still on the phone, I click open Facebook on my laptop and type in "Nicole Bentley." There's a picture of her, smiling brightly and wearing a pair of sunglasses. I click on her page, and the cover picture is Harvard's crest. She has more than a thousand friends, but all of her pictures and posts are private.

"Cal, you still there?" Rae asks. "The girls should be here soon for band practice."

"Huh? Yeah, uh, go ahead," I tell her as I type in *Nyelle Preston*. "I'll talk to you later."

I still have the phone tucked under my chin when I get the results. There's only a *Noelle Preston*—who doesn't look anything like the girl at Crenshaw. I set my phone down on the desk, staring at the screen without focusing on the words.

What happened to Nicole to force her to become Nyelle Preston?

I keep circling back to the night that I can't remember.

RICHELLE

Day After Nicole Moves In

I shovel the last bite of pancake into my mouth and jump up to put my plate in the sink. "Where are you going in such a rush?" my mom asks.

"To see if the new girl can play," I tell her, practically running for the door.

"Richelle, it's early. You might want to give them time to eat breakfast."

"I'm done. Maybe she is too," I holler back and push the screen door open. "Bye, Mom!"

I run across my lawn and stop at the little trees between my house and hers. I poke my head through and listen. I don't hear anything. I step closer to the edge of the driveway, and I hear, "Did you put all your clothes in the dresser?"

They're awake.

I jump over the flowers planted on the edge of the driveway and hop up the front steps. I push the doorbell and wait. But waiting is hard. So I push the doorbell again.

Mrs. Bentley opens the door. "Well, good morning, Richelle. Aren't you prompt?"

"Can Nicole come out to play?" I ask. I've been dying for this day all summer, ever since I knew someone was moving in next door and that they had a kid going into fourth grade too. Cal was hoping for a boy since he's the only boy on our street who's our age. But I'm happy she's a girl.

Nicole pokes her head around her mom.

"Hi, Nicole!" I say. She steps forward and I grab her hand. "Want to come play with me?" I pull her out the door and down the steps before she can answer.

"Nicole, please be careful. And be home for lunch," her mom calls to her.

When we reach the sidewalk, I let go of her hand. She pushes down the skirt of her blue dress like she's trying to make it flatter. She has a matching blue bow in her hair. She looks like she's going to a birthday party with her shiny black shoes on.

"Where'd you come from?" I ask her, heading down the street toward Cal's and Rae's houses. Just then, I see Cal coming out his front door. "Cal!" I run across the street. When I reach the sidewalk, I realize Nicole isn't next to me anymore. I turn around and yell to her, "C'mon, Nicole! We're going to play in the woods."

Nicole continues to walk, not run. She must be afraid of slipping in her shiny shoes.

"Did Phil finish it yet?" Rae hollers to Cal, cutting across her yard.

Nicole finally catches up, and we meet up with Cal and Rae between their two houses.

"No." Cal sighs. "It takes him forever to get anything done."

"God, we're *never* going to have a tree house," Rae complains, like she always does.

"We can still play back there," I say. "Oh, this is Cal and Rae," I tell Nicole, who is standing a couple steps behind me, looking at the ground.

"Hi," Cal says. She looks up at him and quickly looks down again. How could she be afraid of Cal? There's nothing scary about him.

“Hey,” Rae says.

Rae, on the other hand, is definitely scary, but you don’t really find that out until you get to know her. On the outside, she looks like she should be selling lemonade to the neighborhood, with her blond braid and freckles speckled across her face. But once you get to know her, you realize she’d rather dump lemonade over your head than serve it to you.

“What are we going to play today?” I ask, excited to have someone new with us, even though she doesn’t talk.

“Let’s catch bugs and make our own bug zoo,” Rae suggests.

“Or bug circus!” I exclaim, picturing butterflies flying through hoops as I dance around an arena. “Let’s go!” I start running toward the woods, cutting through the tall grass where the wild-flowers grow. Then I stop when I see something hop in front of me. I get down on my hands and knees and look for it.

“What is it?” Cal asks.

“Ssshh.” I’m concentrating on the grasshopper that’s landed on a tall blade of grass. As fast as I can, I cup my hands around it. I can feel it jumping around. It tickles. I squeal and open my hands, dropping it in the grass.

“Why’d you do that?” Rae asks. “You let it go.”

“It felt funny,” I answer, doing a jittery dance, thinking about how it tickled my hand. Someone laughs. I look up and find Nicole giggling. It’s the first sound I’ve heard from her, and it makes me laugh too.

THREE

I wait around the coffee shop the next morning, hoping Nyelle will show up. I leave when I can't wait any longer without being late for sociology.

I'm swearing under my breath as I stalk across campus, taking the most direct route to Stewart Hall. Dr. Tenor likes to embarrass late arrivals, and I'd rather not be today's victim.

I'm jogging down the slope behind the Student Union. Before I start climbing up the other side, I stop. A girl is rolling down the hill. I watch as she tumbles down the steep incline in a blur of hair and blue, dragging a green scarf behind her. She comes to a stop on her back on the flat ground between the two hills, with her arms flopped out beside her. Then she just lies there.

I'm too shocked to move. This isn't something I see every day…or ever. When she doesn't make an attempt to get up, I slowly approach her. She doesn't notice me. Her electric-blue eyes are still directed up at the sky. "Nyelle?"

She blinks at the sound of my voice, focuses on me, and then smiles so wide I can see her bottom teeth. "Cal!"

Not sure what to say to a girl who just voluntarily rolled down a hill, I ask, "Need help up?"

"Not yet. I'm dancing."

"What?" She's not making any sense. I'm beginning to suspect the head trauma theory may not be far off. Or maybe she's drunk.

Her eyes return to the sky again, and she inhales deeply, still wearing the vibrant smile. "I've wanted to do that for so long."

"Um, okay," I say, offering her my hand. She grabs ahold with a cutoff knit glove and hoists herself off the dying grass.

She doesn't brush off the dried blades clinging to her sweater... and everywhere else.

"You have a little something," I say, reaching for the grass stuck in her hair. She shakes her head wildly, her hair whipping around under the brown woven hat. It doesn't help, but she doesn't seem to care. Which is nothing like the girl I used to know. "Where are you going?"

"Class. And I'm late," I say, dreading going.

"I'll walk with you," she offers, heading back up the hill she just rolled down.

I catch up to her. "So do you have a thing for rolling down hills?"

"Nope. That was my first."

"Really?" I question, amused by her answer. "So what made you do it?"

"It was on the list." She says this like it makes perfect sense and I should understand. Except I don't. When she notices I'm waiting for her to continue, she exclaims with a laugh, "And it was *fun*! C'mon, Cal. Haven't you ever had the urge to do something just for the fun of it?"

"Probably." I hesitate. "I just can't remember when."

"Really? That's sad." She truly sounds sorry for me. "You'll have to do it with me next time."

I laugh. "Uh, I'm not sure about that."

We reach the top of the hill and enter the building where my class has already started. I pause in the corridor, about to thank her for the escort, when I hear, "Hey, gorgeous," behind me. I know he's not talking to me.

Nyelle's eyes narrow as three guys walk by us. "Fuck off."

Her words take them, and me, by surprise. I'm not sure who said it, or what he ever did to offend her, but he'll probably never call her gorgeous again. They whip their heads around. "Bitch."

I feel like I should defend her, but the malicious grin on Nyelle's face keeps me silent. I let them walk out the door without interfering. "Do you know them?" I ask her, trying to understand what just happened.

"No," she responds shortly, still staring at the door.

"Then what was that about?"

"They know *nothing* about me," she says between her teeth.

"O-kay," I say with a slight shake of my head, confused by the extreme mood change. They seriously pissed her off. But then I consider who I'm dealing with and what I saw the night of the Halloween party and laugh to myself.

"What?" she asks, turning her attention back to me.

"I've wondered where she went."

"Who?" Nyelle asks, studying me carefully.

"The girl under the mask."

"Which one?" She smirks.

Her answer steadies me. I know she's being cryptic. This isn't the first time. Yet it keeps throwing me off because all I can think about is what she isn't saying.

She turns to walk away. "Bye, Cal."

"Nyelle," I call to her, before she can get too far. She faces me, walking backward. "Do you have plans this weekend? Can I call you?" I hope the request doesn't sound as desperate as it feels, but I can't let her walk away without knowing I'll see her again.

"I don't have a phone," she replies with a small smile. "I'll see you. I promise."

I push through the door to the lecture hall, smiling at the image stuck in my head, of her littered with grass from her hat down to the edge of her sweater. "Well, thank you for making time for us, Mr. Logan!" bellows throughout the room. Every head turns my way. Shit.

I nod apologetically and duck into the back row, taking the first empty seat I find.

I end up only half paying attention to the lecture, thinking back to the girl who is not who she appears to be. Whoever she is, I like her. She's unexpected, and yeah, maybe a little extreme. So different from the perfectionist who refused to talk to me in high school. Regardless of how much I like the transformation, no one changes *that* drastically. Not without a reason.

NICOLE

The Week After Moving

"Nicole, you are a mess," my mom scolds when I come back into the house after spending the afternoon running around in the woods, lifting rocks and rolling logs over to find bugs. I couldn't touch them; neither could Richelle. We'd just find them, scream, and make Rae and Cal pick them up and put them in the buckets.

I look down at my blue dress and notice the smear of dirt from all the times I ran my hands down the front of it. And my black shoes are covered in dirt too.

"You are a little girl," she continues. "You should not be getting dirty! Does Richelle not like playing with dolls? Where did you go?"

I fold my hands and duck my head. "I'm sorry, Momma. She was, um, showing me where these really pretty flowers were behind Cal's house." I've never lied to my mom before. But I'm afraid she'll take my friends away if she thinks they're too messy.

"Who's Cal? You're not playing with a boy, are you?" She makes it sound like playing with a boy will make me sick or something. I shake my head. I don't think I can get away with telling another lie out loud.

"Go clean up and change before your father gets home," she instructs me. "He will be very upset if he sees you like this. We're supposed to make him happy, not disappointed in us."

"Okay, Momma," I respond, taking my shoes off so I don't track dirt all the way to my room.

The next morning I'm in our backyard, setting up the pink table for a tea party, when Richelle comes running over. I don't think she knows how to walk. She's *always* running.

"What are you doing?" she asks as I set the cup on the saucer.

"Playing," I answer, straightening the chair like my mom does at our dinner table.

"Do you want to play with us?" she asks.

"Not today," I answer. I don't want to tell her that my mom told me I couldn't get dirty. That I needed to act like a lady. And that means I shouldn't play in the woods.

"Well, can I play with you?"

I look up in surprise. "You want to have a tea party with me?"

"Sure!" she answers excitedly. "Wait. I'll go put on a dress too." And she runs off, cutting between the small Christmas trees, toward her house.

Richelle came over every morning for the week. Then she'd play with Cal and Rae after lunch. I tried not to be too sad about it, but I was. I could hear them laughing, or Richelle and Rae arguing like they do, from my backyard. I'd try to ignore them and do other stuff so I felt busy. I'd help my mom stick flowers from our yard in vases, put things away in the house, or get dinner ready for Daddy.

The weekend was the hardest because Cal's family had a cookout. They invited us, but we had to go visit my grandma. There aren't any kids where my grandma lives. Only other old people.

Now that it's finally Monday, I can't wait to see Richelle. I stand by the trees, waiting for her. I really want to go over to her house to ask for her to come out, but my mom says it's not polite to invite yourself over. Even though I'm inviting her to *my* house. But my mom still won't let me.

When Richelle finally jumps down her steps, I begin to smile, until she starts walking the other way, toward Cal's house. She almost trips over her shoelace, so she stops to tie it. When she looks up, she sees me. I don't say anything. She waves.

"Hi, Nicole! Guess what?!" She sprints over to me, her pony-tail whipping around. "The tree house is *finally* done. Cal's dad had a bunch of family over this weekend, and the guys helped finish it. Wanna come see it?"

I open my mouth to say yes, because I'm excited to see it too. But then I look down at my pink dress and white shoes and shut my mouth.

"I . . . uh." I want to tell her how I'm not supposed to get dirty, that ladies don't belong in the woods. But I don't want her to think I'm saying she's not a lady. I don't want to hurt her feelings.

Richelle takes my hand. "C'mon." She practically drags me to her house.

"I should tell my mom that I'm coming over," I tell her, looking back at my house over my shoulder.

We enter her house, and her mom comes out of the kitchen.

"Hi," she says. "You must be Nicole. I'm Mrs. Nelson, Richelle's mom."

"Hi," I say, folding my hands in front of me. "Richelle brought me over, but I need to make sure it's okay with my mom first."

"I was actually going over to visit anyway. I'll let her know you're playing. Richelle, where will you be?"

"The tree house," she says.

"Um," I say, my heart beating really fast. "I don't…"

"It's okay," Richelle assures me. "Mom, Mrs. Bentley doesn't like Nicole to get dirty. So I'm going to let her borrow my clothes so she doesn't get in trouble. Okay?"

I can't believe she said that to her mom.

Mrs. Nelson smiles. "I understand. That is a pretty dress. And the woods aren't the best place for white shoes. Go ahead."

Richelle rushes up the stairs, and I hesitate, looking back at Mrs. Nelson because I'm still not sure I won't get in trouble.

"I won't tell, okay?" She winks.

I smile. "Okay."

I climb up the stairs just as Richelle yells, "Nicole, are you coming?!"

FOUR

I drag my feet to the kitchen, pulling a baseball hat low on my head.

"Man, you look like hell. What did you do last night?" Eric asks, perched on the counter, eating a bowl of cereal.

"I couldn't sleep. I kept having these crazy dreams," I tell him, trying to hold on to the broken images of the night I heard Nicole screaming at her parents. It's slowly coming back to me, but not enough that I can make any sense out of it yet. "I need to get to campus to finish my accounting assignment before class."

"Put an extra shot of espresso in your coffee."

I cringe. "The last thing I woke up to was Carly pushing me into a swimming pool–sized cup of scalding coffee. I think I'll pass."

"Yeah, that's going to last all of five minutes," Eric scoffs.

Then he asks, "So the house is having a party Saturday. You want on the list?"

"I guess," I mutter, not really caring about my weekend right now. "I'll see you later." I shove my arms in my jacket and grab my truck keys off the nail in the wall on my way out the door.

Ten minutes later, I'm suddenly aware that I'm driving to Bean Buzz. I'm on autopilot and don't even realize where I'm going until I'm almost there.

I haven't seen Nyelle in a week. And it's not because I haven't been looking. I don't know where this girl goes. But it's nowhere near where I am. I'm thinking she's avoiding me.

So the last thing I expect to hear while standing in line for my coffee is "Hi, Cal. Any chance I can get a ride with you today?"

I'm so tired I think I'm hearing things.

"Cal?"

I turn my head and find Nyelle looking at me oddly. "You okay?"

Maybe she's not avoiding me.

"Oh, hey. Just need coffee," I answer, inching forward in line. "Uh, yeah, I can give you a ride."

"Great! Thanks," she chirps and flops back down on the leather chair with an oversized coffee mug in her hands.

I step up to the counter. "Hey, Mel. Could I get an extra shot of espresso in my coffee?"

She doesn't respond. Instead she looks at the cup she's holding with my name scrawled on it and back at me with a deadly glare.

"Sorry. I didn't mean to throw you off."

"Oh, it's no problem, *Cal*," she says without an ounce of sincerity, dropping my cup in the trash beside her. She nods to the pickup section of the counter, like she's shunning me. She's kinda freaking me out.

I step behind a guy in an overcoat and wait for my order. I can't remember the last time I had to wait. And I continue to wait even after the three people who were standing behind me in line pick up their drinks. Obviously, this is my punishment for not being predictable. Lesson learned.

When I finally walk away with my cup, Nyelle is standing behind me. "What took so long?"

"Don't mess with Mel" is my only response. "Are you ready?"

"Yup," she answers. I realize she's not carrying anything, unless it's under her coat. And considering she's wearing a huge down jacket that looks big enough for a pro linebacker, that's a possibility. The brown coat falls to her knees and covers her hands completely. Her arms swish when she walks, reminding me of the full-body snowsuits we wore when we were kids the few times a year it actually snowed in Renfield.

"What have you been up to?" I ask as we get in the truck, trying to sound casual but wanting to know where she keeps disappearing to and why I can't find her.

"I don't know," she says with a shrug. "I've been doing stuff."

She's not going to make this easy for me, I can tell.

"What's your major?" I ask after we pull away. I'll settle for knowing *any* information, even if it has to be lame.

"I haven't decided yet."

"Me either," I tell her, then wait to see if she'll contribute. Nothing. She's killing me.

"Where'd you go to school last year?" It's hard to believe she could've attended Crenshaw without me seeing her at least once. She'd be hard to miss.

"I spent the year traveling the world."

I have no idea if she's telling the truth.

"The world? Really?" I ask doubtfully.

"Yup." Nyelle reaches deep into the pocket of her jacket without explaining and pulls out a bag of red licorice. She strips one apart from the pack and offers it to me. I shake my head.

"Breakfast?"

"Nope. Just a habit," she replies, sticking the red strand in her mouth.

I give up. We're not really having a conversation—just a string of incomplete sentences. And I'm too tired and out of it to translate. So we drive the rest of the way in silence.

When we reach campus, the caffeine from the coffee is finally kicking in, but I'm already looking forward to the nap I'm planning to take after accounting. My next class isn't until tonight, so I could potentially sleep all afternoon if I wanted. Right now, that doesn't sound like a bad idea.

"I'm going to the Union if you want to come," I offer after we park in my assigned spot. "I have to get the rest of my work done before class."

"I don't have anywhere else to be," Nyelle replies with licorice hanging out of her mouth.

"Then why did you need a ride to campus?" I ask.

"Because I knew you were driving here," she replies, which really isn't an answer. Why do I keep trying?

The cold November air whips around us as we head across campus. I toss my coffee cup in the trash and stuff my hands in my jacket pockets, cursing myself for forgetting gloves.

"Oh crap," I mutter when I spot Corinne walking in our direction across the courtyard. Before I can explain, I duck into the entryway of the law library.

Nyelle takes my lead and leans against the arching brick that covers the entrance. "Is Psycho here, armed with coffee?" she asks in a mocking whisper.

"No," I grumble. "It's not Carly."

Nyelle attempts to peek.

"Please don't."

She looks at me, questioning. "Okay."

I realize how stupid I look hiding from *another* girl, but I can't handle Corinne's overly bubbly enthusiasm right now. I don't have the energy.

"Another ex?" Nyelle smirks.

I clench my jaw and lower my eyes with a slight nod.

"Wow, Cal. How many do you have? And how long does it take you to walk across campus if you're hiding in alleys and doorways the entire time?"

"It's not like that, okay?" I attempt to explain. "Corinne isn't *bad*. She's a sweet girl. But whenever she corners me, I'm stuck listening to her talk about everything she's been doing since the last time I saw her. I was... trying to avoid it this morning."

"This is sooo much better," she says, leaning against the building and looking up at me with teasing blue eyes.

"Trust me. It is."

When Corinne finally passes us, I sigh in relief. "Okay. We can go."

"Really, how many are there?" Nyelle asks, stepping out into the courtyard. "And do all their names begin with C?"

I know she's enjoying this, but I can't say I am. I really don't make a habit of hiding from my exes, although I do avoid them when necessary. Nyelle just happened to be around to see it... twice. This isn't exactly the impression I wanted to make.

"I don't know," I answer evasively, unable to look at her. "There's been a few, I guess."

"Hook-ups or girlfriends?"

"I've dated all of them."

"All?"

I bury my hands in my front pockets again and keep walking with my head down, avoiding the accusatory tone.

"What happened? What was wrong with *all* of them?"

"Nothing really. Except for Carly, who ended up being a psycho. But they're usually really nice. It's just..." I shrug and attempt to pick up the pace, wanting to get to the Student Union faster so we can stop talking about the girls I've dated.

"Then why did you end things, because I'm assuming *you* ended it."

"Usually," I say, barely audible.

"So..." Nyelle pushes, not letting the subject drop. She stops walking just as we're within sight of the doors. "Tell me. What happened?"

I turn abruptly to face her and blurt, "They weren't who I needed them to be, okay?"

She examines me thoughtfully. "*Needed* them to be? What is that supposed to mean?"

I groan. "Coming from the girl loaded with cryptic responses? I think I'll leave it at that." I keep walking without bothering to see if she follows.

"Cal, tell me," Nyelle begs from beside me as I search for an empty table. "Who do you need them to be?"

I don't answer her. I notice a couple guys sliding out of a booth and walk over to claim the table before anyone else can. Nyelle sits down across from me as I set my backpack on the bench.

"Are you hungry?" I ask. "I haven't had breakfast yet."

She recognizes my avoidance and urges carefully, "I'm not judging, Cal. I swear. I'm interested in understanding why you've left a wreckage of broken hearts across campus." I scoff, and her lips curl up into an innocent smile. "Tell me, please. Who are you looking for?"

"I'll be back," I say, needing to stall this interrogation and decide if I'm willing to explain what I meant when I was a little too honest.

I grab a couple breakfast sandwiches and a bottle of water, returning to the table to see her eagerly waiting for me with her chin propped on folded hands.

Against my better judgment, I confess, "I'm looking for the girl I'll regret if I let her go."

Nyelle ponders thoughtfully for a moment. "Your *what if* girl. I like it."

"My what?" I ask with a bite of sandwich in my mouth.

"Your *what if* girl. You serial date so you don't regret passing these girls up, in case one of them is *her.*"

I shrug. "I've never really thought about *why* I date them. Only why I don't stay with them."

"Has there ever been a girl who got away?"

I lean back in the booth and meet her intense gaze. I hesitate before answering, unable to be completely honest. "No. Not really."

"Not even from back home? Where are you from, anyway?"

It takes all my effort not to choke on the food in my mouth when she asks this. I'm doing everything I can to think of her as Nyelle Preston and *not* Nicole Bentley, and then she asks a question that brings it all back, and I can't help wanting to ask her what happened to her. But what if I scare her off and never see her again? It's already hard enough not knowing *when* I'll see her. I don't want to blow it by asking the wrong question too soon.

"I live in a small town in northern California, outside Sacramento." I can't look at her when I say it. It feels like *I'm* the one lying.

"Wow. You're far from home. Why would you choose Crenshaw?"

"It's a good school," I say, without really answering the question. I could tell her I wanted to get away from my family, but I don't. I like my family. I could say they specialized in my major, but I still don't have one. "Truthfully, I was supposed to go to UCLA, but...I changed my mind at the last minute."

She smiles like I've revealed something interesting. "You made a random decision that could affect the rest of your life, just… because?"

"I guess." I shrug.

"Did you serial date in high school too?"

I burst out laughing. If there's anything at all she should remember about me, it's that I was far from the most desirable guy in school. Sure, I had a few girlfriends over the years, but…

I continue to play along. "No," I answer with a shake of my head. "I was…a lot different in high school. I didn't realize how much until I went back home this summer."

A red Jeep stops at the end of the driveway, and Craig Mullins pulls himself up by the roll bar and hangs over the top of the door. "When'd you get home?" he hollers over the music blaring from the radio.

"A couple hours ago," I yell back.

"We're heading to Carter's. Wanna come?"

I look to Rae sitting next to me on the puke-orange and shit-brown plaid couch just inside her garage. She shrugs. "The most happenin' spot in Renfield is the ice cream place. Pathetic." She pushes off the couch and walks down the driveway toward the Jeep. I follow her.

"How's my little Rae of sunshine?" Brady asks from the driver's seat as Rae climbs into the back. She flashes Brady her middle finger. "As cheerful as ever. Nice."

Craig shoots me an odd look when I slide in next to her. "What the hell happened to your hair, Logan? Did you start your own boy band or something?"

I don't bother answering, pushing back the hair hanging in front of my eyes. I didn't plan to grow it out. I've always kept it short. My senior year it was basically buzzed. But I just haven't bothered getting it cut since leaving for Crenshaw, so now it's a flipped-out mess.

"Working for your uncle this summer?" Brady asks, driving out of the neighborhood.

"Yeah," I answer. "What are you guys up to?"

"Same as every summer." Craig turns around to talk to us. "Landscaping for Parker's dad and drinking beers at the lake. Dude, you look... different."

"Uh, okay," I reply dismissively.

"Rae, heard about your chick band," he adds. "Playing any gigs yet?"

"We're still working on material," she tells him.

"Well, you can play at any party I throw this summer," Brady says, looking at us in the rearview mirror.

"Yeah, if we want to play for crickets," Rae scoffs.

"Hey! I throw killer parties."

"Any party in Renfield is a good party," Craig says with a laugh. "This town's too small for everyone not to show up."

Ten minutes later, we're pulling into the dirt parking lot of Carter's Ice Cream. This was the place everyone wanted to work in high school. The most popular kids got their friends hired here each summer. So basically... I never worked here.

It's crowded, as it usually is this time of year. As we approach, I'm trying to prepare myself for the high school reunion that's about to happen.

"Save the picnic table," Rae says as a group leaves. "I'll get you a cone."

Brady sits on top of the table next to me while Rae and Craig stand in the long line.

"Have any epic hook-ups?" Brady asks.

I'm too distracted by the miles of tan skin walking straight toward us to answer. I feel like I'm watching one of those women's razor commercials boasting smooth, touchable skin. It even seems like they're walking in slow motion. Except for Neil Talbert trailing behind them, who might as well be dragging his knuckles. My eyes flick from face to face. Something isn't right. Nicole's not with them.

"Hey, Brady," Heather says as she approaches. "Who's this?" She scans me up and down, not attempting to be subtle about it.

"Uh, this is Cal, Heather," Brady tells her like she's crazy. "Cal Logan."

She tilts her head, confused.

"He graduated with us," Brady adds in disbelief.

I run a hand through my hair to sweep it out of my face, trying not to appear as awkward as I feel.

"Hmm. I don't think I remember you," Ashley says from beside her, gliding her eyes over me as well.

Heather dismisses her comment with a flip of her hair. "You *definitely need to come to the party at Gosland's End tonight."*

"Where's Waldo!" Neil bellows as he comes up behind Ashley, grabbing her ass. She jumps and swats his arm.

"Keep your hands off me, Neil!" she says in disgust. Then she redirects her attention to me. "That's you? Well, you've… grown up." Her suggestive tone makes me wonder what the hell is happening.

The first three years of high school, I was a good five inches shorter, wore round, black-rimmed glasses, and was scrawny and smaller than everyone. Neil used to ask, "Where's Waldo?" wherever he saw me, and it eventually caught on. That stupid-ass saying followed me to every party in high school. It wasn't funny then, and it sure as hell isn't funny now. I've never hit anyone, but I've always wanted to punch that smug look off his face.

"Waldo, what happened to you? You've packed on some muscle. You roidin' or something?" Talbert asks.

"Stop being a douche, Talbert," Craig says, returning to our table and handing Brady a milk shake. "We all know you're the only one with the roid issues. We've seen how small your dick is and that ain't natural."

"Fuck you, Mullins." Talbert takes a step toward him with his fists clenched.

"Don't start acting like a man now, Neil." Vi laughs. "You know he'll kick your ass."

He shoots her a glowering look and walks off. Vi rolls her eyes. Everyone knows they tolerate him only because Nicole dated Kyle for the last three years of high school. Except… Nicole isn't here now.

Because I'm pretty sure she's sitting across from me pretending to be someone else.

"Where'd you go?" Nyelle asks, pulling me out of the memory. I want to ask her the same question.

"Just thinking," I answer dismissively.

Nyelle suddenly shoots her arm in the air and waves frantically. I turn to see whose attention she's trying to get as Tess pushes through the double glass doors. She smiles when she sees us.

"She likes you, you know," Nyelle says quietly, leaning across the table.

"I know," I respond, watching Tess weave her way through the Union.

"Don't let her be another of your victims," she warns. "I'll hurt you."

I turn around, and Nyelle's eyes steady on mine. She's serious.

"Wasn't planning on it," I assure her, not backing down from her stare.

"Hey, guys," Tess greets us, breaking our silent showdown. "What's going on?"

"I'm here to help you study!" Nyelle exclaims, jumping up from the bench. "Wanna go to the library?"

"Uh, sure," Tess replies slowly, obviously surprised by this. "Thanks. I didn't think you had time."

"Change of plans," Nyelle tells her. "See you later, Cal. Thanks for the ride."

I nod. Tess waves bye as they head toward the stairs that lead to the library.

I pull out my accounting assignment, but I can't concentrate. I keep thinking back to the little information Nyelle shared about herself this morning, wondering if she really was traveling last year. And what would bring *her* to Crenshaw? There were only so many coincidences I could accept before I didn't believe in them anymore.

RICHELLE

August—Before Fourth Grade

"Cal and Rae are meeting us at the tree house," I yell back to Nicole as I race across the street. I'm starting to wonder if she knows how to run. I stop on the sidewalk and wait for her to catch up. "Let's pick some flowers first to make it pretty."

"Okay," she answers, tugging at the pair of my shorts she's wearing. She does that a lot too. I think she's never worn shorts in her life. She also borrowed a T-shirt and my mom bought her a pair of sneakers—although she doesn't know that. She thinks the sneakers are mine too. My mom didn't want her to feel bad.

I don't know how she's going to run around in gym without sneakers. Maybe she really doesn't run. It's weird. But she's my friend, so I don't care.

I skip through Cal's yard, toward the woods, and start picking the wildflowers. I really like the white daisies the best, so I get as many of those as I can. Nicole picks some pink and purple flowers. It's not easy to break the stems. Some come right out of the dirt by their roots. I shrug. They still look pretty.

"I love flowers," I tell Nicole, sniffing them—except they don't really smell.

"My mom lets me help with her flowers," she tells me. "She belonged to a garden club where we used to live, and I'd go sometimes. There were so many beautiful flowers there."

"I think I like wildflowers best," I explain. "They just grow wherever they want. No one has to plant them. And then their seeds blow in the wind, and they find a new place to grow."

Nicole stops to think about it and nods. "I think I like wildflowers best too."

I take the flowers from her hand and run into the woods, stopping a couple times for her to catch up. It's hard waiting, so sometimes I just run back and catch up with her before running ahead again. She's definitely not in a rush to get anywhere.

When we finally get to the tree house, Rae is sitting on the ground, leaning against the tree, with Cal standing beside her.

"Finally," Rae huffs, standing up. "Cal, can we go up *now*?" Then she sees the flowers I'm holding. "No way. You are not putting *flowers* in the tree house. It's a *fort,* not a dollhouse."

I ignore her and start for the ladder. She steps in front of me, crossing her arms.

"Come on, Rae. Get out of the way!" I demand. She doesn't move. "Cal, tell her that I can put flowers in the tree house."

I turn toward Cal. He looks to Nicole. "What do you think?"

Nicole looks from me to Rae. I'm afraid she won't say anything because she doesn't talk much... ever. "Richelle was excited to pick them for the tree house. I think it will make her sad if she can't."

I smile.

"Rae, let her put the flowers in the tree house," Cal says. He's used to being the tiebreaker, and usually whatever he decides is what happens. Otherwise, he doesn't really care what we do—as long as we're not playing house or dolls.

"Come on, Nicole," he says to her. She walks in front of him, and he waits for her to start climbing before following.

"Fine," Rae grumbles. "They're going to die anyway."

"And then I'll just pick more," I snap back. I start up the ladder. Cal looks down at me and I smile back up at him.

FIVE

"Excuse me."

I look up and realize there's a line of people trying to get out of the row and I'm still sitting. The screen of my MacBook is dark. I have no idea what happened during class because I spent the entire time wondering when I'd see Nyelle again. And now… it's over. I'll have to borrow notes from the guy who sits next to me.

"Sorry," I say to the girl shuffling by.

I snap my computer shut and grab my bag. I'm still thinking about Nyelle as I follow the drove of backpacks through the exit. I get anxious each time she walks away. I hate not being able to get ahold of her. I'm at the mercy of her random appearances, and it sucks. Last time, it was a week before I saw her again. I wonder how long it'll be this time.

I push through the double doors into the blinding sunlight. Now that we're nearing December, the temperatures can fluctuate between arctic and a crisp fall day. The weather's cooperating today, and I only need a sweatshirt. It actually feels like Renfield's weather, which reminds me, I should probably check on Rae to see how she's dealing back home. I know she feels trapped there. But she'll be here soon enough.

I pull out my phone but hesitate when I notice the wavy brown hair bouncing next to me. Nyelle's walking alongside me. Where'd she come from?

"Hi."

"Hey," she responds casually.

"Two days in a row. That's... unexpected," I say.

"Are you keeping track of when you see me? Aw, Cal. I'm flattered." She's teasing me, and now I wish I hadn't mentioned it.

I'm about to cross the street when she takes a left. "Where are you going?" I know she would've kept going if I hadn't said something.

Nyelle pauses and turns around. People continue to pass between us, making it difficult to see her. "The Frosting Tree. Wanna come?"

"Sure," I answer warily. I've never heard of it.

I cut through the steady stream of pedestrians and continue walking with Nyelle as she leads us away from campus. She's wearing the big brown jacket again, despite the warm day.

"Aren't you hot in that jacket?"

"I'm not wearing anything underneath it," she replies flatly.

My eyes widen. She laughs.

"Wow, Cal. Relax. I was only kidding. I need this jacket, and I'm wearing a tank top underneath. But thanks for your concern."

I press my lips together and nod.

We cross a street that takes us off campus and into a residential neighborhood. I don't spot anything that resembles a store or a restaurant.

"Where is this place?" I ask when we cut down another street.

"Not too much farther," she explains. "When's your next class?"

"In about an hour."

I follow her down another street. "Here we are."

Across from us is a large park with a baseball diamond, basketball court and playground. I'm trying to figure out where the Frosting Tree is when she walks in the direction of a bench. Maybe she changed her mind. I'm about to sit on the bench when she approaches the tree behind it.

She sticks her foot into a deep V where the main branches split and grabs ahold of the branch above her head to hoist herself up. My mouth opens, but nothing comes out. Nyelle continues to climb up another five feet before looking down. "Are you coming?"

"You want me to climb a tree?"

"You don't have to, but I am. Besides, when was the last time you climbed a tree?"

"Uh, not since I was a kid. And where we...I'm from, they're mostly huge evergreens. Not too climbable."

"C'mon," she encourages one more time. "Climb a tree with me."

I look around to see if anyone's watching. This is crazy. But I follow after her anyway, up the tree.

Nyelle picks a thick branch toward the top to sit on, and I choose a sturdy-looking one across from her, keeping hold of the limb above me. I never thought I had an issue with heights, but the fact that I can't see the ground through the crisscross of branches and that we're higher than the power lines is making my palms a little sweaty.

"I like it up here," Nyelle says with a deep breath, like she's at the peak of a mountain, taking in the view. She has her back against the bark, with one leg resting on the branch and the other dangling. "This is a great place to think."

"How often do you do this?" I ask, eyeing a group of kids approaching the tree, dribbling a basketball. They continue to the court without noticing we're above them.

"Think? Only when I need to," she replies sarcastically.

"Nice," I respond. "No, how often do you climb this tree?"

"This is my first time."

"You've never been here before? But you seemed to know where you were going." This girl continues to confuse me.

"I knew there was a park over here," she explains. "So I figured there would be a frosting tree too. The perfect tree to sit in and… reflect on life."

"Another first for you, huh? This on the list too?"

She nods.

"Why do you call it the *frosting* tree?" I ask.

She thrusts her arm, elbow-deep, into her jacket pocket and pulls out a tub of vanilla frosting. "I like to have something sweet while I'm thinking."

"Of course you do. I should've known." I shake my head with a laugh. "And that's why you're wearing the huge jacket—to carry your groceries. What else do you have in there?"

"What else do you want?" she responds with a smart-ass grin. She pops off the plastic cover and peels back the foil before dipping a finger in and removing a huge glob of white frosting that she plops into her mouth. She tilts the container toward me.

I hold up my hand. "I'm all set."

"Try it," she insists. "It'll make being up in this tree so much better." I hesitate another second before giving in, scooping out a conservative helping. When I put it in my mouth, Nyelle notices my expression. "Good, right?"

I nod. "You were right. The tree makes so much sense now."

"I love frosting," she says dreamily, ignoring my sarcasm. She scoops out another helping. "What could you eat every day without getting sick of it?"

After swallowing down another fingerful, I answer, "Cereal. I'm convinced I could eat it for every meal."

"You're such a guy." Nyelle laughs. "I'd eat potato chips every day for the rest of my life. I'd mix it up and have a different flavor or brand each day. I love chips."

"And frosting," I note, watching her mindlessly consume the whipped sugar.

"Have you ever dipped potato chips in frosting?" she asks excitedly—like it's the best idea.

"No." I grimace. "That sounds disgusting."

"No way. Salty and sweet is the best combination. Now that I'm thinking about it, I'll have to try it."

I chuckle, expecting her to reach in and pull out a bag of chips from her pocket. But she doesn't.

Nyelle becomes distracted by a flock of birds flying overhead and watches them land on a tree across the park. A light gust sweeps a few strands of hair across her cheeks. Her eyes flicker with thought, although her face remains calm and content. "If you could have a superpower, what would it be?" She glances over at me, and I realize I haven't taken my eyes off her. I blink and look around.

"Uh," I stall. Not expecting the question. "Are we *reflecting*?"

"Yeah," she answers with a smile. "Don't worry. What's said in the tree stays in the tree."

I wonder just how honest we're about to be. "Okay." I nod, hoping I'm not going to regret this. "I think . . . superstrength. Probably because I was such a scrawny kid."

"You don't look very scrawny now," Nyelle observes, tilting her head to look me over, causing me to shift uncomfortably.

"Yeah, but it doesn't change my childhood. What about you?"

Her translucent blue eyes scan the sky. She's sitting back so casually, like she's sitting on the bench below us—not at the top of a tree. "I'd fly. But more like…float. Let the wind carry me and set me down wherever it wants." She arches up with her eyes closed, like she's tempting the wind to take her. Her chest rises and falls dramatically, filling her lungs with the air she wants to be a part of. When she opens her eyes and looks at me, I sit up straighter and focus on the leaf above her head. I keep getting lost in her. She's unlike anyone I've ever known.

"Do you ever wish you could do something over again?" she asks, her tone more serious. Her eyes are dark and troubled. I'm wondering where her thoughts took her in that quiet moment in the wind. "There are so many times I think about a decision I've made and wonder, 'What if I had done it differently? Who would I be? What would my life be like? What if…?'" She takes a deep breath, leaving the thought unfinished.

Without warning, the storm passes from her eyes and a mischievous smile cuts across her face. "What if you could do something over again? What would you choose?"

I open my mouth but don't know what to say. The irony of her question keeps the words trapped. If anyone has something to confess, it's the girl sitting across from me.

"Don't torture yourself," Nyelle says with a laugh. She looks off in the distance at two little girls running down the sidewalk. "What if I had one more day?"

"For what?" I ask automatically.

She presses her lips together, not saying more. I guess these confessions are meant to be as cryptic as everything else about her.

I look around for inspiration and observe the boys playing basketball. "What if I'd practiced more?"

Nyelle follows my line of sight and grins. "You sucked at basketball?" I shrug. I wasn't very good at basketball. I made the team—just to warm the bench. Guess that wasn't hard to figure out. Or maybe I suck at being cryptic too.

"Okay," Nyelle says, scrunching her face in thought. "What if I had been a better liar?"

I laugh. Isn't that what she's doing right now? "You regret not being able to lie?"

"What can I say?" Nyelle smiles. "I can keep a promise for an eternity, but don't ask me to lie. I will avoid having to lie to a person like you avoid your exes."

Wow, I mouth. "I promise to never ask you to lie for me." I just wish she'd stop lying *to* me.

"Thanks," she responds. "Are you a good liar?"

"I have done my share of lying," I admit, unashamed. "But only to keep from hurting someone. Or to not get in trouble as a kid. Stupid stuff. Nothing morally corrupt or anything." This entire conversation is causing me to break out in a sweat. I have no idea how she's remaining so calm. Unless…she doesn't really believe she's lying.

"I see what's going on, Cal. You look all nice and innocent. Then you break these poor girls' hearts while lying to them about why." She shakes her head in disapproval, but the teasing spark in her eye gives her away.

"I'm pretty sure they've all recovered," I defend with a forced smile.

"What if you could date one of them again? Would you?"

I take a deep breath and try to consider her question seriously. I flip through the girls' faces in my head, but don't pause on any, except one. But we were just kids then, and now I don't know where she is. "Nope."

Nyelle's mouth opens in surprise. "Really? You have no leftover feelings for any of them?"

"I don't think I really had strong enough feelings to begin with. I liked them. Still do for the most part, but..." I shrug, feeling heat creep up my neck. "What about you? If you could give one of the guys you dated another chance, would you?" I hold my breath, anticipating some sort of reaction.

She starts laughing, hard. Not the reaction I was expecting.

I'm afraid she's going to fall out of the tree when she grabs her stomach and shakes her head. It takes her a minute to pull herself together, wiping the corners of her eyes.

"That bad?" I'm thinking of Kyle Talbert, the guy she dated throughout most of high school. And I'm assuming she is too.

"The worst."

I couldn't agree with her more, except if she dated his younger brother, Neil—that would've been *much* worse. But then why did they stay together for so long? This may be the strangest non-conversation I've ever had.

"I definitely want a do-over." She shudders, causing me to laugh loudly. "That and my first kiss." Nyelle's nose scrunches with the thought of it as she sticks out her tongue in disgust. "Yuck."

"You're starting to make me feel sorry for you," I tease. "You had a horrible boyfriend. And your first kiss was evidently... disgusting."

"It was!" she says adamantly. "My first kiss was all tongue and slobbery. I really wanted to ask him if he could taste what I had for dinner, but I wasn't bold enough. I had to find a way to wipe my face with my sleeve after. So gross."

"Yeah, that is bad." I cringe, having no idea who her first kiss was. "I've kissed girls who were... all over the place. Not my first. But still. It's not a turn-on, so I can empathize."

"I'm sure you can," she says with a roll of her eyes. "Tell me this, if you *could* go back and do your firsts over again, would you?"

"My first kiss?"

"First kiss. First time having sex..." Nyelle clarifies.

I laugh awkwardly. "Okay. We're going *there.*" She nods in encouragement. "Being honest—I don't care who it's with—I think everyone's first time is kinda awful."

Nyelle laughs. "You think so?"

"C'mon. For a guy, there's so much pressure to perform, but there's no way you're going to. You have no idea what the hell you're doing, no matter how many... Anyway, it's not going to be good. And for a girl, it hurts. How can that be any fun?"

"I'd like to think there are a few exceptions." Nyelle smiles thoughtfully.

"Yours didn't suck?" I question, completely shocked. I wouldn't expect Kyle to be very attentive. Even if he's two years older. Unless there was someone else before him... I really don't want to be thinking about this.

"Who was your first?" Nyelle presses.

"Um... Lily Graham," I answer carefully, watching for a sign of recognition because I know she knows her... or did, when she remembered things. Nothing. Just an anticipatory brow raise, encouraging me to continue. "Nothing romantic. We'd been going out for a couple months our junior year. She invited me over when her parents weren't home, so we decided to do it. There was a hot tub. Clothes came off. We ended up getting the couch soaking wet. She cared more about her parents being pissed about the couch than the fact that we'd just had sex for the first time. It was... fast."

"What happened?" Nyelle leans in closer, scooping another fingerful of icing out of the tub without taking her eyes off me. There isn't much more to the story, but she's sitting on the edge of her branch in expectation.

"What do you mean what happened?"

"To the two of you? Did you love her? Why'd it end? Did you break her heart too?"

"Uh, no. We weren't in love or anything. I mean, we were in *high school*. We actually broke up two days later."

Nyelle's shoulders sink with a disheartened "Oh."

"Sorry to disappoint."

"What about your first kiss?" she asks, perking back up.

I stop to recall my first kiss. I've always considered there being two. The *first* was technically part of a game. The other was by choice. It doesn't matter—they were both with the same girl. My mouth slides into a small grin. I can't share this with her. Especially considering she was there.

"This is the dumbest game ever," Rae complains, sitting with her legs crossed on the floor of her living room, leaning against the plaid couch.

"You won't be saying that when the bottle lands on me," Brady says with a wink.

"Ew, gross!" Rae grimaces. "I'd rather kiss a snake."

"Oh, you want tongue," Brady says with a cheesy grin, making us all laugh. Rae flips him off.

"Okay, there's three girls and three boys," Richelle declares. "Alternate, and whoever the bottle points closest to is who you have to kiss." She narrows her eyes at Brady. "And there's no tongue, sicko."

"Boo!" Craig protests.

"Nicole, you go first," Richelle instructs.

Nicole's face turns bright red. "Me?"

"Yeah. Go ahead," Richelle repeats.

Nicole looks to me quickly, and I nod in encouragement. I won't admit it, but I want it to land on me. We've been friends for two years, since she moved here in fourth grade. But I like her. I always have. Even if she is a little shy. She's not bold like Richelle. And Rae is more of a guy than Brady is. Nicole may not have much to say, but I still think she's . . . perfect.

I'm holding my breath watching the Mountain Dew bottle spin in a circle. It doesn't spin around many times before it lands between Richelle and Brady.

"Lucky girl," Brady says with a smile. My teeth clench, ready to push him over if he touches her.

Nicole leans over the circle so she's on her hands and knees. Brady leans in, probably expecting more than the quick peck that he receives. I don't even think she kisses his lips.

"That's it?" Brady grumbles. "My grandmother kisses longer than that."

"You're disgusting." Rae scowls. "This game is probably the only time you'll be kissed by a girl in your life, so you'd better stop complaining."

"My turn," Richelle announces.

"Hey! I thought I was next. I'm next to Nicole."

"Girls first," Richelle tells Craig, who rolls his eyes.

Richelle gives it a forceful spin, but it ends up bouncing across the floor.

"Easy there, sugar lips," Brady teases, handing her back the bottle. Richelle ignores him and spins it again.

The bottle whips around and around, eventually pointing right at my knee. Richelle presses her lips together to keep from smiling.

"Glasses off, Cal."

I take them off, and the room is immediately out of focus. I blink. But it doesn't matter. Craig could be kissing me, and I'd have no idea.

"Just close your eyes," she instructs me. I hear the guys' stifled laughs when I do. I wait.

Then something warm presses against my lips. I didn't know lips could be this soft. And they stay against my mouth for what feels like a long time. I don't mind. I like it. And when she pulls away, I can feel the blood rush throughout my body, and I immediately try to sit in a different position. The guys start dying laughing. I want to tell them to shut up, but I don't want the girls to notice what they obviously do.

"So immature," Richelle huffs. I shove my glasses back on and find her looking at me, her cheeks a bit flushed. She smiles a little, and I smile back.

"That must've been some kiss," Nyelle says softly, pulling me from thoughts of Richelle. Her reflective blue eyes shift and fall on me. Neither of us says anything for a full minute. Our knees lightly touch as we sit there staring at each other, neither of us looking away. I lean over and brush the stray hair caught on her lips. She draws in a quick breath. And in that second, I'm tempted to kiss her.

Nyelle blinks, like a light's being flashed before her eyes, and just like that, the moment's gone. I pull back, holding on to the branch with two hands again.

"I liked this," she says, inhaling deeply with her eyes closed, drawing her shoulders up. She relaxes them with a strong exhale and smiles brightly. "Thanks for finding the frosting tree with me, Cal. Not many guys would do this."

"I have to agree with you," I respond with a nod, still needing a moment to get over what almost happened. I look down at the tangle of branches and wonder: Why *did* I follow her up here? And how the hell am I supposed to get back down?

"We should get going so you're not late for class."

Nyelle secures the lid on the frosting and sticks it in her cavernous pocket. She steps down to the next level, and then she's off—practically hopping down the tree. She does it so effortlessly. It takes me a lot longer. I brace myself as I step on each branch, expecting it to snap beneath my boot.

When I finally reach the ground, Nyelle is already at the street. "I'll see you around, Cal."

My gut floods with the familiar anxiety I get when she's about to leave me. "Nyelle." She stops in the middle of the street to turn my way. "Want to do something tomorrow night? My roommate's fraternity, Delta Ep, is having a party."

"Tomorrow night?" After a thoughtful pause, she responds, "Maybe."

Before I can figure out how to get in touch with her, she's walking away again—but not toward campus. I'm tempted to catch up with her, but I need to get to my next class.

"*Maybe*," I mumble. "What am I supposed to do with that?"

NICOLE

October—Fourth Grade

I step off the bus and start walking toward my house, adjusting the straps of my backpack on my shoulders.

"Hey, Nicole," Cal says before I walk too far. "Where's Richelle?"

"At the dentist," I tell him softly. "Where's Rae?"

"She and her mom went to pick up Liam at their dad's."

"Oh," I exhale.

"Do you want to come over? My dad finally finished putting up the tire swing."

I run my hands down the front of my purple dress. "Um... I guess. I have to do my homework first."

"Okay. See ya," he responds, adjusting his glasses on his nose before running off toward his house.

I watch Cal run down the street. But as I turn to my house, I realize I can't play on the tire swing with him. Richelle isn't home, which means I don't have play clothes to change into. And it's very important to my mom that I stay clean, so that we can look nice for Daddy. I try to decide what to do while I finish my homework. Maybe we can play something inside instead.

"Momma, is it okay if I go over to Cal's house to play with him and Jules?" I ask. Cal's sister, Jules, is in kindergarten. She's too little to play with us. But it will make my mom feel better if she thinks Jules is playing too.

"Did Mrs. Logan invite you over, honey?" she asks from the kitchen. I hear the oven door plunk shut.

"Cal did," I tell her.

"Let me call first to make sure it's okay with his mom."

I wait quietly while she calls Cal's mom. When she gets off, she tells me, "Okay. She says you are welcome over. Be sure to use your manners, and please be home by five thirty so you can help set the table for your daddy's dinner."

"All right, Momma," I call before pushing the screen door open.

Cal is waiting for me in his driveway. He has his hands in his pockets and is scuffing his sneaker into the pavement.

"Hi, Nicole," he says. "I know you can't get your dress dirty, so if you want, I put some clothes in the bathroom so we can play on the tire swing. My mom says it will leave black marks on clothes, and I didn't think you'd like that."

I can feel my face get hot. "*Your* clothes?" I'm thinking that maybe I should go back home. I can't wear a *boy*'s clothes.

Cal shrugs like it's no big deal. "It doesn't really matter who they belong to. When they're on you, they're yours."

I think about what he said for a second and then smile. He looks up from the ground and smiles too, just a little.

"Thanks, Cal," I tell him. "That's really nice. I'll be right back." I walk toward his house to change.

Cal is about the same size as me and Richelle, so the shorts and T-shirt fit. The shoes are a little big, but that's okay. I decide it doesn't really matter that they're boys' clothes, even if it has a basketball on the shirt. *I* still look like a girl.

When I come back outside, Cal doesn't say anything about how I look. We just walk toward his backyard, then cut across the wildflower grass and into the woods.

"Wow," I say when we get to the biggest tire I've ever seen. "I think six of us can fit on that thing." It's a giant black tire hung from a big, thick branch high above by chains, keeping it flat like a doughnut.

"I think that's kinda the idea," Cal says. "Get on. I'll push."

I have a hard time getting up on the tire because it's so big. I think it must have come from a dump truck.

"Here, let me help you." Cal stands next to me and laces his fingers together. "Put a foot on my hands and I'll give you a boost."

I'm a little nervous, but I do it anyway. He lifts me up easily. I didn't realize he was so strong. He doesn't look very big. I grab the chains and crawl onto the gigantic tire to sit, dangling my feet through the hole in the center.

"Are you ready?" Cal asks. I hold on tighter and nod. "Okay, I'm going to spin you. Tell me if you get too dizzy."

Cal walks the tire around and around, and I watch the chains twist above my head. When it's too hard to push anymore, he says, "Ready. Set. Go!" And he steps back.

The swing starts to unwind slowly. But the next thing I know, it's whipping around really fast. Everything blurs by me and the wind blows my hair. I start laughing, and I don't stop until the swing does. My head's fuzzy. The world still feels like it's spinning really fast.

When I can finally see right again, Cal is smiling up at me like something's funny. I'm afraid my hair is stuck up or something.

"What?" I ask, suddenly embarrassed.

"You should laugh more. I like it."

I laugh again. And Cal laughs too.

SIX

"Who do you keep looking for?" Eric asks, distracting me from constantly checking the face of every girl in the room.

"No one," I answer, giving up with a heavy breath. If she's going to show, she will. There's nothing I can do about it. I should know that by now.

"Let's get a shot." Eric leads us to one of the bedrooms down the hall. It has an old-fashioned barber's chair set up in the center of it.

A girl gets in the chair. Although she adjusts her short skirt, I can still see her red underwear when she lies back. Most of the guys in the room tilt their heads for a better view. Guess I'm not the only one who noticed.

A guy with a backward baseball hat tips a bottle over her open mouth and then another wearing a cowboy hat helps him spin the chair while everyone cheers her on.

"I'm not going in the chair," I tell Eric. He chuckles and holds two fingers in the air to one of his frat brothers doling out shots. The guy steps up onto a wooden chair and says, "Open up."

I lean my head back and let him pour the contents of the bottle into my mouth, gulping way too many times by the time he's done.

"Shit." I shudder and step away so Eric can take his turn.

I hold my hand up with a shake of my head when Eric offers

me a beer from their cooler. "I'm done." He gives it to me anyway, but I don't open it. I'm sure I'll be feeling whatever I just did an upside-down shot of soon enough. Besides, hangovers are not my friend. "Really. I need to drive. Are you staying here tonight or coming back to the apartment with me?"

He takes the beer from me and double fists it. "Depends on how the night goes," he says, eyeing a blonde walking by.

I don't know when I lose him. But somewhere on the second floor, when I catch myself looking around for Nyelle again, I realize Eric's gone. Which probably means he's going to be crashing here tonight.

I stay upstairs for a while, watching people annihilate themselves as they go from room to room taking shots. Each room offers a different flavor and some asinine way of drinking it—whether through a beer funnel, hanging upside down on a bar suspended from the ceiling, or by dunking their head into a pool filled with vodka-infused Jell-O. It's entertaining, at least until I sober up.

"Hi."

I slowly turn around.

"Want to get a drink?"

I grin at the cute girl with long black hair and big brown eyes smiling up at me.

"Uh, sure." I can handle one more drink…for her. I'd be stupid to say no.

I lead the way to the basement, where the official bar is set up. She grabs my hand so we don't get separated, and I walk closer to her to make sure we're not pulled apart.

"What would you like?" I bend down and ask in her ear. She smells sweet, like strawberries.

"They have this blue drink that's good."

I order for her and take a beer for myself.

"I'm Cal," I holler over the deafening music.

"Jade." She smiles, exposing deep dimples that make her ten times cuter. "Are you with the house?"

"My roommate is."

A laugh cuts through the crowd, and I instinctively turn my head. I search the underlit room but don't see her.

"You okay?" Jade asks, appearing concerned.

"Uh, yeah. Sorry. I thought I heard someone I know." I need to quit being an idiot and stop looking for Nyelle. She didn't want to be here with me or else she would've shown. But there's a girl who *is* interested right in front of me.

"An ex?" She scrunches her nose.

I shake my head. "No. Not an ex." Although bumping into one of them is a probability that I'd rather not think about.

I try to have a conversation with Jade. It's not working. This isn't the place to get to know someone. And the drunker everyone else gets, the more sober I feel. I'd rather end this with her still remembering me.

"I have to give my roommate a ride home," I lie as she starts wiggling her hips next to me, an indication that she wants to dance. And I don't dance.

"Let me have your phone," she requests, holding out her small, manicured hand. "I'll give you my number and we can go out sometime." I hand it to her. She taps in her number, then calls herself. "Now I have yours too."

I lean down to give her a hug, and she brushes her lips against my cheek. "Good night, Cal," she purrs in my ear. I'm suddenly second-guessing my departure, but then she's off, hollering to some girls on the dance floor.

At least tonight wasn't a total waste.

There's a sledgehammer slamming against my head. I press my face into the pillow, begging it to stop. Then I realize the banging isn't inside my head. Someone's knocking on the door. I squint my eyes open, trying to focus in the dark room. I have no desire to get up and answer the door. I roll over with a groan, hoping whoever it is will go away. But the knocker is persistent.

I wait for Eric to answer it.

The pounding echoes through the apartment again.

Shit. Eric's not home.

Grumbling, I throw back the covers and push myself off the bed. Half-asleep, I shuffle to the door that might as well be a mile away.

"Coming!" I yell as another booming knock shakes the door. When I finally open it, I'm immediately blinded by the harsh light in the hallway. I squint and find electric-blue eyes peering up at me. I run a hand through my hair and blink again, not convinced she's real. "Nyelle?"

"Hi, Cal," she says, humming with energy.

"Um… what are you doing here?" I open the door wider so she can come in, but she stays in the hall.

"I came to get you."

I shake my head, trying to understand what's happening. "How'd you know where I live? And why are you holding a sleeping bag?"

"I asked around the dorm. Figured one of the girls dated you at some point. A girl whose friend dated one of your roommate's fraternity brothers told me where you live."

I'm so confused.

"Do you have a sleeping bag?" she asks when I stare at her too long.

"Uh, yeah," I answer tentatively, trying to remember if that's the truth. "Why?"

"Get it and meet me at your truck," she instructs and then walks past me, grabs my keys from the nail in the wall, and disappears down the hall.

"Now?" is my automatic response. I have no idea what time it is, but I know I should still be sleeping.

"Yeah," she calls back over her shoulder before exiting the building.

I rub my eyes, trying to force myself awake.

Then I hear my truck starting in the parking lot.

"She's serious," I say with a heavy breath. Where the hell is she taking me in the middle of the night…with a sleeping bag? As inviting as it sounds to crawl into a sleeping bag with Nyelle, I'm pretty sure that's not what *she* has in mind. And, apparently, I don't have a choice, so I drag myself back to the bedroom to get my things.

I glance at the clock and blink hard when I read *4:12*. No wonder I can barely focus.

I eventually walk outside, dressed and carrying a sleeping bag I had stashed on the top shelf of my closet. I grumble under my breath at the dark sky. I should *not* be awake.

"You're driving?" I climb in the passenger side. Something I haven't done since my older brother, Devin, owned the truck. But I'm too tired to care—and probably to drive safely—so I shut the door and slump against the seat, dropping the sleeping bag on the floor.

Nyelle shifts the truck into reverse and backs up with a small jolt when she releases the clutch too quickly. After fighting for first gear, and a rough transition, we pull onto the road. I clench my teeth as she grinds through the gears, until she eventually gets a feel for the clutch.

"Here." Nyelle hands me a thermal cup that was sitting in the holder. "I don't know if it's any good. I've never brewed coffee before."

I slide it open, and the bitter potency of the coffee makes my nose hairs curl. "Whoa. I haven't even tasted it yet and I can tell it's strong."

"It'll wake you up," she says with a playful grin.

I brace myself and take a swig—my jaw automatically tightens. "Damn. I think I'll be awake for three days now." Nyelle laughs. "So... where are we going?"

"To watch the Leonids," she responds.

"The what?"

"A meteor shower. As long as the sky stays clear, we should be able to see them around five o'clock. And then I figured we could watch the sun rise."

"Oh" is all that I can manage to say. This is crazy. I look over at Nyelle, and she smiles back, her eyes lit up with excitement. Yup, this is definitely crazy. But then again, so is she. In a good way. And I like that about her at any other *reasonable* hour of the day.

We drive through the deserted streets in silence. I lean my head back against the seat and close my eyes.

I'm jerked awake when the truck bounces violently. We've turned onto an abandoned road that's overgrown and rutted with deep tire tracks. "Where are we?"

I grab the bar above the door as we continue to rock along the rough terrain.

"Found this place when I went for a walk the other day," Nyelle explains, concentrating on the dark road lined with dense woods. "I kind of got lost, and well... you'll see. It's pretty cool."

"You walked out *here* by yourself?"

"Are you afraid, Cal?" I can see her mocking smile in the glow of the panel.

"You realize you're just begging to meet an ax murderer out here, right?"

Nyelle laughs.

The road opens up to a clearing. She parks in front of a lodge with *Camp Sunshine* carved into a sign above the door. With the headlights shining on it, I can see that it's old and in serious need of repair. The boards on the porch are broken, and the screen door is hanging from its hinges.

"Tell me again why we had to come way out here to watch the meteor shower?"

"Don't worry. I won't let anything happen to you," Nyelle says with a smirk. She pulls her sleeping bag out from behind the seat, then shuts the door. Between the crack coffee, the *Friday the 13th* backdrop, and the frigid temperatures, I'm wide-awake. I pull my gloves from my pockets and put them on, then pick up my sleeping bag to follow after Nyelle toward a dock that juts out into a lake like an exclamation point. Considering the cabins are a strong wind away from falling over, I don't think walking on the dock is the best idea.

"You're not going out there, are you?" I holler to her, jogging to catch up.

"That's where we're going to watch the meteors," she informs me, her breath a billowing cloud against the cold air.

Standing on the hardened ground at the end of the dock, I look down the long row of weathered planks. It's too dark to really see how worn the boards are, but they *seem* to be intact.

Nyelle walks out on the dock without hesitation. I'm expecting her to fall through at any moment. The wood creaks, and the dock rocks gently in the water, but nothing breaks.

"Here goes nothing," I murmur, following her.

I can feel the boards bow slightly beneath my weight, but they hold me.

Nyelle is studying the sky when I reach her. "Which way is north?"

I take out my phone and open the flashlight app with a compass on it. I point toward the right. "That way."

She orients herself and unrolls her sleeping bag.

I scan the reflective surface of the lake, inhaling the frigid air. What am I doing out here? Then I look at Nyelle with her legs buried in her sleeping bag. I watch as she removes a thermos from one of her Mary Poppins pockets and a bag of marshmallows from the other. I smile. Yeah, I know exactly why I'm here.

"Do you have a heater in there too?"

She rolls her eyes. "Stop being ridiculous. Come sit."

I release the buckle on my sleeping bag and roll it out next to her. She opens the thermos, releasing a trail of steam.

"Let me guess. Hot chocolate?"

"It's not just *any* hot chocolate. It's my favorite." She pours some in the lid. "Here, try it."

I sit on top of my navy-blue sleeping bag and take it from her. It smells like chocolate but . . . sweeter.

"Don't trust me?"

"I do," I respond defensively. I take a small sip. It's pretty damn good. "What is it?"

"It's Milky Way hot chocolate. I put caramel and mocha in it."

"That's actually my favorite ice cream."

"Weewy?" Her words are muffled by the marshmallow plugging her mouth. I laugh at her.

She sucks in the marshmallow and giggles uncontrollably. I lose my laughter at the sound of hers. I've heard Nyelle laugh before, but this light, girly sound is different. It's one I remember so distinctly. *This* laugh is one of my favorite childhood memories.

"What?" she asks. "Are you okay?"

"Uh, yeah," I say, snapping out of it. "Still waking up."

"We shouldn't have to wait too much longer," Nyelle explains, lying back on the dock, pulling her sleeping bag up to her chin.

"What are we looking for exactly?"

"Shooting stars, but lots of them, and brighter."

After a few minutes of sitting and waiting, I'm fricken freezing. So I slip into my sleeping bag and lie next to Nyelle, resting my head on my gloved hands.

We lie there in silence. The sky is speckled with countless stars, despite the large moon low in the sky.

"I was hoping to see you tonight," I say without looking at her.

"You did see me tonight," she says with a small laugh.

"I meant at the party."

She's quiet. I look over and find her eyes are still, like they're steadied on a single star.

"I thought about it. But most people annoy me, and after I drink, I tend to let them know it."

I laugh. "So no parties for you?"

"I'll go, but one a month is my quota."

"Have you met your quota this month?" I ask, still watching her. Her profile is soft lines, accentuated by the fullness of her lips. I've never really noticed her lips before—always too caught up in her eyes.

"Nope. Not yet." She darts her eyes toward me, then back up at the sky.

"Then...next weekend, go to a party with me and my friends?" I suggest. I'm hoping that if it sounds less like a date, she'll show up. I've been trying to figure out how to make sure Rae gets to meet her anyway.

"Where?"

"Not sure yet. *This* weekend is still happening, so I'll tell you when I see you at Bean Buzz on Thursday." This is my way of guaranteeing I see her again this week.

"Um...okay."

I return my focus to the sky with a smile on my face.

We're quiet again. I can hear the water lapping against the dock. It's sedating. Waiting eventually makes my lids heavy.

"There's one!"

I open my eyes. Nyelle's arm is extended, a finger pointing. But I've missed it.

"We're only going to see the brightest ones because of the full moon."

We don't see another one for five minutes. I watch it move across the sky like a single headlight traveling down a highway. I want to call out, "Padiddle!" But that would sound stupid. It just accounts for how tired I am.

"I love looking at the stars." Her voice is quiet and distant, like a memory. "They can take away your pain if you let them. And when the sun comes up, all that sorrow disappears."

When I take in all the stars in the sky, I can't help but think that's a lot of hurt. "What about the shooting stars?"

Nyelle turns her head with a jerk at the sound of my voice, like she forgot I was beside her. "You wish on them, for another chance to get it right."

"Do you believe you can do that? Just start again?"

"Every day," she says in a whisper, staring at the stars.

Two bright streaks rush across the night sky, crossing each other directly above us.

"Now we each get a second chance," I say.

"Do you know what you want to do differently, now that you get a do-over?"

"I need to think about it," I lie, not ready to be that honest. "Do you?"

"Yeah, I do," she answers. When I look at her, her eyes are closed and her chest rises with a deep inhale, like she's wishing it this very second. A slow smile emerges on her lips right before she opens her eyes. She angles her head toward me, still smiling.

I can't look away from the light caught in her eyes. I search them for whatever it is she's not saying. I want to ask her what she wished for, but when she redirects her attention back to the stars, I lose my nerve.

I turn away and stare into space. It occurs to me, as I watch another meteor gliding along the tree line, that tonight the sky is full of second chances. Nyelle continues to call out each sighting. But after a while I give in to the weight of my lids and everything fades to black.

"Want to have sex?"

"What?" My eyes flip open. I blink quickly, trying to appear alert. "What did you say?"

"I knew that would wake you up." She starts laughing that giggly laugh that I love. I've missed hearing it. It's real—and full of life. I smile back at her.

I prop myself up on my elbows and look around. The horizon is lightening behind the trees. "Sorry. I didn't know there would be so much waiting."

"Yeah, they're not exactly celestial fireworks."

"I don't get why they call it a meteor *shower* then." I yawn, sitting up to stretch my arms over my head.

I can hear birds chirping and the rustling of early morning.

"Want to go canoeing?"

I start to ask if she's serious. But then she stands up and starts toward the lodge, where a green canoe is leaning against the side of a small hut, hidden under leaves and pine needles. Of course she's serious.

"Let's do this." I exhale, slowly standing. My body is stiff from lying on the dock in the cold for—I check my phone—the past hour.

Nyelle is already pulling the boat toward the icy shore when I reach her.

"I've got it," I tell her. "Why don't you look for a paddle?"

I tip the boat upright and drag it to the shoreline. Scooping some of the leaves out of the bottom of the canoe, I try to assess what kind of condition it's in. It's old and sun-worn. But I can't find anything wrong with it. Then again, it's difficult to really check it out with years of leaves plastered to the bottom.

"I found this." Nyelle holds up half of a wooden paddle. "And this." In her other hand is a child-sized faded orange life jacket. The kind that feels like it's choking you, not saving your life.

"You really want to do this?"

Nyelle pulls the life jacket over her head and tosses me the paddle. I catch it with a laugh. She looks ridiculous, but undeniably cute at the same time.

I push the boat on top of the ice that's already starting to form around the lake. As soon as she gets in, the boat cracks the surface and floats on the water. I push it in a little farther before jumping in. I bend over the side and shove us off the thin ice.

"Which way?" I ask, practically falling out of the boat in order to row.

Nyelle points toward the sunrise. We clear the ice and glide alongside the dock, slowly veering toward the golden hues.

We're about fifty feet from the end of the dock when icy water begins soaking into my boots. I pick up my foot and look down at the saturated leaves. The water continues to rise above the leaf line.

"We're leaking," Nyelle says matter-of-factly, lifting her feet out of the water and setting them on the crossbar.

"No," I correct her. "We're *sinking*."

I try to whip us around in the direction of the dock. But I might as well be using my hands. If only I could paddle as fast as my heart's pounding.

In less than a minute, my feet are completely covered in freezing water. The more that seeps into the boat, the slower we go and the faster we sink.

"We're going to have to swim for it. We'll be underwater before we get there."

"Bet you're wishing you had one of these awesome life vests right about now, aren't you?" Nyelle laughs.

How could she possibly think this is funny? But she does. When I look across at her, she appears completely amused.

I ignore her and paddle faster. The bath of ice water is beginning to make the muscles in my calves cramp. I press my lips together to keep them from trembling.

Nyelle's smile falls when she notices. "Cal, you're freezing, aren't you? And here I am thinking this is the funniest thing ever. I'm so sorry."

"It's okay," I assure her. "It'll be funny *after* it's over. Right now, it just sucks." I try to conjure a reassuring smile, but my teeth end up chattering instead.

Nyelle starts unlacing her boots.

"What are you doing?"

"Taking off my boots. They'll be like cement if I try to swim in them."

She has a point. I abandon the paddle, pull off my gloves, and struggle to untie my cold, wet laces.

Nyelle fastens her boots together, removes the child's life vest from around her neck, and replaces it with the boots. She sinks her feet in the water and gasps. "Holy shit. How are we not skating on this lake right now?"

"Give it another week and we will be," I say between chatters.

We both eye the twenty feet we have to swim to the dock.

"This is going to suck," I say in a breath.

"No doubt."

Nyelle wraps the vest under her arms, leans over the side of the canoe, and glides into the water. There isn't much of the canoe left above water at this point. Trying not to submerge my head beneath the icy water, I do the same—minus the life vest.

The air is sucked from my lungs upon contact, and my muscles tighten into knots. I kick and swing my arms overhead in a crawl. I don't feel like I'm making progress, probably because I can't *feel* anything. I focus on Nyelle to make sure she doesn't go under.

Her hand reaches out in front of her, stretching for the ladder at the end of the dock. I give her the last push she needs to grab it, and she pulls herself up. I hold on to the side of the ladder as she struggles up onto the dock. Her entire body is shaking uncontrollably.

I climb up after her and blink hard when she peels her

drenched jeans down, exposing white lace underwear. I understand what she's doing, but I'm still not prepared for it.

I run, or pretty much stumble, to the truck. Nyelle, thankfully, left the keys in the ignition. I hop in and start it up, cranking the heat on full blast, giving it time to warm up.

When I return to Nyelle, her clothes are in a sopping heap on the wooden boards, and she's curled up in a ball inside her sleeping bag, shivering so bad I can hear her teeth colliding.

I don't bother to ask when I bend down and scoop her up, sleeping bag and all. I carry her as quickly as I can to the truck and set her in the passenger side. She doesn't make a sound other than a low hum through her chattering teeth.

My entire body is painfully numb and stiff when I rush back out onto the dock to get her clothes and my sleeping bag. I feel like I'm outside of myself and the only thing keeping me moving is staying focused on what I need to do to get out of here.

I toss her clothes in the bed of the truck and shed mine down to my boxers. I actually feel warmer being practically naked in the winter air than I did with the wet clothes on. Wrapping my sleeping bag around me, I climb into the truck.

Nyelle is buried deep within her sleeping bag. I can't see her face, but I can still hear her shivering.

I need a minute, not sure I can actually drive shaking this bad, although sitting here isn't warming me up any faster. When I'm finally able to function, I turn the truck around and drive us in the direction we came.

I take a guess which way to go when I reach the main road, since I was asleep when we turned into the camp. After a minute, I see a sign I recognize and veer down a road that leads back to my apartment.

The heater finally starts blasting hot air, and I slowly begin to defrost. At least my hands aren't cramped around the steering wheel anymore. But the cold has seeped into my bones, and I can't stop shivering.

I glance over at Nyelle, who has the sleeping bag wrapped around her head with big blue eyes peering out.

"I'm sorry I chose the *Titanic* to go across the arctic water," she says quietly.

I can't help smiling. "And I didn't even get the chance to declare myself the king of the world. I kind of feel cheated."

"Yeah, we missed *all* the fun stuff—posing nude, steamy sex in the back of your truck. Although we did get almost naked." She glances at me out of the corner of her eye. I know she's smiling underneath the sleeping bag. And yes, I'm very aware that she's wearing just her bra and underwear. Not *all* of me is frozen.

"Go ahead. Keep messing with me. It's going to come back to get you eventually," I warn with a grin. "How are you doing? Any warmer?"

"I'm a Popsicle," she says, making me laugh.

At this point, the sun is up, but it's still before the rising hour of any sane college student on the weekend, unless they're just getting home. The parking lot is deserted when we pull in.

"Can you walk?"

She nods.

"Okay. Ready?" I hand Nyelle the keys to my apartment, and she rushes to the door. Her bare feet poke out from under the black fabric of her sleeping bag as she runs the short distance to the entrance. I grab our clothes with one hand, cinch my sleeping bag around my chest with the other, and follow after her.

When I enter the apartment, I hear the shower running.

I toss our clothes in the stacked washer/dryer and dump some detergent in. Realizing Nyelle doesn't have anything to change into, I find a sweatshirt and a pair of sweatpants for her to wear.

I knock and slowly open the door to the bathroom. "I'm putting some dry clothes for you on the counter. Okay?"

"Thanks," she says from behind the curtain. I don't linger. But it's hard not to think about her behind that curtain, without the bra and underwear that are now lying on my bathroom floor. I shake off the thought of her naked before it can fully torture me.

I stay wrapped in the sleeping bag until she comes out with her damp hair twisted in a pile on top of her head. And…she's wearing *my* clothes. I grin. They're way too big, but she makes anything look good. I could get used to seeing her in my things.

"Your turn," she says, crawling into my bed and pulling the covers up to her nose.

"Feel better?" I ask. But her eyes are already closed. I smile and head to the bathroom.

When I get out of the shower, she's snoring lightly with just the top of her head visible.

I throw our clothes in the dryer, figuring I'll take her back to her dorm when they're done.

My entire body still aches. I don't remember ever feeling this tired in my life. I slip under the covers on the other side of the bed.

A slow smile spreads across my face at the sight of her hidden under the comforter, breathing deeply. Rolling over and wrapping myself in the blanket, I'm very aware of the warmth of her body along my back, even though we don't touch. As my eyes slide shut, I'm thinking about second chances, knowing that the one I wished for tonight is lying next to me.

RICHELLE

July—Before Fifth Grade

"I think I should be the singer. Richelle, you sound like a dying cat," Rae says from behind an old drum set that's held together by duct tape.

I know she's just trying to make me angry so I'll give up being the lead singer. Never going to happen.

"Drummers don't sing," I argue, holding the hairbrush that is also my microphone.

Cal leans against the wall with his plastic guitar, waiting for us to stop arguing, or until he has to say something to make us stop.

"I brought new music today too," I say, plugging my iPod into the radio.

"If it's Britney Spears, I'm going to throw up," Rae complains, making gagging noises. "And if I can't sing, then I get to pick the music."

"Your music doesn't even make sense," I tell her. "It's just screaming."

"You don't even know what real music is."

I'm about to tell her that it wouldn't be on the top forty if it weren't good, but I notice what time it is and don't bother.

"It's time to get Nicole. I'll be right back."

"Why doesn't she just come over? I don't understand her weird rules."

"You know her mom says she has to be invited first," I say with a sigh. Rae can be so frustrating.

"What is she, a vampire?" Rae laughs.

"Rae," Cal scolds. "Knock it off."

This shuts Rae up. When Cal speaks up, it usually does. I run off down the street and press the Bentleys' doorbell, out of breath. I ring the bell the same time every day, and every day Mrs. Bentley answers it like she doesn't know why I'm here.

"Hi, Richelle. What can I do for you?"

I want to roll my eyes, but I don't. I smile and say the same thing I said yesterday, and the day before yesterday—as far back as the first day Nicole moved into the neighborhood. "Hi, Mrs. Bentley. Can Nicole come out to play?" But today I add, "And can she sleep over at my house tonight?"

"Yes, Nicole can come out. But I will have to call your mother and check with Mr. Bentley about sleeping over."

Nicole is standing behind her mom like she always does when I come to get her. As soon as she hears she can play, she lets me take her hand.

"Be home by five thirty, Nicole," Mrs. Bentley says as we skip away. "I'll have spoken to your father by then."

I don't know why she has to ask him if Nicole can sleep over. She's done it every Friday this summer.

"Okay, Mom," Nicole calls back.

We skip together all the way to Rae's. Nicole still doesn't run, but at least I got her to skip. It's better than walking, even though it still feels too slow for me.

As we approach, Cal is walking across the yard to his house.

"Where are you going?" I ask.

"Rae had to go pick up Liam with her mom. And I have to get ready for baseball. I'll see you guys later."

Rae's brother lives with their dad. And he comes over every

other weekend, except we never really see him or Rae when he does because their mom wants them to have family time. And Cal plays on a baseball team Tuesday and Friday nights with Craig and Brady.

"Oh," I answer, disappointed. "Well, I guess we can go to my house."

We play fashion models in my backyard with an old camera my dad doesn't want anymore. Nicole is allowed to sleep over, just like I thought. We eat pizza and watch a movie before we're supposed to go to my room to sleep. But we don't sleep. We're too hyper, which makes us laugh a lot.

"Can I tell you a secret that you have to promise not to tell anyone ever?" I whisper in the dark.

Nicole is on the bottom bunk. My sister, Kara, and I used to share a room. But when she started middle school last year, my mom and dad let her have my mom's old office. She even gets her own TV. I don't care because I got to keep the bunk bed.

I hang my head over the side, holding on to the edge so I don't fall.

"I promise not to tell anyone, ever," Nicole whispers.

I smile before I say, "I'm going to make Cal my boyfriend this year."

"Really?" Nicole asks with a giggle. "Are you going to *marry* him too?"

I know she says it to be funny. But I mean it when I say, "Yup. When we grow up, we're going to get married and live in a big white house. I'm going to drive a Mercedes and he's going to drive a BMW. I'm going to sell houses, and he's going to be a rock star."

Nicole giggles. "Well, I'm going to go to college at Harvard and be someone respectable like my daddy wants me to be."

"Why do you want to go to Harvard?"

"Because my mom and daddy want me to. They've been putting money in the bank since I was a baby so that I can go there. It's where important people go, and my daddy wants me to be important. He says I have to be the best in school before I can go there. And I have to be a good person that everyone will like and listen to."

"But you don't ever say anything in school," I say, confused.

"I guess I haven't found anything really important to say yet."

"My mom and dad tell me they want me to be happy. Besides, college is so far away. I can't think about that."

"But don't you get married *after* college?" Nicole points out.

"Yeah, but that's just pretend," I defend, feeling light-headed from hanging upside down for so long. "Except I *am* going to make Cal my boyfriend this year."

SEVEN

I peek out of one eye, undecided whether I really want to be awake. It's after two in the afternoon. Then I remember Nyelle and roll over. She's not here. All that's left are my sweatshirt and sweatpants, folded neatly on top of the pillow.

I sit up when I hear a cabinet door shut.

"Nyelle?" I call out. I listen. There's footsteps, but no answer. "Nyelle?"

"Who?" It's Eric. I let out a heavy breath. She left. I'm not surprised, but I can still feel the weight of disappointment in my chest.

"Forget it."

Eric pokes his head in my room. "What happened to you last night? Did you leave with that cute brunette I saw you talking to?"

I yawn, twisting to stretch my back. "No. I met up with another girl and ended up nearly drowning in a frozen lake."

Eric laughs. "What?"

"Yeah, it's funny now," I admit. "But it wasn't when it was happening." I give him the abbreviated version. And he laughs louder.

"Who is this girl?" he asks, still chuckling.

"That's what I'm trying to find out," I reply, eyeing the stack of clothes on my bed.

Nyelle's avoiding me again. Or at least that's what I've convinced myself. She left without a word, and I haven't seen her in four days. Now I'm sitting on the couch at Bean Buzz, bouncing my knee and rubbing my hands together with my eyes trained on the door, hoping she'll show up. I didn't say what time I'd meet her here today. I just said Thursday. Maybe I screwed up.

I'd wait here all day for her except I can't be late for class. I have a midterm. I pull my phone out of my pocket to check the time again. There's a message across my screen.

JADE: WANT TO SEE ME THIS WEEKEND?

I try not to judge girls by their text messages. I've learned that tone can get lost in translation. Still, it says a lot when the girl texts first. It's bold.

I'm tempted to ignore the message, but decide it might distract me from the anxiety in my stomach that's about to swallow me whole. And I have an easy out since Rae's flying in tonight.

ME: I HAVE A FRIEND VISITING THIS WEEKEND.

JADE: SO . . . DITCH HIM.

I shake my head. What? There's not much to misinterpret about that statement.

ME: NOT MY STYLE. HOW ABOUT AFTER BREAK?

JADE: AW! THAT SEEMS TOO FAR AWAY.

JADE: IS YOUR FRIEND A GUY OR A GIRL?

I hesitate. Maybe I should have ignored her text. Insecurity is not attractive. Jade and I didn't talk much the night we met, and regardless of intention, there are warning signs in the few texts she's sent. I must take too long to respond, because she texts again.

JADE: NO WORRIES. I'LL SEE YOU AFTER BREAK. HAVE FUN THIS WEEKEND.

She redeems herself. Or tries to anyway.

ME: YOU TOO. I'LL TEXT YOU WHEN I GET BACK.

I know I shouldn't have sent the text because I have no intention of seeing her again.

I notice the time on the screen. I have to go. I can't wait for Nyelle any longer. When I start for the door, Tess walks in. My shoulders relax, thinking Nyelle is about to walk in after her. But Tess is alone.

"Hi, Cal," she says with a bright smile.

"Hey. Nyelle with you?"

Her smile falters as she shakes her head. "I don't know where she went this morning. She was gone before I woke up."

"Okay," I say, then add because there isn't another option, "There's a house party on Lincoln Street Saturday night if you and Nyelle want to meet up with us."

Her smile reemerges, exactly what I was afraid of. "Really? That sounds great." She reaches in her purse. "Here, let me get your number and I can text you."

After exchanging numbers, I leave for class, hoping Tess didn't get the wrong impression and that she'll convince Nyelle to go to the party.

I hate not knowing where Nyelle is or when she'll show up. I expect her to jump in front of me at any moment, but she never does. Each time I'm with her makes it harder to let her go, because it kills me to have to wait until the next time—fearing there might not be one.

I keep playing back Sunday morning in my head, not sure if I did something or said anything that would've freaked her out. It makes me crazy that I still can't get in touch with her. Where the hell is she and why is she avoiding me?

"Hey!" Rae calls out when she enters the apartment. I exit my room and stop short. Rae drops her bag by the door, scanning the apartment. "Not bad. It's very... college."

Then she notices I'm staring at her, speechless. "What?"

"Uh... that's quite the look you've got goin' on," I say, eyeing the torn skintight black pants and the oversized shirt with a provocative pierced tongue printed on it. Her dark round eyes are dramatically lined in more makeup than I've ever seen her wear in her entire life. But it's the shaved bright pink hair that's really throwing me off. That and the loop through her eyebrow and the stud above her lip. She already had a nose ring and metal lining each earlobe. "Aren't you a little old to be going through your rebellious stage?"

"Fuck you," she bites halfheartedly. "It's my new image. Blond hair and freckles weren't working for an all-girl punk band."

"You still have freckles," I tease. This is going to take some getting used to.

"I like it," Eric chimes in. "It's badass."

It would be badass if she weren't barely five feet tall. Although she does have the skinny rocker look going for her.

"Want a beer?" Eric asks from the fridge.

I shake my head. "I have a paper to finish for tomorrow."

Rae holds out her hand. "I'll take one—or three." Eric laughs and hands her a can. She takes it and flops down on the couch.

"Eric, thanks for picking her up," I say. "That midterm sucked." I might have done better if I'd been able to concentrate.

"Cal, did you realize I've never actually met Eric before today?" Rae pops the beer can open.

"What? Of course you have..." The sentence drifts away when I realize she's right.

Eric and I were roommates last year in the dorms. He's met my entire family. My brothers, when they visited during homecoming for the football games. Jules and my parents, when they came out for parents' weekend. But both times Rae visited last year, he wasn't around. We never met up with him either time because of the asinine things he had to do while pledging Delta Ep.

"I never thought of that," I finally say. "I guess I talk about you guys so much, it felt like you already knew each other."

"I mean, it does seem like I know her," Eric agrees, sitting in the beat-up recliner. "That's why I didn't mind getting her. But on my way to the airport, I realized I had no idea what she looked like."

"I don't think my description would've helped." I glance at Rae with a shake of my head.

"Hilarious, Cal," she says. "I've seen him on Facebook, so it worked out."

"Rae, what's the name of your band again?" Eric asks, typing on his phone. "I need to follow you guys. Do you have anything I can download?"

"Ragin' Bitches," Rae tells him. "Not yet. We're supposed to record a demo when I get back. We're a few songs away from a set, so I'm hoping to book our first gig soon."

"Really?" I ask. This is the first time she's mentioned it. Rae usually complains that the girls can't agree on anything whenever I talk to her. "Will I get to see you play when we go home?"

"Maybe. If the neighborhood doesn't revolt against us. Your mom's trying to make peace by sticking earplugs in all the mailboxes. You'd think they'd be used to music coming from my garage. It's been that way since we were kids."

"Yeah, Rae told me about that." Eric laughs. "She also told me you were a complete dork growing up."

"Nice, Rae. Thanks," I remark with a shake of my head.

"Whatever." She shrugs. "I didn't mean it in a bad way. You just... were."

"*And* she said that you think Lake Girl is actually a girl from your neighborhood you've been obsessing over your entire life."

"Wow. Leave much out, Rae? And I'm *not* obsessing over her," I say in defense. "I wish you'd stop saying that." But considering how much I've been thinking about Nyelle lately, Rae's not totally off.

"Have you met her yet?" Rae asks Eric. He shakes his head. "Nicole, the girl we grew up with, was nothing like the girl he tells me about. She was super shy when we were kids. Then she became a stuck-up bitch in high school."

"Rae," I say sternly.

"What? She was," Rae argues back. "Nicole was too consumed with being perfect to give a shit about the rest of us. Seriously, when was the last time she spoke to either of us, other than to tell us to leave her alone?"

I drop my eyes to the floor. "Nyelle's different."

"That's right. Because it's *not* her. When do I get to meet your delusion anyway?"

"Not sure," I reply. "I'm hoping she'll show up at the party tomorrow night with her roommate."

Eric turns to me. "If you're so sure Nyelle is Nicole and you've known her most of your life, why don't you just say something to her?"

"It's...complicated. I want her to trust me. Rae, don't say anything when you see her, okay? If she's lying, there must be a reason. And if she really believes she's Nyelle, something must've happened to her. I think it would only make things worse if we confront her."

I focus on Rae, silently pleading.

"Whatever," she grumbles. "It's *not* her."

We sit in awkward silence for a moment with Rae pulling the tab of her beer and Eric looking between me and Rae, trying to figure out what we're not telling him.

"How's Liam?" I ask, needing to change the subject.

"A fricken pain in my ass," Rae responds. "But he's staying out of trouble."

"Your brother?" Eric confirms.

"Yeah. He's the reason I'm not here yet," Rae tells him.

"You're supposed to be at Crenshaw?"

I watch Rae carefully as she nods. It's not easy for her to talk about what she's given up for her brother.

"I'll be here next year unless my music career takes off," Rae tells him with a cocky grin.

"So why aren't you here now?" Eric asks, not following.

"Liam tends to be attracted to assholes. They probably remind him of our father," Rae explains, rolling her eyes. "Last year he got arrested for possession with intent to distribute. Dumbass."

"Wow," Eric responds with wide eyes. "So you're, like, his... parole officer?"

"Yeah, feels like it," Rae says with a laugh. "I just need to get him into college without him doing anything monumentally stupid to screw up his life. Once he graduates, he can clean up his own shit."

"What about your parents?" Eric asks.

Rae chugs the rest of her beer. I don't expect her to answer. She doesn't open up much, not even to me. I'm pretty sure she started playing drums when we were kids so she could beat the shit out of something. It's how she copes.

"They split when we were younger. My brother lived with our dickhead father until he took off, leaving my mother with a mortgage and a shitload of debt on top of having to support us. So she works doubles at the hospital all the time and we hardly ever see her. I basically grew up at Cal's house, since his mom works from home."

Eric looks a little lost. "And so... how does this Nicole chick fit into all this?"

"Richelle and Nicole lived down the street from us," Rae explains. She takes in a deep breath. "Until they left us."

"Come on, Rae. Richelle *moved*. And we don't know everything that went on with Nicole... obviously," I say. "Maybe we never did."

"Give it up, Cal," Rae says with a shake of her head. "You need to stop defending her."

That's never going to happen. Not until I know what's really going on.

NICOLE

August—Before Fifth Grade

I walk up to Cal's door and ring the doorbell. Mrs. Logan opens it.

"Hi, Nicole. It's nice to see you. Cal's out back."

"Thank you, Mrs. Logan," I respond and continue around the house to the backyard. Cal's mom called my mom to ask if I could come over. She said Cal had something he wanted to share with his friends.

When I reach the backyard, my mouth opens into a big, huge smile. Cal is running around with a yellow puppy chasing after him.

"He's so cute!" I exclaim, not taking my eyes off the fuzzy little thing that keeps trying to bite the rope in Cal's hand.

Cal stops running, and the puppy jumps up on his legs, chomping at the rope. "Hi, Nicole."

"When did you get him?" I bend down and pet the puppy on the head. He jumps on my knees and licks at my face. "Ow." His little claws are sharp.

"Henley, get down," Cal demands, pulling him away. "Sorry. Did he hurt you?"

"He didn't mean to," I say, kneeling on the ground, making sure my dress covers my legs so he can't scratch me. "Come here, Henley."

"My dad brought him home today." Cal sits on the ground across from me as we both play with the puppy. He can't seem to sit still—jumping back and forth and running around us. "I don't think my mom knew about it, but she says we can keep him. I'm going to help my dad build a doghouse for him."

"My dad thinks animals are too dirty," I say. And watching Henley roll in the grass, chasing after a butterfly, I think he's probably right. But Henley's just *so* cute.

Cal and I play with Henley for a while before I realize it's just the two of us.

"Where's Rae and Richelle?" I ask, squeaking a plastic frog at the puppy, who isn't quite sure if he wants to bite it or run away from it.

"I don't know. I called them, but they weren't home."

It's not weird being alone with Cal. He's nicer than a lot of the boys at school. When Brady and Craig come over, they end up acting kind of dumb, and Cal has to tell them to shut up a lot. Richelle says they're so immature and no girl will ever want them to be her boyfriend. I'm not sure I'm ready for a boyfriend.

Richelle says that it's the best thing in the world to have a boyfriend. You get to tell him secrets. Hold hands. Go to the movies together. And kiss.

I think the only thing I'd like is the movies part, and I already do that with Cal and his friends. Except none of them is my boyfriend.

I watch Cal for a moment as he runs really fast with Henley chasing after him. His dark hair is sweaty and sticking to his forehead. His knees are dirty from rolling on the ground. His glasses are sliding off his nose like they always do. Would I want to *kiss* Cal?

I scrunch my nose up at the thought.

"What's wrong?" Cal asks, breathing fast from running. "Did a bug fly in your mouth?"

"Ew. No," I say. "I was just thinking about..." I almost say it. My cheeks feel hot.

"What? Tell me. I promise not to tell anyone."

I kneel on the ground again where Henley is lying on his back with his paws in the air. I scratch his belly and laugh at how funny he looks lying this way. He's breathing fast too. I can feel his little heart beating.

I don't look at Cal when I ask, "Have you ever kissed a girl?"

Henley flops over onto his belly, stretches his tiny jaw into a yawn, and rests his head on his paws. Cal and I continue petting him. Cal's hands are dirty, even under his nails. My mom would make him scrub them all day before sitting down at our dinner table.

I look at my hands, and even though I've been playing too, I was very careful not to get dirty. Our hands look so different next to each other, moving along the gold fur.

"No," Cal answers. "I've never kissed a girl. I don't think I want to yet either."

"Yeah," I agree, without looking at him. "Kissing's gross." Our hands touch. We stop petting Henley, who's fallen asleep, but don't take our hands off his belly. It rises and falls with his breathing. I hold my breath and move my hand so it's over Cal's.

His hand is warm, and it's softer than I thought it would be. I curl my fingers between his and he squeezes them gently. I keep my eyes on our hands, afraid to look at him, but I'm smiling. My heart is beating like a butterfly is flapping inside my chest. I may not be ready to kiss a boy, but I do like holding Cal's hand.

EIGHT

"Are you sure they're coming?" Rae asks, pressing against the frame that separates the living room from the kitchen, allowing two girls to squeeze between us.

"I'm not sure of anything when it comes to Nyelle," I confess. "But Tess's text said they were on their way."

"Yeah, but that was like an hour ago," Rae notes, tipping the beer bottle into her mouth.

I shrug. "Nyelle likes to walk. It might take them a while."

"They're walking from *campus*?" Rae says. "What is she, crazy?"

I grin without answering.

I'm about to ask where Eric disappeared to when Nyelle enters through the back door.

"She's here."

Rae turns to look, but she's too short to see over the crowd in the kitchen.

Nyelle's wearing her hair down, the way I like it, wild waves falling over her shoulders. The top of her head is sprinkled with snow, and her cheeks and the tip of her nose are red from walking in the cold. Her blue eyes sparkle as she searches the crowd. She stops when she spots me. I wait to see how she'll react. When she smiles, I release my breath and smile back.

Tess waves to me while mouthing an apology and rolling her eyes toward Nyelle.

The smile on Nyelle's face falters. She's too far away for me to see what's happening. My eyes dart around the kitchen, trying to figure out which guy said something to her.

"Nyelle!" Tess yells. I look back just as the door slams shut.

"I'll be right back," I tell Rae. I push through the crowded kitchen and find Tess outside on the back steps.

"Nyelle, what are you doing? I'm freezing from walking all the way here, and I really need to warm up. Please come inside with me."

Nyelle isn't listening. She's pacing back and forth in the small yard, grumbling under her breath.

"Tess, go ahead in and wait with Rae. She's the one with bright pink hair. You can't miss her." When she hesitates, I assure her, "We'll be right there."

Tess sighs and says, "Nyelle, I'm going inside. Don't leave without me." She goes back into the house, muting the music and voices with the closing of the door.

Nyelle continues pacing with her fists clenched by her sides, mumbling incoherently. Every so often I pick up a word, mostly swearing. I can't make sense of it.

"What the fuck?!" she blurts. Then she rants about other nonsensical things, with an "I can't do this" thrown in there.

"Nyelle? What happened?"

She stops abruptly, biting her lip. She looks up at me with wide, frantic eyes, appearing confused. I know *I* am.

I shiver as the cold wind gusts through the button-down I'm wearing. "It's cold. And snowing. Just come in for a little while to warm up. Then I'll take you anywhere you want to go. Even if it's to roll down a hill with you."

Nyelle takes a deep breath to collect herself, then smiles ever so slightly. "It is snowing, isn't it?" She tilts her head up toward the sky, watching the flakes float down onto her face.

I'm met with a rush of warm air when the door opens and Rae comes out. "Is she catching snowflakes on her tongue?"

Nyelle has her mouth open and her tongue sticking out, letting the crystals drift down and soak into it. I smile. "Yeah. She is."

"What the...?"

Nyelle lifts her head and her eyes steady on Rae. With a deep breath, she says boldly, "Hi. I'm Nyelle. I go to school with Cal."

"Hi," Rae falters. "I'm Rae. Cal's friend from back home."

"Nice to meet you," Nyelle replies with an exaggerated smile. "Now let's go *rage*." She thrusts her fist halfheartedly in the air and unenthusiastically hollers, "Woo-hoo," before marching between us into the house.

Rae turns her head up toward me with her mouth agape. "Holy shit, Cal. What just happened? And *who* was that? Because that girl looks a hell of a lot like Nicole Bentley."

I release a breathy laugh. "That...*all* of that, was Nyelle Preston," I say and follow after her into the house.

Tess is waiting for us inside the door, but Nyelle is halfway through the kitchen, heading toward the living room. I start in that direction, then look back to Rae and Tess.

"Go ahead," Rae encourages. "We'll get drinks and meet you in a sec."

I nod and excuse myself through the crowd of people drinking and talking.

Nyelle is leaning against the back of the couch when I finally reach her.

"Hey." I stand across from her, close enough to touch her. When she looks up at me with a weak smile, I'm tempted to. But I don't. "Are you okay?"

She unzips her jacket and pulls it off, stuffing it between her knees. Underneath is a large orange and red sweater that hangs off her. She's cut holes in the sleeves for her thumbs to stick out, like she did with her other sweater.

And then it hits me...I've never seen her hands. I know this is a weird thought. But the realization comes out of nowhere, and now I'm staring at the tips of her fingers, which are barely sticking out of her sweater. Why have I never seen her hands?

"Yeah, I'm fine," Nyelle responds. "How are you?" When I don't answer, she waves her hidden hand in front of my face, snapping me out of it.

"Oh, uh, I'm great."

"I didn't know you had a friend visiting from home," she says, resting her hands beside her hips on the couch.

"I didn't get to see you this week to tell you," I say, trying *not* to look at her hands.

"How long is she going to be here?" Nyelle asks, searching the crowd in the kitchen. I study her darting eyes. She still seems...riled. Did someone say something to her to piss her off? Or is this about Rae? Did she recognize her? Is that really what the backyard was all about?

"We fly back home together on Wednesday for Thanksgiving break."

"Oh" is her only response. She draws in a deep breath, like she's still trying to calm down.

"Are you sure you're okay?"

Before she can answer, Eric comes up beside me and claps a hand on my shoulder.

"Hey, I'm Eric," he says without waiting for an introduction. He's staring. I can understand *why* he's staring, but I'm tempted to elbow him in the ribs to make him stop.

"Eric, this is Nyelle."

"Oh! Lake Girl!" he exclaims with a laugh.

Nyelle smiles. "You told him about the *Titanic*?"

I nod.

"That was completely my fault," Nyelle tells him.

"Yeah, well, guys do stupid things for a girl when we want to get laid." Eric laughs.

"You wanted to get laid?" Nyelle gawks at me.

"What? Me?! Not in the boat, no," I fumble. This time I do elbow Eric, and he fights to hide the pain with a short cough as his face reddens. It would make my life so much easier if he'd think before he spoke. The guy has no filter.

"Yeah, well, we did get practically naked," Nyelle adds, looking me in the eye with a playful grin.

"You did? Hey, you didn't tell me that part," Eric complains.

"No, I didn't," I respond, still connected with Nyelle.

"Don't look now, but Liza's at your five o'clock," Eric whispers loudly so we can all hear him.

"Oh, I liked Liza," Rae says, sneaking in beside me with Tess next to her. Tess passes Nyelle a drink, and Rae hands me a beer.

"Thanks," I reply, taking it from her. I catch Liza's eye and she smiles. I liked Liza too. She's pretty, intelligent, funny, but…

"Hi, Cal. Eric." She greets us with a nod, then looks to everyone else, waiting to be introduced.

"Hi, Liza. Um. This is Nyelle, Tess and Rae."

"Oh, *you're* Rae!" she says excitedly. Then pauses and tightens her eyes. "I'm sorry, but I guess I always thought you'd be…taller.

Maybe it's the way Cal always talked about you; he made you sound..."

"Badass?" Eric offers. Liza laughs.

"How's your brother?" Rae asks her. Liza's brother was in a serious car accident at the end of last semester. Maybe that's why we broke up. She had to go home to be with her family. I think about it. No. That's not it. That happened *after* I ended things.

"Wow, you do tell her everything, huh?" Liza teases me. "Um, he's good. Fully recovered. Thanks." She glances up at me and smiles. "Well, it was good to see you, Cal. Have fun tonight, guys."

Then she disappears back in the direction she came from.

"I remember her," Eric adds. "I liked her too."

"She's another of your broken hearts?" Nyelle confirms.

"You know!" Rae exclaims, instantly bonding with Nyelle over my relationship failures. I should've seen this coming.

Nyelle leans over and whispers loudly to Tess, "I told you he'd break your heart."

Tess's eyes grow wide and her mouth drops open in shock.

"No, no, no." Rae shakes her head. "Don't go there, Tess. You seem like a really nice girl. Stay away from him. He's relationship challenged. Really."

Tess chokes. Her face is turning redder by the second.

"Tess, let's go get you a drink," Eric offers gently, taking her by the hand.

"I have one," she says quietly, holding up her cup.

"Well, then, let's just move into the other room until your face returns to the color it's supposed to be."

I want to apologize. But I know it'll only make things worse because she won't know if I'm apologizing because it's true, or because they just called her out on liking me and I can't reciprocate. Either way, it's better that she walk away.

"I'm trying to remember the excuse you used when you broke up with Liza," Rae says, concentrating. "What was it?"

"My question is: Do you regret it?" Nyelle asks.

"No," I answer without hesitation. She grins. Rae looks between us suspiciously. When her focus lingers on Nyelle a little too long, I nudge her to make her stop.

Nyelle doesn't notice. She's too busy digging gummy bears out of her front pocket. "Want one?" she offers us with her sweater-covered palm held out.

"No, thanks," I respond, taking a swig of the shit beer in my hand. Rae picks one up and bites its head off before tossing the rest in her mouth.

"I think we should go back to your place," Rae announces after chugging the rest of her beer. "This party's lame. We could do so much better on our own. Let's pick up some Jack on the way. Nyelle, wanna come back to Cal's?"

Nyelle hesitates, then focuses on me as if she's waiting for some sort of assurance. I raise my brow in encouragement and she replies, "Sure."

Rae cuts through the kitchen, pockets a couple more beers, and hollers to Eric and Tess, "We're out of here. Let's go." Effortlessly parting the crowd, she struts to the back door.

Nyelle looks after Rae and smiles. "I like her."

I laugh. "Yeah. Me too."

I'm leaning against the kitchen counter, staring at the bathroom door, waiting for Nyelle and Rae to come out. They've been in there since Eric left to bring Tess back to the dorms. That was twenty minutes ago.

"No way!" I hear Nyelle shout through the door.

Rae laughs. "Seriously, it's true!"

I'm afraid to know what they're talking about.

The door opens, and Eric walks in. "Hey. Where are the girls?"

I direct my eyes toward the bathroom just as a burst of laughter filters through.

"What are they doing in there?" he asks, standing next to me with his arms crossed to watch the door.

I shrug. "Who knows. What *do* girls do in the bathroom together?"

"Talk about guys," Eric replies. "Except Rae doesn't like guys. Which means they're probably talking about you."

I stiffen. "What?" I've been worried that Rae's drunk enough to let something slip. Or bitter enough to unleash the grudge she's been holding all these years. But the laughter doesn't sound hostile, which makes me paranoid that they *are* talking about me.

"Oh, and I don't understand why you don't like Tess. She's a cool girl," he continues. "I got her number. But would that mean I'm getting your sloppy seconds?"

"That doesn't even make sense! There's nothing sloppy about Tess, and it's not *seconds* because I never asked her out. She's great, but I'm not interested in dating her."

"Because you want her roommate," he says, nodding toward the bathroom. "Why didn't you tell me Lake Girl was fucking hot?"

Nyelle's hysterical laughter moves my feet toward the door.

I knock. "Hey, are you two coming out?"

"I already did our freshman year, remember?" Rae hollers back.

Nyelle laughs. "You were there. It was fucking funny. I thought Brady was going to have a heart attack."

"Yeah, I was there," I respond with a sigh. "Come out of the bathroom. You've been in there for over a half hour."

"So I was hoping to talk to you about something," Rae says to me as we're waiting for Brady and Craig to show up. They called a while ago and said they were riding their bikes over. They also said they scored a bottle of vodka from Craig's parents' liquor cabinet. If it's the same bottle we drank from last summer, then I know it's half water, so it's not that big of a score.

"Yeah, what's up?" I respond, not looking up from the video game on my phone.

"Cal." Her voice is serious and stern. It's the voice she uses with her brother when he's in deep shit.

I close the gaming app and give her my full attention.

Rae opens her mouth, then closes it. She's nervous, and Rae is never nervous about anything.

"Are you pregnant?" I blurt.

"No!" She punches me in the arm. "I'm not pregnant, *you loser. I'm—"*

"I know you missed me!" Brady yells, rolling up the driveway on his bike. Rae sinks back into the couch and closes her eyes. I know she won't tell me now. "Come on, my Rae of sunshine. Tell me how much you missed me."

"Not even a little," she grumbles.

"You'll come around," he says with a wink.

Craig pulls out a bottle of Jack Daniel's, not vodka. Rae stands up abruptly, opens the bottle, and takes a huge swig, then coughs from the burn.

"Nope. I never will, Brady." She coughs again and then clears her throat. "Because I don't like dicks." Then she takes another shot straight from the bottle.

"Easy there," Craig warns, holding his hand out to take the liquor back.

"That's kinda harsh," Brady says, feigning heartbreak.

"You're not listening. I. Don't. Like. Dicks."

We freeze. Brady with a hand over his heart. We stare at her. It's silent until I utter, "Makes sense that you're not pregnant."

"We'll be right out!" Rae yells back.

I groan in frustration and rest my head on the doorframe. Behind me, I hear Eric tear open a bag of chips.

The door opens.

"You have chips!" Nyelle exclaims. She walks right past me without a glance and straight to Eric.

I stare at her. "You heard him open that bag? You mean that's all I had to do to get you to come out?"

Nyelle laughs and scoops out a handful of Doritos.

Rae follows after her. I watch her, looking for some hint on her face as to what they talked about for so long. She sits on the end of the couch wearing the most frustrating grin. What the hell?

I sit on the other side of the couch and make eye contact. I widen my eyes, silently begging for any assurance at all. She continues to wear a tilted grin. I want to strangle her.

I raise my hands in frustration and she smiles wider, torturing me. We're interrupted when Nyelle bounces down on the cushion between us, kicking off her shoes and crossing her legs.

"God, I love Doritos. Except they make your breath smell for hours after."

"Truth." Eric agrees with a dramatic nod of his head.

"Oh! I remember why you dumped Liza!" Rae exclaims suddenly, making everyone turn toward her. "She wanted you to meet her parents. So you ended it."

Eric starts laughing. "Yeah. That's right."

It comes back to me too. "We'd only been dating a month. I wasn't ready to meet her parents."

"But couldn't you have told her that instead of dumping her?" Nyelle asks, brushing the Dorito crumbs off her jeans. "Maybe she would've understood."

"Yeah, right," Rae scoffs. "Cal does *not* have the awkward conversations. He totally walks away from any kind of confrontation. Seriously, he'll go out of his way by miles to avoid it."

"Yeah, I know," Nyelle says, smirking.

I suddenly find the stain on the couch worthy of my attention when Rae starts laughing. This conversation needs to end now.

"So why do you walk away? Are you afraid of hurting their feelings or something?" Nyelle asks.

And just to make it worse, Eric chimes in. "Cal is that laid-back, let-the-world-happen-to-me kind of guy. That's how he gets the ladies. They always approach him because he comes off as *the nice guy*. I don't think he's ever hit on a girl. So the dude's never had to experience rejection."

"What are you talking about?" I interject, feeling the need to defend myself, even if he is telling the truth.

"Who was the last girl you asked out?" Rae challenges.

I look to Nyelle out of the corner of my eye, because technically it was her.

"No, you didn't," she says, reading my mind. "You were super-casual about it, making it sound like a bunch of you were going out."

"He asked *you* out?" Rae gawks.

Nyelle shakes her head. "No. He didn't."

Eric raises his eyebrows, as if to ask, *What the hell is wrong with you?*

Unable to listen to them analyze me any longer, I stand up and walk to the fridge. "Anyone need a drink?" I grab a beer. Eric raises his hand, so I toss him the can.

"Do you have Coke?" Nyelle asks.

"Me too," Rae adds. I take out the cans of soda along with another beer and hand them off to the girls. Rae mixes hers with Jack Daniel's, and Nyelle takes a huge gulp and swishes it around in her mouth.

"Are you gargling with Coke?" Eric laughs.

"Rinsing out the Doritos from my teeth," she explains after swallowing. Then she shifts on the cushion to examine Rae.

"What?" Rae demands, tightening her eyes.

"Can I touch your hair?" Nyelle requests, holding her hand above Rae's head, waiting for permission.

"Are you drunk?" Rae asks.

"I don't really like to drink," Nyelle replies. "It makes me angry."

"And you don't want to see her when she's angry," I note with a shake of my head, thinking back to the guy pinned up against the house with the blade under his chin.

"Does she turn green and rip through her clothes?" Eric says, laughing hysterically at his own joke.

Rae laughs too. I grin.

"Fine, go ahead," Rae finally says with a dramatic sigh when she realizes Nyelle's still waiting for an answer. Nyelle's eyes light up and a smile erupts on her face as she gently brushes her hand along the buzzed pink hair.

"It's so soft," Nyelle says in awe. "You know, Rae, you're amazing."

"Why?" Rae asks cautiously.

"You're so secure with who you are. Come on, you started your own punk band! I just…I'm going to give you a hug now." Before Rae can respond, Nyelle wraps her arms around her and pulls her in for a quick, tight hug. Rae's eyes widen with shock. "You make me happy." Then Nyelle sits back against the couch, squeezes her hands, and asks excitedly, "Okay. What do we do now?"

No one moves. We just stare at her.

"What was that?" I mutter.

"I think it's the gummy bears," Rae murmurs.

"I have fireworks," Eric blurts.

"We can blow stuff up!" Nyelle exclaims, clapping her hands together.

"Well…they're sparklers," Eric adds.

"Which aren't *fireworks*, you idiot." Rae rolls her eyes.

"Is there something we can climb?" Nyelle asks with a crazed look in her eye. I think she's definitely had too much sugar.

"Umm…there's the barn," Eric suggests. "Or—"

"Nyelle, that's not a good idea," I implore, but it's too late. She's off the couch with her shoes on her feet, walking out the door, holding her jacket…and my truck keys.

I collapse against the back of the couch. "Eric, really?"

"What did I do?" he questions, completely confused. "Wait. Did she just take off for the barn?"

"Yeah," I sigh, standing up and grabbing my jacket. "And you two better hurry up or she'll leave without you."

When I step out in the snow-dusted night, I find Nyelle behind the wheel of the truck, waiting. This is not a good idea. But I can tell there's no talking her out of it as she grips the steering wheel in anticipation.

"Scoot over. I'm driving," I tell her when I open the driver's side door.

"But I haven't had anything to drink," she remarks.

"And I've maybe had a beer," I reply. "Besides, do you even know where we're going?" I hesitate, because I'm suddenly afraid to know the answer. "Have you been... to the barn?"

"You've been to the barn?" Eric exclaims in shock, holding the passenger door open for Rae.

"What are you guys talking about?" Nyelle asks. "I've never been there, but you're the one who mentioned it, *Eric*."

"It's still snowing!" Rae complains, interrupting talk of the barn. "Why does it always have to snow when I come here?!"

She slides in next to Nyelle, and Eric climbs in after her. Nyelle moves closer to me so we can all fit. My pulse picks up pace when her thigh presses against mine. And then I'm finding breathing challenging when I reach between her legs for the stick shift.

"Wait. If you hate snow, why are you coming to school here next year?" Eric questions.

Rae glances at me and shrugs.

"You have this strange hold over the women in your life, huh?" Nyelle whispers close. I can feel her breath on my neck and swallow hard.

"Where are we going exactly?" Nyelle asks.

"To have sex," Eric says with a stupid grin on his face.

"Shut up, Eric," I threaten, suddenly feeling the need to crack the window and let some cool air in.

"Someone make sense. Now, please," Rae demands.

"The barn is on this abandoned property just outside town. And as a rite of passage, couples from Crenshaw go out there and..." I let the words trail off, hoping they pick up on the rest.

"Have sex," Eric says. So now they definitely get it if they didn't before. "The walls and beams are carved with the initials of everyone who's been there."

"*That's* where we're going?" Rae asks, sounding horrified. "Who thought this was such a great idea?"

We all look at Eric.

"Hey! I was just thinking out loud," Eric defends. "I didn't know we'd really go there. I don't even know where it is."

"But *you* do," Nyelle says from beside me. I can't look at her. I remain focused on the road.

"Cal?" Rae says. "Are we going to find your initials on the wall?"

Fuck.

"No," I answer quietly. Not because I've never been out there, only because we never made it out of my truck. But there's no way in hell I'm about to volunteer that information.

I can feel their eyes on me, and I refuse to look at them, steering us through the back roads of Crenshaw to where the houses start thinning out and large expanses of woods and farmland take over.

"I'm not going in there," Rae declares.

"Do you want me to turn around?" I ask.

"No," Nyelle says. "Keep going."

I risk a glance at Nyelle. She's wearing an amused grin. Maybe I should say something to clear up the image she probably has of me. But I don't. What would I say?

A few minutes later, I pull down the long driveway of the abandoned farmhouse. The dirt road splits, and I stay to the right toward the dark wooden barn and the rusted white silo standing beside it.

"It stopped snowing," Nyelle announces as we get out of the truck. Then she pauses in front of the truck, her gaze directed to top of the silo. A brilliant smile erupts on her face.

"Oh no," I say. "Don't even think about it."

Too late.

Nyelle is already walking toward the silo.

"Where's she going?" Rae asks from beside me. "She's not going to..."

"Yeah, she is," I answer. I blow out whatever common sense I have left and proceed after her.

"No way, Cal," Rae says urgently. "Are you insane?"

I don't look back for fear of losing my nerve. I remain focused on making sure nothing happens to Nyelle—it keeps me from thinking too much about what could happen to me. She's my courage. If it weren't for her, there's no way I'd be holding on to the rungs of a ladder, climbing up a silo that has more rust than paint streaking its sides.

"C'mon, Rae," Eric reassures her. "I've got your back. Let's go."

"I can't believe I'm doing this," I hear her say in the distance. I concentrate on my hands, unable to look down.

Nyelle doesn't hesitate when we reach the grated platform. She reaches for the ladder leading to the top of the dome just as I open my mouth to stop her.

Shit.

My hands are shaking by the time I'm sitting next to her. I've convinced myself it's adrenaline, and I'm going with that.

Nyelle's out of breath, but still wearing the kid-on-Christmas-morning smile.

"This is amazing," she says, lying back with a hand behind her head. "Look at the stars with me, Cal."

I lie back, and Nyelle threads her arm through mine, pulling herself close to me. I take a deep breath and try to focus on the sky. The storm clouds have thinned into wispy strands that weave across the sky, allowing pockets of stars to shine through.

"You found your something to climb," I say. "But I think I prefer the tree." I fight to keep my attention on the sky and not on the fact that I'm closer to the clouds than I've ever been without being strapped in. There's no sense in looking down to search for the sanity that I left at the bottom of the ladder. I'm up here. With Nyelle.

"I did," she sighs. "I'm surprised you came all the way up here with me."

"Me too," I say with a short laugh.

"I'm not coming up there!" Rae yells from below.

"Sit here next to me," Eric tells her. "I brought our friend Jack."

Nyelle moves her face close to mine and says so only I can hear her, "She's your best friend, huh?"

"Yeah, she is," I reply, watching the light flicker in her eyes.

"Do you miss her?" Nyelle asks, looking back up at the sky. I continue to watch her, struck by the hint of emotion in her voice.

"I talk to her just about every day," I say. "But, yeah, I miss her."

"I'd miss her too," she says in a whisper. I prop up on my elbow to look down at her. She glances away, swiping the corner of her eye.

"Come down here with us!" Rae shouts up. "We brought the sparklers."

"Ready to get off the top of the world?" I ask her, searching her eyes for the emotion that I thought I'd heard.

Nyelle looks up at me and smiles. "Sure."

Eric and Rae are seated on the platform with their legs dangling and arms hung over the middle crossbar, the bottle of Jack Daniel's set between them.

I step down behind them next to Nyelle.

Rae hands us each a sparkler, and Eric passes around the lighter. Each rod ignites in a shower of sparks. Nyelle waves hers around in the air, leaving behind a trail of smoke and the ghost of streaking light imprinted in the dark.

Eric and Rae have some sort of sparkler sword fight with theirs. I lean over the railing and let the sparks rain below like fireflies being set free. The night echoes with laughter as Rae declares herself victor and Eric demands a rematch.

Nyelle slides along the rail to stand beside me after our sparklers are extinguished, our arms brushing. She doesn't say anything. She just stands there staring out into the night. The stars are becoming brighter as the thin veil of clouds trails away. A light streaks across the sky.

"Make a wish," I whisper, leaning over. Nyelle closes her eyes, a slow smile emerging. I'm about to ask what she wants to do over again when her hand slips into mine and she threads our fingers together. Warmth rushes up my arm. I squeeze her hand lightly and take in the starlight reflecting in her eyes as she says quietly, "I wished for a butterfly."

NICOLE

September—Fifth Grade

I'm nervous, and my hands feel sweaty. I'm more nervous than when I have to show my daddy I got less than a hundred on a test. I'm so nervous, my stomach hurts.

I keep watching out the window until I see Cal running in from the soccer field after they make the first announcement that recess is over.

"Miss Hendricks, I'm going to go now, okay?" I've been helping her clean up the art room all recess.

"Thank you for helping, Nicole," she says from the sink, where she's rinsing out the paintbrushes. I grab the rolled-up paper with the blue ribbon tied around it and walk really fast to the doors where they come in from recess and stand to the side so everyone can pass me.

I see Cal. His hair's all sticking up from running around. He has a grass stain on his elbow, probably from falling. And his glasses have slid down to the tip of his nose.

I make sure he sees me and wave him over to underneath the stairs so people won't notice us.

"Hi, Nicole. How come you weren't at recess?"

"I was helping Miss Hendricks. And umm...I made this for you."

He holds out his hand to accept it, and I almost don't let it go.

"Don't look at it now, okay? I don't want anyone else to see it."

"Okay," he says. "Thanks."

My chest has the butterfly in it again.

"What's that?" Richelle asks. I don't know where she came from, but she's pointing to the paper in Cal's hand.

I can't say anything. The butterfly has turned into a hammer, and I press my lips together, wanting her to go away.

"Nicole gave it to me," Cal says.

"Can I see?" she asks, reaching for it.

I want to tell her no. I want *Cal* to tell her no. He opens his mouth, and I hold my breath. But then she reaches out her hand and he lets her take it. I want to cry.

Richelle unties the ribbon and lets it fall to the floor as she unrolls the paper. She looks at it for a long time. I can feel the tears building up in my eyes. She rolls it back up and gives it to Cal. She won't look at me. I know she's mad when she runs away.

"Cal, I told you not to show it to anyone!" I yell at him. "Richelle! Please don't be mad." I run after her, but there's a teacher in the hall making sure we go to class.

After school, when my homework is finished, I sit outside on my front steps, waiting for Richelle to come out. I feel like I wait for a very long time.

Finally, her door opens and she walks over to stand right in front of me.

"My mom told me I need to express my feelings, so I don't hold things on the inside. And I want to tell you that you weren't a very good friend today. I told you I really like Cal. I told you I wanted him to be my boyfriend. And what you did wasn't very nice."

I blink back the tears and squeeze my folded hands in my lap. "I'm sorry."

"Nicole, did you kiss him?"

I pick my head up. "No. I didn't. I swear. He's just my friend, Richelle. I promise. I didn't mean to make you mad."

"You promise you just want to be friends with him?"

"Yes," I answer, but it hurts my heart a little because I know that's not really true. I don't want Cal to be my boyfriend, because I don't want to kiss him. But I really did want to hold his hand again.

"Okay. I don't want to be mad at you anymore," she finally says.

"Good. I don't want you to be mad at me ever again," I respond, and I really mean it. "I promise that I will never like Cal more than a friend." This was the first fight I've ever had with Richelle, and it hurt so bad I don't ever want to feel this way again.

Richelle sits next to me on the step and takes my hand. It doesn't give me the butterfly in my chest like when Cal holds it, but it does make me feel better—like the sun, all nice and warm.

"Richelle, why isn't Cal your boyfriend like you wanted?"

"You told me he said he wasn't ready to kiss a girl. He can't be my boyfriend until he wants to kiss me. I want to be the first girl he kisses. And I don't want him to want to kiss another girl except me... ever."

"Oh," I respond, my heart feeling heavy.

"Let's go to my house," Richelle says, jumping up from the stairs and pulling me after her. "I have a surprise to show you."

NINE

"Why are you stopping here?" I ask when Brady pulls his Jeep up to the curb.

"Dude, your house isn't that far. Get out," Brady demands. "I have to pick up Rae from Nina's. She needs rescuing, and you're too drunk to stand, so it's up to me to save her."

"I can come—"

"No. You need to go fall on your face in your bed. I'll see you tomorrow."

Reluctantly, I get out of his Jeep.

"Hey," Brady calls, getting my attention. "We fucking graduated!" he hollers with his fist in the air as he drives away. I laugh and watch him speed off down the street. My lids are heavy and everything is moving a little more slowly than it should. I concentrate on my steps along the sidewalk.

There's a dinging in my head. I try to shake it out, but it keeps chiming. That's when I notice Mr. Bentley's Lincoln in the driveway with the door open. That's such an annoying noise.

"You need to calm down." Mr. Bentley's low voice carries out of the house through the open window. "Getting this upset isn't going to make things better."

"Don't touch me!" Nicole screams at him.

I've stopped walking. I can't see anything from where I'm standing behind the car in the driveway. But it's hard for me to focus anyway. I sigh. "Overreacting just a little, Nicole?" I mumble. "Kyle's a douche. You're better off without him."

Who am I talking to? I shake my head. I start toward my house again when the sound of shattering glass turns me back around.

I jolt awake. Blinking, I slowly ease out of the night after graduation and return to the confines of the plane taking us back home for the holiday break.

"You okay?" Rae asks, eyeing me carefully.

"Yeah," I reply. The fragmented memory fades with the dream. I still don't know what really happened that night.

Rae goes back to reading the issue of *Rolling Stone* spread on her tray table.

I press my forehead against the window and watch the clouds pass below us. I grin, reminded of Nyelle. She disappeared again. We didn't see her after that night at the silo. I'd say I was used to it, but I'm not.

"She kind of reminds me of Richelle," Rae says. "The way she gets excited about the dumbest things."

I let out a small laugh at the comparison. "Yeah, I guess." Rae didn't want to talk about Nyelle after we dropped her off Saturday night. I didn't push it. I knew she'd talk when she was ready.

"But she's not the girl we grew up with."

I scrunch my brow together in confusion. "You don't think she's Nicole?"

"I'm saying that whoever she is now is *not* Nicole. She looks a lot like her. If she didn't have the same laugh, I might be convinced of the separated-at-birth theory. But other than that, there's nothing left of the girl we knew—not the bitch or the princess." Her voice is deflated. "I think we need to tell someone. Maura will know—"

"No," I say adamantly. "Don't say anything to my mother."

"What?" Rae stares at me like she didn't hear me right.

"Not yet," I beg. "I just need a little more time."

"For what? What are you waiting for? For her to jump off a bridge?" Rae says passionately.

"She wouldn't—" I pause, thinking better of it. "Okay. Maybe she would. But not because she's suicidal."

"No, because she's *crazy*. I'm serious. There's something wrong with her. She didn't even flinch when I talked about Renfield or when I brought up people she's supposed to know. There wasn't the tiniest tell on her face that she knew who I was talking about. It totally freaked me out."

"What *did* you talk about?" I ask. I've wanted to know since the second they stepped out of the bathroom.

Rae drops her serious expression, replacing it with a teasing smirk. "You're afraid we were talking about you, aren't you?"

"Were you?"

"Of course we were." Rae laughs.

"What did you say?"

"She wanted to know how many girls you've dated," she says, with a taunting smile. "I told her I lost count."

"Rae!"

She starts laughing at me. "It's true! Do you even know how many girls you've been with?"

"Yes," I reply quickly, then clench my teeth together when I can't come up with the number right away.

"Omigod, Cal! *You* don't even know!" Rae is laughing so hard now, she draws the attention of the man in the suit on the other side of her.

"Whatever. It's not *that* many," I defend. "What did *she* say?"

"She thought it was funny. Because it is."

I groan. "Please don't tell me that's what you were laughing about for a half hour."

"No." Rae takes a breath to calm her laughter. "She asked me a million questions about . . . everything. She pretty much wanted to know my entire life story from when we started . . ."

Rae stops, her shoulders round like she's had the wind knocked out of her.

"What just happened?"

It takes Rae a minute to say anything.

"She asked about high school. My brother. The band. You and me," Rae answers quietly. "Basically, she wanted to know everything that's happened to me since . . . we stopped being friends."

Rae tips her head back and rests it against the seat, her jaw tight. I don't know what to say. I've never seen Rae upset like this before. This is about the time she usually shuts herself away in her garage.

"We need to find out what happened to her," she says quietly. "Is she still friends with Richelle? Maybe she'll know."

"I don't know," I answer. "They stayed friends in high school. But I haven't heard from Richelle in a few years."

"Why did she stop talking to you?" Rae says harshly. "Oh yeah, that's right. Because you *let* her."

"Hey! This isn't my fault." I'm suddenly on the defensive,

and I don't even know what I did wrong. This is the most intense conversation I've ever had with Rae. I have no idea how to handle this surge of emotion coming from my best friend, who was okay with shutting everyone out up until two minutes ago. She's needing me to be her drums right now, so if she needs to pound on me a little, I'll let her.

Rae presses her palms over her eyes. "I know. Sorry. I'm just... angry. She was our friend. They both were. And now...I don't know. It sucks. I hate this."

"Why didn't you ever talk to Richelle after she moved?" I ask, struck with the lingering guilt of letting our friendship slip away.

"Richelle and I never really *talked*," Rae reminds me. "We... hung out. You know?"

"Right." I nod. "Do you...still hate Nicole?"

"I never hated her," Rae says. "I just hated who she became. And now I don't think she even knows who she is."

Rae takes a deep breath.

"One month, Cal." Rae turns to me, completely serious. "You have one month to figure out what's wrong with her before I bring Maura in on this."

I nod. It's not that I don't trust my mother. I know she'll do whatever's right to help Nyelle. But maybe what's right isn't what I want. Or what Nyelle needs. Truthfully, I don't know if I want her to get "better" if it means not being Nyelle anymore.

"Who's picking us up?" Rae asks as we walk toward baggage claim.

"Devin," I reply. She groans.

I'm pretty close with my family, despite the age differences. Sean is older by six years, and Devin by four. They had each other growing up. And I had Rae. Jules is the youngest, born five years after me. She probably would've been friends with Liam, except he didn't move back until he was thirteen. And now they're way too different. Jules is the quiet, artistic type. And Liam's . . . trouble.

Rae and I were the target of my brothers' torment whenever we crossed paths. They took pride in torturing us. It didn't really get to me. If anything, it helped me not to give a shit whenever someone tried to humiliate me in school. Whereas Rae would fight back every chance she got. She never won. They usually ended up laughing at her. But that didn't keep her from trying.

"You can't *still* have an issue with Devin," I claim, weaving through the slow-moving holiday travelers. "He hasn't lived at home in more than two years. He has a real job now and is forced to wear a tie every day. I'm sure he's outgrown harassing you."

"Doubt it," Rae grumbles.

We reach baggage claim and find Devin leaning against a post with his attention on his phone. He glances up briefly, and his eyes pass over me at first. Then he looks up again. His expression changing from confusion to surprise.

"What the hell happened to you two? I haven't been away *that* long."

"Not long enough," Rae shoots back. He wraps his arm around her neck and aggressively rubs the top of her head. "Ah! Stop it!" she hollers.

"Oh, Rae. I've missed your smart-ass mouth," Devin says, keeping her in the headlock until she punches him in the side. "You need to start hitting the weights if you ever expect that to hurt."

He redirects his attention to me. "Geez, man, you're fricken taller than Sean now. And your hair seems to have grown with you. Maybe we can get Jules to braid it for you."

"Hey, Devin," I say, holding out my hand, and he pulls me in for a one-armed hug with a firm pat on my back. "How've you been?"

"Livin' the dream, baby." He smirks. "Except I miss Mom's cooking."

"Yeah, looks like you've lost some weight," I chide, knowing he's more fit than he's ever been.

"Dude, you've packed on some muscle. Finally!" He whacks me in the stomach as he leads us to the parking garage. "Been lifting?"

"Eric and I go to the gym a few times a week, yeah," I respond, rubbing the sore spot on my stomach.

Devin and Sean were different from me in every possible way growing up. They were popular in school, involved in just about everything. They're natural athletes, excelling in every sport without an issue.

I was always lost in their shadows, sucking at sports no matter how hard I tried. So even though we're probably about the same size now, I still feel smaller. Hell, I even *look* different, with my brown hair and hazel eyes, in contrast to their light hair and blue eyes.

"Just to warn you, *the uncles* have arrived. They're not staying at the house, thankfully. But they're pretty much there all the time, so it's a fricken zoo."

"Great," Rae responds unenthusiastically. "I'm not going anywhere near your house until dinner tomorrow."

We throw our things in the back of his Jetta and get in.

"Have you two figured out what dessert you're making for tomorrow?" Devin asks, pulling out of the parking spot.

"Shit," Rae breathes out. "I knew I forgot something."

"Typical." Devin reaches into his jacket and hands me a folded piece of paper.

Our family is huge—with aunts, uncles, and cousins coming to our house each year. And we only get half of them at a time. My mother is one of seven. Anytime we get together for the holidays, it's a monumental event. To keep it from being a nightmare for her in the kitchen, we're assigned dishes to make for dinner. Rae and I are responsible for a dessert this year. Which we aren't prepared to make.

I open the paper Devin gave me and find a recipe. Thankfully, my mother has little faith in us. "Looks easy enough," I say. "Seems like it's basically just cake and pudding tossed together with whipped cream on top."

"Thank you, Maura," Rae praises from the backseat.

"We'll stop by the grocery store on the way home. Sean and I are in charge of the stuffing, and there's a few things I need to get."

"If you screw up the stuffing, I swear I'll hurt you," Rae warns.

"Relax, little one." Devin laughs. "We've got this. And unless you start eating whatever Cal's been eating, we'll always take you down."

"Oh, I don't need strength to get you," Rae threatens in a low voice.

Devin flashes me a look of concern out of the corner of his eye. I laugh.

The grocery store is worse than the airport with last-minute shoppers crowding the aisles.

"You've got to be kidding me," Rae complains when we walk into the bedlam. "They've only known that Thanksgiving was coming since *last Thanksgiving*."

"So did you." Devin chuckles.

"Yeah, but I'm twenty. Procrastination is considered a life skill. These are grown humans with families and shit. What the hell?"

"C'mon, Rae. Let's get what we need before you start biting people," Devin says, leading us through abandoned shopping carts and shoppers absently stepping out in front of us.

At the far end of the spice aisle, I spot Nicole's mother with her smooth black hair tied back in a low bun. I nudge Rae and nod in Mrs. Bentley's direction.

"Devin, why don't we split up and meet back at the car," Rae suggests, keeping her eyes locked on Mrs. Bentley.

"Yeah, sure," he agrees. He leans in and says to me, "Keep her close." He smirks at Rae. She sneers back.

"What should we say?" Rae asks as we start down the aisle.

"I have no idea," I mutter. "Maybe we shouldn't..."

Too late. We're standing in front of her, and she's looking at us curiously like she's trying to place us. I want to turn around, and Rae must sense it because she grabs ahold of my elbow, digging her fingers in.

"Hi, Mrs. Bentley," Rae says with a charming smile.

Mrs. Bentley's eyes twitch, probably trying to decide if she should run away or return the greeting. "It's me, Raelyn Timmons. I live on your street. I was friends with Nicole growing up."

Mrs. Bentley's eyes widen in recognition. She smiles sweetly. "Hi, Raelyn. My, you've had a little makeover. I barely recognized you." She laughs uncomfortably.

"Yeah, it's a phase I'm going through," Rae replies in a mumble, squeezing my arm a little tighter. I press my lips together to keep from smiling.

"And you're..." She looks to me, trying to come up with my name.

"Cal Logan."

"Cal!" Mrs. Bentley says in a surprised tone. "Well, you've both changed so much over the years."

"I haven't seen Nicole around in a while. Is she home for Thanksgiving?" Rae asks.

The corners of Mrs. Bentley's smile tighten ever so slightly. "No. She's staying in Cambridge with friends for the holiday. She has a lot of work to do at Harvard. But we're hoping she'll make it home for Christmas."

"So how is she liking Harvard?" Rae continues with the questions. I'm studying Mrs. Bentley's face. She maintains the plastic smile that's she's perfected over the years. Now I know why Nyelle can fake it so well.

"It's kept her very busy, and unfortunately, away from home. But I know she's doing what she needs to do to make something of herself," she answers stiffly.

"Have you been to see her? Like... in person?" Rae fires as soon as she's done answering. I want to elbow her to *shut it*, fearing she's crossing the line.

Mrs. Bentley eyes us curiously. "I have. Her father and I visited during parents' weekend. She's getting along quite nicely." Her frozen expression never falters. "Well, it was lovely to see you two. I have to hurry home to start prepping for tomorrow. We're hosting the family this year, and my house is nowhere near ready."

"When is she—"

"Happy Thanksgiving, Mrs. Bentley." I cut Rae off and smile politely as Nicole's mom pushes her grocery cart past us.

"What are you doing?" I demand, pulling my arm out of Rae's claws. "You might as well have just called her a liar."

"But she *is* lying! She thinks she's hiding it with that stupid

Barbie smile," Rae grumbles in annoyance. "Her daughter's at *Crenshaw*. She has to know *you're* at Crenshaw from talking to your mother. She wouldn't have tried to pull all that *Harvard* shit with us if she knew where her daughter was."

"So you think they're covering something up?" I ask, continuing toward the bakery.

Rae stops in the aisle, making irritated shoppers walk around us, her face distorted in anger. "Hell yeah. Something's not right, Cal."

I exhale slowly. Things just got way more complicated.

Sitting around the mile-long Thanksgiving table filled with my family, I'm caught up in the buzz of voices, laughter, and bickering—like every holiday in my house.

Across the table, my ten-year-old cousin, Tommy, is daring our eight-year-old cousin, Henry, to eat the mashed potatoes without hands. Just as Henry bends down to shove his face into the whipped pile, I hear, "Henry David, don't you dare!" The voice rises above the noise from the other end of the table *before* he's even done anything. I let out a short laugh and lean back in my chair, soaking in the chaos. It's comforting in a weird way. The holidays wouldn't be the same without it. I wonder what Nyelle's doing right now.

"What are you thinking about?" Rae asks from beside me, unplugging an earbud from her ear. She claims that listening to music, instead of my younger cousins, keeps her from stabbing someone. Her family has become an extension of ours over the years. Although her mother usually has to leave early, preferring the double time of a holiday shift over our Thanksgiving madness.

"My family's insane," I tell her.

"Truth."

"But I couldn't imagine not having *this* every year," I continue. "So... what is *she* doing right now? We know she's not with her family. So she's probably at Crenshaw... alone."

"Yeah. I was just thinking that," Rae says quietly.

We pick at our food without another word, the weight of that probability robbing us of our appetites.

My mother's loading the dishwasher when I enter with my plate and Rae's.

"Thank you, Cal," she says as she takes the plates and sets them in open slots. "Would you mind covering those bowls in plastic wrap and putting them in the fridge?"

I take a deep breath to gather my nerve before saying, "Mom, I'd like to get back to school a little early."

"What do you consider early? You're only here for the weekend."

I swallow. "Tomorrow."

My mother rolls the rack into the dishwasher. "Why do you need to go back so suddenly?"

I expected her to question me, and it's the reason I hesitated to ask. But then I think of Nyelle by herself and... I can't stay here.

I scan the kitchen floor, not wanting to lie. I hate lying to my mother, but I can't tell her the entire truth just yet. "There's a friend there I'm worried about."

"In what way?" she asks, leaning against the counter with her arms crossed, focusing on me.

"Ready for dessert?" my aunt Mary asks, walking into the kitchen with the last of the serving bowls.

"Not quite yet," my mother responds politely. "I'll call you once we've finished in here, and we'll get the coffee brewing."

Mary looks between us and nods, leaving us alone again.

"Why are you concerned about this friend?" my mother pursues.

"She stayed on campus for the break, so she's alone today, and . . . I don't think she should be," I answer as honestly as I can.

"Ah." My mother nods. "This friend's a *girl*." I avoid her assuming gaze. "Now I understand."

After a moment of consideration, she says, "Okay. I guess you can go back tomorrow. You'll be back here in less than a month, so I can't be too upset that you're choosing a girl over your mother. Go ahead and change your flight." She smiles teasingly.

"Thanks, Mom," I reply with a small smile. "You know you're the only woman in my life who matters."

"Yeah, right." She laughs lightly, swatting me with the dish towel.

"I've been trying to find a way to make fun of you for doing this," Rae says as she pulls up along the curb at the airport. "But I can't. I like that you're going back to be with her."

"But I'm not sure where to find her when I get back."

"Start with the first place you saw her," Rae suggests. When she sees I'm confused, she says, "*Bean Buzz*. Not the party."

"Right." I nod.

"Here." Rae reaches in the backseat for a small bag from RadioShack.

I take it from her and look inside.

"It's a drug phone . . . for Nyelle, one of those disposable ones like they use in the movies. We need to be able to get ahold of her."

"I think they call them *burner* phones, but whatever," I say with a laugh. "How did you buy this anyway? I mean, you don't exactly have a job other than being your brother's parole officer."

"Yeah, well, I didn't pay for it. You did," she replies. "I stole money from your wallet while we were at Brady's last night and went out to buy it this morning at the ass-crack of dawn with all of the Black Friday lunatics."

I laugh. "I didn't know you had it in you."

"Me either," she admits with a smirk. "I don't know what the hell's going on, or what happened to make her act like she doesn't know who we are, but she shouldn't have to go through it by herself. Oh, and I went on Brady's Facebook account last night. Nicole hasn't posted anything since graduation."

"Really?" I can't ignore the bad feeling in my gut. "Since graduation?"

RICHELLE

April—Fifth Grade

"You have to come see this," I say, excited to show Nicole what we found.

"I'm supposed to leave in a little bit to go to a dinner for my dad," she replies, frowning.

"But they're baby birds in a nest," I explain urgently. "We can see it from the window of the tree house. They're so cute." I look at the frilly yellow dress and white shoes she's wearing and know that she really can't come see it. "Maybe…tomorrow."

Nicole runs her hands down the front of her dress, straightening it like she does all the time. "Well…maybe if I'm careful." She opens her front door and hollers to her mom, "Momma can I go with Richelle? She wants to show me something and then I'll be right back."

Mrs. Bentley comes to the door. "I don't know, Nicole. We have to leave in twenty minutes. We can't be late for your daddy's dinner."

"I know. I promise it will be real quick."

Mrs. Bentley presses her lips together and finally says, "Okay. Ten minutes, and then I expect you to be right here, ready to go."

Nicole smiles brightly. I hold out my hand for her to take and we skip off toward Cal's house.

"It won't take long," I assure her as we walk through the tall grass. She parts the blades and steps likes she's balancing on a tightrope. "Grass won't get you dirty, Nicole."

"But my shoes," she explains, continuing to tiptoe. If she keeps this up, it's going to take us ten minutes just to get there. I wait for her at the edge of the woods, trying my hardest to be patient.

When we finally get to the tree, I'm pretty sure our time is up. But Nicole doesn't seem worried about anything except the dirt touching her shoes. She's walking like she's trying not to touch the ground at all.

Rae and Cal stick their heads out the door and the side window. "We just saw the mom feed them. They ate out of her mouth. It was so gross and awesome!" Rae yells down.

Nicole waits for me to go first, probably because she has a dress on. When I get to the top, she's barely halfway up the ladder. I shake my head, watching her take careful steps on the boards. She's being extra, extra slow today. I climb into the tree house, and Cal makes room for me to look out the window where we can see the birds a few branches down.

Then I hear a scream and a big thud. "Nicole!" I yell, rushing to the door. I look down and she's lying on the ground. I scoot out and climb down as fast as I can. Cal and Rae are right behind me. I can hear her whimpering before I get to her.

"Oh no. Oh no. Oh no," she cries.

I kneel down next to her. "Are you okay?"

Then I hear a sharp inhale and look up. Rae is staring at her leg. I cover my mouth to keep from screaming when I see the stick poking through her skin, into her thigh.

"Rae, go get help," Cal orders her. She doesn't move. "Rae! Go. Now!"

Rae takes off running.

I hold Nicole's hand, trying hard not to cry.

"Keep looking at Richelle. Okay, Nicole?" Cal says, really calm. "Don't move."

Her blue eyes are teary, but no tears have come out yet as she stares at me. It's like she's waiting for me to tell her what to do.

"Everything's going to be okay," I tell her, but it feels like something is stuck in my throat. "Don't think about it. Just keep looking at me."

Cal crouches next to her and spreads his sweatshirt over her leg so she can't see the stick in it. It's not bleeding much from what I can tell.

We suddenly hear footsteps crashing through the woods, and then I see Cal's big brother Sean.

"What happened?" he asks, breathing fast.

"Close your eyes, Nicole," Cal says. She squeezes my hand and her eyes shut at the same time. Cal removes the jacket and Sean makes a sound through his teeth.

"Okay, I'm going to pick you up so we can take you to the doctor," Sean says.

"Oh no! That means we're going to be late," she cries.

"Don't worry," I say. "You have to get your leg fixed first."

Sean scoops her up and Nicole screams in pain.

"Sean! You're hurting her," I yell. "Don't hurt her!"

"Richelle, he has to get her to her mom," Cal explains, holding me back to keep me from pulling on Sean's shirt.

Sean takes off in a really fast walk. Cal and I have to run to keep up. Mrs. Logan is at the edge of the woods, waiting.

"What happened?" she asks. Then she sees Nicole's leg. "Oh, honey. It's okay. We're going to take care of you."

"She fell off the ladder," Cal says.

"Rae went to get your mom," Mrs. Logan explains. "Sean, can

you slide into the backseat of the car with Nicole, without moving her around too much?"

"I think so," he replies. I run around to the other side of the car and watch him duck down. Nicole yells out again, and I clench my fists as tears pour down my face.

"Stop hurting her!" I demand.

Cal stands beside me. "He doesn't mean to."

"Nicole? Oh! What happened?" Mrs. Bentley is walking quickly up the driveway with Rae beside her.

"We need to take her to the hospital," Mrs. Logan says. "She landed on a stick, and it punctured her leg."

"It what?" Mrs. Bentley asks. She bends over and looks in at Nicole and covers her mouth. "Oh no. What did you do, Nicole? Your father's going to be so upset. Why would you go into the woods?"

She says it like Nicole did something wrong.

"She just wanted to see the baby birds," I say, trying to stand up for her.

"We should get going," Mrs. Logan says. She turns to where Devin is standing on the steps. I didn't know he was there. "Take the kids to the Nelsons', okay?" He nods.

"Wait, um..." Mrs. Bentley looks confused, or maybe scared. "We're supposed to go to a dinner with my husband. I don't..."

"Your daughter's hurt, Vera. I'm sure he'll understand."

Mrs. Bentley shakes her head, then looks toward her house. She seems really confused. I hear Nicole cry. My heart is beating so fast. Why haven't they left yet? What is she waiting for?

Mrs. Logan takes a big breath and says, "Dr. Xavier has a private clinic ten minutes from here. He's a friend, and he'll take care of her. Why don't you follow me, and once you know she's all right, you can go meet your husband. I'll bring Nicole back to your house and stay with her until you get home. Does that sound okay?" Her voice is soft, like one of my teachers giving us instructions before a test.

Mrs. Bentley nods and begins to walk away. She trips on something, but doesn't fall. She keeps nodding and walking away.

"We'll be right back," Mrs. Logan says. She looks at me and says calmly, "Nicole's going to be just fine. I promise."

"Okay," I choke out. I still feel like something's caught in my throat.

We all take a few steps back and they drive away.

I sit on Nicole's front steps with Cal and Rae until she gets home. My mom tries to get us to come in for dinner, but I can't eat. My stomach hurts too much.

It's dark when Mrs. Logan's car pulls into the driveway. I jump up and run to the car. Nicole is on Sean's lap in the backseat. When the door opens I can see that she's asleep.

Mrs. Logan leads them to the house with crutches in her hands. "She's fine, like I promised. It wasn't too deep. She just needed some stitches and has to use crutches to keep off it for a little while so it can heal."

"Can I see her?" I ask. "I won't wake her. I just... Please?"

She nods, and I follow them into the house and upstairs to Nicole's room. After Mrs. Logan tucks her in the bed, she leaves the room. I kneel next to the bed and take her hand.

"Please don't ever get hurt again," I whisper, trying not to cry. "You're my best friend. When you hurt, I hurt too. Please. I don't want anything to happen to you again."

TEN

I look up when the door opens. It's not her. I've been here half the morning, and I'm beginning to think she's not going to show. Honestly, I'm not sure I can handle another cup of coffee. My hands are starting to shake. This much caffeine can't be good.

The door opens again, and a rush of cold air sweeps through. And there she is, wearing her gargantuan brown jacket, knit cap, and cutoff gloves. She's also holding a large white plastic garment bag. I watch as she takes her place in line.

Now I don't know what to do. Do I wait for her to see me? What if she doesn't? Do I call to her across the coffee shop, or approach her? Or do I pretend to bump into her?

I'm so wrapped up in my own head that it takes a minute for me to realize she's looking at me. When our eyes connect, she smiles and waves with her free hand. Well, that was easier than I anticipated.

Hi, I mouth, trying to appear casual. I point to the bag with a questioning look. She gestures with a single finger to wait, which means she's coming over. I can feel my smile widen. But my hands are shaking—still blaming the caffeine.

I wait for her to get her hot chocolate, and then she walks over and plops down next to me on the couch.

"Hey, Cal. Wasn't expecting to see you!" she says jubilantly.

"I . . . wanted to get away from the chaos," I fumble. "Big family. It gets a little crazy. You're back too, huh?"

"I decided to stay and have dinner with friends," she says without any hint of distress. And here I am, worried about her being alone. Although I'm not really sure who her *friends* are.

"What's up with that?" I ask, nodding toward the white bag.

"It's a wedding dress," she says, her eyes twinkling like they're lit from within. I must not hide my shock very well because she begins to laugh.

"It was given to me today. I was leaving Elaine's—"

"Elaine's?"

"She owns this consignment shop a few blocks from here. I help her out a couple days a week, and she lets me keep whatever clothes I want in payment."

"Is that where you got the linebacker's jacket?"

"Maybe," she answers, making a face at me. "Hey, I happen to like the big pockets. And it doesn't matter who it belonged to. When it's on me, it's mine."

My eyes tighten. I've heard that before.

"So tell me the story behind the dress. Did you get proposed to since I last saw you?"

"It's an interesting story, actually," she says, taking a sip from her cup. I haven't moved, because she hasn't said, "No." She realizes I'm holding my breath and laughs. "Stop it. I'm *not* getting married. But I am going to wear it."

"Please explain," I ask patiently, trying to filter through the confusion coming out of her mouth.

"I was on my way to the shop when I saw this woman sitting in a car in the parking lot, holding this bag in her hands. She kept looking at the store like she wasn't sure what to do. Then I noticed she was crying, so I knocked on her window and asked if she was okay. She told me that she wanted to give her dress to the shop but couldn't bring herself to do it. I thought it was because she wanted to hold on to the memories of her wedding. But she started crying harder when I told her she should keep it.

"Apparently, she never wore it. The engagement was broken off, and she thought that by giving it away she'd get closure. Except she can't stand the thought of someone else getting married in it. So I offered to take it and promised that no one will ever wear it on their wedding day."

"That's kind of crazy," I blurt honestly. "So now what are you going to do with it?"

"I'm not sure." She pauses in contemplation. "I think it deserves some good memories, you know?" She takes a sip of her hot chocolate and then looks at me like she just had the best idea. "Let's have a wedding!"

"What?"

"Not a *real* wedding. Stop looking all paranoid. Let's show this dress the best day of its life. I feel like by doing that, we're helping this woman move on. Besides, it'll be fun. We'll just be... ridiculous, for an entire day."

"And that's different from any other day?"

Nyelle swats my arm and I chuckle.

"Be nice, or I won't ask you to come." Then she looks at me, expecting a response. "So, do you want to come?"

I pause and take a deep breath. There really isn't a proper answer other than "Sure."

Her eyes grow wide, like she can already envision it. She clenches her fists, barely able to contain her excitement. She looks like a little kid being granted a wish. "Great! I'll plan everything. Don't worry."

Right. Nyelle's in charge, and I have no idea what I'm in for. Why would I worry? "Meet me here tomorrow morning at ten thirty. Wear a tie," she instructs. Then she downs the rest of her hot chocolate like she's chugging a beer. "Okay, I gotta go."

"Where are you going now?" I ask, standing up, wishing I knew how to make her stay... or take me with her.

"To work." It's a simple answer. But again, not at all what I expect to hear, especially since I thought she'd just gotten off from work. "See you tomorrow, Cal."

I walk out the next morning to find snow. Big, fat, cottony flakes floating down from the sky and coating everything. As I'm cleaning off the few inches accumulated on my truck, I feel bad I didn't offer to pick Nyelle up at the dorm.

I drive by her building and continue to Bean Buzz, hoping to spot her along the way. And I do, just as she's walking up the sidewalk to the coffee shop. Or I think it's her. She's the only one I know with that huge brown jacket. But there's a giant hood covering her head, so I can't see her face. Then again, who else would be carrying a white garment bag?

I park the truck and hop out.

"Nyelle!"

She looks up. "Hey, Cal."

"I was trying to find you so you wouldn't have to walk in this."

She peeks out from beneath the hood. "Oh, it's okay. I liked walking in the snow. It was... quiet." A mischievous smile emerges on her face. "So... I have something for you." Nyelle removes a paper bag from under the garment bag and hands it to me.

"What is it?" I ask, peering inside. "Oh, great. It's a tux." There isn't a hint of enthusiasm in my voice.

"I found it at Elaine's!" Nyelle tells me, carrying all of the excitement in hers. "I thought it would be fun if we were both dressed for a wedding."

"Fun?" I'm skeptical.

"C'mon, it *will* be." She flashes me a pleading smile, batting her long lashes. "Please."

I sigh.

She jumps around, doing a ridiculous little dance, not needing me to say yes to realize that I just gave in.

"Let's change here, and then we'll go, okay?"

"What are we doing?"

"Something I've always wanted to do," she answers, without really telling me anything. Nyelle continues into Bean Buzz and heads straight to the bathroom.

The coffeehouse is quiet, thankfully. The town pretty much disappears when college is out, and the storm is keeping most sane people indoors.

I glance at Mel behind the counter as I walk past her on my way to the bathroom. She eyes me curiously, probably trying to decipher the look of dread on my face. Knowing that I get to spend the day with Nyelle is the only thing keeping me from walking back out to my truck.

It's even worse when I pull the tux out of the bag.

"You've got to be kidding me," I mutter to myself, holding up the white jacket with the oversized lapels. Then I remove the matching bell-bottom pants and groan out loud. I prepare myself for a ruffled tuxedo shirt, but it's just a regular shirt. That's a relief... but then I put on the pants and have to suck in so tight to zip them, it's almost painful. The pants cling to my thighs like they're painted on, flaring out below my knee.

The jacket barely hides the snug fit of the pants. This is *not* comfortable. I try to adjust myself, and I suddenly have a newfound respect for male ballet dancers and feel bad for making fun of them when we saw *The Nutcracker* in fifth grade.

I hesitate before opening the bathroom door. "I can't believe I'm doing this," I grumble. I put on my coat to cover up the lapels that extend to my shoulders. Smothering all self-respect, I step out into the coffee shop. I can't move for a second, and it has nothing to do with the restrictive pants.

Standing next to the couch with her hands folded in front of her, wearing the biggest smile on her face, is Nyelle. She looks… beautiful. Her hair is pinned up high on her head in loose curls, circled by a ring of white daisies. I grin, reminded of the flower necklaces she and Richelle used to make. She's even wearing a little makeup. Her eyes look electric, lined in black, and her lips are shiny.

Her neck and arms are covered in lace, but I can still see her skin beneath. I eye the cutoff lace gloves suspiciously, wanting to know what she's hiding beneath them. Then there's a whole lot of satin that crashes down to the floor, with a big beige sash around her waist. The dress doesn't fit her right, but yet again, she looks gorgeous because *she* is. It has nothing to do with the dress.

"Wow," I breathe. "You look…" I hesitate, not wanting to incite bodily injury by complimenting her, "like you're ready for a wedding."

Nyelle beams. "So do you."

I look down and cringe. "I don't think any man should ever wear this much white."

"I agree," Mel says, appearing in front of me. She hands me a tiny cup. "Mazel tov."

“A shot?” I ask, hopeful.

“Of espresso,” she clarifies. She shakes her head at me. “You just threw that dignity right out the window, didn’t you?”

“Hey,” Nyelle says, as if *she’s* offended. “He looks cute.”

I take the shot of espresso and shudder. It was way more potent than I’d expected from that little cup. Mel laughs and continues her low chuckle as she returns behind the counter.

Every single person, granted there’s only five of them, is staring at us. I don’t blame them.

I zip up my jacket as Nyelle pulls on hers, covering up most of her dress. I don’t have that luxury with white flaring out around my boots.

“Where to?” I ask, offering her my elbow.

“To church,” she answers.

“Excuse me?” I choke out.

“Stop it,” she says with a quick laugh. “We’re not going *in* the church. I’ll show you when we get there.”

We step out into the storm. “At least I have camouflage working for me,” I state, looking around. Nyelle smiles. I leave my clothes in the truck as Nyelle ducks into the alley, returning with two sleds.

“I thought we could go sledding,” she says, handing me a blue saucer. “It’s something I’ve always wanted to do, so I thought it was appropriate.”

“You think sledding in a wedding dress is appropriate?” I confirm, shaking my head.

“Who cares?! Today’s about starting again. We can do whatever we want!”

“Okay. Let’s go sledding.” I shrug in concession, offering her my elbow again. She slides her arm through mine, carrying a long red sled in her other hand. “Where’d you get these anyway?”

"Someone was throwing them away," Nyelle explains.

"You have this thing with saving what others leave behind, don't you?" I tease.

"Maybe it ends up being the thing I've always wanted," she states, like she's trying to make a point. Except I'm not really sure what it is.

We continue around the corner, heading away from the stores and restaurants on the main street.

The snow continues to fall steadily, covering up our tracks as if they were never there. The air is still and heavy. Nyelle was right; it is quiet. The snow has put the world on mute.

Nyelle kicks up the piles around her feet as we walk. Black boots poke out from under the dress. I hadn't thought about what she might be wearing for shoes, but this makes me laugh.

"What?" she asks.

"I like the boots. They're a nice touch."

"Well, it *is* snowing," she points out. "I kept my jeans on too." She lifts the hem of the dress to reveal her pants.

"I can hardly breathe in these," I say, pointing to what's basically spandex on my legs, "and you're in jeans. Doesn't seem fair."

"Your pants are polyester," she says unsympathetically. "They'll stretch."

"I hope so," I say, pulling down on the thighs. "Are we really going to a church?"

"Yeah," she answers, just as the small, steepled church comes into view atop a large hill. "Look at that hill. It has to be the best sledding spot in town."

I chuckle with a nod. "You're probably right."

Nyelle hands me her sled and lifts up her skirt to keep from walking on it as we head up the church's long driveway.

"Let's go around back," Nyelle suggests, trudging through the knee-deep snow that's accumulated over the past week.

As we stand at the top of the hill, it feels like we're on our own island, surrounded by a sea of white snow with headstones jutting out like jagged rocks. The cemetery stretches to the right of the church, all the way to the road, bordered by wrought-iron fencing. Large trees break up the untouched white canvas, twisting out of the ground toward the sky, collecting snow along their barren limbs.

"It's beautiful, isn't it?" Nyelle asks from beside me.

I turn to look at her. The chilled air has brushed her cheeks pink. A cloud of breath floats from between her shiny, full lips. Her eyes are such a pale blue, it's almost as if they're coated with frost too. There's an energy floating off her that's full of possibilities. "Yeah. Beautiful."

Her smile's bright enough to part the overcast sky as she reaches for the red sled under my arm.

"I'll go first, okay?"

I can only nod. I'd almost forgotten why we're here.

Nyelle sits down on the long plastic sled, folding the skirt on her lap. She scoots forward, packing the snow beneath before shoving off. She doesn't go very fast, plowing the snow out of her way and leaving a trail behind her. She comes to a slow stop at the bottom just as it levels out.

She hops off and looks up the hill, still wearing that radiant smile. "Your turn."

Sitting on the blue saucer brings on a whole new layer of discomfort. I shift, but it's useless. I hold my legs out in front of me, since there's no way in hell I can cross them. I wouldn't fit on this small sled even if I could.

I dig my hands in the snow, pushing forward until gravity takes over and I'm following Nyelle's path. Still not going very fast, but the hill is steep enough to get me to the bottom.

It takes a few more runs before I'm able to pack the snow enough to pick up speed. The snow pelts me in the face as I move over the surface that's now as slick as ice.

Nyelle yells out when she catches air going over a bump on her way down. Watching her fly down the hill on a sled wearing a wedding dress is a memory I don't ever want to forget.

"We should try one together," Nyelle suggests on our way back up the hill. "That saucer can't be very comfortable."

"Not really. I'm probably bruised," I admit, having felt every groove and bump as if I were sliding down the slope on my bare ass. "But I'm having fun, if that makes you feel better."

"Of course you're having fun! We're sledding in a snowstorm wearing wedding clothes. How could you not?"

I laugh.

"How are we going to do this?" I ask when we reach the top and Nyelle sets the sled down. It's not very big. There's no way the two of us will be able to fit on it without her sitting on top of me. Actually... I like that option.

"Let's stand."

"What?" I shoot back. "And kill ourselves?"

"What's the worst that can happen? We fall in the snow..."

"And kill ourselves."

She laughs and grabs my lapels through my partially unzipped coat, shaking me. "Where's your sense of adventure, Cal? Let's snow surf!"

I stare at her for a moment. She dares me without blinking. I grumble in defeat. Those damn eyes win every time.

"Fine. But if we fall, I'm using you and that huge dress as a cushion."

Nyelle shakes her head at my weak threat. She steps on, holding my shoulder with one hand for balance and gripping the thin nylon rope looped through the front of the sled with the other.

I carefully step on behind her, wrapping my arm around her waist and holding on to the rope too. I would be enjoying this right now, if I weren't looking down the steep hill, foreseeing the wipeout that's going to hurt like hell.

I widen my stance and bend my knees to balance better.

"Ready?" I murmur in her ear. She nods. I swear I can feel her heartbeat speed up. "Hold on." I shift my weight forward, inching us to the edge and down the hill. The cold wind rushes in my face. I can't feel the snow hitting me. My legs give with each bump, and adrenaline courses through me. I'm almost convinced we're going to make it when we hit the bump, and my feet leave the sled.

Nyelle yells out and topples forward, grabbing my hand and taking me with her. We crash into the snow and tumble down the hill. I come to a stop, sprawled on my back, unable to see anything past the snow covering my face.

"Nyelle, are you okay?" I ask, tipping on my side. She doesn't answer. "Nyelle?"

She's buried in the snow, with just her boots sticking out. I crawl over to her, clearing off the avalanche.

"Nyelle?"

When I finally find her face, she's laughing so hard, no noise comes out. Her chest spasms, and her mouth is open wide. I remove my glove to clear the snow from her cheeks.

Tears are welled in her eyes when she calms enough to focus on me.

"Are you okay?" I ask again, looking down at her, encased in snow. She bites her bottom lip, still smiling, and nods. I'm suddenly very aware of her and her slow, drawn breaths. My hand is still cupping her cheek, and I'm transfixed by the emotion captured in her eyes. Just as I'm bending down to kiss her, she sits up, and her head slams into my cheek. I groan, falling onto my back in pain.

"Oh, Cal, I'm so sorry," Nyelle says in a rush. "Are you all right?" She leans over me, concerned. She places a glove on my cheek, covering my face with snow.

"Thanks, Nyelle. I'm fine," I sputter, brushing it off. She laughs and stands to offer me her hand, so I let her help me up.

"Well, since we're already a mess," Nyelle says, still holding my hand, "let's make snow angels."

My eyes widen. "What?"

"Over here." She pulls me along, slogging through the snow to a flat spot that hasn't been touched. "Turn around."

With her back to the snow, Nyelle steps to the side so that her arms are extended. She glances over at me in expectation, waiting for me to extend my arms too.

I sigh. "Okay."

She smiles. "Ready? Fall back on three. One. Two. Three."

We fall backward into the deep snow. I'm in a small white cave, peeking up at the stormy sky.

"Sweep your arms and legs, Cal!" Nyelle instructs me. So I do. Rae would never let me live this down if she could see me.

When I've flattened the area around my arms and legs, I stop and watch the flakes drift down, mesmerized. They land on my face, melt into my skin, and get caught in my lashes.

"Cal?"

"Yeah," I respond, unable to see her beside me.

"Have you ever been in love?"

There's silence for a moment. I'm not exactly prepared for the question.

"No. Have you?"

"No. I wonder what it's like." Her voice sounds like an echo in the stillness. "I think it will be like falling backward in the dark. Terrifying. Exhilarating. Having to trust that there'll be someone there to catch you."

"Or you land in the snow and freeze your ass off. Or on some jagged rock and break your back. Or..."

"Cal!" Nyelle hollers, sitting up. "That's not romantic at all."

I laugh just as a snowball lands on my head.

"Hey!" I sit up, and she's smiling at me innocently. "Oh, that's how we're playing this."

Her mouth drops. "Don't you dare!" She jumps up and tries to run across the snow just as I push up and rush after her.

I grab her around the waist and dump her in a deep drift, falling down beside her. She releases my favorite laugh, shoveling a pile of snow in my face in order to escape.

I crawl after her, pulling her back down.

"I give up," she cries out, holding her hands up in surrender. Her face is flushed red, and she's breathing in quick pants with a huge smile on her face. The thought of trying to kiss her again enters my mind, but I'm afraid if I try, I'll end up with another bruise. So I stand and hoist her up.

She looks down at my pants and covers her mouth to hide her laugh.

"They're split open, aren't they?" I ask, closing my eyes, silently cursing. With her mouth still covered, she nods. "Yeah, it's time to go before everything that's important to me freezes."

She nods again, still speechless.

We pick up the sleds along the way and head back to the truck. I can feel the air rush into the slit between my legs as we walk, but I'm just resigned to let it be what it is and don't bother looking. Nyelle keeps laughing in bursts. She's trying not to, but it *is* funny. Only I can't bring myself to laugh just yet.

"At least you have white boxer briefs on," Nyelle says, trying to make me feel better between giggles.

"Don't." I shake my head, knowing for certain my dignity is buried somewhere back there in the snow. "Just don't."

Nyelle laughs again.

When we get to my truck, Nyelle waits inside the cab while I clear off the snow.

"Want to come back to my hotel room to warm up?" Nyelle asks when I get back in the truck.

I swallow, hard. "Excuse me?"

She smiles. "*That's* not what I meant. I have ice cream. We can make sundaes."

"Um, ice cream is not going to warm me up."

"It'll make you feel better," she says with big eyes. "Ice cream *always* makes everything better."

"I'm not sure I believe you, but okay," I concede, backing out of the parking spot. "Where are you staying?"

"The Trinity Hotel."

"And why are you staying there?" I shift and slowly start down the plowed road.

"The dorms are creepy when they're empty," she explains.

Nyelle wipes her window when we reach an intersection. "Will you turn here?"

"Uh, sure," I respond, taking a right down a narrow road with an old factory on one side and broken-down buildings on the other. "What's down here, other than someone waiting to kill us?"

She rolls her eyes.

Nyelle wipes the window again, squinting her eyes in search of something, or someone. "Stop."

I press on the brakes, looking around. The road is dark, filled with tall shadows like the buildings are determined to block out the daylight.

"Nyelle," I call to her as she opens the door and hops out.

I shut off the truck and follow after her, not about to let her go off by herself.

She disappears into an alley as I walk around the truck. Then I hear, "Is that you, my angel?" The voice is low and gravelly, strained with age.

"Gus, where's your jacket?"

"The shadows took it," he rasps.

I reach the corner of the building and stop. A man is huddled under a torn awning on a piece of cardboard. Nyelle takes off her jacket and hands it to him.

"No. No. The shadows will take it," he says, trying to give it back. His scraggly beard is twisted with black and gray, and wiry tendrils of the same shades hang over his ears. His face is lined with life, weathered and dirty. He's old, but how old is hard to tell because of the fatigue that creases his brow and the sallow tone of his skin. His dark eyes stare at Nyelle like he can't trust his sight. I can see why he would think she's an angel, especially in that dress—even if he is delusional.

"They won't take it from you today," she assures him, bending down to wrap the jacket around his shoulders. "I was hoping to see you at the shelter this week."

"No. I stay in the dark. I like the dark," he mutters, repeating himself over again while rocking.

"I know. I was just hoping."

"Are you going to take me today? Please?" he pleads, his eyes dark.

She smiles down at him sorrowfully. "Not today, Gus. I'm sorry." Nyelle bends down to look into his eyes. "Stay warm, okay? I'll come find you again soon."

Gus begins rocking again, staring at the ground with the jacket pulled tight around him.

Nyelle stands up and turns. She pauses when she finds me watching. I take off my jacket when she reaches me and wrap it around her shoulders, holding her by my side as we walk back to the truck without saying a word.

As I turn the truck around to put us back on course, I ask, "How did you two meet?"

Nyelle stares out the window. "I volunteered this month at the shelter, and sometimes I go out with the street team to hand out meals to the people who don't...*won't* come to the shelter."

"How often do you help out at the shelter?" I ask, still trying to put the pieces of her life together.

"I play with the kids a couple days a week so their parents can look for work," she answers, turning her head toward me. "I try to help them just be kids so they can forget the things kids shouldn't have to worry about, even if it's just for a little bit." She looks back out the window.

"Is that where you were the other day? Who you spent Thanksgiving with?"

"Yeah. They were short staffed in the kitchen, so I helped. It was probably the best Thanksgiving I've had in a long time." She turns to me. "You'll have to tell me about your crazy family sometime." I can tell we're done talking about her. I never know what she'll willingly tell me each time I see her. But no matter how much she reveals, it's never enough.

"Yeah," I say with a laugh. "I wouldn't even know where to start."

"I bet family weddings are huge."

"I think I like this one better," I reply, pulling into the parking lot of the hotel and picking a spot next to a car buried in snow.

"Me too," Nyelle says, her eyes brightening. As we're about to get out of the truck, she pauses. "Um...do you want your jacket to wrap around your waist?" She raises her eyebrows at the tear in the pants, trying to restrain her smile.

"Oh, yeah," I respond, feeling the heat creep up my neck. I reach behind the seat for the bag with my clothes in it and pull out the button-down I originally had on, knotting it around my waist. When Nyelle closes her door, I also grab the RadioShack bag and shove it in with my stuff.

I determinedly keep my eyes on the ground as we walk through the lobby. I know we're drawing attention in our wedding attire, covered in snow. I swear I can hear whispering, but there's no way I'm looking up to find out.

When we reach the elevator, Nyelle hits the button for the fourth floor and starts laughing. "This is seriously one of my favorite days ever."

I look over at her. "Really?"

She nods, still smiling. I smile back just as the elevator dings and she exits.

As soon as we enter the room, I head straight to the bathroom to peel off the wet—and torn—clothes. The pants aren't any easier to take off than they were to put on, and my legs are screaming red from being so cold. I want nothing more than to crawl under the blankets of that bed, preferably with her, but I'm sure that's not an option.

When I exit, there's music playing from the clock radio, and Nyelle is sitting cross-legged on the bed, still wearing the dress. I notice her wet jeans hanging on the back of the desk chair, with her boots tucked beneath.

She's holding a bag of chocolate hearts and a can of whipped cream. She takes out a chocolate, shoots whipped cream on top, and drops it in her mouth.

"Chocolate?" she asks.

"Um . . . sure," I answer reluctantly. She hands me a chocolate. I hold it while she squirts it with whipped cream, and I pop it in my mouth in one bite. "Thanks."

She tips the can upside down and fills her mouth with whipped cream. "Wan sum?" she asks, her mouth full.

I laugh with a nod.

"Sit," she demands. I sit on the bed in front of her, expecting her to hand the can to me. "Open up."

I tilt my head back reluctantly, and she sprays whipped cream in my mouth. A huge smile erupts on her face when I have to extend my cheeks like a chipmunk to swallow it.

"You have something . . ." she says, and before I can wipe the back of my hand over my mouth, she reaches over and slides her thumb gently across my lower lip, removing a smudge of whipped cream. I can't move a single muscle as I watch her lick her finger clean.

"Do you want some ice cream?" she asks, about to get off the bed.

I blink. "Uh, can I take you up on that another time? I can't feel my legs, and there's no amount of ice cream that will make that better."

She settles back on the bed. "You're wrong. Trust me. I'm an expert. But I'm not going to force you to eat ice cream."

"Thanks," I reply. Suddenly remembering, I stand up to grab the bag. "Oh! I have a wedding gift for you."

Nyelle's eyes widen. "You do?"

"Technically, it's from Rae and me, but...here." I hand her the RadioShack bag.

"I feel bad I didn't get you anything," she says, taking it from me.

"Don't worry about it," I tell her as she removes the phone.

She looks completely perplexed.

"Rae calls it a drug phone. She has a disturbing fascination with gangster movies."

Nyelle laughs. "Why did you guys get me a phone?"

"Well...in case you need us. We want you to be able to get ahold of us." I'm hoping she won't hand it back.

She turns it on. "Does it have your numbers in it?"

"It does," I tell her. Then I reach into my back pocket, pulling out my wallet. "And here's a couple cards to add minutes to it. It comes with some, but not much."

She takes the cards. "No offense, because this is a really thoughtful gift, but I don't plan on using it. So don't expect me to start sexting you or anything."

I grin. "I won't. But will you keep it with you, just in case...for emergencies?"

She nods, bowing her head.

In a burst of unexpected enthusiasm, Nyelle's eyes light up. "Ooh, I love this song." She sets the bag and whipped cream on the side table and turns up the radio, then jumps up to stand on the bed. "Dance with me, Cal."

"I don't dance," I tell her, holding my hands up with a shake of my head.

"But you know how to jump." She begins to hop, jostling me on the bed.

"Cal, jump with me!" She holds the skirt of the dress up, exposing her bare legs, and jumps higher.

"Fine. I'll jump," I concede, standing up on the bed with her. I begin jumping up and down, but not with nearly as much vigor.

Nyelle bounds in the air and spins, her skirt flaring around her. When the beat of the song speeds up, she lifts her dress and runs in place really fast. By the time the song ends, I'm laughing so hard my stomach hurts.

We crash down on the bed, sprawled on our backs in an attempt to catch our breath.

She sighs contentedly. "Thank you for today, Cal," she says, still focused on the ceiling.

"I think we ended up showing the dress the best day of its life." I shift to look at her, taking in the infectious smile on her face. I can no longer picture her as anyone other than who she is in front of me. She exudes so much life. I can't imagine what could have made her need to start again. To me, she's always been Nyelle. And whatever happened to Nicole doesn't matter anymore. Because I'd rather have *this* girl here . . . with me.

I stand, and she accepts the hand I offer to lift her from the bed. Her cheeks are flushed, with a few loose curls clinging to them. I brush my thumb along her jaw, freeing the strands. She looks up at me in expectation, her eyes so blue, it's impossible to look away. She runs her hands down the front of her dress nervously. And in that second she's the young girl I once knew, and I can't breathe.

"I'm going to kiss you now," she says ever so softly.

My pulse quickens as she extends on her toes, pressing her lips to mine. They're warm and soft, and taste like chocolate. With the gentle touch of lips, my entire body ignites. I slide a hand around her waist. My world stands still in that moment—her in my arms and her lips connected with mine. Too soon, she slips away, with her eyes still shut and her mouth shifting into a blissful smile.

Even in its brevity, that kiss was everything. When her dark lashes finally flutter open, I still can't move.

"That was the perfect first kiss," she says, letting out a slow breath. Then she steps back. "You should probably go before you get snowed in."

"Right," I say, wishing for an avalanche to keep me trapped in this room with her. I slide on my jacket and she walks me to the door, opening it for me.

"So…I guess…I'll see you," I say, anxiety flooding my stomach as I look into her eyes, trying to read what she might be thinking. She's acting so casual, like nothing just happened between us.

"Yeah. I'll be around," she responds without committing—as always.

Just before she closes the door, I quickly say, "Nyelle."

She opens the door wider. "Yeah?"

I stuff my hands in my jacket pockets nervously. "There is something you can do, you know, as your gift."

"What's that?" she asks with an eyebrow raised assumingly.

"Don't disappear on me."

Nyelle stares at me for a second, her mouth opening like she's struggling with how to react. She nods once and answers quietly, "I won't."

I exhale in relief. But right before the door closes behind me, I hear her murmur, "Not yet."

NICOLE

January—Sixth Grade

"It's so nice to have you over for dinner," my mother calls to Richelle from the kitchen while we set the table in the dining room.

Richelle places the silverware at each setting. As I set down the plates, I rearrange the forks and knives, one thumbnail from the edge of the table, like they're supposed to be. I don't correct her. It's easier to just do it myself.

"Thank you, Mrs. Bentley," Richelle says. "It smells great."

My mother comes in to set the trivets on the table.

"Your father should be home soon," she tells me. "We need to be ready."

"I know," I murmur, placing the glasses directly above the dinner knives. Eyeing the clock in anticipation of hearing his car in the driveway at any minute. "I just need to put the napkins out." I don't make eye contact with Richelle. I should have prepared her for this. I mean, I tried to...but it's not easy to describe. I just hope she doesn't say anything that will make my father upset. He won't care that *she* said it—it will be like it's coming out of my mouth.

I remove the linen napkins from the drawer of the credenza and set them on each of the plates.

"Am I going to need to remember my manners?" Richelle whispers to me, eyeing the napkins.

"It's just my dad" is my response. "He has a thing about dinner."

"Gotcha," Richelle replies. "Best behavior, I swear." She smiles, trying to make me relax. I can't.

I'm grateful she gets it without me having to say anything. But she has no idea what it's *really* going to be like. It wasn't my idea to invite her over. It was my father's. He's never really met Richelle because I'm always at her house. I prefer that. But for some reason, after two years, he wants to know more about my best friend, other than that she lives next door.

My mother sets the platter with the roasted chicken on the table just as we hear his car pull up in the driveway. The little relief I had has disappeared, replaced by a stone in my chest. *Please let tonight go okay.*

My mother rushes to the door as it clicks open.

"Good evening, darling," she greets him, taking his jacket and briefcase as she does every night.

I stand in the dining room by Richelle in anticipation. I don't look at her as I wait for him to enter.

My father is an intimidating man in his height alone. I don't think I look like him, although people say I have his eyes. I hope not. When he looks at me sometimes, I feel... cold. I don't want anyone to ever feel that way when I look at them.

"Good evening, Daddy," I greet him, waiting for him to take his seat at the end of the table before approaching and kissing him on the cheek.

"How are my girls?" he asks as he does every night, but there are no answers, because he doesn't really expect them. My mother and I pull out our chairs and sit. Richelle follows our lead. I keep my eyes on my father, afraid to see Richelle's reaction. I know this is nothing like her family dinners, and I'm so afraid of what she's thinking.

My father's attention falls on Richelle. "So, you're Richelle," he says in his deep voice that I swear sounds like thunder. "It's nice to have you over for dinner."

"Thank you," Richelle says. Her words turn my head. There isn't a hint of timidness in her voice. She sounds just like she always does—no fear. Her eyes connect with mine, and she smiles slightly, almost like she's trying to tell me everything's going to be okay.

Richelle reaches for her fork, but my mother subtly covers her hand to stop her. Confusion appears on Richelle's face for a split second. My mother reaches out to take my hand, and I place my other in my father's large, expectant hand. I know Richelle is looking at me, or at least it feels that way, but I'm focused on my father.

"Thank you for all you do to put the food on our table, for all the hours you work to make our lives comfortable. We are grateful for everything you do for us."

My father lifts his head as my mother concludes and says, "You're welcome."

I'm holding my breath. Richelle is frozen. I want to slink under the table. I wish I could erase the stunned look on her face. I didn't realize just how different my family dinners were until recently, after eating over at Richelle's and Cal's houses.

We wait for my father to fill his plate before serving ourselves.

"Nicole," he says. My chest can't pull in air. I had hoped he wouldn't talk about it tonight. Not in front of Richelle.

"Yes, Daddy," I say, connecting with the icy blue eyes that send a chill down my spine.

"What happened with your history exam? An eighty-nine? That's not acceptable."

The chicken in my mouth is tasteless.

"I tried my best," I answer.

"You didn't," he responds. His voice has no indication of just how disappointed he is in me. It's never his voice. It's always his eyes. And I'm too afraid to look into them now.

"I got an eighty-two," Richelle announces, like she's proud. "It was a really hard test. I mean, I think the highest grade was a ninety-one."

My father is silent. I can't swallow.

"Interesting," my father says. Now he knows that I wasn't the best. Disappointing my father is the last thing I ever want to do.

The rest of the meal is eaten in the most awful silence. I stare at my plate, afraid to face the eyes looking at me, because I know they all are.

"Would you mind if Nicole comes over to my house for a little bit after dinner?" Richelle asks. "I need...help with math. And she's the best in our class."

I glance at her real quick and she grins. We're not in the same math class. I'm in the highest-level class, and Richelle hates math.

"For just a short time," my father agrees. "She has to study for history tonight."

"Great!" Richelle exclaims. My mother's fork scrapes her plate. "I mean...thank you."

After my father withdraws into his office, we're allowed to leave the table.

We bring our plates into the kitchen.

"You girls go ahead over to Richelle's," my mother tells us in her fake, sweet voice. I know she wants tonight to be over as much as I do.

"Are you sure, Momma?" I ask, feeling guilty leaving her with the mess.

"Absolutely. Come back in twenty minutes," she tells me. "Then go straight to your room to study, okay?"

I nod.

Richelle grabs my hand, practically dragging me to the door. She picks up our jackets but doesn't even give us time to put them on.

"Richelle..."

But we're out the front door and cutting between the small evergreens before I can finish my thought.

"Mom! I'm back," Richelle yells as she opens the door.

"How was—" Mrs. Nelson begins, looking up from the computer on her lap. Her eyes widen. "Oh."

"Yup," Richelle responds, continuing to drag me through the house and into the kitchen.

"Hi, Nicole," Mrs. Nelson calls to me as we rush by her.

"Um...hi, Mrs. Nelson," I reply over my shoulder.

Richelle drops our jackets on a chair at the kitchen table, opens the freezer, and pulls out a tub of chocolate ice cream with marshmallow swirl.

"What—"

"Don't. Just eat it," Richelle demands with all seriousness, removing a spoon from the drawer and thrusting both at me.

I take the ice cream and the spoon, not knowing what she expects me to do.

"Go ahead," she encourages. "Take a bite." I've never eaten straight out of the carton before. She stares at me in anticipation.

I scrape the spoon over the surface and put it in my mouth. I close my eyes with a sigh, letting the sweetness melt over my tongue. I take another spoonful. Richelle joins me and we eat in silence for a moment.

"Better?"

I nod.

"Ice cream makes *everything* better. Even dinner with your father."

ELEVEN

"She never went to Harvard," Rae says over the phone.

I'm walking across campus, running late again because I waited for Nyelle too long at Bean Buzz, like I've done for the last three days. Three days. And I haven't seen her. Considering I want to see her every day, if feels like three months. I don't think I'll ever get used to this.

"What do you mean?" I ask, narrowly dodging a girl who cuts in front of me, texting.

"Well, I did something I *never* do and actually talked to people. I started to ask around about her. I found out from Nina and Courtney that Nicole never enrolled last year."

"How do they know?"

"They go to Boston University, and when they went to visit last year, they convinced a guy who works in housing to look her up. He told them that she was never assigned a dorm. Freshmen stay on campus, so..."

"She said she was traveling. Maybe she was," I say, trying to find a path of logic in all of this.

"Or she was locked up in a padded room in some hospital."

"Rae," I say sternly, wanting her to stop questioning Nyelle's sanity.

"I'm just sayin'," she defends. "Cal, I like her, remember? I don't *want* her to be crazy. I just haven't ruled it out yet."

"Cal!"

I stop short, about to slam into the petite brunette standing in front of me.

"Uh, Rae, I have to call you back." I hang up without waiting for a response. I need to get this over with or else I'll be late... again. "Uh, hey, Jade. How are you?"

"I thought you were going to text me when you got back," she says, trying to sound casual, but there's nothing casual about the accusation.

"Oh, yeah, uh... I've had a busy week," I say, willing a way out of this.

"So, are we going out this weekend?" Her eyes flutter in expectation.

"Sure," I blurt without thinking. Shit. I shouldn't have said that. Now I'm stuck. "How about... Friday night?"

"Perfect. I'm in Fredericks Dorm. Text me what time, okay?"

"Okay, I will," I reply. "I'm late for class. I'll see you Friday."

She reaches up, expecting a hug that I return awkwardly. "I can't wait," she whispers in my ear before releasing me and continuing on her way.

That's not how that was supposed to go.

Jade reaches for my hand in the dark. I unwillingly wrap my fingers around hers. My back stiffens when she leans her head against my shoulder.

I shouldn't be here with Jade. She's not the one whose hand I want to be holding, or whose head I want on my arm. But because

I was put on the spot and didn't have the balls to reject her to her face, I'm sitting with her in a crowded movie theater—and the rolling credits can't come soon enough.

Jade wasn't impressed when she found out we were going to the movies. It's the worst possible place for a first date. There's no talking. No chance for intimacy. No interest in getting to know each other. I'm hoping it's a dead giveaway that this won't go beyond tonight. But this girl is determined to make the most of it, or . . . can't take a hint. I silently groan when she runs a thumb over my hand.

My phone vibrates in my pocket and I shoot out of my seat. Jade pops her head up in surprise. "Everything okay?"

"Sorry, I've got to take this," I blurt, without knowing who's calling. Her eyes widen and I hear some guy demanding I sit down. I instantly feel like an asshole. "I'll be right back."

I start up the aisle, checking my screen to see who I should be thanking for interrupting my date. Nyelle. My stomach drops. She said she'd never use the phone. Assuming the worst, I answer before I'm through the doors to the lobby.

"Nyelle?"

"Cal!" she yells way too loudly on the other end of the phone. "I got in a fight. You should have seen it. I punched him!" She laughs hysterically. She's drunk.

"You punched someone? Are you okay?" I'm standing in the middle of the lobby. A little kid bumps into my legs, spilling popcorn on my shoes.

There's silence.

"Nyelle? Can you hear me?" I head for the doors.

There's a heavy breath. "Um . . . I don't know if I'm okay." Her voice is suddenly so somber, I falter in my steps. "Cal, can you come get me?"

"Yeah," I answer automatically, practically at my truck. "Where are you?"

"I don't know," she answers quietly. "I'm sitting in a tree. Oh. I'm sitting in the frosting tree."

I think for a moment, trying to recall exactly where that is. "Okay. I'll be right there. Wait for me, okay?"

"I tried to forget, Cal," Nyelle says barely audibly. "I really wanted to forget."

I don't know what she's talking about, but I can feel her slipping away. I need to get to her. "I know. Stay on the phone with me, okay?" I can't dig the keys out of my jeans pocket fast enough.

"I wanted to leave tonight," she says quietly. "I didn't really care where. I just wanted to…go away. Disappear." Her voice drifts away, like she's lost in her head. And my nerves are shot, knowing I'm nowhere near her yet.

I turn on the engine and back out of the space in practically the same motion. I have the phone tucked under my chin as I shift into first.

"What made you stay?" I ask, not sure if that was the right question to ask. But at this point, my only concern is to keep her talking.

"You," she answers. It isn't the answer I expected, but it's the one I wanted to hear. There's a brief silence between us as I pull onto the road, heading toward campus. "I promised not to leave yet."

"And I don't want you to leave yet," I respond with the faintest smile.

I turn down a road leading toward the park, where I hope to find the tree Nyelle is sitting in.

"You should tell Rae I'm on the drug phone!" Nyelle says with a sudden burst of laughter.

"Yeah, I'll tell her," I reply, the sudden mood change taking me by surprise. "I'm glad you used it to call me. Now tell me about this fight. What happened?"

Nyelle breaks out into another fit of laughter, edged with hysteria. It makes me nervous.

The laughter stops abruptly and then she's yelling into the phone, "Because I want to, so fuck off!"

"Nyelle? What's going on?" I ask, concerned by the hostility in her voice.

I hear a man yelling back in the distance, but I can't make out what he's saying.

"I'd like to see you try, fucker!" Nyelle hollers and laughs. "Cal?"

"Yeah, I'm still here." I make a rolling stop at an intersection, estimating I'm another five minutes away. "Everything all right?"

"Just people giving me shit," she responds. "Like they've never seen someone in a tree before. Stupid." I can imagine her rolling her eyes. "What were we talking about?"

"What you were up to tonight. Where were you—"

"Cal!" Nyelle yells suddenly. I almost slam on the brakes, thinking she's about to fall out of the tree. "Cal! I see your truck!"

I sink against the seat in relief. "God, Nyelle. I thought... Where are you?"

"Can't you see me waving to you?!"

I pull the truck along the curb. "Don't wave. Hold on to the branch. I don't want to take you to the emergency room."

I jump out of the truck, searching the stark branches of the tree in front of me. I spot her within the shadows near the top, her arm frantically pumping.

"I see you." I prepare myself for a moment before I say, "I'm comin' up." I end the call, stuff the cell phone in my pocket, and take in the obstacle course of branches before me. It was easier before when all I had to do was follow her up.

I stick my foot in the V of the trunk and grab ahold of the lowest branch to pull myself up.

"Cal!" Nyelle yells down to me. "You're here!"

"Yup, I am," I grunt, maneuvering through the thicket of tiny branches that snag my sweater. I test out another branch that I hope will hold my weight and continue to climb.

When I step onto the final branch, Nyelle throws her arms around my neck, almost knocking me backward. "I can't believe you're here!"

And if my heart wasn't already racing, it is now. I let go with one hand and gently pat her on the back. "Yeah, I'm here." I sit on the branch across from her. "How are you? Are you okay?"

Nyelle smiles lazily, her eyes glassy. "I'm great. Let's talk. Cal, we're in our tree!"

Wow, she's more intoxicated than I thought.

"We can talk for a minute. Just don't let go, okay?"

"Okay," Nyelle agrees with an overexaggerated thrust of her head. "Where were you tonight? Where's your jacket?"

"I was... Oh shit." I grind my teeth together.

"What?"

I close my eyes with a groan. "I left her."

"Who? Wait. You were on a date?" Nyelle smiles, then chuckles, which leads to a full-on laugh. She reminds me of Rae when I'm forced to hang up the phone on her. But I can't hang up on Nyelle, so I wait it out. "You left your date for me?! Oh, Cal. I'm sorry. I suck."

"No, it's okay," I tell her. "You're worth it. But we should probably go get her since she's stranded." I sigh, not looking forward to what's about to happen. "She's going to be pissed."

"What's her name?" Nyelle asks.

"Jade."

"Is she a stripper?" Nyelle laughs.

"No, she's not a stripper," I say with a grin.

"But she's not *her*, is she? Your *what if* girl?"

"No, she's not," I answer simply. "Not even close."

"Then why are you on a date with her?"

"Because I didn't say no." The truth of that is pathetic. I know this.

"That's a problem for you, isn't it?" Nyelle teases.

I shrug.

She laughs. "Well, you should probably go get her. I can walk back to the dorm." Nyelle begins weaving down through the branches effortlessly, never second-guessing her footing, even in her drunkenness. What's with this girl and climbing things?

"No, I want to hear about your night. Come with me?" I don't want to leave her alone. I'm still concerned about how she sounded when she first called me. Nothing about this feels right. Besides, this is the first time all week I've seen her. So I'm not letting her disappear again. Not tonight anyway.

Nyelle pauses on a branch and tips her head back to look at me. "Okay."

She eventually hops down from the last branch and waits for me to catch up.

"So how did you meet Jade?" Nyelle asks, linking her arm through mine and collapsing against me as I support her to my truck. How was she able to navigate the tree without killing herself?

"At the party you never showed up at," I tell her. She releases a quick laugh.

"Guess I should've shown up," she says, still smiling.

I smile back. "So, tell me about this fight. Where were you?" I ask, opening the passenger door to allow Nyelle to crawl inside.

"At a bar," she answers, scooting all the way to the middle and putting one leg on either side of the stick shift.

"You're twenty-one?"

"Cal! You know how old I am," she says with a shake of her head. I close the door and pause before walking around the truck, trying to decide if I should take advantage of her drunkenness and ask her whatever I want. But is this the way I want to find out?

Just as I'm opening my door, my phone vibrates. I look at the screen. "Shit," I mutter before answering. "Hey. So sorry. I'm on my way back. It was a..." I look at Nyelle, leaning against the back of the seat, grinning at me with her head lolled to the side. "It was important." She smiles wider. "I'll be there in ten minutes."

I hang up without allowing Jade to say a word. I don't need to hear what she has to say. It doesn't really matter. I'm looking at the only girl who does. And she's about to pass out before I can find out what happened to her tonight.

"Nyelle," I coax, climbing in and starting the truck. "What were you doing in a bar?"

"Drinking. C'mon, Cal." She laughs and shoves my arm clumsily. "What else would I be doing in a bar?"

"They didn't card you?"

"Nope. I think they were just happy to have customers."

Her head flops to rest against my shoulder, her eyes half-open.

"Who did you get in a fight with?"

"Some huuuge guy," she says with a yawn. "He grabbed my ass, so I punched his face."

"You... punched him in the face?" I'm trying not to laugh,

because I can actually picture it in my head and I'm wishing I was there to see it.

I've never punched anyone, but my brothers have been in enough fights that I know it can hurt like hell. "How's your hand feel?" I try to get a look at it, but it's concealed by the cutoff knit glove.

"I can't feel it," she mutters, her eyes sliding shut. "But he never saw me coming," she says in a rush of air, like it's taking all of her energy to talk. Her weight settles into my side, and I can feel her fall asleep.

"I bet," I say with a quiet laugh, glancing down at her face squished against my arm. I never saw her coming either.

When I pull up in front of the movie theater, Jade is on the curb with her arms crossed, holding my jacket. And she *is* pissed. Understandably.

She opens the passenger door and stops, staring with her mouth open.

"Omigod, seriously?! *This* was your emergency?" She gets in the truck, tossing my jacket on the floor. "This is why you left in the middle of our date? For a girl? Why didn't you tell me you were seeing someone?"

I pull out of the parking lot, trying to think of the fastest route to her dorm.

"I'm not."

She eyes Nyelle like she wants to shove her out of the moving truck.

"Right. Then why didn't you just say you didn't want to go on a date with me? I mean, *the movies*, really? What are we…in middle school?"

"I should have. I'm sorry." I can't look at her, but I can feel her eyes burning into me. Nyelle's hand grips my leg, and I cringe. She's listening. This night can be over anytime now.

"Are you kidding me? You *didn't* want to go out with me? Omigod. This is the worst date ever," Jade snaps. I risk a glance in her direction. She's seated with her arms tightly crossed and her body shifted against the passenger door.

I pull up in front of her dorm a couple minutes later, and Jade jumps out of the truck before it's come to a complete stop, slamming the door behind her.

Without opening her eyes, Nyelle maneuvers her body so her legs are curled up on the seat, with her head resting on my leg.

"She was grumpy," she mumbles, tucking her hands under my thigh.

I release a breath, looking down at her dark brown hair hanging in front of her face. I gently brush it back so I can see her. Her eyes are still closed. I like this—having her snuggled up against me—even if she is drunk.

"Nyelle, why did you get so drunk tonight? Did something happen?" I ask, running a finger along her hairline.

She's quiet. Just when I think she's not going to answer, she whispers, "I miss her."

"Who?"

"You," she says in a soft breath.

"I don't understand," I reply. She remains quiet. Afraid she might've passed out, I ask, "Nyelle, do you want me to bring you to your dorm?"

"I don't have a key," Nyelle grumbles sleepily.

"Is Tess there?"

"Nope. Grandmother's birthday."

"Won't they let you in if you show them your ID? I mean, you can crash at my place. I don't mind…"

"Okay," she sighs. "Cal, I don't go here, you know."

She says it in a jumbled murmur. It sounds like one long mumbling word. I'm questioning if I heard her correctly.

"You don't go to Crenshaw?"

She shakes her head ever so slightly and shifts to get more comfortable, drawing in a deep breath.

Well, that answers that question. Except I don't understand why she's here and how she's able to stay in the dorms if she's not enrolled. And… what does she do every day? My head is spinning just thinking about it. Every question I've asked her tonight has only left me more confused.

By the time we arrive at my apartment, Nyelle is out cold, so I end up carrying her in.

Kicking the door shut behind me, I take her into my room and lay her down on my bed—which is thankfully unmade. With my hands on my hips, I study her peaceful face. Wondering exactly what happened tonight. And if she'll ever trust me enough to tell me.

I unlace and pull off her combat boots before rolling her onto each side to remove her jacket. Then I eye her gloves, hesitating.

Removing them would be like revealing a secret without asking. I can't do it. When I cover her with the blanket, she rolls over, tucking her hands beneath the pillow.

When I return from the bathroom, she's breathing heavily with her mouth open in a drunken sleep. I consider sleeping on the couch, but I can't fit on the stupid couch. So I slide in the bed next to her like I did before, lying with my back to her, listening to her breathe until I eventually fall asleep.

NICOLE

July—Before Seventh Grade

"If you start talking about what it's like to kiss Cal, I'll puke," Rae threatens Richelle.

"What are we supposed to do at a sleepover if we don't talk about boys?" Richelle demands, sitting on top of her sleeping bag.

"We could go scare the boys," Rae suggests with a devious smile.

I laugh.

"See? Even Nicole likes that idea," Rae says.

"Aren't they sleeping in Cal's backyard?" I ask, looking from Rae to Richelle.

This is the first time I've slept over at Rae's. Sleeping in the basement in sleeping bags is so much different from sleeping in the bunk beds at Richelle's. But I like it. We have a TV, and her mom is on the second floor, so we can stay up all night without her hearing us.

Richelle grabs the bag of Doritos and sits back against the orange and brown sofa.

"Okay. So what should we do?" she asks, after taking a sip of her Coke.

Rae rubs her hands together, grinning. "Come with me."

She leads us through a curtain to the laundry room, where she sifts through the clothes in a basket, pulling out two hooded sweatshirts and handing them to me and Richelle. "They're my mother's boyfriend's. Put them on." She takes out a flannel shirt, putting it on over her Rancid T-shirt.

I look to Richelle. She shrugs and pulls the sweatshirt over her head. I do the same. The clothes are big on us, but I think that's the point.

Rae stretches up on her tiptoes, trying to get a hat on a shelf. I reach up to grab it for her.

"Thanks," she says, putting it on her small head. It looks huge too.

"Rae, you still haven't told us what we're doing," Richelle says. Rae opens a door on the other side of the laundry area, flipping on a light.

It's creepy in here. A dim bulb hangs from the ceiling. Everything's covered in dirt and it smells like old things. I don't follow her in.

"We're going to sneak up on the tent," she explains, rifling through the rakes and shovels leaning against the wall. "One person shines a light so we look like big shadows inside their tent. And the other two will…" She holds up a small ax with a grin.

"We're not going to hurt them, are we?" I ask, staring at the rusted blade.

"Relax, Nicole," Rae sighs. "We're only going to wave it around and yell. It's just to freak them out. It'll be funny."

I nod, not convinced. Richelle walks around the shadowy basement with Rae, searching too. She picks up a pitchfork. "Perfect." She looks to me and asks, "Do you want to hold the flashlight?"

I nod again.

We sneak through the house, and Rae stops by the back door to hand me a large yellow flashlight with a handle. "Here."

I take it from her and we slowly open the door.

We can see the tan dome tent from the back steps.

"Are they awake?" Richelle asks. Rae shrugs.

They creep across the grass. I follow a little ways back, carrying the flashlight. As we get closer, we can hear them talking. Rae holds up her hand for us to stop, listening.

"I can't go," Cal says.

"What, you need permission from your *girlfriend*?" Brady says, teasing him.

Richelle turns to me. She looks confused, and a little worried.

"No, that's not what I'm saying," Cal answers. "Stop being an idiot."

Rae waves us forward. They creep up to the tent.

"Ready?" Rae whispers, looking to me and Richelle. Richelle nods.

"Did you hear something?" Craig asks really fast. The boys are quiet.

Rae nods to me, and I turn on the flashlight, shining it from the ground at an upward angle like Rae told me to, casting tall shadows of the girls on the side of the tent.

"Aaaahhh!!" Rae and Richelle holler in deep voices, waving the ax and pitchfork above their heads.

The guys scream. Actually, Brady sounds like he's shrieking. Rae, Richelle and I laugh hysterically.

"It's the girls!" Craig yells.

I shut off the flashlight at the sound of the zipper. Richelle and Rae screech and drop their weapons by the tent when the boys holler, "Get 'em!"

They burst out, armed with large yellow squirt guns, and start shooting water at us. We scatter. I duck behind the bushes next to Cal's house, watching them run by.

When I think it's safe, I slowly step out, just as Cal runs around the corner. He aims the squirt gun at me. I hold up my arms to protect my face, but nothing happens. When I lower them, he's just standing there.

"I won't squirt you," he says with a small smile.

"Nicole! Run!" Richelle's running around the corner with Craig right behind, squirting her.

Cal whips around and starts squirting her too. She squeals and races toward Rae's house, as I hide behind the bush again.

"What is going on out here?" I hear Mrs. Logan say from the back porch. We all freeze.

"It was their fault," everyone says in unison, pointing.

TWELVE

I'm awake. And I really need to use the bathroom. But I don't want to move. Nyelle is lying behind me, on my pillow, breathing on my neck. Her body is so close, I can feel heat coming off her. Her bare leg brushes against the back of my thigh. There's nothing on her legs, so that means she took off her pants. Yeah. I don't want to move because then she probably will. I'd rather lie here and be tortured by the need to go to the bathroom, knowing I can't turn around and touch her. Because I should probably brush my teeth before I do that.

Shit. I need to go to the bathroom. *And* brush my teeth. Shit.

I gently slide the covers back and try not to disturb her, getting off the bed in one motion. She rolls over to her side of the bed with a groan. I sigh.

I walk over her sweater, pants, bra and gloves on the way out of my room. I'm not sure what's left under the blanket, but sliding back in bed with her should be interesting…or completely inappropriate.

When I step out of the bathroom, Nyelle is sitting on the arm of the couch, slumped forward with her hair hanging in front of her face. She's wearing a pair of my boxers and a Crenshaw sweatshirt that hangs over one shoulder, revealing a tank top strap.

Rubbing the cuff of the sleeve over her face, she grumbles, "Do you have an extra toothbrush? I have the worst taste in my mouth."

"I think so," I answer, opening the small closet just inside the bathroom. I shift some things around and pull out a blue toothbrush in cellophane. "It's one of those cheap ones the dentist gives you. That okay?"

"I don't care," she mumbles, standing unsteadily, holding out a hand that's barely poking out of the sleeve. I give it to her and step out of her way as she stumbles into the bathroom with her eyes half-closed.

After throwing on a hoodie, I sit on the couch and turn on the TV, not confident enough to return to bed now that she's awake.

The bathroom door opens. "How are you feeling?" I ask, although the answer to that is evident when she drags her feet to the bedroom. She may have grunted as she passed.

A couple minutes later, she reemerges with a pillow under her arm, dragging a blanket behind her.

Nyelle tosses the pillow on my lap and lies down without a word. Pulling the blanket up to her nose, she falls back to sleep.

I'm watching a college football game when I hear the key in the door. Nyelle still hasn't woken up. I'm starving, but I refuse to move her from my lap. I'm focused on the game with my hand on her shoulder when Eric enters.

"Hey, man."

I look over as he walks in, carrying fast food bags. "Please tell me you bought something for me," I beg as he tosses the bags on the counter.

"I did," he responds, then gets a better look at me. "Uh... your date go well?"

"Not at all."

"Then..." Eric nods toward Nyelle. "Who's that?"

"Hey, Eric," Nyelle croaks from beneath the blanket.

Eric creeps over to get a closer look, trying to figure out who she is. Nyelle pulls the blanket down.

"Did you bring any hot chocolate?"

"Lake Girl! Holy shit!" Eric exclaims. "Was *not* expecting you under there."

"Ow. Not so loud," Nyelle pleads, squinting up at him. I rub her shoulder in empathy.

"Got a little wasted last night?" he asks with a grin. "Did you go all Hulk and hurt someone?"

"I did," she replies in a rasp.

"Oh, yeah," I say, suddenly remembering. "How's your hand?"

"Wait. You really did hurt someone?" Eric's mouth drops open. Then he starts laughing. "Did you punch Cal and I missed it?"

I shoot him a look.

"Why would I want to punch Cal?" Nyelle asks. "My hand's okay. Although my head hurts so bad, I can't feel anything else."

"Let me see it," I request.

She slips her hand out from under the blanket. It looks so delicate, I can't imagine it forming a fist and punching someone in the face. I slip my hand under it to examine it more carefully, taking in the details of her uncovered hand. Her knuckles are red but not cut. It's a good thing she was wearing her gloves.

"Doesn't look bad," I say. But before I can turn it over, she pulls it back under the blanket. I didn't find what she didn't want me to see. But she's definitely hiding something.

"What did you bring us?" I ask Eric.

"Well, I didn't know I was feeding three people," Eric responds.

"I don't want food," Nyelle says, and makes a noise like even the thought of eating is making her sick.

"Don't we have Powerade or some other sports drink in the fridge?" I ask, still not willing to get up.

Eric eyes Nyelle lying on my lap and replies dramatically, "Well, let *me* go check."

He returns with a sports drink and a bag of food.

"Thanks." I take the bottle from him and open it. "Nyelle, you should drink this. It'll help your head."

"So, what are we doing today?" Eric asks, leaning back in the recliner before unwrapping a burger.

"Nothing," Nyelle answers, carefully lifting her head to take a sip.

"Well, that sounds exciting," Eric responds sarcastically. "There's a party—"

"No," Nyelle snaps quickly. "No parties. Please."

I laugh and shrug. "No parties."

Eric crumples up the wrapper of the burger he just inhaled. "I'm meeting some of the guys at the gym to play ball. I was supposed to ask you..." Then he looks at Nyelle and stops. "I guess I'll see you later."

"Thanks for getting the food," I say, watching him disappear into his room.

Nyelle shifts onto her back so she's looking at me upside down. I brush the hair out of her face. She smiles weakly. Then she closes her eyes and falls asleep. I watch her hidden eyes shift beneath her lids and rub her arm. I know *she's* miserable right now. But I'm not.

"Henley, get down," I tell him as he jumps up on the couch next to Nicole.

"It's okay," Nicole says, digging her hands into his fur and rubbing behind his ears. "Hey, Henley. So good to see you."

He jumps back on the floor and she brushes his gold fur off her skirt.

"How was your baseball game?" she asks, kicking off her shoes and lying down on the small pillow so her head is right next to my leg. She folds her hands over her stomach and lies perfectly still with her legs straight.

I look down at her and she's staring up at me with her bright blue eyes.

"Bad day?" I ask, setting down the controller for the video game. Nicole usually does this whenever something's bothering her. I tease her that it makes me feel like she's lying on the couch of a psychiatrist's office. Although I know psychiatrists don't really have couches for patients to lie on—at least my mom doesn't.

"Lance asked me out today," she says quietly.

My heart skips a beat.

"And what did you tell him?" I feel like I have sandpaper in my throat.

Nicole sits up on the cushion next to me. "That I don't want to go out with anyone."

"Oh," I say in relief. But then... wait. "You don't?"

She looks at me and shrugs. But she doesn't look away. It's like she's waiting for something. "Are we supposed to want to now that we're in middle school?"

"I don't know," I answer. I haven't asked anyone out since we entered the sixth grade a couple months ago. But then again, the only girl I'd want to ask is looking at me right now.

Nicole takes my hand and closes her eyes. "It's so confusing. I don't want to have to think about it yet."

I want to wipe my hand, afraid that it's sweaty. But she doesn't seem to care. She does this too sometimes, just sits here with her eyes closed, holding my hand, like I have some magic power to make her feel better. It never used to bother me, and it still doesn't. But now it feels different, or at least I want it to mean something different.

"Hey!" Richelle hollers from the top of the stairs.

Nicole's eyes fly open. She releases my hand and practically jumps to the other side of the couch as Richelle comes down the stairs, carrying an empty Mountain Dew bottle.

"What are you guys doing? Come over to Rae's. The guys are here. I thought we could play a game." She looks at me and smiles.

"What are you thinking about?" Nyelle asks, her eyes open. I look at her hand wrapped around mine and I grin.

I shake my head. "Nothing. Are you up for watching a movie?"

"Do you mind if I take a shower? It might help me feel better."

"Sure," I say. "Want me to get you something to eat?"

"Peanut butter and jelly?" she requests.

"I have that," I tell her. "Grape or strawberry?"

Nyelle pushes off the couch. "Strawberry."

I have a paper plate with a peanut butter and strawberry jelly sandwich and a handful of Doritos waiting for her when she gets out.

"So much better," she says, tossing the empty sports drink in the trash. She searches the cabinets for a cup and fills it with water, then sits on the couch next to me. "This is perfect! Thanks." She begins to eat like she hasn't in weeks. She doesn't make a mess, but she barely swallows between bites.

"Just don't breathe on me after," I tease.

"What? You don't think peanut butter–Dorito breath is sexy?" she says, crunching on a chip.

"Not really." I chuckle. The next thing I know, she's straddling me, breathing in my face. I try not to laugh as I hold my breath, turning my head away. She leans in closer, so I grab her wrists to keep her back. She's laughing as she struggles against my grip.

"Smell my peanut butter–Dorito breath, Cal! I know you want to."

I flip her onto the couch and I'm between her legs, pinning her arms above her head.

She smiles up at me. I don't move. Suddenly, I don't give a shit what her breath smells like and drift toward the mouth I was trying to avoid just seconds ago. She frees a hand and runs it through my hair.

Just as I'm about to kiss her, she says, "You need a haircut." Then she pops up, her head nearly colliding with my mouth. "Oooh. Can I cut it?"

"You want to cut my hair?" I ask, sitting back on the cushion, defeated. Trying to kiss this girl is dangerous.

Nyelle leans over and finishes the last bite of the sandwich. "Yes. And I promise to brush my teeth first. Do you have clippers? Or scissors? Or a razor?"

She's off the couch and in the bathroom before I can react.

"No razors," I say adamantly, images of bloodshed flashing in my head. I can hear her digging through the contents of the closet in the bathroom.

She returns carrying the black bag with Eric's electric clippers in it.

"Scissors?" she asks after setting the bag on the coffee table. I don't remember saying okay to this.

"In my room, in the desk drawer," I tell her, figuring if it sucks, I'll just buzz it short like I did in high school.

She returns with the scissors, pulling my desk chair behind her.

"Sit here," she instructs me, placing the chair in the middle of the open space.

"Have you ever done this before?" I ask, sitting on the chair.

"Not exactly, but kinda." That wasn't an answer.

"So, basically, you have no idea what you're doing,"

"Basically," she agrees, plugging in the clippers. She puts a towel around my shoulders, then stands in front of me and studies my head, running her fingers through my hair. My eyes shut with her touch.

Then I hear the clippers buzz into action and my eyes pop back open.

"Keep them shut," she says. "I don't want to get hair in your eyes."

I should be concerned. But I'm not. What my hair looks like is not that important to me. But I could sit here all day, letting Nyelle run her fingers through it.

The clippers hum as I absorb the tingle of her fingers sliding through the hair around my neck, over my ears, and eventually the sides of my head. When she shuts them off, I ease my eyes open, sedated.

"I like the way it kinda curls up," she says, tousling the hair on top of my head that she has yet to cut.

I force myself to focus on her face with her standing this close. If I look forward, I'll be staring right at...*Crenshaw.* And not looking is taking all of my effort. She's torturing me right now, and she doesn't even know it.

Nyelle picks up the scissors. I release a tense breath when she stands behind me. I need a moment to get my shit together, breathe deep, and think about football.

She trims the top of my head. When she's done, she removes the towel from my shoulders and stands back to admire her work.

"I like it," she declares with her hands on her hips, still looking at my hair and not really at me. She sets the scissors down and steps forward until the sweatshirt is practically brushing my nose, flipping my hair with her fingers. I can't resist. I slide my hands onto her hips.

She stills within my grasp, her fingers easing through my hair. I reel her in gently so she's straddling one of my legs. She still won't look at me, but I'm watching her eyes, waiting for a sign that I should let go. She inhales deeply, expanding the letters of *Crenshaw* across her chest. Then she brushes a hand down my cheek.

I take it in mine, and that's when I notice the scars. It looks like she slammed her fist down on miniature razor blades. Tiny crisscrosses run along the side of her hand. It's shaking.

The rest of her is motionless. I don't think she's even breathing. I press the side of her hand to my mouth, kissing the marks she's been so determined to hide. She slowly eases herself onto my lap. Her eyes are dark and have yet to blink, watching me apprehensively. I run my hand along the soft skin of her cheek. Her eyes shut with my touch, like I've hit a switch.

Her mouth opens ever so slightly, in anticipation. I keep my eyes focused on her lips until I'm too close to see them anymore. And all I can do is feel them. Her arms slide around my neck as I pull her into me, pressing against the soft give of her mouth that tastes of mint.

I run my tongue along her lips and they part for me. The kiss is slow and careful but edged with a heat that makes my muscles tighten. I wrap my arms around her waist and start kissing with a little more need.

I've waited my entire life to kiss this girl, and I could never have prepared myself for it. I'm burning up on the inside. And I don't want her to pull away. I can't let her pull away. And when she exhales against my mouth, I come undone. I'm an inferno.

I slide my hand under the sweatshirt, running my fingers along her skin. Her back arches and she eases back, separating us. A smile creeps across her red lips. "Want to watch a movie?"

I shake my head. Before I can kiss her again, she laughs and slides off my lap. I can't move. My body hasn't cooled enough yet. The flames are still lapping under my skin, and if I'm going to sit on the couch with her without attacking her, I need to extinguish them.

"Where's your broom?" Nyelle asks from behind me.

"Next to the refrigerator," I choke out. I ease myself up off the chair and roll it back into my room, taking the biggest breath of my life. "Holy shit," I murmur, gripping the back of it tight while staring at my desk.

"You play the guitar?"

I whip around to find Nyelle in the doorway, looking across the room at the acoustic guitar leaning against the wall.

"Sorta," I answer, clearing my throat. She wouldn't know this about me since I didn't start playing until high school. "Rae usually brings her guitar when she visits, and we mess around. She's better than I am. I just try not to suck too bad."

Nyelle walks across the room, picks it up, and sits cross-legged on the bed. She supports it across her lap and plucks at a few strings, having no idea how to play. I lie down on my side with my head propped up, watching her. She's concentrating like she can figure it out just by touching it. I like watching her fingers fumble through the chords, knowing she doesn't feel she needs to hide them from me anymore.

"Can I ask you something?"

Nyelle stops and nods, looking me in the eyes intently, like she's bracing herself.

"Last night when you were drunk...You said you didn't go to Crenshaw—how are you living in the dorms?" I've tried to figure out how, or when, to ask her about this since she confessed. I don't want to ask too much too soon. She's just beginning to trust me, and I can't screw that up.

"Why are you here if you don't go to the school? Crenshaw isn't exactly exciting."

Her shoulders relax, and a small smile appears. "It was on the list."

"'Fake attending Crenshaw' was on the list?" I ask in amazement. "Why? And what is this crazy list?"

"It just was." Nyelle shrugs. "It's a list of things I need to do. And Crenshaw was on it. I'm only here for a semester."

I open my mouth to speak, but I can't—this upcoming week is finals week. The last week of the semester.

Nyelle continues like she doesn't notice the shock on my face, although I'm not doing anything to hide it.

"The day after everyone moved into the dorms, I followed some girls into the building. I hung around the lounge like I belonged there and listened. Girls like to talk. I found out who had single rooms and that Tess was one of them. I showed up, claiming to be her new roommate. Tess is too nice to question it, so she let me in. I get into the building when other girls enter and don't go to our room unless Tess is there. She thinks I knock all the time to be polite, in case she's with a guy. She's always bright red when she answers the door. I mean, she's *never* with a guy. But she's too embarrassed to admit it."

Nyelle laughs.

I've barely heard a thing she's said. "So you're leaving next week? After finals?"

She shifts her eyes down, running her hands along the guitar. "I have to."

"Don't," I say quickly.

"What?" she asks, as surprised as I am by the desperation in my voice.

I've been afraid every day since I first saw her in Bean Buzz that there'd come a day I'd lose her again. Now she's telling me it's going to happen... and when. And I can't let her.

"Don't leave," I plead.

"Cal." She laughs. "I don't go to school here. Didn't you hear what I said?"

"So. Stay here. You can... move in with us," I offer, sitting up.

She studies me for a moment, then shakes her head. "I can't. Cal, I'm sorry."

I swallow. My thoughts are racing. I'm trying to figure out what I have to say to convince her to stay.

"How about... just till the end of break?" I suggest, my words coming out in a rush. "Just hang out with me for a little while longer. I feel like I just met you, and... I'm not ready for you to leave."

She smiles softly. Nyelle runs her eyes along my face thoughtfully. I'm afraid to move. I'm afraid that if I blink, she'll disappear.

"Till the end of break," she repeats in contemplation. "That's... a month from now, right?"

I nod. She presses her lips together, hesitating.

"Okay." The word comes out so quietly, I'm not sure I hear her.

"Okay?" I confirm. She nods. I feel like I just won... the Super Bowl. I want to grab her, throw her down on the bed and kiss her. But I don't. I can't freak her out. Just because she's saying okay now doesn't mean she won't change her mind.

I'm suddenly feeling bolder than usual, because any other day of my life, these words would never come out of my mouth. "Stay here with me after finals. Eric goes home for break, so I'll sleep in his room."

"You're not going home?"

I grimace. I'm *supposed to* go home. My mother will kill me if I'm not there for Christmas. She might still kill me when she finds out I'm not coming home for the entire break.

"I will for Christmas—"

"Cal, don't stay here because of me. Your family—"

"Is going to be there. Forever. Trust me. They're not going anywhere. You're giving me one month. They'll get over it."

Nyelle's cheeks grow pink as she studies the guitar. "That's sweet." Then she whips her head up at me with a scowl. "I'm not going to be one of your girls, Cal!"

"Uh," I say, backing away with my hands raised in defense. "Of course not. That's not... Wow. I won't touch you. I promise." Then I add, "Unless you want me to."

Her frown deepens.

"Or never again."

She smirks.

"Just don't leave," I request sincerely. "Not yet."

"Not yet," she agrees under her breath, flipping her fingers over the guitar strings.

RICHELLE

December—Seventh Grade

"What are you staring at?" I ask, pushing my way past the people standing in the hall.

When I get closer, I see Cal bent down, holding Nicole's hand, talking to her quietly. She's sitting on the floor, leaning against a locker, shaking her head. She doesn't react to whatever he's saying. She's staring at the wall with the saddest look on her face.

"What happened?" I ask, kneeling beside her. "Nicole, what happened?"

"He's going to be so disappointed in me," she says, slowly facing me. In her other hand, she's gripping a piece of paper. Her report card. There's black ink smeared on it. It's also on the tips of her fingers and on her skirt. "I can't show him this."

"Let me see," I say, removing it from her fist. I flatten it out and examine each grade. They look fine to me. I hear whispering behind me and stand up.

"What are you looking at?" I holler, getting in the face of the closest person hovering behind us.

"Uh, nothing," the short boy with the pimply face says. He moves on, and the rest of the crowd reluctantly breaks up too when I continue to glare at them.

I turn back to Nicole. "Okay, let's get you off the floor." I reach down and help Cal lift her by her elbows. She still looks like she's in a trance, and it's creeping me out. "What grade?"

"History," she murmurs.

"You got an eighty-nine," I report. "And a ninety-two last quarter, so it's still an A average. That's not bad."

"He doesn't think like that," Nicole responds, looking at the floor. "It's a B. It might as well be an F." She lets out a huge sigh. "I really hate history."

A small laugh escapes from Rae, who's leaning against a locker. I scowl at her.

"What?" she says. "The way she said it was funny."

I need to think. Her dad is ridiculous, and I know she has to get into Harvard or she'll pretty much not exist to him. Which is dumb, since we're only in seventh grade. I bite my lip, thinking.

"What happened to your fingers and your dress?" I ask, looking Nicole over. I'm afraid she might pass out.

"I broke my pen when I saw the grade."

"Okay," I say with a heavy breath. "This is what we're going to do. Cal, take Nicole to the shop room to use that smelly soap to wash her hands. Rae, come to Mrs. Wilson's office with me."

"What are we going to do?" Rae asks, her eyes perked up with excitement.

"We're going to change her grade."

Cal's mouth drops. "What?"

"Don't worry about it," I tell him. "Take her to get cleaned up."

"We're going to break into the computer?" Rae asks, practically bouncing as we head toward the main office.

"Kind of," I say. "I'm an office aide, so I know where she keeps her passwords. She tapes them in her drawer, which is so obvious. She doesn't give us enough credit. We're not stupid. Whatever. She'll never know."

"What do you need me to do?" Rae asks.

"Be the lookout. Stop Mrs. Wilson from coming into her office until I can print a new report card."

"I can do that," she says confidently. I never doubted it. Cal would be an awful distraction. He'd choke on his own tongue before he could find an excuse to keep her out. Rae can talk her way out of anything. I'm not worried.

I walk behind the counter like I belong in the office. Ms. Kelly is busy announcing the buses, and everyone else is out in the parking lot, making sure no one gets run over. Ms. Kelly looks at me.

"I forgot my purse in Mrs. Wilson's office," I tell her. She nods and goes back to her announcements.

Within minutes, I have the program open—it helps that she never closed out of it. Nicole's ID is typed in, and the eighty-nine has become a ninety-one. Save. Print. And out the door.

"Have a nice day, Ms. Kelly," I say to her with Nicole's pristine, straight-A report card hidden under my jacket. Ms. Kelly doesn't even notice me leave.

"Did you do it?" Rae demands as soon as I step into the hall.

"Of course I did," I gloat, heading back to Nicole's locker, where she and Cal are waiting.

I smile and hand her the corrected report card. She throws her arms around me, and I stumble back.

"You're not allowed to cry," I say into her hair, feeling her whole body shake. "You can't let him make you cry."

She lets go. She still looks like she's about to fall apart into a thousand pieces. I take her hand. "I have an idea." I start down the hall, but Cal and Rae stay behind.

I turn back. "You guys coming?"

"Sure," Rae answers for them both, and they follow us.

We walk down the hall and out the door at the back of the

school. There's no one around. I lead us to the edge of the field, still holding on to Nicole's shaking hand.

"I think... we should scream."

"What?" Nicole asks, completely confused. I know it sounds crazy.

"You're still super stressed, and you need to get it out before you collapse," I explain. "So scream. Ready?"

They're all looking at me like I've lost my mind. And maybe I have. But if I had to live in Nicole's house, with her father expecting perfection at all times, I *would* go insane. I don't know how she hasn't lost it yet.

I take in a deep breath and close my eyes, and I scream. I scream for her and everything she has to put up with that I can't do anything about. And then... she's screaming with me. The next thing I know, the four of us are screaming, the sound echoing across the field. And it's so... freeing.

Then Rae starts laughing, and soon we all are, because we do look like lunatics.

"We missed the bus," Rae says as we walk around the side of the school.

"That's okay," I tell her. "We don't live that far. Besides, Nicole likes to walk."

THIRTEEN

"Shit, if it was going to be that easy, we should have asked her why she was at Crenshaw from the beginning," Rae says on the other end of the phone. "Now ask her why she's pretending to be Nyelle."

"She was drunk when she told me about Crenshaw. And it's not like she admitted to anything that'll help us."

"Yeah, like why the hell Crenshaw would be on her list. Cal, this has to do with you, don't you think? The coincidence is too weird. No one else we know goes there."

I've thought about that too, but I can't quite bring myself to believe that she's here because of me. Especially considering how much she avoids me.

"I can't believe you convinced her to stay with you over break." Then she gasps. "Omigod, you're going to have sex with her."

"No. Uh, not... no," I fumble.

"You were going to say 'not yet,' weren't you?" Rae accuses. "Cal, you can't screw this up by sleeping with her. She's already unstable. Don't make it any more complicated."

"How's the demo coming?" I ask, redirecting the conversation.

Rae grumbles under her breath.

"I think the band's breaking up." Her tone is flat and depressed.

"But you haven't even played a show yet."

"I know," she says in a short, angry burst. "Girls are...complicated. And dramatic. And exhausting."

"Tell me about it."

"But I did meet someone, and she's pretty awesome." Suddenly there's way more excitement in her voice, and I'm not sure how to react to it. Rae's almost never excited, except when she gets a new instrument.

"Uh...that's...great."

"Dude, we don't have to talk about it. I know how much you suck at relationships, so it's all good. I have Maura to talk to."

"My mother?"

"Yeah. She gives great dating advice. You should talk to her. Maybe you'll date a girl for longer than the length of a movie." Then she starts laughing. Again. I already hung up on her once when she couldn't stop laughing after hearing about my date with Jade.

"Rae," I warn her.

"Wait. Don't hang up," she says, trying to regain her composure. "Where's Nyelle now anyway?"

"Getting hot chocolate and coffee."

"And why aren't you with her?"

"Because I'm supposed to be studying."

"Did you make her walk?"

"She's using my truck."

"Your truck?! Seriously? You let her drive your truck?" Rae exclaims in shock.

"She does it without my permission anyway. I figured, why not?" I'd probably let Nyelle get away with anything she wants. I have a hard time telling her no. Like Nyelle said, it's one of my issues.

My phone beeps. I pull it away from my ear.

"Rae, my mother's on the other line. Please don't tell me you're sitting across from her at the kitchen table and she overheard this entire conversation." It wouldn't be the first time it's happened.

"No. I didn't tell her about Nyelle, I swear. But you should ask her about the repercussions of getting involved with a potentially psychotic girl," she says.

"Going now," I say, clicking over. "Hi, Mom."

"Hey. Were you on the other line? Do you need to call me back?"

"No. It was Rae. We were done."

"Oh. Okay. Did she tell you about Jackie?" she asks excitedly.

"I... uh... not... yeah."

My mother laughs. "She's cute. You'll like her. Anyway, I got a notification that you changed your flights. What's that all about?"

I clench my teeth. I forgot the account was attached to her name even though I paid for the changes.

"Sorry. I was going to tell you about that."

"Tell me? And why would you need to tell *your mother* that you're not spending the holidays with your family?" I know she's giving me shit, but I also hear the note of disappointment in her voice.

"Mom, I'll be there for Christmas," I assure her. "Remember that friend I was telling you about?"

"The girl?" She says it as an accusation.

"Yeah, her. Well, she's transferring next semester, and I want to spend some time with her before she leaves."

This conversation is killing me. I know my mother can sense I'm holding out. She's way too smart to not see through my evasiveness. I just hope she doesn't ask too many questions. I *really* don't want to lie to her... too much.

There's silence on the other end of the phone.

"Cal."

"Yeah?"

Silence again. I run my fingers through my…much shorter hair. Still getting used to it.

"Am I going to meet her? This girl?"

"Probably not," I answer honestly.

She sighs. I clench my eyes shut, feeling like I'm betraying her or something.

"How's Dad?" I ask, using her silence to change topics.

"He's working on my office above the garage…again. Oh! I almost forgot," she says suddenly. "It's actually the reason I'm calling, other than to tell you how heartbroken you've made me. But I suppose I'll have to get over it."

"What is it?" I ask. She knows how to lay on the guilt, and it's working.

"The strangest thing happened the other day. Vera Bentley stopped by to drop off flowers from her garden, which is very bizarre since she never really speaks to me anymore. But anyway, she asked about you and how you liked Crenshaw. Then she asked if you still spoke to Nicole. You don't, do you?"

"Cal, I got—"

I turn as Nyelle appears in the doorway of my bedroom. She doesn't continue when she sees I'm on the phone…silently hyperventilating.

"Uh, no, Mom. I haven't spoken to her in years." I'm staring at the lie I'm telling. Nyelle's eyes flinch ever so slightly. Otherwise, she hasn't moved a muscle. I think my heart's about to pound out of my chest.

"That's what I thought. Did I just hear a girl? Ooh. Is it *the girl*? Let me talk to her. If I'm not ever going to meet her, then I should at least be able to hear the voice of the girl who is keeping my son away from his mother."

"Not going to happen," I tell her. "I should go. It's rude. See? You taught me something."

"Very funny," my mother whips back. "I love you. Tell this girl your mother says hello. And I'll see you in *two weeks* instead of on Friday like I'm supposed to. Just saying that out loud breaks my heart."

"Love you too, Mom. Bye."

"Bye, Cal."

I hang up the phone.

"For you," Nyelle says calmly, handing me a cup. "Your mother?"

"She says hi," I say without thinking. Then I want to shoot myself in the head when her eyes widen.

"You told her about me?"

"No," I say quickly. Nyelle's eyes narrow. "I mean, she knows you *exist*. But she doesn't know... Fuck."

Nyelle closes her eyes and shakes her head with a laugh. "I forgot about your whole meeting-the-parents phobia. I'm not offended that you didn't tell your mother about me. I mean, we're not... dating... or anything, really."

I nod, needing to swallow all words before I make a bigger jackass of myself.

"I should go," she says.

And now I'm panicked, afraid I just screwed this up and freaked her out. "You don't have to."

"It's okay," she assures me. "Tess should be back, and you need to study for finals. I'll see you on Friday."

"Friday? Why Friday?" I clamp my mouth shut. I sound like a desperate girl. The girls I avoid at all costs. "Sorry. That came out worse than... Anyway... What are you doing all week? You're welcome to hang out here if you want."

"No. You study. I have things to do," she explains.

"Will you ever tell me what it is you do, now that I know you're not in class?"

"I do go to classes," she responds. "I sit in on different ones all the time."

"Just for fun?" I ask in disbelief. The thought of it makes me want to pluck my eyes out.

"Yeah, just for fun," she says with a laugh. "The reason for just about everything I do. And yes, I'll tell you what I do when I see you on Friday. Actually, if you want, I'll show you."

"Really?" I ask in surprise.

"Really," she responds with a smile. "Bye, Cal."

"Do you need a ride?" I ask, following her into the living room.

"No. I want to walk."

And then she's out the door without looking back. I slump against the arm of the couch with an exhausted breath. I think I've screwed up every conversation I've had today.

"Smooth. Real smooth," Eric says from behind me. I turn around to find him in the recliner with a textbook on his lap. "You're never going to see her again after that."

"Shut up, Eric," I shoot back, heading back into my room and slamming the door behind me. I lean against the door with my fists clenched, afraid he might be right.

I have no idea how I got through finals. There's a good chance I bombed every single exam. All I could think about was Friday and whether I'd see Nyelle again.

"I was thinking about coming back the first week in January," Eric says as he's dragging a bag of dirty laundry toward the door. "That cool with you?"

"Uh, yeah. Why?" I ask, washing the last of the dishes. I've spent most of the morning disinfecting the place. I know Nyelle's been here before, but now she's going to be living here for the next month. I don't want her to think we're disgusting...which we can be.

"You're staying in my room, right?" he confirms. Then smiles. "Or you're not."

"I am," I insist.

"Right. Well, Merry Christmas and all that shit. I'll see you in a few weeks."

"Merry Christmas," I return as he walks out the door.

I place the last bowl in the cabinet and scan the apartment. Other than Eric's room, which only I will have to deal with, it looks pretty good.

Now what? I don't know when she's coming, or if I'm supposed to pick her up. We never talked about it. I wish she'd turn her stupid phone on.

So, I call Tess.

"Hey, Cal!" she answers, like she's surprised to hear from me.

"Uh, hi, Tess. How were finals?" I ask, feeling the need to attempt a conversation before asking for her roommate.

"Glad they're over. Are you leaving today?"

"Not yet." I pause. "Is, um, is Nyelle there?"

There's silence. I crush my teeth together, knowing how much that just sucked.

"Yeah," she says quietly. "Hold on." I hear her say in the distance, "Nyelle, it's for you."

"Hello?"

"Hi."

"Cal? What's up?"

"I thought I'd pick you up."

"Um, okay. Pick me up at four and you can go to work with me."

"Work? Uh, sure."

"See ya," she says, hanging up.

When I approach the entrance at four, Nyelle is outside with a backpack and one rolling suitcase by her feet. That's it. I was expecting more. Especially for a girl.

Her eyes light up when she sees me. She runs up to me and practically knocks me over when she throws her arms around my neck. I blink in surprise.

The shock disappears quickly with the touch of her lips. The entire world disappears with that kiss.

She pulls back, smiling. "Hi."

"What was that for?" Dumb question, I know. "I thought I'm not supposed to touch you."

"I like kissing you. That okay?"

"I can handle that," I reply with a grin. I can definitely handle that.

"But I'm still not one of your girls," she says before turning back to get her bags.

"Don't even compare," I say under my breath, reaching for the suitcase as she slings the backpack over her shoulder and walks toward my truck.

Nyelle sits with her leg pressed against mine, straddling the stick shift, despite having the entire seat to herself. We sit with the engine running. I look up at the dorm and then back at Nyelle, who's watching me curiously.

"Did you tell Tess you weren't coming back?" I ask.

"I left her a note."

I nod. Then I ask the question that's been stuck in my head since I spoke with Rae earlier. "Why Crenshaw?"

"What?" she asks, taken off guard.

"Of all the colleges, why is Crenshaw on your list?"

She smirks. "You tell me, Cal. Why Crenshaw?"

Nyelle tightens her blue eyes, willing me to answer. And I can't.

"I don't know," I mumble.

"Exactly. I don't know."

I shake my head and laugh to myself. That got me nowhere.

I lean over and kiss the side of her neck. "Where to?"

Nyelle smiles and lays her head on my shoulder. She continues to confuse me with every conversation we have. But this girl makes me happy. Frustrated too. But mostly happy. And so I'm going to take advantage of every second I have with her.

Following Nyelle's directions, we end up in front of a two-story office building twenty minutes later.

"This is where you work?" I ask, trying to read the names of the offices on the tall sign by the road.

"Technically, Lynn is employed here. But she pays me cash to cover for her on Mondays and Fridays so she can work her second job."

"How long are we here until?"

"Seven thirty."

"And how do you know Lynn?" I ask, still trying to find a connection between Nyelle and Crenshaw that isn't just me.

"I met her on campus," she explains as I follow her up to the second floor. "I helped her study for a biology exam."

We walk through a glass door that has something about medical services printed on it.

"But you don't actually attend classes," I say, baffled.

"I like biology," she says with a grin, continuing past an empty reception desk to a row of cubicles lining the windows.

"Hi, Keith," Nyelle says to the only other person in the office. He's sitting in front of a computer, wearing a headset and squeezing a stress ball.

"Nyelle." He nods. He glances at me without a reaction. Then turns to face the computer again.

"He doesn't talk much," Nyelle explains, stepping into the next cubicle. "And that's funny, since that's what we're paid to do."

She unwraps two headsets and plugs them into a phone before logging on to the computer.

"Here, you can use the training set," she says, handing me one of the headsets. "There's a chair behind you."

"What do you do exactly?" I ask, pulling up a chair behind hers in the tiny cubicle.

"I…talk." She smiles at me over her shoulder, typing on the computer.

I put the headset on when she does and hear a phone ringing.

"Hello?"

"Hi, Marla. It's Lynn. How are you today?"

"Oh, it's *Friday Lynn*. I'm doing okay, sweetie."

"How's Roger feeling? Has he started physical therapy yet?"

"He was finally able to get out of bed on Monday. So he starts next week."

"That's so great! How are Heath and Allie?"

"A pain in my ass." Marla laughs. "But that's their job, right? And before you say anything, I sent in a payment yesterday. I swear."

"Oh, only if you can afford it. Don't you dare send these doctors any money if your kids need anything. The doctors aren't starving. I promise you that."

Marla laughs. "I know. You're too sweet. But it's okay this week."

"Well, I'll talk to you again soon, okay?"

"Bye."

Then the line is disconnected. Nyelle spins in her chair with a grin.

For a moment all I can do is stare. Every time I'm with Nyelle, I realize how much I don't know about her. And…how much I want to.

"You're supposed to be collecting *money*," Keith hollers from over the cubicle wall.

"He's by the book," Nyelle explains with a roll of her eyes. Then she says in a whisper, "But I hit the call quota, and I guarantee I bring in more money than he does, even when I tell my people they don't have to pay."

I laugh.

I listen to her *talk* for the next few hours. Every person she calls loves her. They tell her about their kids. Their parents. How hard their lives are. Or about a new job or classes they're taking. It's almost never about money, or paying the bill they owe. And she's so patient with them, genuinely invested in their lives.

At seven thirty, she wraps the cords around the headsets and puts them in a drawer. "Now we get paid."

"By Lynn?" I ask as we walk out of the cubicle. Keith is already gone.

"On Fridays, she's Jasmine," Nyelle says, pushing through the glass door. "She works at Starlight on Mondays and Fridays, but she doesn't want her husband to know. I help her keep her minimum-wage job so she can make enough cash to put herself through college."

"She's a stripper?"

"She's a *student*," Nyelle corrects me, getting into the truck. "She just happens to have a killer body, and guys are stupid enough to give her money to look at it."

I chuckle. "Yeah, guys are dumb like that." Then it hits me. "Wait. Are *we* going to Starlight... now?"

"You can stay in the truck if it makes you uncomfortable," Nyelle says with a smirk. "But I thought we could eat. They seriously make the best burgers in town."

"We're going to have dinner at a strip club," I say, more to myself than to Nyelle. "O-kay."

I've never been to Starlight. It's on the other side of town, away from campus. I know it exists, because I hear the guys talk about it. I've just never been... tempted.

The small black building doesn't look like much. I wouldn't even know this was the place except for *Starlight* painted across the side in some sort of script, the "i" dotted with a star. There aren't a lot of cars in the icy dirt parking lot when we pull in.

Nyelle strides through the entrance, immune to the surroundings, heading directly to the bar. I pause inside the heavy metal door, taking in the dark club, which pulses with light as a strobe light flashes onstage. A pole extends to the ceiling in the center of a runway off the main stage. And upside down on that pole are legs... long legs.

Nyelle pulls my jacket before I can follow those legs down to a face. I blink out of the fog-induced haze and sit on a stool at the bar.

"Hey, Jimmy," Nyelle says with a smile, sliding out of her jacket and setting it on the stool.

"How are ya, Nyelle?" Jimmy is a muscled guy in a tight black T-shirt, his black hair slicked back. And he's way too tan for winter in upstate New York. "Your regular?"

"Yes, please. Can you make it two?" Nyelle nods toward me.

"How do you want it cooked?" he asks, staring me down.

"Uh, medium-rare, thanks," I say, trying not to look around, but it's fricken hard.

"Cal?"

Nyelle and I slowly turn on our stools. There's a blonde with big, wavy hair down her back, wearing a ton of glittery makeup and not much else.

It takes me a minute to place her. She doesn't look like anyone I know, dressed in a sparkling black string bikini top and super short cutoffs. Then I see the butterfly tattoo above her hip bone. "Micha?"

Her glossy pink lips widen into a smile. "How are you? Omigod, I never would have thought I'd see you *here*."

"Uh, I'm getting dinner?" It sounds more like a question, because I know it's a strange thing to say at a strip club.

"You know Micha?" Nyelle says with an amused laugh. "Of course you do."

"Yeah, we dated for like... three weeks?" Micha says, looking to me for affirmation. I nod with a quick shrug. "Oh, so you're here with Nyelle?" She sounds surprised.

"Hey, Nyelle. I'll let Jasmine know you're here," she says, setting her tray on the bar next to me. "I'll be back for those drinks in a second, Jimmy."

Then she saunters off in the tallest heels I've ever seen.

"How does she walk in those?" I ask.

"Are you looking at her shoes or her shorts?" Nyelle asks. I glance up, and the side of my mouth quirks up, because the shorts cover less than most bathing suits.

"That too," I say. Nyelle swats my arm. "What? I hadn't even noticed until you mentioned them."

"You dated Micha," Nyelle says with a shake of her head.

"I didn't know she was a stripper," I tell her.

"She's not. She's a cocktail waitress," Nyelle explains. "And would it have mattered if she was?"

I pause for a second, scanning the scattered crowd sitting in the dark, focused on the bodies being flaunted in front of them. There's no way I would be comfortable letting these guys watch a girl I was dating dance naked.

"Yeah, it would."

"How many girls have you walked away from, Cal?" Nyelle asks me.

"Uh... What?" If the lights were on, my face would be bright red.

"Twenty?"

"No! Not that many," I say, wiping the sweat off my palms. "Why does it matter?"

"Just curious," Nyelle says with a tilted smile. "And you walked away from all of them?'

"Sometimes they're the ones walking away," I tell her, uncomfortable with the judgment.

"And you let them?" When I don't answer, she asks, "Why?"

I look behind Nyelle at a tall black woman with flowing dark hair hanging to her waist. She's slender but with the definition of an athlete.

Nyelle turns to see who has my attention.

"Hey, Jasmine," Nyelle greets her happily. "This is Cal."

"Hi," I say, now understanding how she makes enough money here to put herself through school.

She looks me up and down without a word, and just nods.

"Cute boy-next door type," she says to Nyelle, handing her a hundred-dollar bill. "Rusty wanted me to tell you the offer still stands. I told him you were leaving town, but he's stubborn."

"That's so nice of him," Nyelle says with a small laugh. "But it would be embarrassing for everyone involved if I got on that stage."

"Had to ask." Jasmine returns her attention to me. Her tone is low and almost threatening. "I don't think I've seen you here before."

"Cal's not the strip club kind of guy," Micha says with a wink, appearing beside me. She picks up the tray of drinks, and I almost jump off the stool when I feel something slide into my back pocket as she passes behind me. I watch her walk away, unable to move. What was that about?

Whatever it was, I'm not about to reach into my pocket to find out, especially when I look back at Jasmine, who has her arms folded in front of her and her eyebrow cocked.

"Nyelle, what are you doing with this guy? Do you trust him?"

Jasmine's accusatory tone instills instant guilt—even though I haven't done anything wrong.

Nyelle examines me like she needs to think it over. I'm suddenly afraid that if she doesn't say yes, Jasmine's going to kick my ass.

"I'm living with him," Nyelle answers. I blink, hard. "And yes, I trust him."

I don't hear what Jasmine says before she struts away. I don't hear what Nyelle says in response. I don't even notice when the burgers are set in front of us.

"Why are you looking at me like that?" Nyelle asks, about to pick up her burger.

I tuck my hand around the back of her neck and pull her to me, kissing her. She presses her hands on my chest, kissing me back. When we part, she's breathless and flushed.

"What was that for?" she asks.

"You trust me," I reply, grinning.

NICOLE

August—Before Eighth Grade

"What do you mean you're moving?" I say, hoping I didn't hear her right.

"We're moving to San Francisco," Richelle says, sitting on my bed. Her eyes are red from crying.

"When?" I ask. My throat tightens and tears flood my eyes.

"Tomorrow."

"No!" I shoot back, shaking my head. "No. You can't. You can't leave, Richelle."

Tears are leaking out of her eyes.

"Why tomorrow? I don't understand. Why so fast?"

Richelle shrugs. "My dad has a new job. And . . . my mom wants to move now. She says . . . we have to."

This doesn't feel right. It's too fast.

"Did you tell Cal? Or Rae?"

Her face twists, and she's crying into her hands, shaking her head. "I can't."

"Why? You have to tell them. They're our best friends."

"It hurts so much just telling you. I can't say good-bye to them. Especially Cal. I just . . . can't."

"You're just going to leave?"

"I wrote him a letter. I was hoping you could give it to him after I'm gone."

FOURTEEN

I have no idea how I've restrained myself the past four days, waking up next to her. Nyelle insists that I sleep in my bed... with her. She says she trusts me. "I trust you." The same words I wanted her to say are now the worst words in existence. Those words are a concrete wall dividing my bed in half, with me on one side, balled up tight to keep from busting it down. And Nyelle on the other, rolling around, occasionally flopping an arm or leg on my side so our skin touches. She doesn't seem to give a shit about the wall. But I do. "I trust you." She might as well have castrated me.

And then every day I receive a call or a text from Rae, demanding progress. Like now that Nyelle is staying with me, she'll suddenly open up and tell me all her secrets. If anything, she's even more evasive. Speaking in her cryptic sentences with their unknown meanings. Having conversations with her about anything that pertains to her life is like playing dyslexic Scrabble.

When she kisses me, I'm not concerned with who she used to be. Only that she's the one kissing me now. I live to feel those lips. I'd like to feel more, but I'm letting her pace us. I don't want to move faster than she's willing.

Each time we connect, I'm combustible. The fire from the touch of her burns up every inch of my body. Whenever I think we're about to take it farther, she stops. Without warning. She gets up and walks away. I have no time to calm down. She should just go ahead and dump a tray of ice cubes down the front of my pants.

I refuse to believe she's torturing me on purpose. The right thing to do would be to talk to her about us. Where this is going. What we want out of this. But when it comes to girls, I have yet to do the right thing. Just because I'm actually invested doesn't make communicating easier.

There's a reason Rae's my best friend. She talks through her drums. I just…don't talk.

"Where are you going today?" I ask Nyelle as she slides on her jacket. She's about to disappear, as she does every so often without notice. Even though she's staying with me, it's hard to watch her walk out that door.

"Want to come with me?"

Jumping off the couch, I grab my jacket. "Sure."

I always say yes whenever she invites me. I never know what I'm agreeing to, but whatever it is, it's always unexpected.

Sunday, Nyelle said she wanted to play pinball. So we played pinball…all afternoon at an arcade that only the local gamers seem to know about. It's old, dark, and smells like stale fries and mildew. Not the best combination. But the place houses every old-school video game in existence. I had blisters on my fingers when we left.

Yesterday, she bought thirty latex balloons filled with helium and tied the message "You are loved" to each string. Then we drove out to the abandoned farm and stood in the middle of the snowy field to release them.

Just before we set them loose into the world, I asked, "Is this on your list?"

"Sorta."

I waited, knowing there was more.

"What's actually written on the list is: Relive the happiest day of your life."

I looked up at the cloud of colorful balloons. "You've done this before?"

"No." She smiled brightly and shook her head. Then she let them float away into the overcast winter sky, blasting color where there wasn't any before. "But now I'll get to do it again sometime."

I laughed. Then I pulled her into my arms and kissed her. A moment like that deserved a kiss at the end of it, and so I made sure to give it the best ending possible. I continued to kiss her as the colored dots floated away above our heads.

So, today, I don't know where she's taking me. And I'm okay with that. No expectations. Because I know Nyelle is beyond every expectation I could ever have.

"Where to today?" I ask, starting the truck.

"We need to go to Elaine's first," Nyelle tells me, sliding in close beside me.

"And then?" I prompt.

"And then...we're going to make the world a little more happy." She bounces up on the seat, giving me a kiss on the cheek.

There never seems to be an answer in her answers.

After retrieving several bags of what appear to be the materials to construct a spaceship from Elaine's, Nyelle gets in the driver's side. She doesn't even ask. And I don't bother arguing. She obviously doesn't want me to know where we're going until we get there. But the last place I expect to arrive is the children's hospital.

Crenshaw has a reputable medical school, and people come from all over to be seen at the hospitals. I've heard they have some cutting-edge studies. It's one of the reasons students attend the university.

It's not my reason.

I'm trying to prepare myself for whatever we're about to do, following Nyelle down the halls of the hospital. But there's really no way to prepare for this. It's not like stretching before a race.

"They're just kids," Nyelle says, pulling me out of my head. She looks me over and produces a reassuring smile.

"That obvious?" I ask.

"You look a little pale," she notes, reaching for my hand as the elevator dings. "We need to help them remember."

"Remember what?" I ask, letting her lead me down the corridor.

"That they're kids. No matter what they're going through, they're still kids."

I look at the shimmer in her eyes and nod. I don't *not* like kids. I'm just never around them, except for the few times a year that my family gets together.

I take a deep breath and squeeze Nyelle's hand. How bad can this be, really? It can't be worse than meeting a girl's parents.

We cut down another corridor, and Nyelle reaches for a glass door with *The Shea Clinic: Outpatient Services* printed across it. She holds it open for me. I'm bombarded with noise when we cross the threshold—kids talking and laughing, babies crying, video games beeping and the voices of characters broadcasting from a television.

"Hi, Maddie," Nyelle says to the woman behind the reception desk in a medical coat covered in smiling snowflakes.

"Hi, Nyelle," Maddie replies pleasantly, glancing past her to me. I act like I'm supposed to be here, faking the confidence. From the concerned look on her face, I know she sees right through it. It could be the beads of sweat across my forehead.

"Nyelle!" A woman with cropped red hair appears behind the desk. "I'm so happy you're here. The kids were starting to ask for you."

"Hi, Rose," Nyelle says. "Rose, this is Cal. The guy I told you was going to help out today since Elaine couldn't make it."

"Of course! Welcome, Cal," she says to me. "I just have a few forms for you to fill out and I need to make a copy of your ID."

"Sure," I respond, giving Nyelle a quick questioning look. I pull out my ID for Rose, and she walks into a back office area.

"Elaine used to be a nurse here," Nyelle explains. It's not exactly what I wanted to know. "Now she volunteers once a week. I've been coming with her for the last two months."

"Okay," I respond. "What exactly are we doing, Nyelle?"

"Here you go," Rose says, handing me a clipboard before I receive an answer. "And these are your volunteer badges. As soon as you're done with the papers, hand them to Maddie and you're all set. Thank you so much for being here today!"

"Not a problem," I answer, still not certain what I'm volunteering for.

An ear-piercing scream suddenly erupts from a room down the hallway, and my entire body goes rigid.

"Kids don't like needles," Maddie tells me when she notices my wide eyes.

"Neither do I," I reply, feeling the blood drain from my face, hoping I'm going nowhere near wherever that kid is.

"I'll be right over there," Nyelle informs me, pointing to the far corner of the open space, where a large table is surrounded by plastic chairs. I nod.

"Nyelle!" I hear a bunch of young voices cheer as she approaches.

I sign the last form and hand the clipboard back to Maddie. "Thanks."

I walk through the waiting area where parents are reading and talking and past the boys at the gaming console. I stop a few yards away from the table, watching Nyelle spread out what look like art supplies.

"They can smell fear," a nurse says from behind me, spinning me around.

I swallow.

Nyelle looks over her shoulder. "You coming?"

I cautiously approach, feeling like a trespasser. And from the strange looks I'm receiving, they must see me as one too.

Nyelle takes my hand and eases me toward the table. "They don't bite... usually."

Someone laughs. I glance over my shoulder at a father with a little boy on his lap. He looks down, trying to hide his smile. That didn't help.

"Who are you?" I find a small girl missing her two front teeth and wearing a colorful scarf wrapped around her bald head peering up at me. She's holding on to a metal pole with a machine pumping clear liquid down a tube that's hidden underneath her pink sweater.

I open my mouth, but nothing comes out. I'm intimidated by a little girl. Not cool.

"This is Cal," Nyelle tells her. "He's a little shy." She grins at me, and I roll my eyes.

"Hi," I finally say. "Who are you?"

"Tally," she says. "I'm six."

"What are we making today?" a boy with a head full of dark curls asks, leaning over the table and picking up a pink flower with a worried expression. He's not hooked up to a machine. "Not girl stuff. I'll puke."

"We're making these." Nyelle pulls a sword out of the bag. The blade is wrapped with tinfoil, and the hilt is decorated with plastic flowers. Heart stickers run the length of the blade. "Don't worry, Jacob. You can design yours however you want. You don't have to use the flowers. Unless you want to." She smiles at him.

"Ew!" he exclaims. He reminds me of Rae as a kid, making me laugh.

"Do you have anything for princesses?" a girl with the biggest blue eyes I've ever seen asks. Her little bald head only makes her round eyes that much bigger.

"Princesses can have swords," Nyelle says, sitting in a blue chair next to her.

The girl looks confused. "But then what about the prince?" She looks up at me. My eyes widen. "Doesn't he need a sword to rescue you?"

Nyelle laughs. "I don't need any rescuing. And neither do you. That's why you get to make your own sword, so you can fight for yourself. Maybe we'll have to rescue *him*." Nyelle leans in and whispers, "I think you look like you could slay a dragon all by yourself. Him . . . not so much."

The girl glances at me and giggles.

Something is pulling at my pants. I look down. There's a small boy wearing a baseball hat staring at me. A machine is beeping next to him. I kneel down.

"My mom says I'm not supposed to play with guns or swords," he tells me in a low voice.

I pause, looking to Nyelle to bail me out. But she's working with the blue-eyed girl. "Um . . . I guess we'll just have to make you a shield then, huh?"

The boy smiles and nods.

We spend the next several hours helping construct shields and swords. The kids are pretty funny. And they don't care that I have no idea what I'm doing.

"That's a pretty cool flame sword," I tell Jacob, helping him wrap the handle in black electrical tape

"I know it is," he brags, taking it from me and thrusting it into the air.

"I didn't know you were artistic," Nyelle says, as I help a boy make his sword look like a road with trucks driving on it.

"I'm not," I respond quietly, so the boy doesn't overhear. "But they're not that critical."

Nyelle nods toward the girl with the big blue eyes, who's been sitting next to me the entire time. She's strategically placing heart stickers on her rainbow sword. "I think Isabel has a crush on you."

When I look over at the girl, her face lights up with a bashful smile.

"Yeah, I think she's got me," I lean over and whisper to Nyelle. "It's the blue eyes—they make me weak." Nyelle's cheeks flush.

Isabel approaches me while I'm picking up the last of the stickers, getting ready to leave. I squat down so I'm closer to her size. She holds her hand up to my ear and whispers, "You don't have to be afraid. I'll rescue you."

"Thanks," I whisper back. She places a heart sticker on my hand and rushes away. I look down at it with a smile.

I watch Nyelle give hugs and high fives before we go. The happiness that she brought into their world is etched on their faces. Despite everything they're going through, they're still just kids. And regardless of what she went through to be here, she shouldn't be anywhere else.

"Kids aren't so bad. Well, at least these kids aren't," I admit while we're walking to the truck.

Nyelle laughs. "These kids are *amazing*."

When we get to the truck, I turn toward her, pulling her to me with my hands on her waist.

"So is there anything else?"

Nyelle eyes me curiously. "What do you mean?"

"Well, let's see... You voluntarily walk the sketchiest streets in Crenshaw to make sure a homeless man doesn't freeze to death. You help little kids fight their dragons. You tutor a stripper..." I quickly correct myself when Nyelle glares at me. "I mean, student in biology, while *not* collecting money, and attend classes at a university you're not enrolled in. Oh yeah, in your free time you roll down hills, climb trees, and punch assholes in the face. And you make sure every day is all about having fun. Am I missing something?"

"Um... that sounds about right," Nyelle replies with a grin.

"So what else is on this list you haven't done?" I wrap my arms around her, pulling her against me.

She stiffens.

"Nyelle?" I ask when she pushes away. "What's wrong?"

She turns from me in an attempt to hide her glistening eyes.

"Hey. What's going on?" I have no idea what just happened.

Nyelle doesn't say anything. Just presses her lips tight and walks to the other side of the truck.

"Did I say something wrong?" I think over everything I said, but I can't figure out what caused her to pull away from me.

"Can we get some ice cream?" Nyelle asks before slipping into the truck.

I get in and close the door. "You're not going to tell me, are you?"

Nyelle shakes her head. "I just need some ice cream."

"Okay. Let's get ice cream," I concede, deciding not to push it. "It makes everything better, right?"

She releases a broken laugh. "Exactly."

I'm not sure what triggered the tears she refused to let fall, but Nyelle's back to being her vibrant, carefree self as soon as we pull into the ice cream place, like nothing ever bothered her.

I haven't figured out how to get her to tell me all that she doesn't want me to know. I like everything about Nyelle just as she is—despite the fact that I don't know *why* she became her. And I'm not really sure I want to know anymore. I'd rather just let her be exactly who she needs to be.

The rest of the week is over way too fast, and now I'm supposed to be flying to Oregon in the morning to spend Christmas with my family.

"Explain your family to me again," Nyelle requests, sitting next to me with a bowl of popcorn and a box of Goobers. "Your mom is one of…six?"

"Seven," I correct. "She's the second oldest. The way we think of it is there's *the uncles*, who are two years older and younger than her. Then the next three are *the aunts*, who are separated by four years and there's two years between them. And then there's Zac. He's the mistake."

"Cal, that's awful," she scolds.

"Well, he is. He's eleven years younger than my aunt Helen. He's only a year older than my brother Sean. There was nothing expected about him."

"And it's his house you're going to tomorrow?"

"Yes. It was their family vacation home when they were

growing up. But Zac lives there now. Half of us go there, and the other half go to my aunt Livia's in Ohio. We switch it up every year. There's way too many people to put under one roof."

"I'd love to be a part of a big family," she says, her eyes cast up like she can picture it.

"You can borrow mine anytime you want."

Nyelle stuffs a handful of popcorn in her mouth and shakes some Goobers in on top of it.

I cringe. "That can't taste good."

"It's the best thing next to ice cream and frosting," Nyelle claims. "Stick out your hand."

I reluctantly obey. She places a few pieces of popcorn and a couple Goobers on my palm. Skeptical, I dump them in my mouth.

"Hmm," I say, pleasantly surprised. "Way better than the chocolate-drizzled Fritos. That was disgusting."

Nyelle laughs.

"You're okay with staying at Elaine's? I'll leave you the key if you feel like coming back here."

"No. It's totally fine. We have some things planned." She clenches her fists and her eyes light up like they do when she can barely contain her excitement. "She has this attic of antique clothes. I'm way overdue for a tea party."

"Those words will never come out of my mouth."

Nyelle smiles. "Yeah, you always disappeared when we picked flowers." She stuffs more popcorn in her mouth.

I'm trying not to react. I'm trying so damn hard to let it slide. But I can't.

"Do you remem—"

"Are you going to date Micha again? She's waiting for you to call her," Nyelle says, talking over me.

"What?" There's no way I heard her correctly.

"Micha. She said she asked you to call her," Nyelle repeats. "Didn't you break up because she thought she was going to transfer? She's not anymore. So, are you going to call her?"

"No," I say quickly. "I'm not... What are you doing? Why would you want me to call her?" I'm staring at Nyelle in complete disbelief. "Seriously. You *want* me to... date her?"

"I like her," she says with a simple shrug, avoiding the shock covering my face.

I need to clear my head. I stand up and walk to the refrigerator to get a beer. After chugging half the can, I ask with my voice coated in anger, "You're okay if I date?"

"I'm leaving, Cal," Nyelle replies, sounding way too calm. She's doing that thing she does when she removes all emotion from her voice. She's pulling away.

I feel like I just got sucker punched in the gut, and I'm trying to catch my breath. I drain the rest of the beer.

"Right" is my only response.

"Want to watch a movie?" she asks, acting completely unaffected. "Before I eat all the popcorn?"

"Sure," I say flatly and sit back down next to her on the couch.

She's right. She *is* leaving. This, whatever *this* is between us, is evidently nothing. Tell that to whatever it is that's gutting my insides right now.

So when she lies down on the couch, resting her head on my leg, I can't handle it. But instead of saying something to her, I shift out from under her and stand up.

"I think I'm going to pack. My flight's pretty early."

She looks at me oddly and nods. "Okay. Should I leave tonight? I can have Elaine pick me up."

"Leave whenever," I say, walking into my room and closing the door behind me. As soon as I do, I clench my teeth. I sounded like a dick and I know it.

I grab my duffel bag out of the closet and start shoving clothes in it, not really paying attention to what I'm selecting. The sound of the television in the next room kills me. She has no idea how what she said affected me. None.

"Cal?" Nyelle's head peeks into the room. "Are you okay?"

Okay, maybe she has *some* idea.

I nod, lowering my eyes.

"I called Elaine. She's on her way." She opens the door wider to enter and picks up her backpack from the end of the bed.

I close my eyes, trying to think clearly enough to say the right thing.

"Don't go. I didn't mean it the way it sounded."

"No. It's okay. She's not much of a morning person anyway."

Nyelle takes the backpack and suitcase into the living room. I drop my bag on the floor and sit on the end of the bed, running my hands through my hair, desperate to fix this. To convince her not to leave tonight.

Just as I stand up, Nyelle steps into my room. We look at each other for a long second. Her eyes shift to the floor with a saddened sigh. Then her brow creases. "What's that?"

I turn toward the closet. There's a folded note and a rolled-up piece of craft paper on the floor. They must have fallen out when I grabbed my duffel bag off the shelf. Nyelle bends down to pick them up. It hits me what she has in her hands right when she unrolls the paper.

"Nyelle, don't—" rushes out at the same time her mouth opens in a silent gasp.

Nyelle looks from the painting to me. Her eyes flicker with confusion. She slowly lowers herself to sit on the bed, holding the paper like it might disintegrate between her fingers. It quivers in her grasp as she looks it over, a deep impression between her brows like she doesn't know what to think or how to react.

With a small exhale, she gently strokes her fingers over our childhood. I watch as her fingertips brush over the girl with blond hair playing a guitar under the tree, and the girl with the blue ribbon in her hair and the boy wearing black glasses sitting in the treehouse, holding hands. Then her trembling hand hovers above Richelle, picking flowers in the field.

When she raises her head, I'm taken aback by the pain reflecting in her eyes. I've never seen someone hurt like this, and I don't know how to save her from it. I'm tempted to tear the painting from her hands and shred it, to try to stop whatever it is that's making her look like she's shattering on the inside.

"Why'd you keep this?" she asks in a broken whisper, her attention back to the picture she made for me so many years ago.

"I don't know," I answer quietly.

"We had our first fight over this painting," she murmurs, her voice fading, weighted with suffering. She picks up the letter Richelle wrote to me right before she moved away.

Nyelle closes her eyes and shakes her head, her face distorted in a tortured expression, her lips trembling and her jaw tight. This is hurting her more than I ever could have anticipated. And I want to make it stop.

"Nicole?" I say her name quietly. She keeps her eyes shut without responding.

When she does open them again, the emotions she's been fighting have disappeared. The pain and confusion possessing her a moment ago have been tucked back behind the mask. I'm too stunned by the transformation to speak. It's like Nicole was here for a second, and now she's gone.

A buzzing comes from her pocket. She removes the small black phone. "Elaine's here."

Nyelle sets the painting and letter on the bed, calm and devoid of emotion. She makes a move for the door, and I step in front of her. She refuses to look at me.

"Don't go."

"I have to," she says in a whisper, stepping around me. I follow her into the living room, my heart pounding in full panic. If she walks out that door now, I'm going to lose her.

She grabs her jacket and shifts her backpack over a shoulder, rolling her suitcase toward the door.

"Nicole!"

She turns, propping the door open. Her eyes are ice, staring into mine. "I'm not her. Not anymore."

I'm stunned, frozen in the middle of the living room, watching the door click shut. Panic pushes me forward and I reach for the door. But I stop with the handle in my grasp, unable to turn it. I rest my forehead against the door, letting her walk away.

RICHELLE

May—Eighth Grade

"So what are you going to do this summer?" I ask Nicole as she sits on the end of my bed, flipping through a magazine. She slept over last night, like she does the last weekend of every month since I moved to San Francisco. Her mom brings her here on the train. Sometimes she's able to talk her mom into coming down more than once. But that almost never happens.

"I don't know." She shrugs, not looking up.

"Are you still friends with those girls?" I ask, pulling the blanket up on my lap, still tired. We didn't get much sleep. We usually don't when Nicole stays over, no matter how many times we're told to go to sleep.

"They're not really my friends," she says. "You know that."

"Right," I say. She seems quieter than usual today. It's probably something to do with her father. "You don't have to hang out with them if you don't want to."

"It makes my mom happy," she says quietly. "She's wanted me to be friends with them since we moved there, because my father works for one of their dads. And she likes having their mothers over. They're in the PTA together... It doesn't matter."

No. This is about Cal and Rae.

"Nicole," I say, making her look up at me. "You can talk to them, you know? Cal and Rae. You just can't tell them everything."

"I can't be friends with them," she says sadly.

"He asks about you when I talk to him." This only seems to make her sadder. I hate that they stopped being friends. It's not what was supposed to happen.

Nicole smiles to make me feel better, but I know it's fake. "It's fine. I swear. It won't be forever, right?"

"Right," I agree. Then an idea comes to me that spreads a real smile across my face. "Want to do something crazy?"

Nicole nods slowly, without saying anything.

"Want to cut off my hair? You know, like Britney did when she went all crazy? Just maybe not as short. Then we can dye it blue. Rae will be so pissed she didn't do it first."

"You want me to cut your hair supershort?" Nicole asks, like she can't believe I'm even suggesting it, forget about being serious. I know it will make her laugh, and I like it when she laughs.

"Yeah. It's only hair. And it'll look so cool when we're done," I tell her, excited by the idea. "Get my dad's clippers from the hall closet. Just don't let my mom see you."

FIFTEEN

"Why is there a moving truck in front of the Nelsons' house?" I ask my mother, eating breakfast and watching the men load wrapped furniture into the back of the truck.

Mom peers out the window. She doesn't answer me for a moment. "Oh, Cal. I'm sorry. Rick must have gotten that job in San Francisco. I wonder why Diane didn't call to tell me."

"What?!" I exclaim. I'm up from the table and out the front door before my mom can yell at me for not putting my bowl in the dishwasher. I sprint to Richelle's house.

I'm about to walk through the front door when I hear, "Can I help you, Cal?"

I turn toward the truck to find Richelle's dad.

"Um, hi, Mr. Nelson. Is Richelle around?" I ask, my heart racing, and not just because I ran as fast as I could over here.

"No. Sorry, Cal," he says quietly without looking at me. "She's already in San Francisco with her mother, getting the new place ready for when the truck arrives."

"I didn't know you were moving," I say, trying not to sound as angry as I am.

"It happened pretty fast," he explains, walking past me toward the house with his shoulders slumped forward. "You

can always e-mail her, Cal. I really am sorry about this." But he sounds flat and tired, like he doesn't mean it.

"Thanks," I mutter, shoving my hands in my jeans pockets and walking back to my house with my head down.

"What's going on?" Rae asks from the end of her driveway.

"The Nelsons are moving to San Francisco." The words taste bitter in my mouth.

"Why are they moving?" Rae demands, like the thought of it doesn't make sense.

"I guess her dad got a new job or something," I mumble.

"You didn't know?"

"Did you?" I snap.

"No," Rae grumbles.

"That's messed up. We're supposed to be her friends. I'm supposed to be her boyfriend. *You'd think she would've said something." My voice is getting louder as the anger reaches the surface.*

"It's not her fault."

I turn to find Nicole behind me. She looks like she's been crying—her eyes are red and puffy. "She didn't want this to happen. It's not like she had a choice or anything. So you can't be mad at her."

"Then why are you upset?"

Nicole doesn't answer. She wipes a tear off her cheek. "She wanted you to have this." She hands me a folded piece of paper and walks away.

"Are you going to mope all week?" Rae asks, sitting next to me on the leather couch in my uncle's office.

"I'm not moping," I reply defensively, staring out the window.

"You're afraid she's not going to be there when you get back, aren't you?"

"Yeah." My voice is barely audible.

"Why didn't you go after her when she walked out on you, Cal? Why did you let her leave like that? Especially after what she said about being Nicole."

"No. She told me she *wasn't*, remember?" I haven't been able to get that pained look on her face out of my head.

"But she also said *not anymore*. Which means she's running away from something."

"What was I supposed to say, Rae? Huh?" I demand, raising my voice. "I asked her not to leave. I—"

"But you didn't ask her what happened to her," Rae argues back. "You didn't ask why she's not at Harvard, or home with her family, or why she's pretending her life before never happened. You didn't ask her anything, Cal! And now...she's probably gone, and if anything happens to her—"

I stand up, cutting her off. I never told her how hard it was to watch Nyelle struggle with the memories of our childhood, like going back there was some form of torture.

"We have to tell Maura," Rae states adamantly.

"No." I glare at her.

"Why are you being so stubborn?!" Rae yells in frustration.

"Because I don't care!"

Rae doesn't move. Anything she's about to say is frozen in her mouth.

"Maybe I like her the way she is and don't care what happened to make her this way! Maybe I don't want to know."

And I won't force her to remember if it's going to hurt her. I can't put her through that again.

"What's going on?" my mother asks from the doorway. "What are you arguing about?"

Rae stands up.

"Rae," I say sternly. "Don't. You promised to give me a month."

My mother looks from Rae to me, questioning.

"You're being stupid, Cal," Rae snaps, walking past my mother out the door. "I need a drink."

"Hey, you're not twenty-one *yet*, young lady," my mother calls to her over her shoulder. She turns to me. "What was that all about? Why are you driving Raelyn to drink?"

I sit back down on the couch and run my hands over my face.

"Cal?" my mother prods carefully. "Is this about that girl? The one you're going back to Crenshaw for tomorrow? What's her name anyway?"

"Yeah," I respond, resting my head on the couch, staring at the ceiling. "Her name's Nyelle." My mother sits next to me and sets a hand on my knee.

"I know you never talk to me about girls. But I haven't seen you this upset over one since Richelle left when you were in eighth grade. So if you need to..."

"It's okay," I tell her. "I'll be fine, Mom. Thanks."

"Okay," she says, standing up. Before she reaches the door, she turns to face me. "You really care about this girl...Nyelle, don't you?"

I let out a heavy breath. "Yeah. Since the first day I saw her."

Sean opens the office door two hours later. "Come on, GQ. We're playing football."

I sit up on the couch.

"No more being lame, man. Let's go," he demands.

There's no arguing with Sean. He's used to getting his way. So I stand up and follow him out of the house.

Sean messes up the hair on top of my head. "I like this new look, man. It's sexy as hell."

I knock his hand away. "Shut up, Sean."

"You get Cal," Devin declares. "He can't catch worth a damn."

"Screw you," I argue, hopping down the steps, holding up a hand to my uncle Zac. He tosses a spiral right at me and I catch it, flipping my brother off.

"Cal!" my mother scolds from the porch.

Devin and Sean laugh at me for getting caught.

"Rae, you gonna play?" Devin calls to her.

"I'm all set," Rae says, sitting next to my mother and her sisters on the porch with Henley curled up at her feet. Her mother and Liam must've left while I was in the office.

She refuses to make eye contact when I look at her. I hate it when she's pissed at me.

"Hey, do you want to earn back some of that money you wasted changing your flights for a girl?" Zac asks when we stop for a water break. "You're never going to afford that custom drum kit for Rae if you keep spending the money you've saved for it."

I look to the porch where Rae continues to glower at me with her arms crossed.

"I'm heading back tomorrow," I tell him. "But I'll be here for spring break."

"Well, if you change your mind, I could use your help in the garage. Custom orders have been picking up. I'll be away on a hiking trip next weekend, but I plan to be around other than that. You can bring the girl with you if you want."

"Wouldn't that be spending even more money to fly the two of us out here?" I counter.

"Well, I want to see this girl for myself," he admits. "I've never seen you like this before."

"Like what?" I ask uncomfortably.

"Hey! Are you playing? Or are you still crying over the girl who dumped you?" Devin calls to us. Zac looks to me and chuckles.

I check to see that Mom's not looking before flipping him off again. Nothing's sacred in this family.

The game ended up being a good distraction. When I climb the porch steps after the guys, I'm sweaty and tired.

I collapse on the rocking chair vacated by my mother moments before. Rae's still sitting there with her arms wrapped around her legs. I can't take her being upset with me.

"Still mad at me?" I ask her.

"No," she says quietly. "I still think you're being stupid, but I'm not mad at you."

After a moment of rocking in silence, she asks, "Can I ask you something? And you can't give me some lame answer."

"Okay."

"Why'd you really go to Crenshaw? You were all set to go to UCLA. It was even listed on the college board in the office. What made you change your mind?"

I take in the view of the tall evergreens surrounding the property, continuing to rock.

"I don't really have a great answer. I accepted on an impulse. No other reason than that. But Richelle's why I applied in the first place," I confess.

"Uh...what?"

What I'm about to tell her isn't going to make sense, but she asked, so I'll tell her the truth.

"Hey," I say, answering the phone.

"Hi," Richelle replies. "What are you doing?"

"Nothing. Just watching basketball." I lean back on my pillow with my arm behind my head. "What are you doing?"

"Watching paint dry."

"Seriously?"

"On my toes." I can hear the smile in her voice.

"Funny."

"How were the campuses you visited?"

"Fine. Just like every other campus." I pick up the Nerf basketball and start tossing it in the air.

"Still don't know where you want to go? This is our junior year. We're supposed to have some idea what we want to do with the rest of our lives," Richelle says mockingly.

"Yeah, right. And I have so much life experience. How am I supposed to make a decision like that? It really doesn't matter where I go. What about you? Have you decided?"

Richelle is quiet for a minute. "Going to any college sounds good to me. Except Harvard."

I laugh. "Do you still talk to Nicole?" We haven't mentioned Nicole in a long time. It's hard, knowing Richelle's been able to stay friends with her, while she treats Rae and me like we don't exist.

"Yeah. She had a ballet recital in San Francisco last weekend."

"Really? I didn't know she still danced."

"You would if you talked to her."

Now I wish I hadn't brought her up.

"I know. I promised to let it go," she says when I stay quiet. "I just hate that you're not friends anymore."

"Whatever," I reply. I'm not going to admit that I miss Nicole. Not when she hasn't even looked at me in three years. I'm not about to beg her to be friends with me again.

"Let's pick a college, and we'll go there together," Richelle says, pulling me out of my angry thoughts. "Pick any college. And if we both get in, and don't have a better option, then that's where we'll accept."

I laugh. "Why not? Where are you thinking?"

"Um . . . what teams are playing right now?"

I look up at the TV on top of my dresser. "Memphis and Crenshaw."

"Where's Crenshaw?"

"New York. A little north of Ithaca and Cornell, I think."

"Sounds good to me." She laughs. "Out in the middle of nowhere. I love it."

"You're really going to apply?"

"I promise."

"All right. Let's do it." I know this is never going to happen. We'll end up somewhere local, most likely at completely different universities. But there's something about the randomness of it, doing something I never would have done, that made me agree.

"Cal, you won't even send in an application."

As soon as she challenges me, I'm committed to this ridiculous pact. And it's . . . liberating to do something for no other reason than just . . . because.

"What if I do?"

She laughs. "Then I guess I'll see you at Crenshaw."

"But Richelle didn't go to Crenshaw," Rae says, confused.

"I know. When I accepted, I was hoping she'd be there," I reply. "I'm not sure where she ended up. She stopped talking to me not long after that."

"You never told me what you did to make her stop talking to you."

I shrug.

"Did you ask her? Or did you just let her walk away, like you always do?"

"I *did* try, Rae. But she never responded to anything I sent."

I called Richelle and sent her texts and e-mails for weeks. She never responded, not once. And then I got too angry to keep trying. It pissed me off that she just blew me off like that, for no reason… at least not one that I understood.

"You had to have done *something*."

"Then I have no idea what it was. Did *you* ever hear from her?"

"We communicated through you, remember? We were friends, but it wasn't like the two of you. She was fricken in love with you even when we were little kids."

"No, she wasn't," I scoff.

"Are you serious?" Rae counters, sitting up to gawk at me. "*Yes*, she was. How could you not know?"

"Umm…the letter made it pretty clear she wasn't," I countered, still feeling the burn of rejection, even after all this time.

"What letter?"

"The one she had Nicole give me after she moved, breaking up with me," I explain. It was bad enough not knowing she was moving until after she already left, but then to have her break up with me in a stupid letter was even worse. I have no idea why I kept it.

"Oh. *That* letter. You changed after she left, you know," Rae says, recalling the worst summer of my life.

"We don't need to talk about it."

"We never did then either," Rae says. "You just shut down and refused to talk to anyone for, like, a week."

"Seriously. Let's not go there, Rae," I reply. I know we were just in middle school, but I lost my girlfriend and best friend that day. It took a while to recover . . . or maybe I never did.

"Whatever she said in the letter couldn't have been that bad. I mean, you became friends again," Rae continues, ignoring me.

"We should have just stayed friends," I mumble, resting my head on the back of the rocking chair. "It wasn't the same after. We never even saw each other again. So I'm pretty sure she *wasn't* in love with me."

"Trust me, she was. She probably just knew it would never work. I mean, a long-distance relationship when you're thirteen is pretty pointless." Rae sighs and hugs her knees to her chest. "You have no clue how girls think."

"I'm not going to argue with you on that," I admit.

We don't say anything for a minute, silently rocking. Then Rae's mouth rounds as if she's been struck by a sudden epiphany. "You said something to her about a girl, didn't you?"

"When?" I'm trying to follow her girl-speak but can't.

"When she stopped talking to you. You told her about some girl. I know it."

I try to think back. It seems so long ago now.

"Oh," I breathe.

"What?"

"Lily. I told her about Lily," I say, recalling how quiet she was after I confessed what a disaster my first time was.

"You're such an idiot," Rae says, shaking her head. "You don't tell the girl who's in love with you about losing your virginity to *another* girl!"

"She was one of my *best friends*! I told *you*," I reply.

Rae rolls her eyes. "You're so clueless. No wonder you can't stay in a relationship longer than a month."

"You *really* think Lily's the reason she stopped talking to me?" I ask, still skeptical.

"Definitely." Rae lets out a quick laugh. "You should try calling her. It's not too late, you know. And if she stayed friends with Nicole, she might know what happened to her."

"I'm not sure she'll talk to me now. It's been, like, three years."

"What do you have to lose?"

She has a point. I already lost her once. What's the worst that can happen? "I'll call her later, if I can get a signal out here."

Reception in the middle of the Oregon woods is sketchy. There isn't a need for a cell tower for the hundred or so recluses who prefer nature to civilization, my uncle included.

I still have Richelle's cell phone number programmed in my phone. So I find the spot where it flashes two bars and try to call her.

"Hey. This is Richelle. I'm not around right now. So leave a message and I'll call you back if I want to talk to you."

The sound of her voice brings back an onslaught of memories. I've missed her, and it took hearing her voice again to realize just how much.

"Uh, hey, Richelle. It's Cal. I know it's been a while. And I'm sorry I haven't called. Was wondering how you are and where you ended up going to college. I'm at Crenshaw. Bet you didn't expect that, did you? Anyway, you have my number. Hope you'll call me back."

NICOLE

September—Freshman Year of High School

"How's high school?" Richelle asks when I enter her room.

"Stupid," I mumble, sitting on the beanbag chair in the corner. "It's all about what you wear. Who you talk to. Who likes you. It's stupid."

Richelle laughs. "It can't be *that* bad."

"I don't even want to talk to anyone. It's exhausting," I say with a groan. "Besides, Ashley, Vi and Heather talk more than enough, so I doubt anyone would ever notice if I didn't."

"You never used to talk before anyway." Then her brown eyes light up. "You can be the mysterious hot girl who never speaks." Richelle says it in a seductive voice, grinning.

I know she's trying to make me feel better. But I really do hate high school. There's so much . . . judgment.

"Who cares," she throws out there when I try to smile but fail. "Don't talk. Watch. You'll become the most popular girl in school without ever saying a word."

"Seriously?" I have to smile at that one.

"People are stupid," she notes matter-of-factly. "Example. Look who you're forcing yourself to hang out with. Those girls don't have a brain cell between them."

I laugh, and she smiles in return.

"You have no idea," I say, still smiling. "I honestly have to tune them out most of the time and just nod my head so they think I'm paying attention."

"I wish you were brave enough to dump them. I know you don't want to upset your parents, but those girls are..." Richelle huffs in exasperation. We've gone over this before, many times.

She continues. "As I was saying, people are dumb and superficial. You are those girls' beacon to anything with a penis."

"Richelle!" I gawk.

"You know what I mean. You're gorgeous. Guys flock to you, which means guys flock to them. They win by default."

"That's so sad when you say it like that." I shake my head, cringing.

Richelle and I don't really talk about it, but she knows I don't see myself like everyone else does. I'm a package, wrapped up nice and neat by my parents. Filled with expectations of perfection—from my hair, to my teeth, to my perfectly pressed clothes. There is nothing real about the person I present to the world, and so I don't see anything but a mirage when I look in the mirror. The way I look is as fake as I feel.

No one has any idea who I am under the perfect bow tied in my hair. Except Richelle.

"I wish I could be there to watch you silently rule the school."

"I wish you were there too," I sigh. "You're the only real friend I have."

"Same here." Richelle grins.

"So, we'll have to get through high school together, even if we're apart," I declare.

Richelle is quiet. She looks down at her hands.

"Don't do that," I tell her. "It'll be fine. You have to believe that eventually you'll come back to Renfield. Besides, I already started our list for after graduation."

"You did?" she asks, perking up. "What's the first thing on it?"

"Spending the summer backpacking through Europe."

"Your parents will *never* let you," Richelle says with a laugh.

"Actually, Harvard encourages students to spend their first year abroad, to experience the world. They'll think it's a great idea, trust me."

"Then let's spend a whole year doing it, instead of just the summer. We'll travel around the world. When else will we be able to take an entire year off?"

"True. I'll change it." I take the lined yellow paper out of my purse and cross out "for the summer" and add "for a year."

"Let me see it," Richelle requests, holding out her hand.

I stand up and join her on her bed, handing her the paper.

Richelle reads off, "Travel around the world for a year. Take a hot air balloon ride. Help someone who doesn't want to be helped." She looks at me and smiles. "I like that." She pauses, then says, "Ooh. Then let's do this."

She takes the pen and writes, "Help kids remember they're kids even when their lives suck."

This squeezes my heart…in a good way.

She starts reading out loud again. "Fall in love." Then she writes "with Cal" in parentheses. And adds, "Lose virginity to Cal."

"Richelle! This is a list we're supposed to do *together*!"

"I'll put his name in parentheses here too. You can lose your virginity and fall in love with whoever you want."

"Yeah, that's never going to happen." The idea of *liking* a guy, forget about falling in love with one, seems impossible. Most of the guys I know drive me crazy…except Cal. Although I don't talk to him anymore. Besides, I could never do that to Richelle—she's my best friend. I even promised her years ago that I wouldn't.

"Let me see." I hold out my hand to take the list back. "Roll down a hill? Really?"

"When was the last time you rolled down a hill?" she challenges.

"Never," I say quietly.

"Exactly."

I write, "Relive the happiest day of your life."

"What day is that?" Richelle asks.

I smile. "I don't know just yet."

SIXTEEN

I collapse onto the broken-in leather sofa at Bean Buzz, exhausted and defeated. I spent the entire day driving around Crenshaw in search of Nyelle. But I couldn't find her.

I checked every possible place that I could think of: the hotel, the homeless shelter, Elaine's, the hospital, the medical office, Starlight, and back here again. I drove down random streets in hopes of finding her walking. I called her. I texted her. I did everything except scream her name—although I did consider it. She's gone, and I have no idea what to do now.

"Bad day?"

A cute girl wearing a low-cut sweater is sitting next to me with a book in her lap.

"Very," I answer, sinking farther into the couch. My body feels like it's about to collapse in on itself.

"I'd be happy to buy you something stronger than coffee if you want to leave here," she offers sympathetically.

I smile politely. "Thanks, but—" I grunt when someone pounces on me, landing on my lap. I'm paralyzed when I find Nyelle straddling me.

Before I can react, she says, "I take it back. I don't want you dating anyone." She wraps her arms around my neck and kisses me in front of everyone. I'm still trying to catch my breath when she pulls away. "Okay?"

She's back. The carefree girl I met in this coffee shop. I can torture myself wondering where she's been, or trying to figure out what happened to Nicole. But right now, I don't care. Nyelle's sitting on my lap, smiling down at me, and that's all that matters.

"Hi. How was your Christmas?" she asks happily. There's not a hint of the distress in her voice or sadness in her eyes that have been haunting me since I let her walk out.

The girl with the revealing sweater is gawking at us. Actually, just about everyone is staring. I should be used to being stared at in this place by now—I'm convinced I'm a legend at this point.

Someone clears her throat.

We look up. Mel is standing next to us with her hands on her hips. "I know you two are still going through your honeymoon phase and all, but this is a family establishment."

Nyelle smiles at her. "That's okay. We were just leaving."

She stands and takes my hand.

"Uh... sorry, Mel."

Nyelle yanks me from the couch and leads me out the door. When we're outside in the cold, she turns around and throws her arms around my neck again. My brain is hesitant to accept that she's really here, standing in front of me. And... is genuinely excited to see me.

I pull her in for a hug, burying my face in her hair. "You have no idea how happy I am right now."

"You thought I left, didn't you?" She squeezes me back.

"Yeah," I say with a heavy sigh. "I did. I'm sorry I didn't go after you when you walked out. I should have. I just..."

"It's okay," she says, peering up at me. "I'm still here." Her eyes connect with mine. "We don't have to talk about it."

And so we won't. The last thing I want is for her to walk away again. Instead, I respond by leaning down and kissing her warm lips. She runs her fingers through my hair, pressing into me. The kiss picks up pace, along with my pulse.

She murmurs, "Let's go back to your place," with her lips still touching mine. I think I answer, but it might have come out as a low groan.

"Excuse me." We turn our heads. Mel is standing on the steps with her arms crossed, glaring at us. "Seriously?"

"Uh . . . yeah. We're *really* leaving," I utter, my face flushed. I take Nyelle's hand and walk to the truck.

Nyelle's bags are already in the front seat when we get in. I smile, knowing she stashed them here when she realized the truck was unlocked. There's still a part of me that believes I'm dreaming all of this.

Especially when we enter my apartment and she goes straight to my bedroom, dropping her jacket on the couch and pulling her shirt over her head. This better *not* be a dream.

When I enter the bedroom, her boots are off and she's unbuttoning her jeans.

I drop my jacket on the desk chair.

"Are you sure about this?" I ask, unable to take my eyes off the skin she's just exposed.

She bites her lip and nods. Lowering her jeans and peeling off her socks, she lies back on my bed. I'm watching her eyes, waiting for any hint that she's messing with me. Which would be cruel, especially when I glance down the length of her—it would be *very* cruel.

I grab my T-shirt from behind my neck and pull it off, tossing it on the floor. I refuse to look away, fearing that if I do, even for a second, I'll wake up. I've had this dream before.

"Wow." She raises her eyebrows. "I wasn't expecting to see that under there."

I freeze. I don't even have my pants off yet. Then I realize she's talking about my chest. And I don't know how to respond. What do I say? Thanks? I decide not to say anything, and lean over her on the bed as she glides her hands along my skin, rousing an eruption of goose bumps. I kiss her softly, holding myself over her.

"Just tell me what I should do," she murmurs into my mouth. I'm not expecting her to be so forward. But there's something about the way she says it that makes me stop.

I pull back and look down at her. "What do you mean?"

"Just... let me know how to do this." Her blue eyes search mine with a hint of nervousness.

"Wait." I stand back up. "Nyelle, is this your first time?" But it can't be. There's messed up, but this is beyond that.

"Well, yeah," she answers, propped up on her elbow. "That's okay, right?"

I nod, trying to process this. "But..." I'm about to ask her about Kyle. At the last second, I stop myself. "You dated... for a long time."

"I know," she responds, sitting up.

"Then, how are you still a virgin?"

"I never wanted anyone to touch me," she responds bluntly. "But I trust you. I've always trusted you."

Oh shit. Those words again. "I trust you." They're words weighted with expectation. Damn, I really hate those words right now. And on top of that, what I said in the frosting tree about everyone's first time sucking is coming back to kick me in the ass. No pressure or anything.

I pick up her clothes and hand them to her.

"What?" she asks, taking them from me. "You don't want to have sex with me?"

"Oh, I definitely want to have sex with you," I assure her, pulling my shirt back on. "But now I need to be the exception."

"What does that mean?" she asks, holding her clothes on her lap, not moving.

"Do me a favor? Get dressed in the bathroom and wait until I come get you. Okay?"

She nods slowly, still confused. When she stands up, I gently grasp her arms and place a soft kiss on her lips.

"I need a minute."

"Okay," she says quietly before walking out of the bedroom.

I shut the door behind her and close my eyes, running a hand through my hair. Shit. I take a quick breath and then go to my closet. There's a box in here somewhere filled with... Here it is. Candles. I spread the votives around the room and light them. Fold back the covers of the bed. Plug in my iPhone. Select a decent playlist. And shut off the lights.

I stand back and check out the room. Much better.

Before I leave, I take a condom out of my dresser drawer and set it on the table next to the bed. I'm usually not so obvious about it. I like to make it seem like it appears out of nowhere. But there's going to be a lot of pressure as it is, and I don't want to be searching for it when the time comes.

Last minute, I decide to take off my boots and socks. They're always the worst mood killer. There's no subtle way of removing them. When I step out of the room, the shower turns off. Wasn't expecting that. I grin, already anticipating the scent of her clean skin.

I still can't believe Kyle and Nicole never had sex. I'm not complaining. But I could have sworn...

RAE: WHERE ARE YOU?

ME: DOWNSTAIRS

RAE: AT FRONT DOOR. COME GET ME.

"Rae's here," I tell Brady and Craig, who are playing some sort of drinking game with darts. "I'm going upstairs to get her. I'll be right back."

"Okay," they respond in unison without looking at me.

I cut through the crowd and up the steps. No one's upstairs, since the party's in the basement and outside. I have no idea why Rae needs an escort, but whatever.

"Where is she now?" Vi huffs. "I'm not waiting around here forever."

I pause before I turn the corner.

"She's upstairs with Kyle. God, they've spent the entire summer together. You'd think they could keep their hands off each other for one party," Heather adds in that tone that drives me crazy. So much drama out of one person.

"I wouldn't be able to keep my hands off of him either," Ashley says with a seductive lilt in her voice.

"Ashley!" Heather giggles.

I almost bump into them when they come around the corner. They don't acknowledge me directly, but sigh dramatically, like I'm in their way.

When I reach the front door, Rae isn't there. Actually, no one's around.

I pull out my phone.

ME: AT FRONT DOOR. WHERE ARE YOU?

RAE: BATHROOM. WAIT FOR ME.

I take a seat on the stairs leading to the second floor and wait. I hear a door click open at the top of the stairs and stand, expecting Rae.

"I just don't want to do it here, okay?" Nicole says. "We're at a party, and that's not exactly what I had in mind."

"Do you ever have me in mind?" Kyle demands.

"Hey, you're getting exactly what you want out of this," Nicole snaps back.

"Okay. Listen, I'm sorry," Kyle says, "but I've wanted you for so long, and you're about to go to college—"

The door clicks shut again, thankfully. The last thing I need to hear is Kyle telling Nicole how much she means to him.

"Ready?" Rae asks, appearing in front of me.

"Let's go," I reply, following her downstairs.

Looking back, I guess I didn't hear that conversation right at all.

The bathroom door opens and Nyelle steps out, pulling her dry hair out of an elastic and letting it fall over her shoulders. She put her clothes back on, which makes me happy. I'd rather be the one to take them off.

"I'm ready," she declares, like she's about to run out onto the basketball court.

"Okay. No rush. No pressure. We're going to take this—"

She jumps up on me, wrapping her legs around my waist. I stumble back a step and tuck my arms under her butt to hold her up. A sexy smile appears on her face. She leans in until her lips brush against mine, teasing. Just the feel of her breath against my skin ignites me. Her mouth moves with mine, slowly.

Nyelle kisses along my jaw and down my neck as I carry her into the bedroom. I set her on her feet, cupping her face to kiss her again, unable to get enough of her. Her hands slide under my shirt, and I help her pull it over my head. I shiver when her fingers dance along my skin, and her mouth finds my chest.

I ease her shirt off, and she reaches for the buttons of my jeans. I'm undoing her zipper as I attempt to kick my jeans off, which is taking way too much effort. We're both standing here in our underwear, staring at each other.

I search her eyes again for any sign of hesitation. I really could spend the night looking into these eyes. She stands up on her tiptoes and whispers, "I want this. I promise."

That's all I need, and I'm sliding my hands along her waist and kissing her with more passion and want than I've ever felt in my entire life. I swear I'm on fire. Every inch of me.

Nyelle slowly lowers onto her back, and I'm right there, over her, kissing her, touching her. Her breath is heavy as I trail my hands down her skin, taking my time—getting to know all of her. I accept that there's not much I can do about the sex itself being uncomfortable for her, but I can make what happens before it worth remembering. And from the sounds escaping her, I believe I do…

I hold myself above her, taking in the girl below me. My heart hurts, she's so beautiful. And she trusts me…

Nyelle is lying quietly against my chest, and I'm tense, waiting for some kind of reaction. I had a hard time deciphering her quick breaths and closed eyes while it was happening. I had no idea what was going on in her head. Still don't.

"Uh..." I finally say. "How are you?"

There's a pause. I remain still, practically holding my breath.

"Different."

"Is that... good or bad?" I ask quickly.

She laughs lightly, drawing circles on my chest. "Just, different."

Nyelle lifts her head and grins at me. Then she leans in and kisses the tip of my nose. I still haven't moved, fearing I just became another horrible first-time statistic.

"Cal, it was our first time," she says—not helping. "I don't have anything to compare it to."

"Oh," I reply, trying to relax.

"So we'll have to do it again," she says lightly, pressing her lips to my shoulder. I grab her waist to flip her onto her back.

"Not today," she states adamantly. "I couldn't do it again today. But we will... again."

"All right. That's good. Whenever... whenever you're ready," I reply, faltering over my words in relief. I pull her to me and kiss the top of her head. "I'm going to go to the bathroom. Okay?"

"Okay," Nyelle says. I lean down and kiss her again before reaching for my boxer briefs.

When I return, Nyelle's wearing one of my T-shirts, which hangs to her thighs. She's pulling a fitted sheet over the last corner of the bed. I throw on a pair of shorts from my dresser before helping her tuck in the sheet and tossing the comforter and pillows on top.

She steps up on the bed and walks across it to where I'm standing, bends down with her hands on my shoulders, and gives me a quick kiss. I slide my hands along her bare thighs, and before I can stop myself, she's toppled over onto her back, and I'm following up her small kiss with a much deeper one of my own.

"Cal," she breathes. I moan in response. "We can't."

I collapse on the bed next to her. "Right. Sorry."

"Oh!" She jumps up, abandoning me. "You're going to love this."

I follow her into the living room. She's crouched in front of her bag, digging around. I sit on the couch and wait, turning on the TV. I hear plastic rustling and a bag of chips opening. I'm a little nervous because I know what's coming.

"Close your eyes," she demands.

"Nyelle, is this one of your chip experiments?"

"This one's going to be good," she promises. "But close your eyes so you get the entire experience. No prejudging."

I close my eyes. Then I feel her sit on my lap. So far, I'm liking this experience.

"Open up," she instructs.

I do. Then there's a marshmallow in my mouth. I bite. And...

"That's disgusting," I complain after swallowing it down. "Was that a Cool Ranch Dorito in the middle?"

"I think it's so good," she says, biting down on one.

"You're the strangest girl I've ever met."

"Gud," she says, kissing me on the cheek with her mouth full of marshmallow.

I open my eyes the next morning and look right into Nyelle's bright blue ones. We're both curled up on our sides, facing each other. Her hands are tucked under her pillow.

"Hi," I say, trying not to breathe too heavily.

She smiles lightly.

"You okay?" I ask when she continues to just lie there, staring at me.

She nods.

"Been awake long?"

Nyelle makes a twisted face.

"Did you sleep at all?"

She reluctantly shakes her head, her eyes darting around.

"Are you sure you're okay?"

She presents a small smile and nods. But there's a strange tension in her smile.

"You're not going to talk to me until you brush your teeth, are you?"

She smiles wider, her lips still pressed together, and shakes her head.

"Okay. Well, I'm going to take a shower now, if that's all right, and then the bathroom's all yours."

She nods, but she still doesn't move—even when I get out of the bed. She remains on her side, staring straight ahead. I glance back at her from the doorway. Something doesn't feel right.

When I get out of the shower, I return to my bedroom. I'm about to open the door, but I stop with my hand gripping the handle. Listening. I swear I hear...

She's talking to herself. I risk opening it a crack to find Nyelle pacing the floor next to my desk, her hands stretching and clenching by her sides, her head down. She's going off on one of her incoherent rants. I can't make out everything she's saying, but she's definitely worked up. "What do I do now?" she mutters. I think I hear her say, "This wasn't supposed to happen." I can only assume it's about me and what we did last night. And now I feel like shit.

I'm about to close the door when she throws herself on the bed and screams into a pillow. I can't move. A chill rushes through my body.

"I'm going to go find the bathroom," I tell Rae and the guys, standing up from the chair I've claimed for the duration of the party. I'm not sure why we even go to these things. We just sit in the corner and keep to ourselves. Well…Rae and I do. Brady and Craig wander off every so often, using us as home base when they strike out with whichever girls they've hit on.

I find the bathroom on the first floor easily, since there's a line of girls waiting to use it.

"Logan, you can use the bathroom in my room if you want," Reggie tells me so no one else overhears. "It's upstairs. Just don't tell anyone I let you. No one's allowed up there."

"Thanks," I say, grateful he's one of the few guys on the basketball team who talks to me off the court.

"Oh. If you see anyone up there, kick them out for me?"

"Sure," I respond, weaving my way to the front of the house. There's a dog gate at the top of the stairs, blocking the landing, with an Off Limits *sign taped to it. I release the handle so it swings open and close it behind me.*

Reggie's door is obvious, decorated with Keep Out *and* Will Shoot on Sight. *Just as I'm about to open the door, I hear someone talking. Great. I really didn't want to find anyone up here.*

I'm about to turn around and wait in the hour-long line downstairs when I hear what sounds like…screaming, but muffled. I freeze. Now I can't walk away without checking to see if everything's okay. I slowly open the door enough to peek in. It's dark, but Reggie's aquarium casts enough light to make out the silhouette of a person . . . a girl, sitting on the edge of his bed with a pillow on her lap. Alone.

She bends over and thrusts her face into the pillow and screams. It's such a painful sound, even muted, it sends a cold chill down my spine. I watch as she replaces the pillow and stands, fixes her hair, and runs her shaking hands along the front of her skirt. It's Nicole.

I close the door and duck into Reggie's sister's room until I hear her leave.

"That was fast," Rae comments when I return. "Did you just go outside?"

I shake my head, searching the crowd for Nicole Bentley. I find her across the room, surrounded by the elites. She smiles at something someone says, appearing composed like she usually does. But just for a moment, our eyes connect, and her brows dip for an instant. Or maybe I imagined it.

Kyle comes up beside her and wraps his arm around her, and she startles when he kisses her cheek, but she doesn't say anything. I watch for just a few seconds longer.

"She never . . . talks," I say quietly.

"Who?" Rae demands. "Who are you staring at?"

"No one," I answer, sitting back in the chair.

Nyelle looks up and inhales quickly, finding me motionless in the doorway. I don't know what to say. Her eyes flicker, trying to read mine from across the room.

She stands and walks toward me. I release the handle, pushing the door open. She places a hand on my chest, glancing up at me sorrowfully before walking past me to the bathroom. My insides feel like they've been fed through the shredder.

I sit on the bed and collapse forward with my elbows on my knees. I can hear the shower turn on in the bathroom. I screwed up. She wasn't ready. And now...she regrets it. Or more like, she regrets me.

I know I should say something to her when she comes back in the room. The awkwardness is going to kill me if I don't. But where would I even start? The thought of apologizing makes me break out in a cold sweat. Because I'm not sorry. I've slept with girls and had it end soon after. Not everyone's compatible. I get that. But this, I don't regret. Not a single second of it.

I wish she didn't either.

I rest my head in my hands and search for whatever it is I need to say.

"You weren't supposed to see that."

I sit up. Nyelle is standing within the doorframe in just a tank top and underwear. Her wet hair is slicked back, and her skin is still damp. I think she's trying to kill me.

"Sometimes I just need to let things out," she explains, moving slowly in my direction. "I've never been very good at it. I let it build until I feel like I might explode. So...I do. It's how I cope."

She sits next to me on the bed, resting her head on my shoulder.

"You weren't supposed to see it, though," she sighs. "I'm sure I looked crazy."

My mind is racing, trying to put this all into perspective.

"Was it me?" I ask quietly. I swear I can feel my heart beating in my throat.

"Is what you? The reason I lost it?" She tilts her head up at me, scrunching her brows together. "Oh no, Cal. No. It wasn't you at all."

A realization flashes across her face. She crawls over me and straddles my legs. "I'm sorry I was being weird this morning." I rest my hands on her thighs as she drapes her arms over my shoulders. "Last night was a big deal. You know that."

I nod.

"Well…it hit me that I'm leaving in two weeks. And then I couldn't sleep, so…I watched you sleep. Which only made things worse because…I don't want to leave you…" She slumps forward and hugs me. I run my hands up her back. "But I have to."

"Why?" I ask, my face pressed against her neck.

"I don't belong here, Cal. You know that," she answers quietly.

"But you don't want to leave, and I don't want you to go. So, it's easy. Stay."

She sits back on my legs with a laugh. "I wish. But I can't."

"I don't understand. There's a lot I don't understand about you," I say, caressing her cheek, silently begging her to tell me. "Help me understand." I know this is a risk. But I feel like I've been fighting to keep her every day since I first saw her here, and now that I have her, I'm not willing to give her up that easy.

"You can tell me anything."

"I'm sorry" is all that she says. "I'm so sorry."

Then Nyelle pushes my shoulders, forcing me onto my back. She places a hand on either side of my head and holds herself over me. "Do you think we could…you know," she says with a seductive grin.

My eyes widen. "Really?"

"You look adorable when you're sleeping, by the way," she murmurs, lowering on top of me, kissing my neck up to that spot beneath my ear. "So I'm here…with you…for two weeks." Then her lips find mine, and in that moment, nothing else matters.

NICOLE

October—Sophomore Year of High School

"My mom should be here in a few to pick us up. Thanks for coming with me," Richelle says, stuffing her books in her messenger bag. "I know this is not exactly how you want to spend your weekend."

"Of course it is. Besides, I had an assignment I needed to get done too," I say, zipping my backpack. Leaning back in the plastic chairs, we wait for Richelle's mom to pick us up before I have to take the train back to Renfield.

"You never told me how the piano performance thing went the other night," Richelle prompts.

"It was okay," I answer. "My dad liked it, so I guess that's all that matters."

"Sadly," Richelle replies. I avoid her eyes, knowing how she feels about him and his need for perfection. "Does Rae still play the drums?"

"Yeah. I hear her in her garage every night. How come you don't talk to her like you do to Cal?"

Richelle lets out a quick burst of laughter. "Rae and I never really *talked*."

"True," I say, remembering them pretty much always arguing about something.

"But it'll be like it always was when we move back."

My heart skips a beat. "Really?"

Richelle shrugs. "My parents say it's a possibility. Depends on how everything goes."

I close my eyes, wanting nothing more than to have her back in Renfield. It'll mean everything will finally be better.

"We can start our own band. For real this time," Richelle says, balancing her chair on two legs. "You can play the keyboard. I'll sing. Rae will be on the drums, of course. And Cal will play the guitar. Do you know if he's any good? I hear him messing with it sometimes when we talk, but I can't tell if he's—"

She stops, knowing there's no way I can answer that.

"Don't say it," I say sternly, having heard it too many times. "I made a promise. And that's more important than being friends with them."

"But *not* being friends with them was never part of that promise," Richelle argues, the same point she makes every time. It doesn't matter. I know if I remained friends with them, I'd end up breaking the promise. And I can't do that. No matter how much I miss them.

My silence makes Richelle roll her eyes. She recognizes the conversation is over... again.

"Oh! Listen to this," Richelle says, crashing her chair back on the linoleum. She pulls her earbuds out of her sweatshirt pocket and plugs them into her phone. She hands me one of the earpieces. "I heard this song and thought Rae could kill it on the drums. We could totally play it."

I sigh, knowing she's not going to stop talking about them like I wish she would. I stick the earbud in my ear to listen. Richelle runs her finger along her screen and selects the song. It starts with a bass guitar, and within a few seconds, the beat kicks in and Richelle starts bobbing her head with her eyes closed.

I can't help but nod in time too. At the anthem-like chorus, Richelle suddenly stands up and thrusts her fist in the air. I laugh at her unexpected move. She's starting to draw attention from other people in the room, but she doesn't seem to care.

The next time the chorus comes on, she starts singing. My mouth opens, releasing a shocked laugh. She takes my hand, demanding I stand, and spins me around. The song ends with the squeal of a guitar chord. And Richelle collapses onto the chair, winded. My face is bright red, because everyone is staring at us.

"Excuse me," a stout woman says to us. I think she's in charge or something. "That's not exactly appropriate—"

"Are you serious?" Richelle challenges her. "Just trying to have a little fun."

A mother sitting on the other side of the room with her son shakes her head in disapproval. The boy grins, thinking it's as funny as I do. The woman hovering over us appears shocked with enlarged eyes.

"At least be respectful of other people and keep it down." She turns and storms away, obviously frazzled.

Richelle looks to me and laughs. "I can't believe people. They need to relax. And live a little!" she suddenly hollers, making the mother's mouth drop in offense. The boy giggles. "Right?"

"Very true," I say, giggling too. "That's what life *should* be about. Having fun."

"Finally!" she exclaims, like she's made a breakthrough. "Just be happy, Nicole. No matter what. Be happy."

SEVENTEEN

"What would you like to do tonight for New Year's?" I ask Nyelle, pouring cereal into a bowl.

"You want to make a big deal out of it?" Nyelle asks, sitting on the arm of the sofa.

I lean against the counter with the bowl in my hand. "Not a *big* deal, but I feel like we should do *something*."

Nyelle scans the ceiling, thinking about it. "Okay. We'll do something."

"Are you going to tell me what it is? Because the thought of showing up unprepared to whatever you come up with scares the hell out of me. And for the record, I'm wearing my own clothes."

Nyelle laughs. "Fine. I'll put away that sequined outfit I had picked out for you."

"You're hilarious, but I have a feeling that this sequined thing exists."

Nyelle grins, then pulls her knees up under her chin. I have no idea how she's balancing on the end of the couch like that, but she looks adorable. I continue to eat my cereal while her mind goes to work.

"I've got it," she declares when I'm rinsing out the bowl. "Let's go back to Camp Sunshine."

"I'm not ice diving," I tell her.

She makes a face. "No. We'll build a fire. Make s'mores. And go tubing on the frozen lake."

"Tubing?"

"You know. We'll buy a couple of those inflatable doughnut sleds and slide across the ice."

I pause, considering it. Doesn't sound *that* crazy. "Okay. I'm in."

Nyelle holds her inflatable sled in front of her, her cheeks red, as we both stare at the frozen lake. "Ready?" I nod. "Set. Go!"

We run along the snow toward the lake's edge. I hesitate for just a step before throwing my body out onto the ice on top of the tube. That one moment of sanity gives her the edge she needs to slide out in front of me, stopping about five feet ahead on the frozen lake—that a little more than a month ago we were sinking in.

"I won!" she declares, thrusting her arms into the air.

"Because I suddenly had a clear image of landing face-first on the ice," I claim in defense. "There was blood. And a broken nose. It wasn't pretty."

She just shakes her head at me.

"Try pushing me," Nyelle requests, turning over to sit on the doughnut.

I carefully stand on the ice. With the thin layer of snow blowing across it, it's not too slick. But I'm not about to try sprinting on it either. I place my hands behind her on the tube and plant my feet as best I can before giving her a hard shove.

Nyelle yells out like she's taking off on a roller coaster, sailing across the lake. Not as fast as when she had a running start, or as fast as a roller coaster for that matter, but she still travels a decent distance.

"Now I'll push you," she says, lying on her stomach and using her feet to scoot back to me.

"You're not going to be able to push me," I say, sitting down on the tube.

"I feel bad," she says, bumping into me. "You were always the one who pushed us on the tire swing. You almost never got a turn."

I know she's slipping up again, talking about our childhood. Before I allow it to sink in too much, I lean over and kiss her. In my head I can hear Rae yelling at me for missing the opportunity to interrogate her. But it's not what I want tonight to be about. A new year is about starting again, not looking back. Right?

"Race you again?" I challenge, standing up and grabbing the rubber handle of the sled.

"Best two out of three?" she suggests. "Winner gets..."

"Anything they want," I propose.

She lifts an eyebrow. "Name it first, so I know what's at stake."

My mind is suddenly all over the place, and so are my eyes. She swats my arm. "Cal! I knew it was going to be something... naked."

"Of course it is," I say with a laugh, not even about to deny it. "If I can get anything I want, and one of those things is you naked, then that's easy. Trying to decide *how* I want you naked is the hard part."

"Fine. Naked it is. In the shower." She pauses, waiting for my reaction, which is complete stillness. "In the dark. And we actually have to wash each other, with shampoo and soap and everything."

"What?" I balk. "I better win because that sounds almost

dangerous. Besides, what's the point of showering together if I can't see you naked?"

"Well, what's yours then?" she demands, with her arms crossed.

"I'll keep with the same theme, but we take a bath together... with the lights *on*. And there's no need for washing, just—"

"Bubbles," she interjects.

I grin, liking that idea. "I can do bubbles."

"You're on." Nyelle sticks out her hand. I grin at her competitiveness, taking hold of her hand. But instead of shaking it, I pull her to me and wrap my arms around her, kissing her.

"That's not fair," she breathes. "You're trying to make me lose focus."

"I think it's a good strategy," I murmur, running my lips along her neck.

Nyelle pushes back. "Oh! Really? That's how it's going to be?" She stomps back to the snow-covered beach and takes off her scarf, followed by her jacket. When she yanks her sweater over her head, she pauses to see if she has my attention, which she definitely does. And then she slowly peels her tank top off, revealing a black lace bra and a whole lot of flesh.

I exhale slowly. "You're evil."

She smirks with her hands on her hips. "Bring it."

I smile, taking in every inch she's unveiled. I should tell her to put her clothes back on. It's about twenty degrees out here. But I'm enjoying this way too much to be practical.

"Wow, boobs make guys dumb," she says with a roll of her eyes.

"I'm not arguing," I say, still admiring the view.

"Stop staring and get over here," she demands, picking up her sled.

I shake my head, trying to regain my composure.

"First win doesn't count," I tell her when I step on land. "Best two out of three, starting now."

"Deal."

Nyelle hugs herself, shivering. "You must be freezing," I observe, tossing some wood on the fire to help warm her up.

"And do you know what will make me warm? A nice hot shower, in the dark," she gloats.

"You got lucky," I claim, shifting the logs.

"No, I had a good strategy," she boasts. "You kept tripping over yourself trying to watch me run."

"Can you blame me? And for the record, this showering in the dark thing is going to be a disaster. It still doesn't make sense to me."

Nyelle pops her head through the hole of her sweater, suddenly looking serious. She opens her mouth, then closes it. I stop messing with the fire, giving her my full attention.

"Would you still be attracted to me if you couldn't see me?"

The question comes out of nowhere. "I'm not sure how to answer that."

"Forget it." She zips up her coat and wraps the scarf around her neck. "How's the fire coming?"

"Come stand by it. It'll warm you up," I say, studying her carefully. She tries to smile, but I know there's something more to that question. I've seen the way she reacts to anyone who calls attention to her looks. Hell, she punched a guy in the face—granted, he did grab her ass, but still. I have yet to comment on how attracted I am to her. Every time the thought reaches my mouth, I silence it. For some reason it offends her, so I don't tell her.

Sitting next to each other on our tubes with blankets on our laps, we roast marshmallows on sticks we found in the woods—that I then carved into proper marshmallow spears.

Rolling my marshmallow over in the fire, I keep thinking about Nyelle's question. And wonder why the way she looks upsets her so much. She was friends with three of the most superficial girls in high school. Their whole world revolved around appearances. So why did she choose *them*?

"Cal!" Rae hollers to me as I'm walking down the sidewalk. "Where are you going?"

I wait for her to catch up. "To Nicole's. She's supposed to be back, but I haven't seen her yet."

"Where was she all summer again?"

"I don't remember," I reply. "Some ballet thing, I think."

Just as we're about to walk up the driveway, the front door opens and out come three laughing girls, all dressed up.

On either side of Nicole are Ashley Kinsley and Victoria North. I know them because their older brothers are friends with my brothers. They don't go to McDermott with us. They're in the other middle school, Canton. But the way they're dressed—short skirts, hair curled, lots of makeup—they look like they're trying to be high schoolers.

"Hey, Nicole," I say, when she doesn't see Rae and me standing behind her mom's car.

"Who are they?" Victoria asks. She inspects us with a disgusted look on her face. I push my glasses up the bridge of my nose and ignore her.

Nicole shrugs without looking at us.

"Nicole?" I call to her again, not understanding why she's being weird.

Ashley's nose scrunches like she smells something gross. "Are they your friends?"

"Not anymore," Nicole answers quietly.

She still won't look at us.

"What the hell?" Rae demands. "Nicole, are you serious?"

Nicole gets in the front seat of the car and closes the door without responding.

What's going on? Why is she acting like we don't exist? This doesn't make sense.

Rae whips around and storms off down the sidewalk. She gets to the next house and turns back. "Cal! Are you coming?"

Mrs. Bentley steps out of the house, locking the door behind her. "Hello, Cal. Did Nicole introduce you to her new friends from the ballet program she attended this summer?"

"Uh, yeah," I say. I don't know why I lie, but I know how important it is to Nicole's parents that she's polite, and despite how she's acting, I don't want to get her in trouble.

"Well, I'm taking them to the mall. I'm sure we'll see you again," she says, smiling in that weird way she does.

"Okay," I reply automatically. I turn slowly and walk toward my house. Rae is already in her garage, beating the heck out of her drums.

Nicole never spoke to us again, and I still have no idea why. I was still recovering from the letter Richelle wrote to me only months before. I couldn't hear Nicole tell me that she didn't care about me either. So I left her alone. She made it clear she had no interest in being friends anymore.

Nyelle lowers herself across my lap, making the tube shift beneath me. "Hey. What are you thinking about?" she asks, sliding her arms around my neck.

I've tried so hard to convince myself Nicole and Nyelle are two different people. But Nyelle *is* Nicole. And I can't ignore the truth forever. I open my mouth to ask all the questions I still don't have the answers to, including why she stopped talking to us all those years ago. But I can't. She's so...happy. And I don't want to be the one to extinguish that glint in her eye.

"You're beautiful" slips out instead.

Her body tenses.

"Don't hurt me," I plead, suddenly afraid of being maimed. "But I think you deserve to know, and I want to be the one to tell you. And it's not just your insanely blue eyes, or unbelievably soft mouth, or painfully perfect body." Her mouth pops open, stunned. Maybe that wasn't the best way to say it. "You're beautiful because you don't care if you are. I think I understand why you get so angry when you're judged for how you look. Hell, it's not your fault you're gorgeous. Blame genetics."

Nyelle continues to stare at me, speechless.

"But what *is* your fault is who you are underneath all that. You can hide under clothes that are too big, or not put any effort into your appearance, but *you're* beautiful regardless. And I'm glad I get to see who you really are. Not just the naked version of you, which...has changed me...forever—" Nyelle's eyes narrow. I laugh, quickly continuing before I lose momentum—or a body part. "But the caring, thoughtful, selfless, and spontaneous side of you. To watch you live is breathtaking. You live a life filled with possibilities. A life most people miss out on. So yes, Nyelle, even if I couldn't see you, I'd still be attracted to you.

"I thought you were the most beautiful girl I'd ever seen from that first day, when you stepped out of the car wearing that yellow dress. And at the risk of you punching me in the face, I still—"

There are lips on my mouth, saving me from my rambling; otherwise I may never have stopped. I'm instantly on fire and melting beneath her touch as she unzips my jacket, running her hands under my shirt, twisting her body so she's on top of me. It could be twenty below zero, and I wouldn't care. I'm taking off my jacket and my shirt and frantically stripping her out of her clothes as if our lives depend upon it.

I wrap the blanket around her bare shoulders. Billows of breath rush out of her mouth when she lowers herself onto me. There's enough heat running through me to melt the lake.

Nyelle leans down and drags her lips against my neck. She whispers in my ear, "You're the first person to ever make me feel beautiful." Then she kisses me so slowly, and so gently, it aches—in a good way. In the most amazing possible way. I don't realize there are tears on her cheeks until they've dripped onto mine.

I pull her against me, kissing her so she knows just how much I meant every word I said.

We watch the seconds tick from last year to the next, the embers from our campfire glowing in the dark. I almost expect fireworks to shoot across the sky, or to hear a hundred voices screaming and those stupid horns blowing when the clock on my phone flashes midnight. But there's only quiet. And it's perfect.

"Happy New Year," Nyelle says, kissing me. She huddles further under the two blankets covering us.

"Happy New Year," I say, wrapping my arms tighter around her. We're trying to fight it, but we're both shivering. "We're never going to do anything normal, are we? Look at us. We're celebrating the New Year naked, sitting on an inflatable tube next to a frozen lake. And I think we need to stop flirting with hypothermia."

"Shower time!" Nyelle bursts out, jumping up with the blankets still wrapped around her, bounding through the snow to the truck in bare feet.

"Holy shit, Nyelle!" I holler, sucking in frozen air, shrinking in every way possible as I scramble to find my clothes. I hear the truck start behind me. "Oh, don't worry. I'll get your clothes," I say to no one because she's already in the truck. I zip my pants and pull my shirt over my head. I don't think I've ever gotten dressed so fast in my life.

After I toss her clothes in the truck and tie the tubes down in the back, I shovel some snow on the fire. By the time I get in the truck, it's warmed up—which is a relief, because I'm officially numb. I rub my hands in front of the heater, trying to regain feeling in my fingertips.

Nyelle is curled up under the blankets with just her face sticking out, reminding me of the last time we were here—painfully frozen. We should probably never come back here again... ever.

"Sorry I left you to pick up our stuff. Just the thought of getting dressed sounded torturous."

"Oh, it was," I assure her. "Good call. But guess what? I'm not carrying you into the apartment. And I might park in the farthest spot from the door, just because."

"Cal!" She pouts. I laugh as we pull out of the camp, hopefully for the last time.

I end up parking right in front of the door, but I do make her walk in her bare feet, wrapped in blankets, naked.

"Ah!" I holler, clamping my eyes shut. "You got soap in my eye."

"Oh, sorry. You're taller than I thought."

"Please explain again how taking a shower in the pitch dark is sexy?" I complain. "I can't see you. I have soap in my eye. And I have no idea where anything is."

"But I can *feel* you," she says, rubbing a bar of soap on my chest in small circles, slowly working her way down.

"Oh!" I exclaim, suddenly getting it. "Okay. I changed my mind."

Nicole laughs with her mouth against my skin.

And yes, even in the dark, with only my sense of touch to guide me, she's still beautiful.

NICOLE

January—Sophomore Year of High School

"Happy New Year," I say, entering Richelle's room with a bouquet of helium balloons.

"Ooh, you brought a party!"

"I'm sorry you were sick for New Year's Eve. I thought balloons with fireworks on them would make you feel better."

"Don't worry," Richelle says, slowly easing herself up in bed, "I had a line of guys waiting to kiss me at midnight, but my dad scared them away."

"Their loss," I say with a quick shrug. She smiles. "How are you feeling?"

"Okay," she answers. "My mother is being a lunatic though. I swear she gets off on the whole Nightingale thing. I mean, how much liquid can a person drink?"

Despite how pale she looks, she's acting like she's feeling better. I wasn't sure if I should visit when I found out she was sick. But I'd honestly rather be here, watching her sleep, than be at home.

"Please tell me you have some hysterically horrible New Year's party story to share with me? Like... someone set off fireworks and lit the neighbor's house on fire. Or a bunch of guys streaked down the street, only to trip and fall on top of each other."

I chuckle. "So, you want me to lie?"

"You're a horrible liar. I guess I'll have to be satisfied with whatever sad story you have about sitting in a corner and watching people drink all night." Then her eyes widen. "Please tell me you actually went to a party. I might have to deny you as my friend for an entire... week, if you stayed home."

"I went to a party," I drone. "And it was horrible. Sort of." My cheeks become hot.

Richelle's mouth rounds. "Tell me everything. Now. Who is he? What does he look like? Is he a good kisser?"

The smile spreads across my face without effort. "His name is Kyle. And he's a senior."

"No way," she gasps. "Do you have a picture?"

I pull out my phone and search for him on Facebook, then hand it to her.

"He's hot! Nicole, I'm so proud of you!"

I laugh. "Nothing happened. He basically saved me from the worst kiss ever."

"You had your first kiss too?! This is seriously an epic New Year's for you. And who was the horrible kisser?"

I take back the phone and pull up Justin Murphy's picture. She checks him out and shrugs. "He's kinda cute."

"But I swear if that's what kissing's supposed to be like, I never want to do it again. I thought I was going to drown."

"That's disgusting!" she exclaims. "And no. Kissing should *never* be like that." She blushes. I know she's thinking about Cal, and I shift at the end of her bed.

"Um... so, Justin kissed me at midnight, basically because I was standing next to him," I share. "But then after, when everyone was all coupled off, Kyle and I went for a walk. He's so nice. His younger brother is a sophomore too, but he's..." I make a disgusted face. "So obnoxious."

Richelle flips back to Kyle's Facebook page. "He plays lacrosse," she notes. "Ooh! And nice beach pictures."

I bite my lip, having memorized each picture by now.

"So when are you going out?"

"Next weekend," I tell her. "We're going to dinner and then maybe a party. Not sure yet."

"I like it," she says with a grin. Richelle settles back into her pillow, suddenly looking tired.

"Do you want me to leave?" I offer.

She shakes her head. "No. Just sit with me," she requests, taking my hand. Hers is cool and damp.

"I'm not going anywhere," I promise, giving it a squeeze.

EIGHTEEN

My eyes flip open as music blares throughout the apartment. The football game I fell asleep to is still playing on mute in front of me. I turn my head when the couch jostles violently and find a half-naked girl jumping on the cushion at my feet.

I lie on my back to get a better view of Nyelle in one of my T-shirts, jumping with her hair flinging around her, singing at the top of her lungs to a song that's about . . . being naked.

I laugh when she hollers the chorus, directing the lyrics at me. Sitting up, I grip the backs of her thighs and pull her down so she's straddling me.

"I think this may be my new favorite song," I say, sweeping the hair from her neck to give me access.

"I thought you might like it," she murmurs, fisting my shirt and tilting her head to the side. "I think we should do what it says."

"I think I like that idea," I return, easing the T-shirt over her head. Smiling when there's nothing underneath but a thong. "Well, that was easy."

Nyelle lowers her mouth to mine as I run my hands along her bare back. She bunches my shirt, separating long enough to jerk it over my head, and tosses it to the floor. I inhale deeply with the touch of her soft skin against mine, holding her close as she maneuvers her legs so they're wrapped around me.

I slide us to the edge of the couch and set my feet on the floor, tasting along her neck to her shoulder, slowly working my way down. She arches her back and draws in a slow breath.

I don't care how many times we've done this now; I'll never get enough of her. The feel of her. The taste of her. The noises she makes when I find the right spot. The way my body lights up like an inferno with just the smallest touch of her.

Nyelle squeezes her thighs tighter around me with a breathy moan as my mouth covers her smooth skin. Needing better positioning, I flip her over so she's lying on the couch and prop myself above her, taking in the light reflecting in her blue eyes.

"I don't think I can let you leave me," I tell her, capturing any argument she might have with my lips pressed firmly to hers. I'm not usually so bold, but I'm a little unfiltered right now. She does that to me.

Nyelle moans when my hand slides up between her thighs. Her fingers fumble with the button on my pants.

I freeze when I hear, "Hey!"

Dropping on top of Nyelle, I try to cover her with my body. She releases a surprised grunt.

"Eric!" I exclaim, looking up at him over the arm of the couch.

"What's going on?" he asks, setting his bag down. When he finally looks at me, his eyes widen in realization. "Oh shit!" And then he starts laughing. I want to strangle him. "Sorry about that."

He walks closer and squints, "Hey, Lake Girl! Didn't see you under there."

"Eric! What the fuck!" I holler.

"Hi, Eric," she responds, her voice strained. Probably because

I'm crushing her with my weight, but there's no way I'm moving until Eric gets the hell out of here.

He looks at us and shakes his head with a heavy breath. "You didn't sleep in my room at all, did you? Not even for one night?"

"Why are you still standing here?!"

"Great," he grumbles. "Now I owe Rae twenty bucks."

"You bet on... Dude, can we talk about this later?"

"Yeah, Eric. He's kinda squishing me," Nyelle says breathily.

"Sorry," I say, kissing her forehead.

"You're right. That doesn't look very comfortable," Eric notes, tilting his head to get a better view.

"Eric!" I yell. "Just get in your room for, like, five minutes. Please!"

"Going." He picks up his duffel bag and strolls into his room at a frustrating pace.

As soon as I hear his door click shut, I push off the couch and grab my T-shirt, shoving it over Nyelle's head and trying to pull her arms through.

"Umm... Cal, I can dress myself," she says, sitting up as I pull it down over her red thong.

"Yeah, uh... I'm sorry. I just don't know if his five minutes is really five seconds," I tell her.

She laughs, standing to adjust the shirt. "I wanted to go for a walk anyway. You guys can catch up."

"Or I can kick his ass," I counter.

"You're not a fighter," she says, bending down to kiss me before entering the bedroom.

———

"Have you heard from Richelle yet?" Rae asks when I pick up the phone.

"No. But there's a chance the message didn't go through or record right with that shoddy signal at Zac's," I say, closing my laptop. "I'll try her again."

"Uh, is Nyelle with you?" Rae asks hesitantly. "She's not responding to my texts."

"She *never* responds to my texts," I reply. "But no, she went for one of her walks. Why?"

"Uh, it's nothing," Rae answers evasively. "We've just been texting about something..."

She sounds weird.

"You and Nyelle have been texting?" I question, strangely jealous, considering I haven't even spoken to Nyelle on her phone since the night she called me from the tree. And it took her being drunk to do that. "What about?"

Rae is quiet for a minute. I'm starting to get nervous. She never holds out on me.

"Rae?"

"I auditioned at Berklee a couple weeks ago," Rae blurts.

Now I'm the one who's silent, only because I'm too shocked to say anything.

"I knew you'd be mad," she says. "That's why I didn't want to tell you until I knew for sure that I got in."

"I'm not mad," I reply quickly. "I just wasn't expecting it. Why didn't you tell me you were applying?" The question I should have asked is why she told Nyelle.

"Because you think I'm coming to Crenshaw to go to school with you."

"Rae, I only want you to come to Crenshaw if you want to be here. Not just because I'm here." Realistically, I know that's the only reason she planned to come to Crenshaw, but I never thought to stop her . . . until now. "This is a huge opportunity for you. And I'd be pissed if you didn't go after what you want."

"Thanks," she says quietly.

"When do you find out if you got in?"

"Not for another couple of weeks," she says with a sigh. "It's killing me."

"Is that why you were looking for Nyelle?" I ask, uncomfortable with how disturbed I am that they've been communicating directly. I guess because I'm protective of Nyelle, and . . . I don't trust Rae not to say something that could make everything fall apart.

"Mostly. So, when are you going to talk to her, Cal? You only have a week left," she demands. Rae has laid off of the month deadline since we saw each other over Christmas. This is the first time she's harassed me for answers since then.

I take a deep breath and flip a pencil around on my desk.

"I'm not going to," I confess.

"What?" Rae asks, her voice raised.

"If you feel like you have to tell my mother what's going on, then go for it. I can't ask Nyelle what happened to her, Rae. I won't hurt her."

"How would you hurt her?" she asks, confused.

I rub a hand over my forehead. "She doesn't want to remember. Whatever it was, she blocked it out for a reason. I'm not going to make her relive it because I need to know. Because I *don't* need to know."

"You're being stupid again," Rae scolds.

"Maybe. But I only have a week left with her, and I'm going to do whatever I want with it."

"You slept with her," Rae groans, like that explains everything.

"That has nothing to do with it," I respond defensively. "I care about her."

"You're *in love* with her," Rae corrects adamantly.

"No" is my instinctive response. But then I shut up.

Neither of us speaks for a minute.

"Your life is about to suck. And it's only going to get worse when you can't ignore whatever she's hiding anymore."

I lean back in the chair with a heavy breath, my head spinning. Is this really happening? Am I honestly sitting here trying to decide if I'm in love with Nyelle?

"You can't love a person you don't really know," she responds. "And I have to tell Maura. I'm sorry, Cal." She hangs up.

I close my eyes and run my fingers through my hair.

I *know* Nyelle. I know exactly who she is. But I wasn't about to get into it with Rae. I feel the same way about Nyelle as I did about Nicole most of my life. That hasn't changed. I've always been drawn to her. Every version of her. Since the day I saw her in that yellow dress. So maybe... it's time I told her.

I take a deep breath. I can't believe I'm doing this. My stomach feels like it's going to twist in on itself just thinking about it. But... she's worth it. And she needs to know it.

"Eric!" I call to him, opening my bedroom door.

"What's up?" he says, poking his head out of his room.

"Can you stay at the fraternity house tonight?"

He rolls his eyes. "Wow. Nice to see you too."

"I just need one more night. There's something I have to do," I tell him, knowing he has no clue what I'm talking about.

"Yeah, no problem."

Not knowing how long she'll be gone, I grab my jacket and the keys to my truck. "Thanks," I say over my shoulder and rush out the door.

I'm sitting on the couch, rubbing my sweaty hands on my pants for the hundredth time, waiting for the door to open. She's been gone for about three hours, and I'm on the verge of going to look for her. But I don't want to risk her showing up here while I'm gone. Especially after spending two hours rushing to get everything in my room ready.

I decide I might as well try Richelle again to keep me from staring at the door. I listen to the phone ring. Just as it picks up, the door opens, and I jump up from the couch, disconnecting the call.

"He's dead," Nyelle gasps as soon as her red, swollen eyes find me.

"What?!" My heart is pounding at the sight of her tear-soaked face. "Who's dead?" I rush over and wrap my arms around her. She leans against me as I kick the door shut and guide her to the couch. I ease her onto the cushion, holding her close and rubbing her back.

I coax softly, "Nyelle, who died?"

She murmurs between sobs, "Gus."

I close my eyes. The homeless man I saw her talking to in the alley the day of the snowstorm. I don't know what to say, so I just kiss the top of her head.

"I thought he was sleeping," she says, her voice muffled with her face against my chest. "But he didn't move when I said his name. He just lay there, even when I touched him. He was so…cold."

I press my lips together. I don't know how to fix this, how to make her feel better. But that always seems to be the problem.

"Hey, man. I lost you at Shannon's. I wanted to ask you what time you're picking me up tonight." I prop the phone under my chin and pull my keys out of the ignition. I spent the day with Brady and Craig, hopping from one graduation barbeque to the next. Rae wants nothing to do with our classmates now that we've graduated, so she opted to spend the day with her girlfriend, Nina.

"Seven," he says. "We have three graduation parties to hit tonight."

"Three?" I reply in shock.

"Yeah, I gotta go. My family just got here," Brady says before hanging up.

I pause in the driveway when I think I see a glimpse of red in the woods. I squint to focus through my glasses. There's movement farther in, near the tree house. I don't know what keeps me walking in that direction, but I do. Henley comes bounding out of nowhere, his tail wagging and his tongue lolling out of his mouth.

"Hey, boy," I say, bending to scratch his head. When I stand up, I look toward the woods again, and I can definitely see someone, but whoever's there is still too far away to make out. "C'mon, Henley. Let's see who's out there."

I wonder for a moment if it's Rae, but I know she hasn't been in these woods since we were younger. Or maybe it's one of the neighborhood kids come to check out the tree house. Considering how old it is, and that it was one of my dad's projects, it's probably not the safest idea. We should seriously take the thing down before someone does fall... again.

The last person I expect to find is Nicole. As soon as I see the red ribbon in her hair, Henley takes off running.

"Henley!" I yell instinctively. My voice turns her head in my direction, her hair falling away from her face. She's crying. I stop.

Henley sticks his nose in her face, demanding attention. She scratches his head as he licks her face, releasing a laugh within a sob. Henley settles down next to where Nicole is seated on the leaf-strewn ground, with her legs straight in front of her and her back pressed against the tree.

I slowly walk toward her, afraid to say the wrong thing. So I don't say anything. I just silently lower myself to the ground on the other side of Henley, whose head is resting on Nicole's knee as she strokes his back. Leaning against the bark, I set my hand on his golden fur as well. I watch her thin, pale hand move along his coat without looking up at her. But I can hear her sobs. Glancing out of the corner of my eye, I notice the bouquet of wildflowers grasped tightly in her fist. Her arm is pressed against her stomach as if she's holding herself. Nicole's hair is a sheet of black, concealing her face, but the spasms in her back reveal each gasping sob.

Neither one of us says a word. We just sit against the tree, petting Henley. And then I feel her cool hand brush my skin, and I stop moving. She sets her hand on top of mine and curls her fingers around it. I look up, but she's not looking at me. Her focus is on the flowers.

I give her hand a gentle squeeze. I still don't know what to say, especially considering we haven't said a thing to each other in five years. I want to ask her what's wrong. I want to make her feel better, to take away whatever it is that's hurting her. But I fail to do anything at all other than hold her hand—until she releases it. She stands up and straightens her red skirt before walking way. I notice she forgot the flowers on the ground next to the tree. But I don't call to her. All I do is watch her disappear.

I just let her walk away without a word, and then I never saw her again. I only heard her screaming at her parents that night. And I still can't remember the details. So this is the last image I have of Nicole, until Nyelle.

I slide my hands on either side of Nyelle's face. Her eyes shine and her cheeks are red and raw from the tears. "He had a hard life. And you were one of the best things to happen to him."

I lower my mouth to hers and press against it, holding the kiss for a long breath before pulling away.

"Thank you," she whispers, resting her cheek on my chest and wrapping her arms around me tightly. "He's been waiting to go for a long time. I knew this was coming. But it still sucks." She releases a drawn breath.

"Yeah, it does," I say into her hair. I hold her until she eases away. When she looks up at me, I stroke her damp cheeks with my thumbs to dry her tears. "What can I do to make you feel better? Ice cream? Marshmallows? Chips? A hot shower in the dark?"

She laughs lightly. "I'll be okay." She stands and starts for the bedroom. I jump up. I don't want her to go in there. Not now.

"How about we go away?" I say in a rush.

"What?" Nyelle turns around.

"Let's get out of Crenshaw," I suggest, my pulse thrumming.

"Where do you want to go?"

I grin at the intrigue reflecting in her eyes. "Uh…Oregon. My uncle's cabin. He's going hiking this weekend. We'll have the place to ourselves. And... there isn't any snow."

She laughs. "A cabin in the woods, just the two of us for a weekend?"

"Or the rest of the week," I offer. "Up to you. He won't care. And I can work for him in the garage while I'm there. I could use the money."

Nyelle bites her lower lip in thought. Then she slowly smiles and says, "Okay. Let's spend the rest of the week in Oregon."

She reaches for my bedroom door, but I rush to intercept her. "I'll get our bags. Why don't you... get your things from the bathroom?"

Nyelle eyes me suspiciously. "Are you hiding something in there?"

"It doesn't matter," I answer evasively. "Let me pack a bag, and we'll leave."

"Right now?" she questions, still scrutinizing me.

"Yeah. Why not? We'll catch the next flight out, even if we have to fly standby and take a couple layovers to get there."

"You know you're being weird right now, right?"

I nod. "I know. But it'll make sense later. I promise."

Nyelle keeps her narrowed eyes on me as she slowly walks to the bathroom, like she's worried I've lost my mind. Which is very possible. "Okay."

When she's safely behind the bathroom door, I slip into my room to pack.

NICOLE

May—Junior Year of High School

"Can you believe he just told me like it was no big deal?" Richelle screams into her pillow as I rub her back, trying to calm her down.

Her face is red and damp with tears when she lifts it from the pillow.

I want to say I'm sorry. I want to tell her that Lily doesn't mean anything to Cal. They already broke up. I want to tell her anything that will make her feel better.

But more than that, I wish I was screaming into that pillow alongside her.

"I'm being such a girl. I know it," she says, sniffling. "But it hurts. And I don't know how to make it stop."

"I know," I console. And I do. My chest felt like it was being crushed when I found out. And then when I arrived and saw Richelle's face, it only made it worse. So I try to be the best friend that she needs and not the heartbroken girl that I am, and listen to her cry as she spills her hurt on her pillow.

Richelle inhales, trying to calm her stuttering breaths. She eases herself up to sit, holding the pillow to her chest.

"Do you know what hurts the most?"

I wait.

"That he didn't even hesitate to tell me. He obviously thinks of me as just a friend. I know I told him that's what I wanted when I broke up with him. But I didn't mean it. I just couldn't tell him…"

"I know," I say when her voice cracks. "You love him and he doesn't know it."

"What if he could never feel that way about me?" She sniffles, crushed. "I don't know what to do. Maybe I shouldn't talk to him anymore. It hurts too much. "

"Richelle, you're hurting right now. But you can't stop talking to him."

"Why not? You have."

"But that's—"

"Because of me," she interrupts.

"No. I was going to say, that's *my* choice. Don't let him go like I did."

Because I regret it every day.

NINETEEN

"You've packed enough sugar to last a month," I remark as Nyelle tries to zip her backpack around the bag of marshmallows sticking out of the top.

"You said we'll be in the middle of nowhere," she says, smiling proudly when she's finally able to close the bulging bag.

"And that's all you're planning to eat?" I ask, throwing my duffel bag over my shoulder. "Besides, I was going to stop by a store on our way to the cabin."

"Now you don't have to," she gloats, putting on her jacket.

I laugh, waiting for her by the door. "Yeah, I do. I can't eat like you. I need something that grows out of the ground every once in a while."

Nyelle rolls her carry-on behind her down the hall. "Will your uncle be there when we get in?"

"No. He's leaving this afternoon to meet up with the guys he's climbing with. I called and told him we're coming, though. He's leaving the light on."

We step outside into the instant freeze. I start the truck, shivering, wishing I'd let it heat up.

"You never told me what you did for him." Nyelle cuddles up close to my side to get warm.

I pull out of the parking lot and wrap my arm around her shoulder. "He custom designs and rebuilds motorcycles."

I don't notice until after we're driving away that Nyelle's gawking at me.

"What?"

"You. And motorcycles? Really?"

I eye her curiously. "I don't get it."

"That's kinda hot."

"I don't *ride* them," I clarify. "And I don't have a single tattoo. There's nothing really badass about me. I just happen to know how to use a socket wrench."

"Don't ruin this for me," Nyelle says. "Let me hold on to this image for just a minute longer." She closes her eyes with a grin.

I laugh. "What's so sexy about a guy on a motorcycle anyway?"

Truth. My mother would *kill* me if I ever rode any of the bikes I help construct. Her uncle died in a crash when she was young, and she won't let any of us even consider riding. Even my brothers are afraid to go against that rule.

"I don't know. It just is. Unless he's a cocky douche. Or three hundred pounds. That's just... Ew." She exaggerates a shiver.

"That didn't really explain anything," I say with a smile. "But I guess it's a good thing I will never be a three-hundred-pound cocky douche riding a motorcycle."

"It *is* a good thing." Nyelle reaches over and turns down the radio.

"Cal?" she asks, leaning in so her head is resting on my chest.

"Yes?" I'm wary of her careful tone.

"You never told me what makes you walk away from all the girls you've dated."

"I thought we already had this conversation," I say, not exactly sure what she's looking for. I walk away because it's what I always do. And it's easier to do it when there's nothing to lose.

"We did. Sort of," she says, playing with the zipper on my jacket. "I just think there's more to it."

"Really?" I respond, not willing to agree or disagree. I'd rather not be talking about this at all. But for some reason she keeps bringing it up. I don't know what she's hoping to learn about me, other than I get out before it starts getting complicated.

"Yeah, I do. I think when you end things, it isn't just that they're not your *what if* girl."

"Okay," I say carefully, letting her come to her own conclusions. So far, she's right.

"You don't have feelings for them, no matter how much you like them."

This is starting to get uncomfortable, especially with her sitting under my arm. When I'm quiet, she leans back so she can see my face, forcing me to remove my arm from behind her.

"You know why you do it, don't you? Why you walk away?"

I grip the steering wheel tighter. "It's not like it's a secret I'm trying to keep from you, Nyelle. It's that I don't really want to think about these girls, especially since I'm here *with you*. You're not one of them. And I don't want you to ever think you are."

"That's sweet." She leans over and kisses me on the cheek. "So tell me."

I blow out a lungful of air and say, "I don't want to hurt them."

She's quiet. When I glance over at her, a sad smile hangs on her face.

"What?" I ask. "Why does that upset you?"

"You walk away before you can hurt them," Nyelle says softly. "So... who hurt you?"

I continue to stare straight ahead, not willing to contribute to this conversation anymore. Because what am I supposed to say... you? You and Richelle crushed me within the same summer, and it's not something I've ever gotten over. That's not about to come out of my mouth. So I don't say anything.

"I'm sorry," she whispers, wrapping herself under my arm and laying her head on my chest. "I don't want to..." She doesn't finish. But I know where that sentence was going.

"It's okay." I squeeze her against me and kiss the top of her head. "I'll be fine."

We both know how this is going to end. She's leaving after this week, even though we haven't mentioned it since the night of the painting. And when she does, it's going to suck. This isn't where she belongs. I know that. But then... where *does* she belong? As much as I want that answer to be "with me," I know it's not the reality. I'm running out of time. There's no avoiding it now. This is *definitely* going to suck.

The winding dirt road veers off down a narrower road that ends at the cabin. I park the rental car next to the garage and turn off the engine.

"Nyelle, we're here," I tell her softly, running a hand along her cheek.

Her eyes blink open and she looks around. "We're here?"

"Yeah."

Henley comes trotting out from behind the cabin, barking and wagging his tail, just as Nyelle opens her door. I step out of the car as she exclaims, "Henley!" Then falls to her knees to receive him. He rushes over to her, licking her face. Nyelle wraps her arms around him, patting his back as he continues to lick her cheek, wagging like crazy.

When she stands, Nyelle is visibly shaken. She grabs on to the passenger door for balance.

"Hey," I say, jogging around to her. "Are you okay? What's wrong?"

Nyelle shakes her head to dismiss me, tucking loose strands of her ponytail behind her ear. "I'm fine," she rasps. She presses her lips together to conceal their trembling as she averts her eyes, scanning the ground.

I reach for her hand, but she quickly pulls it away, turning to shut the door. She appears disoriented as she keeps her hands pressed against the frame of the door for balance.

"Nyelle? What's going on?" I ask, trying to assess what just happened. Henley rubs against my leg. I look down at him, patting the top of his head. That's when I know... seeing *him* did this. Henley stays with Zac while I'm at college, and since Zac knew we were going to be here, he decided to leave Henley behind. I never expected Nyelle to react like this when she saw him.

Nyelle turns to me, lost behind vacant eyes. It's like she's not really here.

"Do you remember Henley?" I ask cautiously as she reaches for her backpack.

I never thought she was pretending not to know me, or making an effort not to recall things she should've known. No one's that talented of an actor. I just stopped questioning it because I was willing to accept her as she is. Now... I can't ignore the trembling girl in front of me, accosted once again by a reminder of a past she's somehow forgotten. I have no idea what to do.

"Sorry. I'm really tired," she murmurs, running a quivering hand over her hair. "Do you think we can go in?"

"Yeah, sure," I say, wrapping an arm around her and picking

up her bag with the other hand. She leans into me as we walk toward the house. She's still shaking, almost as bad as the night I carried her after swimming in the icy lake.

I remove the key from the hook under the stairs and lead Nyelle up to the door. She's quiet, her gaze still directed at the ground, dazed. I unlock the door and flip on the lights, lighting up the large open space.

I climb the stairs to the room I usually stay in and push the door open for her.

"There's a bathroom in here too," I tell her as she slips past me. "I'll get the rest of the stuff."

She nods, and I watch her walk into the bathroom, closing the door behind her. I have a feeling she didn't hear anything I said.

I don't think I can do this. If she has some sort of psychotic break, even worse than she is now, I won't know how to help her. I should call my mother . . . or Rae. She can explain everything to my mother better than I can.

I walk around the front of the house in search of a spot to make the call. But the "No Service" message remains lit. Shit.

Henley follows me back into the cabin as I carry in the rest of our things, along with the couple bags of groceries we stopped to get on the way. I take my time putting them away, glancing up at the door on the far end of the landing every so often.

My nerves are shot, and I'm fighting to keep my shit together. But I don't want to leave her up there alone for too long.

I lock up and shut off the lights before slowly ascending the stairs. I pause outside the door to pull myself together. I can do this—listen to her, hold her, let her scream into a pillow. Whatever she needs. I grab the handle, prepared for full-on female emotions. But I'm not expecting her to be . . . sleeping.

I brush the hair out of her face, and watch her sleep with her hand resting on the pillow. She looks so peaceful, like nothing in the world could be wrong with her. I wish that were the truth.

Crouching beside her, I run the back of my hand along her cheek. I can't help but wonder who's going to be looking at me when her eyes open in the morning. My attention drifts to her hand. The entire side from her knuckle to her wrist is slashed with tiny white lines. "What happened to you, Nyelle?"

Glass shattering has a very distinct sound. Even in my drunkenness, I know exactly what I'm hearing. And it's loud.

"Maybe I don't want to be your perfect little girl anymore." There's so much anger in her voice, and it comes out strained, like she's physically pained to say it.

"Nicole, stop!" Mr. Bentley's deep voice booms from within the house. "What do you think you're doing?"

I find my feet moving toward the house, but they feel like they're made of cement. I stumble across their perfectly trimmed lawn.

"Nicole, you're bleeding all over the floor!" Mrs. Bentley cries.

"Call Dr. Xavier," Mr. Bentley instructs. "Tell him to use the back door."

"Did I disappoint you, Daddy?!" Nicole screams, sending ice down my spine.

Suddenly, Mr. Bentley bursts out of the front door. The veins along his forehead stick out as he rushes to his car. Then he sees me, and stops.

"Cal? It's Cal, correct?"

I nod, trying so hard to appear sober. "Is Nicole okay?"

"Oh." He clears his throat. "Yes, she's perfectly fine. Just had a bad night, that's all. We're taking care of her. Thanks for your concern."

"No problem," I murmur and turn to walk toward the street. I look back over my shoulder when I reach the sidewalk, and he's still watching me, standing by his car.

"Nicolas?" Mrs. Bentley calls out.

I can still hear Nicole's hysterical sobs drifting through the dark as I walk away.

As my eyes open, I roll over to find Nyelle's side empty, forcing me up. With a rush of panic, I'm fully awake. I listen but don't hear any movement, so I flip back the covers and get out of the bed. It's just after two in the morning. Where could she be? She's not in the bathroom. I open the bedroom door. The house is pitch-black.

"Nyelle?" I call out. Nothing.

I turn on the lights as I walk through the house, checking every room, eventually making my way outside. My heart is racing. The dream, or memory, still lingers, and it only fuels the panic.

I walk around to the back of the cabin and stop when I see a strange shape in the grass. When I get closer, I realize it's Nyelle, with Henley. She's on her back with her hair splayed around her, looking up at the stars. A hand rests on Henley's head, which is propped on her stomach.

"Nyelle, what are you doing up?" I ask, still trying to recover. This has seriously been the most stressful night.

She doesn't shift her eyes away from the stars. "Trying to feel better."

"Can I lie down with you?" I ask cautiously, needing to do the same. She nods.

My body releases a quick shiver when I lie down on the cool grass. I'm watching her as she stares intently up at the sky like she's waiting for something to happen. I'm scanning her face, wondering who it is lying beside me.

"I've never seen so many stars before," she says quietly. "A sky full of possibilities and pain. That's such a contradiction. Maybe they're just painful possibilities." Her voice sounds so sad, I almost don't recognize it as hers. Her mask is cracking, and whatever she's been hiding behind it is starting to show. I'm not sure how to put her back together.

"What do you need me to do?" I ask. "I'll do anything. I'm not above freezing to death for you."

There's a hint of a laugh, and I know Nyelle is still with me. "It is a little cold, huh? I didn't really notice."

"Being with you usually means losing feeling in my limbs. I've come to terms with it."

She reaches over and takes hold of my hand. "But you always feel so warm to me."

I squeeze her hand and press it to my lips.

"I needed to feel that," she says softly.

"What?"

"The butterfly." The word comes out in a whisper.

"What does that mean? That was your wish at the silo, but I didn't understand."

"Holding your hand. It makes me feel like there's a butterfly beating in my chest. There's something about it that helps me believe everything's going to be okay."

"Everything *is* going to be okay," I assure her, wanting to believe it too.

"I know. I'm sorry," she says, laughing uncomfortably and

quickly swiping away a tear that's escaped down her cheek. "I'm not supposed to be like this. You shouldn't have to see it."

"Hey." I roll to my side and redirect her attention with a finger under her chin, so she's looking at me. "You can always show me exactly who you are. No matter what."

"I'm not sure who that is," she murmurs, pressing her lips into a tight smile to lock the emotion inside. The forced smile is too much like her mother's. A disturbed chill runs through me.

"Who do you want to be?" I ask.

Her eyes flicker, troubled by the answer. I brush my hand on her cheek. I've never felt so helpless in my entire life.

"I don't know." Her lip trembles and she can't hold back. "I don't know anymore."

I scoot closer and pull her trembling body to my chest, wanting to take it all away.

What would have happened if I'd done something that night I heard her screaming? What if I hadn't walked away? What if I'd gone into her house to help her? What if I'd been the friend she needed? Would she still be lying here, searching for herself in the stars?

"You can be anyone you want with me. And it won't matter, I promise—good, bad or crazy." And it doesn't matter which version of her is looking back at me; she's the same girl. The girl I've wanted most of my life.

She releases a light, breathy laugh.

"Although I might regret saying that later," I say, hoping to get her to laugh again, and she does.

I lift her chin and brush her lips with a gentle kiss.

"Everything's going to be okay," I say again, lying to us both.

NICOLE

August—Before Senior Year of High School

I hang up the phone and lean back in my seat. Curling my fingers around the steering wheel until my knuckles turn white, I stare out the windshield. I need to calm down before I can get out of the car. There are too many people here. I can't lose it now.

I jump when someone taps on the window.

"Nicole, what are you doing?" Ashley demands. My jaw clenches at just the sound of her voice.

I turn it off. The sadness. The anger. The frustration. And *smile.*

"I'm coming," I say, dropping the phone in my beach bag and opening the door.

"Can't believe we're finally seniors," Heather remarks as we walk along the hot sand, searching for the best place to set up. Or, as the girls prefer it, the place where the hottest guys are.

"Ooh, I like this view," Ashley announces, dropping her bag in the sand.

I unfold the blanket and Vi helps me spread it as Heather and Ashley survey the landscape of roided bodies.

I pull my tank over my head and toss it on top of my bag. Just as I'm about to slide my shorts off, a muscled forearm presses into my stomach and I'm swung off the ground. I yell out in surprise.

"Hey, baby," Kyle murmurs in my ear. I groan internally, wishing he'd take his hands off me. He turns me around and kisses me, forcing his tongue in my mouth. I count the seconds until he's done.

"Hi," I say, smiling up at him. "What are you guys doing here? I thought it was a girls' day."

"And miss seeing you in a bathing suit? No way." He winks. I want to gag. Then he leans in and whispers in my ear, "Besides, you've been away all summer, and I haven't had any time with you."

I pull back with wide eyes.

"Don't worry. I stuck to your story," he drones.

I try to relax, hoping he didn't slip up. He's supposed to say he and I were in Malibu after I spent four weeks at the ballet program. I was actually with Richelle and not with him at his family's vacation home. But I fight to keep our friendship to myself, so I have one genuine thing in my life no one else can touch.

He pulls me tight against him. "But it's killing me to see you wearing that bikini, knowing I've never seen what's underneath."

"But that's why I let you do whoever you want on campus," I say low in his ear. "As long as you don't tell, I don't tell."

Kyle is worried about his reputation. Pathetic. He's convinced the guys in our town that we have sex all the time, and in return, I let him have sex with any coed he wants. If his younger brother or any of the elites found out that he's never even seen me without a shirt on, other than at the beach, he would never live it down.

I can't believe he hasn't broken it off with me yet. I've been waiting for it for the past year, ever since he went off to college. But then again, he has a sweet deal. He has this stupid-ass reputation in his hometown of being... whatever it is he claims to be. And he gets to live up the single life on campus.

"Where's Waldo!" Neil hollers. I clamp my teeth shut as he goes up for a pass and runs into Cal, knocking him to the ground. "Oh, sorry, man. Didn't see you there." The guys around us laugh obnoxiously.

"Then maybe you should take your head out of your ass," Rae snaps, getting in his face, but she really only reaches his chest. I press my lips together to keep from laughing.

Craig helps Cal off the ground. I watch him brush himself off and adjust his glasses. He looks...taller. But he's still skinny, which really doesn't matter. I'm surrounded by guys with killer bodies—they're still assholes.

He looks over at me, and for a moment I can't look away. In those few seconds, I'm silently screaming that I'm sorry Neil's a douche. I'm sorry I'm not hanging with them in Rae's garage, listening to music and drinking on that ugly couch she moved up from the basement. I'm sorry that I don't cheer loud enough for him at the basketball games when he gets to play for, like, five minutes. I'm just...sorry.

I break our connection and sit down on the blanket.

"Don't you think so, Nicole?" Heather asks.

"Huh? Oh, yeah," I respond, having learned that's the only way to ever respond. Just agree.

I drive home, exhausted and numb, wishing I could scream at the top of my lungs. But, unfortunately, Kyle manipulated a ride out of me, so I have to keep wearing this ill-fitting smile.

"Pick you up for that party later?" he confirms when I pull up in front of his house. "Eight?"

"Sounds great," I respond with fake enthusiasm.

He leans over and paws me, kissing me aggressively. I let him, reminding myself to keep my eyes shut until he's done.

"Babe, it's your senior year," he says, pulling back, out of breath. "Don't you think it's about time we had sex?"

"Maybe," I tell him, smiling sweetly. "I just want it to happen naturally, you know? When it's the right moment."

Now get the fuck out of my car!

"Of course," he agrees. "I'll see you later."

When I walk into my house, I have nothing left holding me together.

"Why can't I go to San Francisco this weekend?" I demand as my mother folds laundry.

She straightens, surprised by my assertive tone. A tone I've never used with her before. "Excuse me?"

"I was supposed to see Richelle this weekend," I explain, trying to collect myself. "But you called and said I had to stay home. Why?"

"We're attending a company dinner with your father tomorrow night. He needs our support," she explains.

I close my eyes, trying to stay wrapped up in the pretty packaging.

"You know why it's important that I see her," I say slowly. "This is our weekend. I can't miss it."

"Well, your father is more important."

I fall apart. "Sitting next to you and Daddy, smiling like some cheap plastic doll while he kisses ass for three hours, is *not* important. He will not get promoted. He will not get that raise. He will stay in that middle management position he's been in for the past four years, although we have to pretend like he's the ruler of the universe every time he walks through that door. *He's not!*

"I don't know why you let him treat you like his slave—dressing, cleaning and cooking for him. Always perfect. Never wanting to disappoint. Well, maybe I don't give a shit anymore!"

I'm trembling in my rage. My mother blinks at me like I'm a kitten she finds adorable. I want to shake her. I want to unplug her from the program that keeps her from being human.

"Are you done?"

I flinch. The emotionlessness of her words feels like a slap.

"Your father and I are partners in this marriage. I support him by keeping the house clean and preparing his dinner each night, creating a calm and respectful setting where he can feel loved and appreciated. And he puts up with the disappointment of being overlooked in spite of all he gives to that company year after year. Even moving here to fill a position he was overqualified for, so that we can have this life. Saving for a college he was never able to attend, just so you can have every advantage he didn't. So you *will* be at this dinner. You *will* be respectful. And you will *not* disappoint him. Do you understand?"

Defeated, I slip on the perfect-daughter mask and nod numbly. "I understand."

TWENTY

The sun shining through the windows wakes me the next morning. I rub my eyes and stretch, debating whether I should cover my head and fall back to sleep.

I roll over. Nyelle's awake, watching me.

"Good morning," she says quietly, offering a small smile.

I groan, wrapping my arm around her waist and rolling her on her side so her back's pressed against me. "Are we awake?"

"Yeah," she says. "I already showered and brushed my teeth."

"Then I should too." I yawn into the pillow.

"Before you say anything, although I know you won't," she begins, shifting onto her back. She lightly traces her fingers over my hand resting on her stomach. "I'm sorry about last night. I got a little freaked. Thank you for being so patient with me. I'm sure it hasn't been easy."

I prop my head up and focus on her, trying to decipher what patience she's referring to. The fact that she's still lost behind Nyelle, or that being Nyelle can be a little... overwhelming. Now I'm confusing myself.

"I'm sorry I'm not who you expected me to be," she says, her lips pressed into an apologetic smile.

"Nyelle, you are *more* than I ever expected you to be," I respond intently. I can't stand the insecurity in her eyes. It's not her. I need to get rid of it. "I don't give a shit if I haven't brushed my teeth, I'm kissing you."

"No, don't," she pleads, giggling. I push my body between her legs and pin her arms above her. She squirms, trying to get free, laughing in that way that makes all the difference. The laugh that I needed to hear. I nuzzle into her neck and trail small kisses along it. Her body relaxes beneath me, and her hands slide up my back.

I drag my lips down to the dip in her collarbone and she inhales quickly.

"Wait," she says suddenly. I don't move. "Um... I was hoping to make you breakfast."

"Breakfast? I was just about to..."

"Yeah," she blurts, sitting up, knocking me off her. I collapse on my back with a groan. It's painful being denied first thing in the morning. Or any time really.

"Uh... you don't even have to get out of bed. I'll bring it up." She sounds weird.

"What are you up to?" I ask, lifting my head as she walks to the door.

She flashes a devilish grin. "I'll be right back. Don't go anywhere."

"We're in the middle of the woods!" I holler as I hear her footsteps trail down the hall. "Where would I go?"

While I'm waiting, I decide to take a quick shower to wash off the day of traveling that's still clinging to my skin.

As I stand under the stream of water, I'm hoping today is better than yesterday. I sure as hell don't want it to be worse.

I'm not dismissing everything that's happened in the past twelve hours, but I'd rather not jump back into the deep end of the emotional pool so early in the morning. Her apology was heavy enough.

We have a week. I'm pretty certain that it's all going to come out before it's over. And when it does, it's not going to be the best day of my life. So I just want to be an idiot for one more day, if I can.

When I step back into the bedroom, Nyelle is sitting on the bed, in a flannel shirt with the sheet covering her legs. She's wearing a ridiculous smile that makes me laugh. I look around, expecting a bowl of cereal or something.

"Uh...what's for breakfast?" I ask, pulling a drawer open in search of a shirt.

"Me," she answers, turning me around. Before I can utter a sound, she unveils her legs and there are pink hearts painted on them. When I look closer, I see pink hearts on her neck, peeking out from underneath the collar of the shirt.

I grin, relieved that she's willing to be in this bubble of denial with me. Whatever it is that's going to change everything, it can wait.

"Frosting?"

Nyelle nods.

"And we don't even have to climb a tree," I say, moving toward the bed, suddenly starving.

She smiles innocently as I bend over her, tasting her lips.

"There isn't any frosting there," she murmurs against my mouth.

"Just thought it was a good place to start," I reply, working my way down her neck to the heart painted below her ear. I take my time finding each spot strategically marked for me. She gasps at the touch of my tongue on her sweet skin as I move down her body, savoring every inch.

This is most definitely the hottest thing I've ever done. Her breath quivers when I finish with the hidden hearts painted along her legs.

"I love breakfast in bed," I say, returning to her lips once again. "So much better than cereal."

"Did you just compare me to cereal?" she asks, still flushed.

"What? I can have you both every day and never get sick of you," I argue, scanning her naked body. I'm not quite done with her yet. "How is that bad?"

She inhales quickly when I ease on top of her. "Oh, it's not."

"Did you fall asleep?" Nyelle asks, leaning back against me.

"Nope," I say groggily, with my eyes closed. The hot water's sedating. "But I probably could."

"We're losing our bubbles," she says. The water swishes.

"Do you want to get out?" I ask, opening my eyes with a deep inhale. I lean forward and kiss her shoulder.

She holds her hands up in front of us. "My fingers are pruny, so I think it's time."

Nyelle uses the sides of the cast-iron tub to push herself up. I admire the water cascading off her skin. Then I shake the thoughts from my head, knowing we can't spend the entire day in bed. Or... maybe we could.

"I was thinking about going for a walk," she says, wrapping a towel around herself.

"It looks like it's going to rain," I inform her.

"We're in Oregon. It always looks like it's going to rain."

I smile, reaching for the towel on the hook. "True."

"What would you say if I asked to dress you?" she says, walking into the bedroom.

"You want to pick out my clothes? I didn't bring a huge selection."

"No." She laughs. "Actually dress you. I like the thought of it."

I pause, about to make a comment about how strange it sounds. But then I stop myself, thinking back to when I thought showering in the dark was a bad idea. And now that memory will never leave me.

"If you want to," I respond. "Will you let me dress you?"

"Sure," she answers with a smile in her voice.

Watching her bend down in front of me to pull up my pants and then sliding her fingers up the zipper is much more of a turn-on than I ever could've imagined. I'm tempted to ask her to take them back off again.

When it's my turn, I take my time, sliding her arms into her bra and standing close to clasp it behind her. Kneeling before her as she steps into her underwear, running my hands up her legs as I guide them into place.

Kissing her when her head peeks out of the sweater. Then running my lips up her thighs when I pull her pants up. I pause at the small scar on her right thigh, kissing it gently. I smooth my fingers over it. It's so light after all these years. I hadn't really given it much attention until now, too distracted by the other parts of her.

"I can't believe how small it is," I remark, "considering there was a branch sticking out of it. I thought Richelle..."

Her body is suddenly too still. I cringe. I said too much. Shit.

Nyelle reaches for the top of her pants, pulling them over her hips and buttoning them. I stand openmouthed, wanting to take it back. But what should I do? Apologize? Pretend like I didn't say it?

I'm so used to her not flinching at the mention of Renfield or anyone in it. Even the few times she's let a memory slip through, she didn't react. She didn't even seem to realize that she'd done it. But now it's different. The memories are like jolts of electricity, waking her from her oblivion. And they hurt. How do I make it stop?

"Uh...do you want to make pancakes?" I ask, hoping to distract her enough so that she can move past this. She was so excited when we picked up the box of mix on our way here. I'm grasping for anything right now.

"No, that's okay," she answers quietly, sitting on the bed and pulling on her socks. "I think I'll go for that walk before it rains."

I watch silently as she laces up her combat boots. She still won't look at me, and it's killing me.

When she stands, I step in front of her, placing my hands on her hips. "Nyelle." She stares at my chest. "Please look at me."

She reluctantly raises her eyes to meet mine. But quickly looks away when the pain surfaces and her eyes shine with tears. I try to control my expression so she doesn't realize I'm as freaked as I am.

"I think...I think we should talk about it." Holy shit, I've said it.

"I don't want to talk. I can't," she replies in a broken whisper. "I'll be back in a bit."

She slips past me.

"Wait. Don't go," I plead, following after her down the hall. "I know that you're upset. You don't have to hide it. Nyelle, you don't have to hide who you are with me. Remember?"

She reaches the bottom of the stairs and turns back around. "I'm fine," she lies. "I just need to go for a walk and clear my head."

I follow her to the door, but let her leave without stopping her.

I clasp my hands behind my head. Fuck.

Do I go after her? Do I give her time to herself? I'm so far out of my element here. I go back upstairs to grab my phone.

I walk around the house, searching for a signal. Nothing. The overcast sky must be making the reception worse than usual.

I go outside and hold the phone up, waiting for *any* bars to appear. As soon as I see two, I stop.

The sound of the phone ringing breaks up, and I close my eyes, begging for it to go through.

"Cal? Where've . . . been?!" Rae answers. The reception sucks.

"I'm at Zac's," I tell her.

"Where?"

"Oregon. Zac's cabin," I say again. There's no way we're going to be able to have a conversation.

"Nyelle . . . you" is all I get from her before it cuts out.

I grunt in frustration. That was useless. I walk around again, even trying along the dirt road. Nothing.

I sit on the steps of the cabin, and Henley trots over to sit at my feet. I pet the top of his head and stare at the woods for a while, hoping she'll come back.

"So what do you think, Henley? Should I go after her?"

He just looks up at me with his tongue hanging out.

"You're right. *She's* the girl worth going after," I say, scratching him behind his ear. "Let's go get her."

Except when I stand up, I have no idea which way to go. We're surrounded by woods. She could have gone anywhere.

So I just start walking, trying to follow the most natural path. After about fifteen minutes, I stop. This is useless. Then I remember . . .

"The lake," I say to Henley, who tilts his head at the sound of my voice.

I get my bearings and head down the slope toward the lake. I don't know why I didn't think of going there first. I'm hoping she's instinctively drawn to it or something. Either way, I have nothing to lose.

I'm about halfway there when I catch movement out of the corner of my eye. Henley stands at attention, listening. Then he takes off running. I should've just let him lead me to her.

I jog after him through the trees and underbrush.

I slow to a walk when I see her in the distance. Henley is stopped up ahead, waiting for me to follow.

The trees open up, surrounding a large patch of moss carpeting the forest. And in the middle of that clearing is Nyelle. And she's... dancing.

I'm afraid to continue. I don't want her to stop. The idea that she's spinning around in the middle of the woods seems insane. But she's so graceful in her movement, it's actually... beautiful.

I move in closer, hoping she won't notice me. Then I realize she has earbuds clipped to her ears. And her eyes are closed.

I lean against a tree and watch her sweep her hands in the air, dipping back and extending a leg toward the sky, her bare foot pointed.

I knew she danced. I never saw her perform. Seeing this, I wish I had.

She leaps in an arcing movement. Upon touching down, Nyelle lowers to the ground into a seated pose with her legs bent at elegant angles and her arms folded around them. And then she doesn't move.

I slowly approach her. She's still bowed over, her head resting on her arms. Her shoulders shake as she gasps for each breath. She's crying.

Henley jogs up, sticking his nose in her face. She raises her head, looking directly at me with tears streaming down her face. She removes her earbuds without getting up.

Staring into those same blue eyes I memorized so long ago, I ask, "Who's Nyelle Preston?"

RICHELLE

May—Senior Year of High School

"I like it out here," I say, lying back on the blanket, staring up at the stars.

"We probably shouldn't stay out here long. It's getting cold," Nicole replies, her hands folded on her stomach.

"Nothing seems to matter when I look up at the stars," I continue, not worried about the chill in the air. "They're full of possibilities, and they can make everything better by just wishing on them."

"I've always thought of them as everything I haven't done and wished I could. The moments I want back, to do again."

"Your what ifs," I declare.

"Yeah."

"Well, every time you see one streak across the sky, take it back. Do whatever you wanted to do over again."

Nicole lets out a small laugh. "I'd like that."

We lay in silence for a moment. Nicole has been my best friend for most of my childhood. Every happy memory is attached to her in some way. But a part of me always worries about her. I can't help it.

"Are you happy?" I ask her.

"What?"

"All I ever want is for you to be happy. You put so much pressure on yourself to be what everyone expects you to be. I'm afraid that you're not happy."

"I am when I'm with you. You're the only person who doesn't

expect me to act a certain way." She pauses. "Sometimes I wish I could be everything I'm not. Spontaneous. Adventurous. Just do something because it's fun. Not care what anyone thinks about how I look. How I act. Just be... me."

"I think you should do it," I encourage her, smiling just thinking about Nicole being anything but composed and put together.

"I wish," she breathes.

"That's your first *what if*," I proclaim. "The next shooting star we see, you get to do *you* over again."

Nicole laughs.

We lie there for a moment, watching the sky, waiting for that second chance.

"Richelle?"

"Yeah," I respond, still watching for any movement in the sky. I think I see one, but it's a plane.

"Are you... are you happy?"

There's a hesitation in her voice that makes me reach out and grab her hand. "Today I am." Nicole squeezes my hand. "Do me a favor?"

"Anything," she answers quickly. Too quickly.

"I worry about you, you know? How quiet you are. What must be going on in your head. Everyone expecting you to be... perfect. I know you must get sad, and angry, and frustrated. Just... let it go."

"I can't always scream when everything sucks."

I continue to absorb the burning lights above me. "Then... let the stars take it away and make everything better. And when the sun comes up, and those stars disappear, they take all the hurt with them."

"Until the next night when they're there to remind me of everything that sucks."

"No, because then they become possibilities again."

"You being all philosophical is confusing."

I laugh. "Yeah. I don't know if I'm making sense anymore."

"Well, I'll never look at the stars again without thinking of you," Nicole says, holding my hand tight.

"That's not a bad thing."

A streak of light passes above us. We both lift our arms to point at the same time.

"There you go. You get to be her. The messy, crazy, unpredictable girl you've always wanted to be."

Nicole sighs heavily.

"Girls," my mother calls to us from the back deck of the cabin. "Come inside. The last thing you need is to get a cold."

"Isn't that the reason we're here—to get fresh air?" I ask.

"Richelle," my mother says sternly.

"Com-ing!" I reply.

"It's okay," Nicole reassures me. "It *is* pretty cold out here."

I sit up. "Ooh! Maybe she'll make us hot chocolate!"

TWENTY-ONE

Will you please tell me? Who's Nyelle Preston?" I ask again, after what feels like an hour of us just staring at each other.

Nyelle pulls her knees up, hugging them as she remains seated on the mossy ground. "A lie I wanted to be true."

"She seems real to me. How is she a lie?"

Nyelle closes her eyes, her lashes glistening with tears. I want to touch her. To hold her. But then I'm afraid I won't find out what I came here in search of.

Her pained blue eyes rise to meet mine. "I didn't want my life. I didn't want to hurt anymore. So I became the lie I wished for."

She looks down and lets out a breath, like she's trying to release the hurt into the air. She's not making sense. I'm not sure how much has come back to her. And how much is still trapped within the lie she's convinced herself to believe.

"Did you recognize me that night, at the Halloween party?"

"Not at first. You look different," she says, biting at her lip. "But when I knew it was you, I tried to stay away. I tried so hard, because you reminded me of everything that I needed to forget. But each time I saw you, I wanted to see you again. So, I got to know you like it was the first time."

"Then what happened to Nicole?" I ask. Somewhere between

the cabin and here, I found the nerve to ask every question I've been choking on all this time. Not saying it's easy watching her bowed over like she wants to fold in on herself and disappear. But if I'm going to fight for her, she needs to fight for herself too, whoever she is.

Nyelle lays her head on her arm, staring at the moss. "I wished her away." She draws in a deep breath and sighs sadly. Her cryptic answers still confuse me. What if she's been trapped within her lie for so long, she can't find her way out?

A raindrop lands on her arm. I look up at the sky, which has decided that now is the perfect time to open up on us. Of course.

"Let's go back to the cabin," I suggest, moving closer to help her up.

Nyelle slides on her socks and boots before accepting my hand.

I'm about to start running as the rain picks up. But Nyelle walks, unfazed. Which is exactly what I should've expected from her. The canopy of evergreens shelters us from the brunt of the storm. But we're still getting wet.

"Why did you wish her away?" I ask after a minute of walking with our eyes on the ground, the silence suffocating me.

Nyelle glances up at me with a curious smile, like she doesn't understand why I'd ask. "She… The girl I used to be did what everyone expected of her. She wasn't real and I didn't want to be that girl anymore." She bites at her lip, trying to keep from crying again. "It's been so hard remembering her. What I was like. But I'm not her. Not anymore."

"Because you started over," I conclude. "And that's not a bad thing, I guess. Aren't you happier being Nyelle… being you?"

Nyelle stops and turns to me, her eyes glistening. "Yeah," she breathes. "I am. But what if this isn't really who I am? What if I wanted to be Nyelle so bad that I've lost myself along the way?"

I reach for her. The distance between us feels like a canyon, and I can't stand it any longer. She doesn't resist when I wrap my arms around her.

"I don't think you're lost. You've just let yourself be who you've always wanted to be. And that makes you happy," I say into her hair, kissing the top of her head. "And you've made me happy along with you. So, as far as I'm concerned, you *are*... you. Exactly who you're supposed to be."

She peers up at me, wearing a hint of a smile, tears mixed with the rain soaking her face. "I've missed you."

"I've missed you too," I say, kissing her soft, wet lips. "Why'd I have to lose you for all those years?"

She pulls away, wiping the tears from her cheeks with a shake of her head. She's not ready for this part yet. To talk about what hurts.

We start walking again. I don't want to ask her any more questions. I can't. It's taken everything I have to get this much out of her. My chest feels so tight from the anxiety squeezing it, I'm surprised I'm still breathing.

"I made a promise." Nyelle's whisper barely cuts through the rain.

She stops in front of me at the edge of the forest with the cabin in sight, her hands clenched tight.

"Do you still have to keep the promise?" I ask. I'm watching the two halves of her being ripped apart as she struggles with what she has to tell me.

Nyelle shakes her head. "But I've kept it so long, I don't know how to let it go." She covers her face with her hands, sobbing.

Her shoulders shake with each tortured breath, and it's breaking me. I can't handle it. With just the touch of my hand on her shoulder, she collapses against me, unable to hold herself up any longer.

"It's okay," I console her, holding her tight. "You don't have to tell me."

"I will," she mutters into my soaked shirt. "I need to. It just...it hurts. It still hurts so much."

Henley starts barking. I peer over the top of Nyelle's head as my mother's car comes into view. Nyelle twists within my arms, still leaning against me. We remain still, watching my mother and Rae get out of the car in front of the cabin.

I keep my arm wrapped around Nyelle's shoulder and step forward. But she won't move.

"Cal, we've been trying to reach you," my mother says from under an umbrella. My stomach drops at the sight of her pinched brow. Her eyes scrunch, looking at Nyelle, then widen in recognition. "Nicole?"

"What's going on?" I ask, but I don't really want to hear whatever it is that caused the red rims under Rae's eyes. I brace myself.

"You know," Nyelle says beside me, redirecting my attention. She's staring at Rae.

Rae nods. "I know."

NICOLE

Day After Graduation—High School

I stare up at the stars, wishing they'd take all of my pain away. But I know if they did, there'd be nothing left of me.

A shooting star races overhead.

I close my eyes; tears spill out and run along my temples, soaking into my hair.

"I wish I were as brave as you," I murmur to the stars. "I wish I laughed more. I wish I took more chances. I wish I could be the girl you saw in me. Please make it stop hurting, and I promise that I'll be that girl. I promise to let it all go . . . and be happy . . . for you."

"Nicole? Nicole, is that you?" my mother calls to me from between the miniature evergreens bordering our yard. "What are you doing over there?"

She steps out from the shadows.

"Do you realize how late it is?" she continues. "Your father is supposed to be home soon. He had to attend the dinner without us because *you* disappeared the entire day. Now get off the neighbor's lawn so you can clean up before he arrives."

"Are you kidding?" I snap, glaring up at her. I let out a humorless laugh. "Of course you're not." I push myself up off the ground. And storm past her toward the house.

"Wash up, and come back downstairs so we can greet your father," my mother instructs as we enter the foyer.

My jaw clenches. I can taste the bitter anger forming on my

tongue. I whip around and she eyes me curiously. "You didn't tell me! You knew for *two* days and you didn't say a word!"

"You were valedictorian," she responds so calmly that I want to rip her open, convinced there are wires holding her together. "We chose not to take away from the importance of your day."

"She's my best friend! My *only* friend!" I bellow, trembling. "You can't take her away from me like that! You had no right!"

"We are your parents," she replies. "We have every right to do what we think is best for you."

A car pulls into the driveway. My mother's eyes instinctively go to the door. She looks back at me.

"Go wash up."

"Go to hell!" I yell, my hands squeezed so tight my fingernails dig into my palms. A moment later my father enters the house appearing a little frantic. Which is strange. I've never seen him anything but composed. His frigid eyes narrow in on me, and a shiver runs up my spine. He closes the door behind him, and his gaze flickers between us, assessing the situation.

"Getting upset isn't going to make things better." His deep, thunderous voice echoes through me, despite his efforts to sound calm.

I clench my teeth. "You've controlled everything in my life, but you don't get this. You don't get to tell me how to feel."

He steps slowly toward me, and I back up. He holds up his hand, like he's approaching a spooked animal. "You need to calm down."

"Don't touch me!"

He stops, paralyzed by my defiance.

"You can't make it go away by pretending nothing happened." Rage has possessed my body, empowering me. "Because then you might as well erase me too, Daddy. She was the only real thing I had, and without her, I'm no one."

Continuing to move away from him, my back collides with the credenza, rocking it. The meticulously designed floral display tips over and crashes to the floor. My mother's hand goes to her mouth.

I crumple to my knees, sobbing into my hands.

"Pick yourself up and be the girl I raised. *This* is not who you are." He sounds disgusted.

I lift my head and glower at him. "Maybe I don't want to be your perfect little girl anymore." I slam my fists down onto the glass scattered all over the floor, shredding his perfect girl apart.

"Nicole, stop!" he demands.

I glare at him and raise my clenched fists, colliding with the broken glass again. I can't feel a thing. The shards slicing through my flesh aren't enough to mask the pain tearing my insides apart.

"What do you think you're doing?" my father bellows, his voice carrying throughout the entire house.

"What's wrong? Am I not pretty enough? Or smart enough? Or perfect enough?" I challenge, ripping away the pretty packaging and spilling out what's been trapped inside my entire life.

His face twists, repulsed by what he sees.

"Nicole, you're bleeding all over the floor!" my mother cries.

I stare defiantly up at my father as my fists smash into the broken glass again.

My father turns away. "Call Dr. Xavier. Tell him to use the back door. And clean this up." My mother scurries to the kitchen.

"Did I *disappoint* you, Daddy?!" I scream. But he's already out the front door.

And I'm alone.

I collapse in the blood that's smeared across the polished wood and cry, mourning the loss of us both.

TWENTY-TWO

"Richelle's dead," Nyelle utters in a single breath.

I stare at her. I couldn't have heard her right. There's no way she just said...

I turn to Rae. Tears are falling from her eyes. I've *never* seen her cry before. Not even when she tore up her leg wiping out on her skateboard.

I look to my mother. She presses her lips together, and her eyes meet mine in a silent apology.

"No," I say, shaking my head. "No. She's not. She can't be."

"Cal, I'm so sorry," my mother says, taking a step toward me. "Her mother called... after she heard your message."

"I don't understand," I respond. "How?"

"Let's go inside," my mother encourages us, leading the way.

I continue to stand in the rain, unable to move. Something warm wraps around my hand. I look down at it, and there's another hand holding it.

"Let's go inside," Nyelle says softly. I search her stormy blue eyes for some sense of comfort. But they're filled with so much hurt, they're screaming.

I walk alongside her to the steps, where Rae is waiting for us. I catch my foot on the bottom step and grab the railing to keep from falling, although it feels like I already have—off a hundred-foot cliff onto jagged rocks.

Nyelle grips my hand tighter, and Rae stops, but they don't say anything. I straighten and continue into the cabin.

"Why don't you put some dry clothes on?" my mother suggests.

"What happened to Richelle?" I demand.

"She had leukemia," Nyelle says.

I spin around to face her. "You knew..." I stop. Among the chaos tearing through my head, it becomes clear. "That was the promise you made?"

She nods, her chin trembling.

"You promised you wouldn't tell us she had cancer?" Rae asks, like she's accusing her of treason.

Nyelle bites at her lip. "She didn't want you to know. She was worried you'd treat her different because she might...die," she explains, her voice quivering. "She thought when she got better and moved back to Renfield, you'd never have to know. Like nothing ever happened." She swallows. "But you can't make it go away by pretending it never happened."

Nyelle raises her eyes and connects with mine, like she knows I was there and heard her say those words to her father.

My mouth drops. That's what I overheard.

"Graduation," I utter. "That's why you were crying..."

"She died the day before."

Nothing moves. The air is so still, I swear the earth has stopped rotating.

"That's why you're Nyelle, isn't it?" Rae concludes, disrupting the stillness. "You combined your names."

Nyelle closes her eyes, releasing a rush of tears down her cheeks.

I rub my face, even though I can't feel it, and I walk up the stairs. I can't do this.

"Cal," my mother calls, and I turn around on the landing. "Don't shut us out, okay? Change and come back down?"

I nod slightly and continue to the room, closing the door behind me.

I lean against the door with my palm pressed to my forehead, wanting to shut it all off and wake up from this twisted nightmare.

I kick off my boots and tug my soaked sweater off, tossing it to the ground. I start toward the dresser, but my legs give out. I'm hunched over on the floor when I feel her warm arms wrap around me. She presses her cheek against my back. I feel like I'm sinking and she's the only thing keeping me from going under. We stay on the floor, huddled together for...I have no idea how long. And I focus on breathing, because that's all I can do.

When Nyelle releases me, I slowly straighten, sitting on the floor with my back against the side of the bed. Nyelle slides next to me. And Rae lowers herself from the bed to sit on my other side. I wrap my arm around Nyelle and grab Rae's hand. And then we sit in silence. Not moving. We just...sit.

"That's why she moved to San Francisco? Because she was sick?" My voice finally finds the surface. Shadows have filled the room, so I can only assume the sun has set.

"Yeah," Nyelle replies in a breath.

"But I talked to her all the time. She never...I didn't know. I feel like I should've known."

"It's not how she wanted you to remember her. She didn't want you to see her sick," Nyelle explains, her cheek pressed to my chest and her arms wrapped around my waist. "She only wanted to go back to Renfield, to you guys, when she beat it. She went into remission for a short time, and she was excited because her parents were talking about moving back. But then . . . it came back."

"We were her best friends. We deserved to know. We should have been there for her." Rae says, her voice strained with anger.

"But that's not what she wanted. It was so important to her that you only remembered her happy and full of life." She lets out a broken breath, and I squeeze her. "But she was *always* so full of life, even when she was miserable after chemo. Or when she had to have a blood transfusion. She didn't let it break her."

I can't imagine Richelle ill. But I can picture her defiant and determined to get better. That sounds exactly like the opinionated, bold girl I knew.

"What are you doing?" I ask, approaching the girls sitting at the edge of the tall grass behind our house.

"Cal's here!" Rae announces. "Let's do something else."

"We're not done," Richelle says sternly. Then she looks up at me. "We're making flower necklaces." She twists a daisy stem around another.

Nicole is working on a pink and purple strand. And Rae has a bunch of broken flower heads sitting in front of her.

"You should stay, and we'll have a pretend wedding," Richelle suggests happily. "You and I can be the bride and groom. Nicole will be the maid of honor, and Rae will be the flower girl."

"The flower girl?" Rae shoots back, throwing a handful of flower heads at Richelle.

"Uh, I think I'm going to see what Brady and Craig are doing," I say, slowly backing away.

"Push us higher!" Richelle squeals, standing on the tire swing, holding on to the chains with her head dipped back.

I rush toward the tire and push it as far away from me as I can before running out of its way. The tire begins to spin as it flies back.

"I think I'm going to throw up," Rae hollers.

Nicole and Richelle start laughing.

"Higher, Cal!" Richelle demands again with a huge smile on her face. "I want to touch the stars."

"I want your love. Ooh baby, I want your love," Richelle sings, standing on the orange and plaid couch that we just carried up from the basement.

"This song sucks. This song sucks," Rae bellows in the background, crashing the cymbal.

Richelle ignores her.

Nicole carries the melody with the keyboard, and I basically pretend to play the guitar. We're terrible. I'm sure there are dogs howling somewhere in the neighborhood.

Richelle leans on the back of the couch and does a dramatic kick. "I want your love tonight."

Richelle is so into it, she doesn't care what she looks like, which makes me laugh.

"Was that how we're supposed to do it?" I ask, pulling back and looking at her nervously. I want to wipe the saliva off my mouth, but I'm afraid it'll hurt her feelings.

"It felt pretty good to me," Richelle says with a smile. "But maybe we should keep practicing."

"Okay." I'm not going to argue with her.

I lean in to kiss her soft mouth, willing to practice all day if we have to. If she'll let me.

"Then I guess I'll see you at Crenshaw."

"I'll never see her again," I utter in disbelief, remembering her words as if she'd just said them.

"Were you there when she died?" Rae asks. "Did you see . . . ?"

"No." Nyelle answers quietly. "I didn't know until after. But I visited her as much as I could. I went to the clinic with her when she got chemo. I sat by her bed in the hospital and talked about stupid things to distract her. And I lay under the stars with her, wishing for them to make her better."

I close my eyes and swallow against the tightness in my throat.

"She made you keep that promise," I struggle to say. "You were watching her die, and you couldn't talk to anyone about it."

"I was watching her *live*," Nyelle counters, her words wrapped in tears. "Every day I was with her was another day I got to laugh with her, or plan our lives together. She's still the bravest person I've ever known."

"So we lost you both because of this promise, but barely got one of you back," Rae says, leaning her head against the bed with a ragged breath, trying to fight the emotion stuck in her throat. "I hate this."

"I'm sorry," Nyelle offers passionately. "I would've lost her if I told you. And she was my best friend. The only person who knew me. I couldn't…I didn't want to hurt you. I'm so sorry."

Nyelle stops, unable to continue, burying her face in my chest. I rub her arm and kiss the top of her head.

Nyelle wipes her face and takes a deep breath before continuing. "She wanted to start a band with you, Rae. And—"

"Please don't tell me she wanted to sing," Rae blurts.

We stare at her. Her face is damp from crying, and her eyes are bloodshot. She puts up her hands in defense. "What? She was a *horrible* singer."

I press my lips together to suppress a smile. Nyelle releases a burst of laughter. Rae starts laughing too, making me smile wider. The smile feels good but strange. Mixed with the sorrow. Because underneath it, my chest feels like it's collapsed.

Nyelle steadies her gaze on me. "She was in love with you."

"I knew it!" Rae exclaims like she just won a bet.

I stare at her. "Seriously?"

"Dude, you're oblivious when it comes to girls. I just like being right." She sits back, gloating.

I roll my eyes, then ask Nyelle, "I hurt her when I told her about Lily, didn't I?"

"Yeah," Nyelle says, her expression sympathetic. "But it's not your fault. You didn't know."

I'm silent. I'm such an idiot. She stopped talking to me over a girl who didn't really mean anything to me. All because I couldn't see how she felt about me.

"She forgave you," Nyelle says, as if reading my mind. "She tried to call you a few months later, but you never responded. So she thought she screwed up."

"What? I never heard from her."

"Oh." Rae sighs in realization. "That was the summer your dad got the company phones and your number changed. Remember, you were pissed?"

"You've got to be kidding me," I groan. "I wish I'd tried harder. I shouldn't have given up on her."

I look down at the floor and close my eyes. Regret is a vicious beast, clawing deep and pouring salt on the wound when you try to heal. I should have fought for her.

Nyelle and Rae remain silent. "I'm so angry," Rae says after a while. "I can't help it. I am."

Nyelle looks between us with a small smile. "I have an idea that might help."

"I don't want ice cream," I grumble.

Nyelle laughs. "No, not that." She eases herself off the floor. "Put on a shirt. We're going outside."

I turn to Rae. She looks at me and shrugs. "Let's go."

I sigh in resignation and push myself up. My body feels stiff and tired. It takes me a minute to get myself together before pulling on a long-sleeved shirt. I stuff my bare feet in my boots, not bothering to lace them.

My mother watches us come down the stairs from the couch, where Henley is curled up at her feet.

"How are you guys doing?" she asks tentatively.

"I'm pissed," Rae announces. "So Nyelle's going to help me deal."

My mother nods slowly, digesting it. "Well, I'm here too. I just figured I'd give you three some space for a bit."

"Thanks, Mom."

We walk out onto the porch.

"Now what?" Rae asks.

"Scream," Nyelle tells her.

Rae looks at her like she's crazy. Then it hits her. The day we—well, Richelle—changed Nicole's grade, and we stood in the back of the school and released all of our frustrations.

"Okay," Rae replies, gripping the railing.

Nyelle and I line up next to her, facing the dark woods.

Rae inhales deep and then lets go. Her scream is piercing. I know it's scaring small animals in the woods. And then Nyelle begins screaming along with her, with a pitch so high and full of emotion it could shatter all the windows in the house.

I reach down deep and take all the shit that's been thrown at me today and release it too, letting my pain and anger echo in the dark.

We stand on the porch, side by side, screaming at the world for taking Richelle from us. For leaving us here to create memories without her. Moments she deserved to be a part of. For the years I didn't get to be there for her when she was sick. For the friendship I lost. And all the hurt that it caused. I scream for all of us, until there's nothing left.

When we're done, my shoulders sink in exhaustion. Rae collapses against me, drained. I hug her, and then Nyelle comes up behind her and squeezes her too. If Richelle's seeing this, she's laughing, because I know we look ridiculous.

"I miss her," I say quietly, still holding on to the girls. "I've missed her for a long time."

"I miss her every day," Nyelle whispers, looking up at me, over Rae.

"Okay, get off me," Rae demands. "I'm done. I can't cry, scream, or do anything anymore. I'm going to fall on my face."

I grin, releasing her. Nyelle spins her around, grasping her shoulders, and kisses her on the mouth. It happens so fast, Rae is left stunned.

"I love you, Raelyn," Nyelle declares.

I fight to keep from laughing, but fail. "Rae, I—"

"Don't you dare," she warns. "There's already been way too much touching going on tonight. I can't handle all of this love shit too." She walks determinedly into the cabin.

Nyelle turns back to me, still laughing with me. It *feels* good to listen to her laugh.

When she looks into my eyes, her laughter drifts into a soft smile. I don't look away, brushing her cheek with my thumb.

My heart is pounding as I open my mouth to say—

"Are you guys coming?" Rae calls out. My hand falls away along with my words as we both turn to the door.

I poke my head into the bedroom next to mine, where Rae is lying on the bed with headphones covering her ears, tapping her drumsticks in the air to an unheard beat. When she notices I'm in the doorway, she sits up and pulls the headphones around her neck.

"Have you seen Nyelle?" I ask her.

"No. She was downstairs with your mom earlier," she replies. "Not there?"

I shake my head. I've been in the garage for the past few hours, distracting myself with bike parts to keep from thinking about how fucked up this whole thing is—Richelle dying of cancer, Nicole becoming Nyelle to deal with it, and it all happening around me without me knowing it.

"Are you coming back to Renfield with us tomorrow?" Rae asks, standing.

"I'm staying here to work," I tell her.

"I think Nyelle's coming with us."

I feel my shoulders stiffen. "She is?"

"I think that's what Maura was talking to her about downstairs. She offered to help her talk to her parents."

"Where is she, Rae?" I hurry down the stairs. Not liking that she's disappeared right after she discussed facing her parents. I need to find her.

"I don't know," she replies, following after me.

My mother left to get food for dinner. The groceries Nyelle and I bought aren't exactly ideal for family dinners. I'm hoping Nyelle left with her.

We didn't talk much last night, after all the secrets were torn open. The three of us passed out on the shag carpet in front of the fire, emotionally inebriated. And we've each spent today doing whatever we needed to distract ourselves from the pain.

I continue outside and around to the back of the house and stop at the corner when I spot Nyelle behind the cabin, pacing.

She's shaking her head, walking back and forth in quick strides. Her hands clench and release as she mutters a blur of words.

"She's still crazy," Rae says from beside me.

"She's *not* crazy," I defend, hesitating to approach her. "She's coping."

"Because she's crazy," Rae repeats. "What do we do?"

"I've got this," I assure her, watching Nyelle continue to get worked up.

"Are you sure? Maybe we should wait for Maura." The concerned tone in Rae's voice makes me grin. She cares. And I like it.

"It's okay, Rae. Really. I've got this." *I think.* Taking a breath, I walk toward Nyelle, leaving Rae at the corner of the house.

When I get close enough, I ask, "Who do you talk to when you do that?"

Nyelle stops in the worn path she's making on the lawn, looking up at me in surprise. "Oh, hi. What did you say?"

"When you do this, you know, walk back and forth, talking out loud. Who are you talking to?"

She smiles uneasily. "Me, mostly. Sometimes Richelle. It's what I do instead of screaming, I guess."

I'd figured that's what it was.

"I'm going home to see my parents tomorrow," she informs me, blowing out a quick breath. "I'm a little nervous."

"Makes sense," I say, getting closer. "Do you want to see them? You don't have to, you know."

"I know. I don't hate them, Cal. I just don't want to be like them." Her eyes dip when she adds, "Besides, where else do I have to go?"

I'm about to tell her to come back with me. And she must know it, because she cuts me off before I can offer. "We knew this was coming. I told you I had to leave. And I still do. I don't belong at Crenshaw. You know that."

I nod, swallowing the bitterness in my mouth. "Will you go to Harvard?"

"I don't know," Nyelle responds thoughtfully. "That was always my dad's dream. I'm not sure if it's mine."

With a sinking exhale, Nyelle sits on the ground and lies back on the grass. "I'm not sure what I'm supposed to do anymore."

"Well, you're Nyelle for a reason," I say thoughtfully, lying next to her on the cold, damp ground. I should have known it was going to be miserable down here. "Because you wanted to start again."

"Richelle wanted this life for me. For me to be happy. That's all she ever wanted." I glance over at her. Her eyes are closed and her lips are trembling. "I miss her. I miss her so much, Cal. It still hurts, and I don't know what to do without her." Nyelle chokes on a tearful laugh. "God, I don't want to cry anymore."

I reach for her hand and hold it tight. Sharing the secrets that've weighed her down all these years hasn't exactly set her free. Nyelle is still lost and still hurting. And I wish I could be the one to protect her from all the expectations that will keep her from being happy.

"You're not alone," I say quietly.

She rolls her head to look at me, her eyes glassy with unshed tears. "I know." A faint smile emerges. "You and Rae are my best friends. You always have been, even when you didn't know it. And I've missed you guys.

"And I'm so sorry I hurt you," she continues, her voice cracking. "I never wanted to hurt you, I swear. So... please don't walk away from me, Cal. Things are going to be awful when I go back to Renfield. I know it, but I have to do it. So I need you to be my friend. I can't do this without you."

"Of course," I say, having a hard time forming the words. I want to sink into the ground and let it swallow me whole. She wants to be friends. We were always friends. But that's not exactly what I had in mind now. And I can't help thinking about what she said about falling backward in the dark. Well, I just landed in a pit of spears, and it fucking hurts.

"I'm not going anywhere," I say, squeezing her hand as I

redirect my attention to the clouds moving swiftly across the night sky. There aren't any stars to wish on tonight. I could really use a do-over right about now.

With that spear jutting through my heart, I assure her, "I'm not walking away. I promise."

The next morning, I see them off to Renfield, staying behind with Zac and Henley to earn back the money I've spent on airfare. I still plan on buying that drum set for Rae. Hopefully, I'll be able to get it for her before she goes to Berklee, because I'm convinced she's going.

When I return to Crenshaw at the end of the week, everything seems...quieter. I know it's because Nyelle isn't with me. I enter the apartment, not really wanting to be here without her. But she has to figure out what's best for her right now. And I need to let her do that without any added pressure from me. I don't want to be another person putting an expectation on her.

I open the door to my room and I falter, like something inside me just ruptured.

Strewn across my floor are thirty deflated balloons, with "You are loved" tied to each string. I sit down on the edge of my bed, picking up a blue balloon, silently blaming it for making me feel like shit.

I take off my jacket and throw it on my desk chair, but it slides off and lands on the floor. When I bend over to pick it up, I notice a yellow piece of paper sticking out of the inside pocket. I actually didn't know I had an inside pocket until now.

The paper is worn, like it's been opened and closed a hundred times. After carefully unfolding it, I find "Nicole and Richelle's

List," and then in parentheses next to it in another handwriting it says, "Ni-Elle." I laugh. This is *the list*.

There are little boxes next to each item. I smile wide, having been a witness to most of them. "Hot Air Balloon Ride" is circled without a check mark. And there are three question marks next to "Relive the Happiest Day of Your Life."

Sitting on the bed, I continue scanning the checked boxes. Then I stop. The paper flutters within my shaking hands when I see the check mark next to:

"Fall in Love (with Cal)."

EPILOGUE

Spring Break—Sophomore Year of College

"Hi!"

I just about drop the wrench that's in my hand when her voice echoes through the garage.

Then I just about drop to my knees when I see her standing in the entrance. Her hair is back to its natural black, pinned in a messy bun at the nape of her neck. And she's wearing a short yellow dress, looking even more gorgeous than she did the first day I saw her, wearing that same shade. She's still the most beautiful girl I've ever seen.

"Hi," I say, clearing my throat, trying to find my voice. "I wasn't expecting you until tomorrow."

I haven't seen Nyelle since she returned to Renfield two months ago. Although we've texted or spoken just about every day, it still hasn't been easy for her. Being back with her parents, she has to fight the expectations they try to put upon her, so she doesn't become *that* girl again. I hear the pressure in her voice sometimes when we talk, and I say whatever I can to make sure she doesn't give in. Rae's probably a better help than I am. She couldn't stand the closed-off version of Nicole and lets her know it whenever she sees

Nyelle slipping back into the perfected shell. Although I probably need to give my mother the most credit, since she's the one who's introduced Nyelle to a psychologist friend of hers.

Her parents have slowly come to terms with calling her Nyelle, since that's the girl she's always wanted to be. But she did take back Bentley instead of Preston, Richelle's mother's maiden name. And oddly enough, her parents are backing off on the whole Harvard pressure. I can only imagine how hard it is for her father, since it's been *his* dream since her conception.

I look down at my grease-covered hands and back at the form-fitting dress, cursing the world. Nyelle notices the distraught look on my face and laughs. I grab a rag and do my best to wipe my hands clean as Nyelle slowly approaches. If she gets much closer, there's no way I'm going to be able to keep my hands off her.

"I had this whole thing planned for when you're supposed to arrive tomorrow night," I say when she stops to admire the motorcycle, running her hand along the blue flames on the gas tank.

"And you can't do it *now*?" she questions, taking a few steps closer. I haven't moved. The way the dress hugs her hips is too tempting, and I don't trust myself.

I look around the garage. "This wasn't exactly where I wanted to do it."

"Then we can wait until tonight if you want."

I wipe the sweat from my hands. "I don't know if I can wait that long. It's been torture waiting *this* long."

"Then tell me where we'll be, when I arrive tomorrow night," she requests, closing her eyes.

"What?" I ask, confused.

"I'll picture it in my head," she explains with her eyes still closed. "I arrive. It's dark. You come out of the cabin, then..."

I take a breath, feeling my heart thrumming. Here goes nothing.

"I take your hand," I begin.

"Ooh, I like this so far."

"I haven't done anything yet," I say with a chuckle.

"You're holding my hand," she counters, lifting her hand for me to take.

"My hands are dirty."

"I don't care about getting dirty," she says, still waiting with her hand extended.

I step closer so that we're only a deep breath apart and take her hand in mine—hoping she doesn't realize that it's shaking. She smiles.

I stand in front of her, looking at her eyes, which are still closed, trying to imagine the shade of blue they'd be right now if they were open.

"Then we walk to the back of the cabin and lie down on the grass to look at the stars. And it's a cloudless night. There are so many stars it looks like someone scattered confetti all over the sky."

She smiles wider.

"And then what?" she asks when I'm quiet too long, lost in the smile on her face.

What I'm about to say releases a thousand of those butterflies she talks about in my chest.

"We wait until there's a shooting star, so we can wish on a second chance. And when it happens... I wish for you."

Her eyes open. They are so bright, I'm almost blinded by them.

"For me?"

"Yeah. Nyelle, I want to be your best friend. But I can't be *just* friends with you," I explain, taking in the big crystal-blue eyes staring at me. And then…I fall backward. "You're her…my *what if* girl. The girl I will forever regret if I let you go."

In an unexpected motion, Nyelle wraps her arms around my neck and jumps up on me. I catch her, faltering back a step. I'm never prepared when she does this.

"I'm getting your dress dirty," I say, my hands pressed against the curves that the tight dress accentuates so well.

"I don't care," she says, kissing my cheek. "Because that's exactly who I want to be." She kisses my mouth quickly. "And that's the answer to the question you asked me."

"What question?"

"The night we were lying on the grass, and I said I didn't know."

"Who you wanted to be?" I recall.

"Your *what if* girl," she responds, hugging me. "The girl you can't be without."

"You're more than that, you know," I tell her. She pulls back to look at me. "You always have been."

Her mouth is on mine, and I can feel the tension leave me. I've run this entire moment over in my mind a thousand times, with a hundred different endings. This one is better than all of them.

I'm hoping Zac doesn't come in to find us kissing with her legs wrapped around me and her skirt hiked up to her hips with my hands cupping her where the fabric ends and her flesh begins.

She slowly eases away and stares into my eyes, unable to contain her smile. "You know you're never getting rid of me now, right?"

"Sounds good to me," I say, slowly lowering her to the ground but keeping my arms around her.

"So…I sent a letter to Harvard, explaining my situation, and they extended my acceptance."

My eyes widen. "You're going to Harvard?"

She nods. “Rae told me you’re going to BU. It all worked out perfectly, don’t you think?”

“I was waiting to tell you…until you decided what you were going to do,” I explain, feeling guilty, not wanting her to think I was keeping it from her. “You needed to make the decision on your own without me influencing it in any way.”

“I know,” she says, squeezing me with her head pressed to my chest. “Have you declared a major yet?”

“I have no idea what I want to do with my life except to have you and Rae in it.”

A gorgeous smile emerges on Nyelle’s face.

“How come Harvard was never on the list?” I ask, holding her against me.

“I wasn’t sure if going was because *I* wanted to go, or because my father expected me to. But I’ve worked really hard to earn that acceptance. And it’s one of the best universities in the country. As Rae told me, I’d be stupid not to go.”

I laugh.

“So…you found the list?” Nyelle confirms, peering up cautiously.

“I liked the last one,” I say, kissing her gently, letting our lips linger.

Her cheeks are flushed when we part. “I still have one more to check off.”

“The hot air balloon?” I confirm. “We can do that.”

“I think I want to get married in a hot air balloon,” she announces casually.

“What?” I start choking. Literally. I start choking.

She laughs and then keeps laughing, like she and Rae do when they’re messing with me.

“That wasn’t nice.”

"You should have seen your face," she returns, about to start laughing again, but I interrupt her with another deep kiss.

"At least I don't have to worry about your meeting-the-parents fear," she says when she slowly pulls away. "You've already met mine."

"And they scare the shit out of me," I respond. She laughs.

"Come on. There's something we have to do," she says, stepping away and taking my hand.

"What's that?" I ask as we exit the garage.

Standing in front of the cabin is Rae, holding enough balloons to make me worry they might send her floating off into the sky.

"Relive the happiest day of my life," she announces, squeezing my hand.

"What were you guys doing in there?" Rae huffs; then she notices the grease handprints on Nyelle's dress. "Forget it. I don't want to know."

Nyelle takes the balloons from Rae and carefully divides them up between us. They each have the "You are loved" message tied to them.

"These are for Richelle," Nyelle explains, "from us. So she always knows. And we never forget her."

I hold the strings of the balloons with one hand and take Nyelle's hand in the other.

"Ready?" she asks, looking between us. "On three. One. Two. Three."

We release the balloons and watch them drift off.

"I love you," I lean over and say in Nyelle's ear.

"It's about time," Rae grumbles, making Nyelle laugh the laugh that makes everything right. My laugh.

"I've always loved you," she says. "You were my first wish."

A NOTE FROM THE AUTHOR

This is a story that can easily be spoiled, but I ask that it not be by you. If you choose to leave a review, I kindly request that you allow the next readers to have their own journey, to experience whatever emotions this story may stir in them, spoiler free.

I hope *What If* made you *feel.* It's what I strive for each time I create. Every day I am reminded how lucky I am to do what I do. Thank you for choosing to read *this* novel, and thank you so much for being a part of *my* journey.

(Now that you know the ending, you may want to read *What If* again! It's delicately constructed so that it's an entirely different experience when you know the truth. Remember, *everything's* on purpose!)

~ Rebecca Donovan

Bonus Material

NYELLE'S EPILOGUE

You can do this.

Shit. I can't believe I'm doing this.

You've got this.

Fuck. What was I thinking? I shouldn't be here.

It's going to be fine.

"Stop doing your crazy talking-to-yourself thing and help me get all these fricken balloons out of the car."

I spin around, clenching my fists to keep from running my hands down the front of my dress. I've been fighting against those little urges since I returned home two months ago.

I hate that the *perfect* is still rooted inside me. The minute I set foot in Renfield it started spreading its tendrils. I wish I could rip it out.

I won't let it. I won't let it take over.

"Why are you staring at me like that?" Rae asks, opening the back of her mom's SUV.

"Umm...no reason," I tell her, distracted by the voice that fights for who I really am. The voice that keeps me...me.

I know I sound crazy talking to myself. But I refuse to live a life of holding everything in, letting the emotions build up until I feel like I'm being crushed from the inside out. I've been getting help on how to deal better. It's sorta-kinda working.

Obviously, not today.

I walk around the car and duck under the cluster of colorful balloons to gather the strings.

"You're freaking out, aren't you?" Rae says, shutting the trunk as I do my best to untangle the balloons so they separate when we release them. "You're the one who wanted to get here a day early. You can't get all crazy now. Wait…forget that. I prefer the crazy."

Despite the delivery, I know she's saying this because she cares—in her own Rae way. She's worried that I'll get lost under the *perfect* mask again. The one everyone in Renfield expected me to put back on as soon as I returned. Everyone except Cal and Rae.

"That's why I love you."

"Whatever," she grumbles, walking away.

I don't know how I survived all those years without Rae and Cal in my life. Letting them go was one of the hardest decisions I've ever had to make. But it's not one I regret either. Because if I had lost Richelle…

I stutter in my steps, dismissing the cavernous pain that opened up inside me the day I *did* lose her. The pain I fought for two years under the guise of a lie. A lie I wanted so much to believe that it became my reality. I am now the girl I was never brave enough to be. Experiencing life with the wonderment of a child. No expectations. No judgment. I don't care what anyone thinks of me, as long as they let me be myself. Living that lie gave me another chance to see everything and everyone around me for the first time… even Cal.

And now…I'm truly who I'm meant to be.

I eye the garage, and the nervousness erupts again. I've been thinking about this day for so long, I should be excited. I mean, I *am* excited. I haven't seen Cal in about two months, despite talking or texting every day. Today... I'll finally open up and tell him how I feel about him. How I've *always* felt about him.

I bite my lip... or I don't tell him. Because if things don't go like I wished for, then the butterfly that's flapping in my chest will easily be crushed.

Did I say excited? Now I'm terrified.

I close my eyes and take a deep breath.

Release.

It's going to be okay.

Inhale.

Release.

It's going to be okay.

"You're doing it again," Rae calls to me, leaning against the car. "Give me the balloons and go get Cal before you totally freak more than you already are."

"Okay," I agree, more to myself than to Rae. "I'll be right back."

I hand her the balloons, and she's instantly lost behind them. I laugh.

"Are you sure you've got them?"

"Shut up," she says from somewhere behind the bouquet of colors. "Go."

I walk tentatively to the garage and stand at the entrance. The nervousness dissipates at the sight of him, replaced by the calm I always feel when I'm with him.

He's oblivious to my presence. I watch as he concentrates on the partially assembled motorcycle in front of him. His tall, lean body is crouched over as his callused fingers work a bolt into place. His profile is thin lines and sharp angles, the light reflecting off the hint of stubble along his jaw. His dark hair has grown out since I cut it.

It's beginning to flip up at the ends again. I grin, wanting nothing more than to run my fingers through it.

Focus.

"Hi." My voice echoes in the huge space. Cal jumps to his feet.

His hazel eyes widen. "Hi," he croaks out, clearing his throat. "I wasn't expecting you until tomorrow."

Cal scans the length of me, swallowing. Then his eyes lock with mine, and all words are lost. It reminds me of the day I wore the wedding dress, ill-fitting and pooled around my feet. That dress was all about letting go, and moving on.

And this one... this dress that I was drawn to when I saw it sitting in the store window, enticing me like the center of a daisy lures a bumblebee. This dress is all about starting again.

I know the delving look in his eyes has nothing to do with the tight dress. He's always looked at me like this. Like he's seeing who I really am. Even beneath my skin. And he accepts me as I am. No matter who that is.

Cal finally blinks, and grabs a rag from the bench to wipe the grease from his hands. I know he wants to touch me. I can feel the tension. But he doesn't make a move. Watching Cal fidget in front of me, unsure what to do, makes me smile again.

A blush creeps up to my cheeks when I look him over, slowly tracing the curves of his chest and lines of his stomach underneath the worn T-shirt as it clings to him. I run a hand along a bike parked beside me, trying to redirect my thoughts, knowing exactly what *I* want to do to him.

Stop! Stay focused!

"I had this whole thing planned for when you're supposed to arrive tomorrow night," he says. I snap my head up, my cheeks hot.

Hoping he can't read my thoughts, I step closer to him as he remains frozen in place. "And you can't do it *now*?"

His eyes flip around the garage. "This wasn't exactly where I wanted to do it."

I'm fighting the urge to touch him. Forget that. To jump up on him. "Then we can wait until tonight if you want."

He shifts uncomfortably. "I don't know if I can wait that long. It's been torture waiting *this* long."

"Then tell me where we'll be, when I arrive tomorrow night." I close my eyes so I can imagine it in my head as I listen to his voice.

"What?"

"I'll picture it in my head," I explain, keeping my eyes shut. "I arrive. It's dark. You come out of the cabin, then..."

The butterfly within my chest erupts in a flutter as I sense him moving closer. I breathe in the scent that I love so much, especially when he's lying next to me in bed, holding me against him. It reminds me of dewy grass in the morning, enveloped in a soothing fragrance that feels like... home. Or a home I've always wanted anyway.

"I take your hand," he says quietly.

"Ooh, I like this so far." I smile, already feeling the tingles cascade along my arm at just the thought of his hands holding mine.

"I haven't done anything yet." He laughs.

"You're holding my hand," I reply, reaching out my hand, urging him to take it.

"My hands are dirty."

I want to laugh. It's the last thing I'm worried about. "I don't care about getting dirty."

I can feel the wisp of his breath upon my lips as he moves closer and then the warmth of his hand taking hold of mine. My mouth erupts into a huge smile. It's like I can *feel* him holding me together. A calming swell washes away every troubled thought. Like it always has.

"Then we walk to the back of the cabin and lie down on the grass to look at the stars. And it's a cloudless night. There are so many stars it looks like someone scattered confetti all over the sky."

My smile widens, anticipating what he'll say next. I wait. But he remains silent.

"And then what?"

I'm holding my breath. I squeeze his hand tighter. *Please, oh, please tell me. Please.*

"We wait until there's a shooting star, so we can wish on a second chance. And when it happens... I wish for you."

My eyes flip open. I feel like I am that shooting star, flying across the sky.

"For me?" Please tell me he really just said that.

"Yeah. Nyelle, I want to be your best friend. But I can't be *just* friends with you," he says, looking me in the eye like he does. So intensely. So sincerely. Consuming me. "You're her... my *what if* girl. The girl I will forever regret if I let you go."

I can't contain myself anymore. I'm way too fricken happy, and he needs to know it. I throw my arms around his neck and leap up, forcing him to catch me as I wrap my legs around him. I don't care that the dress has practically become a shirt. If it were up to me, we'd both be stripped down and on the floor of this garage in about thirty seconds.

"I'm getting your dress dirty," he says, his hands pressed under my thighs, along the skin that the dress no longer covers.

"I don't care," I say, peppering kisses along his jaw. "Because that's exactly who I want to be. And that's the answer to the question you asked me." I kiss his soft lips. I've missed these lips. Why did I *ever* think I didn't want to kiss this boy?!

And he is my best friend. But he's *always* been so much more.

"What question?"

"The night we were lying on the grass, and I said I didn't know," I answer, continuing to kiss his face.

"Who you wanted to be?" he clarifies.

I was so lost that night. And I just wanted to be found. To know where I belonged in this world. But Cal knew exactly who I was all along, even beneath the mask. And now I'm exactly where I'm supposed to be... with him.

"Your *what if* girl!" I exclaim, hugging him tight. "The girl you can't be without."

"You're more than that, you know." Cal pulls away far enough to peer into my eyes. He has the kindest eyes, and I could look into them for a lifetime. "You always have been."

The butterfly has exploded into thousands of shooting stars, hearing him say this—knowing he's felt the same this entire time.

I press my lips firmly to his and pull him against me. The stubble on his face scratches my skin as he kisses me back, sliding his tongue into my mouth. I release a small gasp as he grips me tighter. I run my fingers up his neck and into his hair, moving my mouth with his. If we don't stop now, Rae's going to walk in on us. And she might see more than Eric ever did.

I slowly pull away. Wearing a satiated smile, I look him in the eye and say, "You know you're never getting rid of me now, right?"

"Sounds good to me." He sets me on my feet, his arms wrapped around my waist.

I tell him about Harvard. And how everything has worked out exactly how it's meant to be, with him and Rae going to school in Boston too. In spite of the pressure my father placed on me my entire life, it's actually something I want.

"How come Harvard was never on the list?" he asks curiously, as I rest my head on his chest, thinking about my best friend.

I lift my head to look up at him.

"I wasn't sure if going was because *I* wanted to go, or because my father expected me to. But I've worked really hard to earn that acceptance. And it's one of the best universities in the country. As Rae told me, I'd be stupid not to go."

He laughs. Rae's candor has kept me grounded for the past two months since I've returned home. I still get lost sometimes, not knowing how I fit in the world around me. My parents are trying to accept who I really am and the decisions I've made. But they still have expectations they can't quite let go of. So when I start sliding on the mask of feigned perfection, Rae helps pull it back off.

I don't know if they'll ever truly understand why I had to leave and find myself, but I do know they don't want to lose me again.

I haven't completely forgiven them for not telling me about Richelle. But I know they didn't take her away from me like I accused them of doing. They never could. She's the bravest part of me.

"So...you found the list?" I ask tentatively. When I tucked it in his inside pocket before I left for Renfield, I knew there was a chance he might not find it.

"I liked the last one," he says, brushing his lips across mine, taking my breath with him when he eases away.

I can feel the heat in my cheeks. He knows.

He knows I love him. I loved him before I understood what love really was.

I casually mention wanting to get married in a hot air balloon, just to see his reaction. And it's so worth it. He seriously has the best reactions when he freaks out. I laugh so hard, my stomach hurts.

Oh, I love this boy.

I take him by the hand and lead him out of the garage. "Come on. There's something we have to do."

"What's that?"

I smile brightly at Rae holding tight to the balloons shifting above her head, like they're begging to be set free.

"Relive the happiest day of my life," I tell him. And it is. It's a day I want to relive over and over again.

"What were you guys doing in there?" Rae demands. Her brows rise when I shift my dress down to its intended length. "Forget it. I don't want to know."

I rescue Rae from the balloons as she swats them out of her face. Carefully separating the strings, I hand some to each of them. Cal flips one of the "You are loved" tags over in his fingers and grins.

"These are for Richelle," I tell them, my throat tightening slightly, "from us. So she always knows. And we never forget her." I can feel the bitter burn of tears in the corners of my eyes. As happy as I am to be here with Cal and Rae, I miss the girl who wore daisies in her hair, and ran everywhere because she was just too excited to walk. The feisty girl who fought for her friends, and screamed at the world. The beautiful girl who loved to live, even for just one more day. I miss her... every day, as I will for the rest of my life.

Cal reaches for my hand. I smile up at him when he squeezes, like he understands more than I've said.

"Ready?" I glance over at Rae. She shrugs. "On three. One. Two. Three."

We release the balloons. I watch them drift up into the sky, scattering into the oblivion, calling out to my best friend: *You are loved, Richelle. Thank you for wishing this life for me. For wanting me to be happy. Thank you for being my friend.*

"I love you." His words drift into my ear and sink straight into my heart, easing through my body with each thumping beat.

"It's about time," I hear Rae mumble behind Cal. I laugh, blinking away the tears.

I look up at the face of the boy who has made me so happy. Who always will.

"I've always loved you," I say. "You were my first wish."

I wished for him after all.

Q&A WITH REBECCA DONOVAN

Interviewed by Brandee Veltri, from *Brandee's Book Endings*

Tell us about creating the different characters in this story. Which character do you think you are most like?

Cal was the only boy his age in a neighborhood of girls. So he needed to be able to handle it. That's why I gave him a laid-back, go-with-the-flow attitude. But there can be something so attractive about the guy who sits in the corner, don't you think? I wanted him to be the *nice guy*, without making him pathetic. I ended up with a crush of my own on Cal.

I love having a voice of reason in my stories, and in this case it's Rae. I liked making the contradiction in her looks and attitude—having this frail-looking girl with freckles on her face have the biggest attitude of them all. Adding some crassness to her realism made her the character that kept me laughing the most.

Richelle reminds me of Ellie from Disney's *Up*. She's boisterous, fun, and full of energy. I can see the huge smile on her face, and her running from place to place because she's just so excited to be a part of anything and everything. I loved how she took charge of her life, and stood up to anyone…even Rae. That meant I needed to create her opposite in Nicole. And of course that made them instant best friends!

Nicole is prim, proper and careful. This quiet girl is so very complicated. Creating her personality and her life challenged me the most when creating this story. I didn't always know where we were going. The revelation of who her father is in corporate America was a surprise to me when Nicole revealed it. But there's a strength in her that I admire, and I liked being inside her teenage head. She's so much more than she appears on the outside!

Later, while Cal is in college, Nyelle is introduced. And she is so full of life, I loved creating her. I've climbed trees with her, rolled down hills just because it was fun. I share her affection for chocolate and caffeine. I admire her living the life she wants, and not letting anyone judge her for who they think she is. She's a force, and doesn't allow fear to keep her from living. I wish I were more like her. But then again, she's the character who has more "me" in her than any other. I suppose that tells you a bit about who I am, doesn't it?!

How did the idea of *What If* first come to you?

From a song...I was listening to "Girls Like You" by the Naked and Famous, and they sing about a girl whose whole existence is based on how others perceive her. And I wanted to write about *that* girl. The girl who looks perfect on the outside, but no one understands what's truly happening on the inside. So I wrote about the girl who was ready to break, or needed to break free. But she wouldn't be able to tell her own story. She's too damaged. *He* had to be the one to tell her story. He needed to figure out what happened to her. And that's when the plot took an interesting turn, and everything got complicated...

The characters' childhood plays a big role in this story. Are there elements of your childhood in *What If*?

I did a lot of reflecting back to my childhood while writing the past scenes—when my friends were the kids in the neighborhood because they lived so close and were the same age. We used to run around in the woods, building forts, searching for bugs and slimy creatures, creating role-playing games that were almost never "house." (I had too many boys in my neighborhood.) I'd have tea parties with the girls, and learned to do a one-handed layup with the boys. We had neighborhood Wiffle Ball and kickball teams. I used to be the terrible lead singer of a mock rock band with my two boy cousins—and they were as critical of my singing as Rae is of Richelle's. There's a bond I share with the kids I grew up with, no matter what happened to us later, when we drifted apart and conformed into different social roles as teens. They're still part of my favorite memories. I hope slipping back into my childhood helped readers remember theirs.

Of the three narrators, who was your favorite to write? Who was the hardest?

I loved writing from the young girls' points of view. It was fun to be transported back to the ages when the silliest things felt like the biggest things. I enjoyed creating the bond of friendship that lasted into their teens. Remembering the sacredness of secrets, crushes, and standing up for your best friend.

Cal was the absolute hardest. I wanted him to sound like a guy. A *regular* guy. Not overly sensitive. Not a bad boy. Just the average twenty-year-old. It took me a long time to find his voice. At first, I was so wrapped up in perfecting his averageness that I actually didn't like him. He was boring. But then I peppered him with internal sarcasm, and we got along just fine.

While *What If* takes place mostly in the present, it regularly flips back into the past. Did you write it like that? Or did you write all the past parts first and then the present?
It was a very complicated process creating the interweaving storylines. The past scenes weren't in the original concept. But I was having difficulty showing why you should invest in these characters by only referring to them in the present. After conferring with a trusted author friend, it clicked. I needed to let the readers in on the friendships when they happened. But I also wanted to share moments when Cal wasn't present. I considered writing the past in the third person, but I have a strong preference for using the first person. I believe it allows me to express emotion better. So I wrote the present and the past at the same time. The past scenes are revealed chronologically, so they almost never directly correlate with the preceding chapter. But they are important to what is happening in the present, even if it hasn't happen yet.

I had to go back and rewrite sentences or details in the previous chapters to make it all connect perfectly because when I wrote about it in the present, details changed. Wooh…that sounds confusing, doesn't it? I feel like Richelle trying to explain her stars. Well, let's just say it was challenging! Everything is interconnected. But you may not realize it until the very end. This is a story I highly recommend reading again. It will be a completely different experience the second time around!

What is *your* "What If"?
I have many. For now I'll reveal one…But before I do, I'd like to say that I don't regret a single second of my life, even at its worst. I've

had a colorful life, but every decision, even the wrong ones (and I still make them), has led me to this moment right now. And for that I am grateful.

What if I had chosen to leave that night when I was terrified and uncertain? Then I wouldn't have known that I was strong enough to make it on my own when I finally did walk out that door.

What would you like your readers to take away from *What If*?
Simply: This is *your* life. And every choice is your own. Be true to who you are, despite how others may perceive you. And . . . be happy. It really *is* what's most important.

SPOILERS—

Cal wondered what would have happened if he hadn't walked away that night, if he had been the friend that Nicole needed. Would Nicole's life have been different if Cal had intervened?
Absolutely. Every decision has a consequence, even if the change is slight. Cal's interference that night would have exposed him to a side of Nicole's life she kept hidden. There's a chance she would have opened up to him in her vulnerability. Or she could have pushed him further away, ashamed of what he'd seen. We'll never know. Because it's not about looking back. It's about living with the choices made, and embracing all the positive moments that came to be because of those choices. If Cal hadn't walked away, then they may not have fallen in love. I like this ending so much better, don't you?

DISCUSSION QUESTIONS

1. *What If* ends with some questions about the future unanswered. The characters are still very much on the brink of some huge life choices. What futures did you imagine for each of them?

2. Did *What If* make you reminiscent about your childhood? What parts of the childhood stories could you relate to?

3. Was Cal's nonconfrontational personality a blessing or a curse for him and those around him? Were any of the other characters guilty of inaction or was Cal the only one?

4. *What If* is filled with rich friendships. Which was your favorite pair of friends and why?

5. Many readers will find themselves begging Cal to confront Nyelle: *Ask her what is going on! Is she Nicole? Does she remember?* But was there ever a point when you reversed direction; when you absolutely did *not* want Cal to confront Nyelle—a point at which you wanted him to leave well enough alone? If so, when was it?

6. In what ways do Cal and Rae provide a perfect balance for each other? What kind of person would Cal have been growing up *without* Rae?

7. As teens, when Rae completely dismissed Nicole and accepted that she'd become one of "the vipers," Cal seems to hold out hope and remains interested in Nicole. Why do you think that is? What was it that kept him from moving on?

8. If you could ask *one* character *one* question, who would it be and what would you ask?

9. Which character are you the most like? Is there a character you *wish* you were more like?

10. Each character is dealing with their own "what if" questions. Share a "what if" of your own.

11. Butterflies, ice cream, shooting stars, masks, gloves, coffee, drums, sugar, snow, and icy water! *What If* is absolutely brimming with symbolism. Which resonated with you the most? What did it mean to you?

WARNING! SPOILERS AHEAD!

12. When, if ever, were you sure that Nyelle *was* Nicole?

13. Nyelle references masks several times in the story. Who do you think was her true self?

14. Was there a certain point where you became aware of Richelle's situation? If so, when was it?

15. It's pretty obvious why Richelle was someone Nicole needed as a friend, but did Richelle need Nicole too, even before the life-altering events?

16. If you were young Nicole, would you have acted differently? Would you have honored your promise to keep your best friend's secret? Why or why not?

There are choices that change everything.

What's one of yours?

Live the life you want, not the one you're given.

What's your "what if"? A decision that changed the course of your life. What positive result came from that choice? Even if it happened years later. This isn't about regret. It's about embracing those moments that change everything. Every choice is a chance to start again!

Join the conversation and share your "what if" moment at:

whatif.rebeccadonovan.com

ABOUT THE AUTHOR

Rebecca Donovan is the *USA Today* bestselling author of the highly acclaimed new-adult trilogy The Breathing Series. Her novels include *Reason to Breathe*, *Barely Breathing*, and *Out of Breath*.

Rebecca is a graduate of the University of Missouri, Columbia, and lives in a quiet town in Massachusetts with her son. Excited by all that makes life possible, she is a music enthusiast and is willing to try just about anything once.

Learn more at:
RebeccaDonovan.com
Twitter, @beccadonovan
Facebook.com/RebeccaDonovanAuthor